T0369540

A Hard Rain

— Book Two of the Shift Trilogy —

By Michael Juge

iUniverse, Inc.
Bloomington

A Hard Rain
Book Two of the Shift Trilogy

iUniverse books may be ordered through booksellers or by contacting:

iUniverse
1663 Liberty Drive
Bloomington, IN 47403
www.iuniverse.com
1-800-Authors (1-800-288-4677)

ISBN: 978-1-4759-0693-6 (sc)
ISBN: 978-1-4759-0694-3 (e)

Printed in the United States of America

iUniverse rev. date: 6/26/2012

Novels of the Shift Trilogy

Ride The Wilderness **Book One of the Shift Trilogy**
2012 *Previously released in 2010 as "Scourge of an Agnostic God"

A Hard Rain **Book Two of the Shift Trilogy**
2012 * First edition released in 2011

Refurbished Soul **Book Three of the Shift Trilogy**
2012

For updates on upcoming works and to follow along with the background music and Google maps, visit www.michaeljuge.com

Acknowledgements

I owe so much of my life's fulfillment to my alluring wife. She is my greatest lover, my best friend and has spurred me on to explore the fullest potential of this trilogy without hesitation. The *Shift* trilogy has consumed me since emerging out of my own apocalypse, which I call "the Panic of '06." When I thought about writing a story exploring the panic through the vehicle of an apocalyptic fiction, my wife enthusiastically supported me. When I wavered on whether to continue, she rallied for me to soldier on. Damn, I love that woman!

There are other people I want to thank, people with whom I have a more… platonic relationship. Megaton from www.postapocalypticforum.com. The man reluctantly picked up *Ride The Wilderness,* (formerly entitled *Scourge of an Agnostic God)* but then, having loved it, he gave it a glowing review, and gave *Ride The Wilderness* mad street cred in the apocalyptic community. Then there's Agent Orange from www.quietearth.us who posted *Ride The Wilderness'* press release (likewise under the former title) up on his website and that despite the goofy title.

To my son and daughter, you do drive me nuts, but guess what? I love you two profoundly, so much that it hurts. And you two gave me the life experience to write as a parent. Liam, my talented Aussie illustrator who created an incredible cover, God bless you, mate. Shanyn, Jennifer and Delana, Kristi and Lynn. And Jenny, my fellow Falcon and a helluva a scary lawyer. Thank you, ladies. Y'all gave *Ride The Wilderness* literary fiction street cred.

Disclaimer

The views expressed in this novel are those of the author, and do not necessarily reflect those of the U.S. Department of State or the U.S. Government.

A Note about the Soundtrack to A HARD RAIN

Hi Reader,

Thank you for picking up *A Hard Rain*. If you purchased this book by mistake, the exit can be found by closing the cover or by pressing the escape button. I wrote the *Shift* trilogy with the intent of providing you with a fully integrated experience. I want you to see what the characters see and listen to on a daily basis. In other words, I want to bring you into their world. With that in mind, I created a multi-media environment, so that you can listen to the music that is either being played in the background or is on the mind of the character. Throughout the story, you will see a prompt that looks something like:

BACKGROUND MUSIC: "Old Man" by Neil Young

Visit www.michaeljuge.com on the *A Hard Rain* page located at http://michaeljuge.com/wordpress1/a-hard-rain/ and select the referenced song in the imbedded YouTube link while you read to get the full sensory experience. You can also study the Google Map to see where you are geographically in the story on the *Maps* page. If you would like to have background music play throughout while you read, tune your Pandora or Last.fm internet radio to David Bowie or perhaps the Rolling Stones.
I hope you enjoy the *Shift* trilogy and remember, keep your bikes ready and peanut butter stockpiled!

Kaplah,
Michael Juge

Virginia 2013

To view an interactive map, Visit www.michaeljuge.com **on the Maps page**

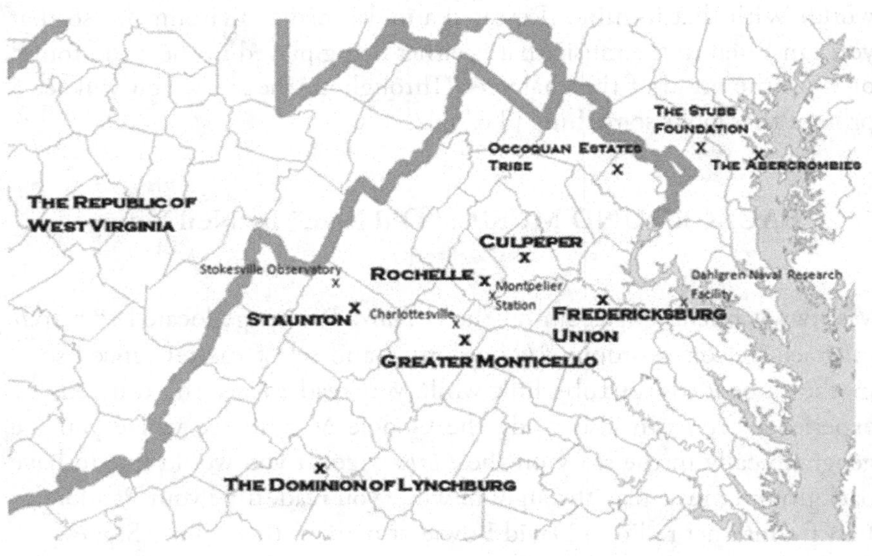

CHAPTER 1

"Jingle bell, jingle bell, jingle bell rock
Jingle bells swing and jingle bells ring..."

Chris Jung shuffled languidly down the aisle as if in a daze. While his ears were still numb from the bitter cold outside, the sudden transition into the tropical heat of the house wares store had Chris sweating underneath his itchy Ross Dress for Less brand suit. The flat screen TVs plastered on the walls had Santa flying all over the store, cheerfully wishing everyone a Merry Christmas without pause while Jingle Bell Rock *blared in surround sound. Across the aisle, Chris couldn't help but notice a painfully attractive young woman wearing black patent leather boots surveying the assortment of blenders, the skirt over her tights leaving little to the imagination.*

"You like?"

"Yes," Chris answered hungrily, before catching himself. He returned his attention to the frumpy-looking older woman wearing the store's smock and a Santa hat. "I'm sorry, like what?"

"This. You like?" the store clerk held up an electronic contraption. "It's called a hand blender. It's a much nicer gift than that," gesturing to the Snuggie in his hand basket.

"True, but I didn't want to, you know, make a faux pas by giving a gift that's so...domestic. Wouldn't it be like giving her an iron or a Stairmaster?" The lady just chuckled.

Chris was a little disappointed to see that the hottie in the boots had disappeared. He was loyal to Meredith and knew he had a good thing, but eye candy was eye candy, and he was a male with a pulse.

"What a bright time. It's the right time to rock the night away. Jingle Bell time is a swell time to go gliding on a one-horse sleigh..." the clerk ringing up his haul sang without seeming to notice that she was singing aloud to the commercialized Christmas tune.

"Looks like it's beginning to snow," she said as she placed the blender inside the bag.

"Yeah, I'd better get going. The toll way is probably going to be a mess."

"You said it. People here freak out whenever it snows. Put in your pin on the keypad. Thanks and Happy Holidays."

Chris buttoned his trench coat and headed outside. The pale grey sky shed snowflakes onto the frozen asphalt of the packed parking lot.

Before he knew it, he too, was singing, "Giddy-up jingle horse, pick up your feet. Jingle around the clock."

When he reached his car his vision started to go shaky. He pressed the key remote to his car when he heard a peculiar whooshing sound. He looked around when suddenly the car waiting impatiently for his parking space exploded in a torrent of gas and shrapnel. People screamed. Out of the bedlam, Chris heard a guttural roar of men and women bellowing, "Onward, Vicious Rabbits!"

Reston, Virginia
December 2012

The parking lot of the Bed Bath & Beyond was packed with vehicles that had lain still for five and a half years now rusting in the elements. Snowflakes drifted slowly onto the cracked asphalt, creating a thin insulating layer to muffle ambient outside noises. It was deceptively serene. Captain Chris Jung knew it was anything but safe as he studied the iconic house wares storefront.

He crouched behind the engine block of a burnt out Lexus SUV as he slammed another magazine into his M4. Beside him was a tall young African American woman. Lieutenant Kendra Baraka was whispering to herself again. It was a nervous habit of hers that Chris had gotten used to over the years. He knew he had no room to complain. He had a plethora of his own quirks.

Chris wished he had better eyes inside the store. The windows had been shattered, exposing the store to the elements. Kendra tried to get a better view with her binoculars. But her muted curse confirmed that she had no better view into the darkened interior.

"They're in there, Captain. Third squad followed them all the way over. But it could be a trap."

Chris peeked over the hood of the SUV for another quick look and sat back down. He stroked one of the braids of his two-pronged goatee meditatively and tried to ignore the freezing moisture of sweat and ice on his skin. The thermal underwear he wore under his type 4 Kevlar vest and homespun BDUs kept the hypothermia at bay, but he felt as though he had been shivering ever since his company had been deployed a week ago.

"I don't think it's a trap, Lieutenant. The weeds aren't worn over the asphalt, and I don't see so much as a soap dispenser inside. If they were planting a trap, they would have also placed some trinkets to lure prey. I think they panicked and ran themselves into a dead end."

Chris honestly didn't know. Like Kendra, he couldn't see what was in the store beyond the cash registers. It was a risk running into a building like this, but risk was part of the deal in the Vicious Rabbits Corps. Besides, his mission was clear: to seek out and destroy the band who attacked the outpost in Culpeper. The bandits were inside that building, and he knew it. If Chris called to withdraw, then these bandits would not only live to fight another day but would have the added incentive for vengeance to attack again. If he stalled and waited, it would only give them more time to come up with a plan. Maybe they even dug an escape route out of the store. Chris had to act.

"Alright Lieutenant, you, me and the squad behind us."

Kendra nodded tersely and signaled to the other squads in sight to lay suppressive fire to cover their advance. It took all his will to push himself up and to expose himself like that, but once he got running Chris was at a full sprint, his vision shaky, reduced to myopic tunnel vision. As exhausted as he was and despite the seventy pounds of gear, Chris covered the distance to the store's entrance quickly; a benefit of relentless training. Along with the occasional snowflake, he could feel the whizzing of rounds passing from behind, rounds fired from his own people covering his approach. He trusted his cavalry, but it was still unsettling being inches from death. Once inside, Chris dove left as Kendra leapt to the right. Another three soldiers followed him, while another four followed Kendra.

The sudden transition from light to darkness put him and the rest of his team at a distinct disadvantage. Were he the bandits, he would have waited right on the other side of the threshold to cap the intruders whose eyes hadn't adjusted to reduced light. Chris stumbled over a discarded rack as it took a couple of long seconds for his eyes to adapt.

The store hadn't been completely picked clean. Miscellaneous items were strewn about: scattered ice trays and cheese graters here, metallic garbage cans over there, a rack of digital clocks, none of which would ever have any use in this world other than as paperweights. As he scrutinized the gutted and vandalized remains of what used to be his wife's favorite store, he knew this was a bad place to be. Chris recalled the way that Bed Bath & Beyond was laid out – not in rational aisles like a Wal-Mart. It was a circular tour. This was great for ensuring that you didn't miss any part of the store when shopping, but it also provided plenty of cover if you were trying to lay an ambush, too. At least the bandits hadn't run into an IKEA. That would have been a real dog's breakfast.

It reeked inside. Unwashed humans left a revolting stench, meaning this store was their den, contrary to what he suggested a couple of minutes ago.

Across from the toiletries section just past the bath towels, Chris saw movement and dove for cover just as a muzzle flash revealed the bandits' position. The gunfire was magnified in the confined space and reverberated throughout the store. One of his people screamed out in pain. Firing back, Chris overrode the flight instinct that threatened to overtake him. Chris and another Vicious Rabbit rushed over, toppling the emptied racks rather than running across the bottleneck of the aisle. Muzzles flashed in front of him and to the side. A loud explosion and a wave of hot air rushed past him. He kept his eyes on the targets ahead and laid down controlled three round bursts. Fire discipline was hard to maintain when he was pumped with adrenaline, but his experience taught him the value of not wasting ammo. The bandits, on the other hand, didn't bother with such tactics. They sprayed the place blindly hoping to hit something. One of them was shooting from the hip like actors did in the movies. A private took the easy shot and the bandit paid for his bravado with a new hole in his head.

Kendra and her team met up with Chris' group and converged on top of the bandits. Chris could smell the feral men long before coming face to face with them. Chris drew out his knife and threw himself on top of one wiry bandit. Chris' broad shouldered muscular frame, maintained by a healthy diet and endless hours of blacksmithing, easily overpowered the scrawny bandit who lived off of pigeon scraps and cans of dog food. Chris didn't contemplate the fundamental inequity of it all, what a bum deal the bandit had and that he could just have easily wound up in the smelly little man's place. Nor did he allow himself a moment of doubt where compassion could inject itself into his response. That would be asking for it. He grabbed the bandit from behind and slit his throat as though he were a cardboard box to be broken down. Out of the corner of his eye, another bandit raised the butt of his empty rifle. Chris maneuvered quickly and used his Krav Maga training to pin the man's neck under Chris' knee, and before he knew what happened, Chris ended the bandit's struggle as painlessly as possible.

It seemed like an hour had passed when in reality the skirmish lasted less than fifteen minutes. The bandits were dispatched efficiently with only one gunshot injury to his people, which the medic said the young man would be all right thanks to the vest. The rest of the company swept the store and pulled the bodies of the bandits and their meager belongings outside to examine them. This little band of wild men was responsible for the recent spate of raids into the settled lands. But they were just one band out of dozens who poked through the porous borders of civilized territory in search of food, loot and girls. Each time it happened, Captain Chris Jung and his Vicious Rabbits First Bicycle Mounted Cavalry Company were called upon to find the ones responsible and neutralize them. Without fail they ended up back in the Beltway region. The only people out here these days were ferals. Some were harmless collections of people scraping the carcass of the dead cities struggling to stay alive another day. He even did business with some of them, trading jars of fresh fruit and vegetables and ammunition in exchange for information. Other ferals were bandits. Bandits raided the civilized territories for food, weapons and medicine. They hadn't been too much of a problem until recently.

Last week, Culpeper had been hit hard, worse than they ever had before. Being on the northern edge of settled territory was dangerous business. Rochelle, a close ally of Culpeper and member of the Orange Pact, contributed to their mutual security and took the initiative to chase down the ones who committed this most recent attack. Chris didn't know if it really made any difference. Five and a half years on, ferals far outnumbered the civilized. And the bandits who raided them seemed to be getting better coordinated in their attacks and more brazen.

The company was camped out in the Bed Bath & Beyond parking lot, their bicycles, weathered and worn but well-maintained, leaned against each other in circular patterns. Some had child trailers attached to carry extra bike parts, spare ammo, food, pup tents and the 3G Stirling radio. Although a lot more reliable than first two generations, the Stirling was still a behemoth contraption composed of thick copper wires and vacuum tubes. At least they worked in the post-Shift environment…sort of. Transmission and reception range was severely limited by the sporadic Shift surges. The ionosphere was still a mess. The Stirling's range, named after the inventor Don Stirling who was a retired TV repairman in Culpeper, was limited to about thirty miles at best.

Vicious Rabbits chatted as they cleaned their weapons, some marveling at the big box storefronts now devolving into ruins. The snow was falling harder. Chris Jung squatted as he washed off blood from his face and arms in a bleach solution. His tunic, which was bloodied from the fight, was placed inside a plastic bag to await a thorough boiling when they returned home. His shoulder-length, brunette hair and his two-pronged chin beard were matted with sweat from all the action inside. He rubbed his beak of a nose, which had been broken three times in the last four years from numerous fights. Fortunately, the bandits he fought with today didn't break anything. He swished some water and spat out a little blood. He had a few less teeth these days as well. He lost three of them to brawls and training. Having a rational fear of seeing the town's dentist with her crude equipment had cost him another tooth. Chris sang as he sponged himself off in the freezing snow-laden parking lot.

"Jingle bell, jingle bell, jingle bell rock
Jingle bells chime in jingle bell time
Dancing and prancing in Jingle Bell Square
In the frosty air."

Chris found it peculiar to be singing Christmas songs even though he hadn't been barraged by the commercialized holiday music in years. Maybe the snow evoked some memories. He drank down some distilled water from his titanium Starbucks travel mug, the same one he brought with him when he, his wife and friends fled Falls Church to Rochelle when the Shift first hit. The ringing in his ears magnified since the firefight. What was even more annoying was this shaky vision he had right now. It usually happened out here in the Beltway. He figured it was stress related. He wasn't surprised how his mind could always come up with new and exciting ways to screw with his head. He could never ignore it, but he learned to at least put it on the back burner in order for him to do his job. His lieutenant walked up to him.

"What's the word, LT?"

Kendra had also stripped off her tunic down to her T-shirt and BDU pants. Her long dark brown arms were remarkably sculpted for a woman, a young one at that, barely twenty-two. Chris stared at the bandage on her left arm. Kendra noticed the concern on his face.

"It's nothing, Captain. I sliced my arm on one of the display racks on the way out after the fight."

"Hmm. How jejune," he mused.

"Yeah anyhow," ignoring Chris' word of the day, Kendra crouched beside him. "They've just finished up with the search. No children in this group."

Chris sighed with relief. Children complicated matters considerably. She continued, "But they've found something odd you should see."

Chris put a hand on his back to assist himself up and they proceeded to the front of the store passing by makeshift tents constructed over vehicles long since dead. His back was acting up again. Back during the Obsidian War, he had sustained injuries along his side and back from a mortar explosion as well as losing a couple of toes on his left foot. Although he officially recovered, Chris noticed that he wasn't quite as nimble. The stabbing pain beneath the scar tissue was manageable; it only aggravated him in extreme heat. But his back was his Achilles heel. It barked at him constantly. Maybe he would have felt that way even if he hadn't played a contortionist flipping over himself when the mortar hit. He was constantly bending over the handle bars or over an anvil. Either way, the back was another way of reminding him that he would be turning forty next month.

Gunnery Sergeant Jay Birmingham greeted the two with his Scottish/ Australian lilt.

"Ay Cap'in, LT. Lookee what we've found 'ere."

The bandits had been stripped naked and their clothes spread out. With a pair of tongs from the store, the gunnery sergeant showed a pair of underwear.

"Notice something odd?"

Chris shrugged his shoulders.

The gunny continued. "They 'ad on clean underwear."

The underwear was not actually clean. Violent death caused them to evacuate their bowels. Chris was about to point that out when he realized what the gunny meant. They had on clean underwear *before* they met their demise. He could see the clean waist band and portions of brilliant white fabric.

Chris bowed his head. "Well, their mothers would have been proud."

"Captain?"

He took another look at the dangling underwear. They were Cream of the Crops. And neither the waistband nor the fabric were well worn, nothing near the shredded pieces one would expect from bandits' undergarments if they wore such things. Hell, even he didn't wear underwear that nice. These were brand new. The only people wearing new pre-Shift manufactured underwear were in Lynchburg. They had an underwear distribution center there, and the city didn't fall. Pre-Shift underwear in original packaging was expensive. What were bandits doing with such a luxury item? The gunny answered his question.

"They must 'ave ransacked a truck from Lynchburg. They've got a whole stash right 'ere" pointing to several boxes with his latex gloved hand.

Chris knelt down to examine the crate full of originally packaged Cream of the Crops underwear, and muttered a mild profanity. "I guess you're right. They must have been from a swiped Lynchburg truck."

"Serves the buggers right it does. Bloody pod knockers, wot?"

Chris didn't know what a 'pod knocker' was exactly, even after having worked with the gunny for five years, but he assumed it wasn't a compliment. People from Rochelle, Culpeper and Monticello had little nice to say about Lynchburg.

"Alright, Gunny. I don't think these fresh pairs need to go into the treasury," referring to the crates of underwear. "Distribute them out to the company, contact our ride to let them know we're heading back and tell the troops we're *imshee*'ing out in thirty minutes."

Corporal Hicks who overheard the conversation proceeded to wind up the bulky vacuum tube radio that was barely small enough to fit on his back and the radio came to life.

Gunnery Sergeant Birmingham grunted and bellowed out, "Roit, you Vicious Rabbits, queue up for your free bloody panties! I said queue up, not crowd like a bunch of 'orny ferals at a brothel! Porkins, 'and 'em out!"

BACKGROUND MUSIC: "Street Spirit (Fade Out)" by Radiohead
Visit www.michaeljuge.com **on the *A Hard Rain* page to listen**

The First Bike Mounted Cavalry Company cruised cautiously down the Dulles Toll Road, weaving around a traffic snarl of dead vehicles here and a pile up there. It was a sight Chris had grown accustomed to even if it was a sordid reminder of the world that was no more. Five and a half years ago, on July 11, 2007, a mysterious series of electromagnetic pulses—EMPs—struck across the globe. Nobody knew what it was at the time or what was causing it. But the result was absolutely devastating. With that first EMP, all solid state electronics, everything with a microchip, was immediately rendered inoperable. Every transistor radio, every computer, every TV, and every iPod plugged to a power source and virtually every vehicle stopped dead. The world stopped dead. Civilization, which had become completely integrated and dependent on the microchip, died with a remarkable quickness. The people in the settled lands of the Orange Pact to include the Rochelle Sovereignty, Culpeper, Greater Monticello and the Fredericksburg Union had come to learn that the EMPs were caused by the earth itself as it was preparing to shift its magnetic poles. They came to refer to this phenomenon as "The Shift."

The first EMP struck at 6:02 PM on that July evening, right in the middle of the evening rush hour, leaving the highways throughout the Beltway region congested with dead vehicular traffic. The infuriating thing to Chris was that contrary to reason, the traffic jam was in both directions. There were almost as many people who worked out in the suburbs and lived in the city as those who had traditional commutes. It wouldn't have bothered him so much except that the two-way snarl significantly slowed his company's approach to the staging area in Manassas.

Chris pushed on the pedals of *The Interceptor*, his Kona mountain bike, ignoring the minor cuts and bruises he acquired in the op. His eyes darted back and forth from the road with all of its obstacles to the highway's walls, which could hide any number of bandit ambushes. Chris didn't like riding on the highway. It was a fatal funnel. If he were to set a trap against an unsuspecting traveler, he would set it inside the miniature canyon of the Dulles Toll Road. The only hope was to move fast and quietly. Stealth was their strength.

Some other outfits used dirt bikes. That was asking for it in Chris' opinion. Post-Shift fuels were corrosive chemistry experiments of random combustible liquids. Between the nasty fuel and the occasional EMP surges, internal combustion engines could crap out at any moment. Once the tank ran out of gas or the engine otherwise went kaput, the rider was stranded leaving a 'perty' faced citizen naked in the wilderness. But most importantly, dirt bikes announced their presence a mile away with their whining chainsaw engines. Horses were an option, but they didn't do well on the hard surfaces for long stretches. Plus, one needed to care for them, which was difficult to do in urban environments.

Mountain bikes were the best way to go inside the Beltway. Although they were slower and couldn't carry as much, bikes were quiet, easy to maintain out in the urban bush and were better than walking. Like the other mountain bikes in the cavalry, *The Interceptor* had been retrofitted with straps, cages and an array of spare parts. Chris' M4 was secured along the top tube of the frame. The fork had been replaced, the tires reinforced with car treads. The same bike on which he escaped DC several years ago looked very different today than it did then. Along with the modifications, he painted his bike black and stenciled the bike's christened name *The Interceptor*.

Snowflakes danced above the eerily silent highway as the company raced up towards the exit to Highway 28. Chris' shaky vision was still aggravating him. He couldn't tell what was more annoying: the shaky vision or the blasted Christmas song that wouldn't get out of his head. He then recalled that the song played in one of his dreams. His dreams tended to be vivid, and they usually were set in the pre-Shift world, "the real world" as it had come to be commonly referred.

He dreamt about the most mundane things like sitting in the living room of his old apartment in Falls Church watching TV, going to the grocery store, getting stuck in the middle of an excessively slow drive thru, screwing around on the internet or some other gloriously mundane task in the real world. Sometimes he would be at work, not as the owner of Jung Fabricators and Armoring or as the captain of the Vicious Rabbits First Bicycle Mounted Cavalry Company. He was at his old job as an intelligence analyst with Diplomatic Security sitting in a cube wasting his life away. The most disturbing of dreams involved him riding on the DC Metro. And it got outright weird when his post-Shift world encroached in the pre-Shift backdrop. The dreams were disturbing reminders of his life before and he was glad to wake up and find it was just a bad dream. The world had ended; he was fine.

Chris was so deep in thought he almost missed the pack of dogs racing across his path along the exit.

"Shit!"

He swerved just in time. Fortunately, the snow wasn't gathering on the ground just yet. The company exited onto Highway 28 and soon they were skirting along the edges of the metro area of Northern Virginia where farmhouses and vast undeveloped fields were enclosed by cookie cutter subdivisions. The grayish daylight was beginning to ebb. Chris looked at his Rolex self-winding watch. It was difficult to say whether they were going to make it back to the busses waiting for them in Manassas before nightfall or not. The roads leading from the edge of settled land in Culpeper to the outer reaches of the Beltway region weren't terribly clogged, allowing the cavalry to hitch a ride in the relative comfort of armored busses—*relative* being the operative term. At least on a bus he could sit and relax instead of hauling himself and the seventy pounds-plus of equipment on *The Interceptor.*

He would have been happy to be schlepped all the way to Reston by armored bus, but unfortunately, the roads were impassable inside the metropolitan area. Again, the timing of the first EMP hitting at evening rush hour conspired to make vehicular locomotion all but impossible. That's why they paid him the big Byrds, the currency minted in the Republic of West Virginia widely in use today in the Shenandoah Valley, to go and hump it manually on his bike to battle. Meanwhile, the busses awaited the cavalry's return at a strip mall located miles away in Manassas.

Chris called for a break and the company pulled off the road into a Jiffy Lube. The Vicious Rabbit with the Stirling radio pulled up to the captain. The young man wound the rotary, charging the battery. Chris breathed steam into his hands trying to warm his fingers frozen beneath his gloves. A medic checked on a wounded Vicious Rabbit who was stuffed into the other child trailer while Gunnery Sergeant Birmingham held the handle bars of the wounded soldier's bicycle. Bikes were way too valuable to ditch.

After a few seconds the young Vicious Rabbit radioman handed Chris the mic, which resembled an old telephone receiver.

"Thanks," he mumbled and pressed the button to speak. "Firefly, Firefly, this is Serenity. Firefly, do you read me?"

After a few long seconds, static crackled through the receiver. "Serenity, this is Firefly. We read you three by five. Go with your traffic."

"Firefly, we're about fifteen clicks from your location, but we got some baggage and the snow's making our approach difficult. We're gonna have to go Holiday Inn Express. I'll give you a wakeup call in the AM."

"Copy that, Serenity. Sleep tight."

Chris handed back the mic to the Vicious Rabbit, took out a power bar mock up and rubbed his legs to push blood down to his toes. While the company rested, Chris studied the AAA road atlas, which was marked up with hand written notes about feral tribes and routes. He had become an expert on the Northern Virginian necropolis over the past few years. He and his company were out here so often he supposed he should have rented an apartment in the wasteland. It was his job to know where to set up camp, to keep tabs of the groups of ferals that inhabited the areas both townie and bandits alike, and to get his people back home safely.

The gunny and Lt. Baraka joined him, and Chris pointed to a blue marked section on the map.

"Over here. Right off of the 28."

The blue scribble was drawn over Occoquan Estates, a gated community that had seen its real estate value increase when a tribe of townies moved in. He had stayed with the Estates Tribe a couple times before. Like most ferals, they lived by and large off the remains of the city; however, this tribe cultivated a field. The Estates Tribe maintained some residue of the civility they'd had before the Shift. Plus, they collected souvenirs for trade. Chris might be able to get some of his Christmas shopping done while he was out here.

"Aye, Captain. The boss man seems right 'nuff," the gunny mumbled.

Kendra nodded. With that, Chris closed the atlas and repacked it. Chris always took his subordinates' opinions under serious advisement, especially the gunny's. The gunny was an actual legacy Marine, not some cube monkey who stumbled his way to leadership like himself.

As he drank from his Starbucks travel mug, Chris saw a small ragtag line of ferals walking along the highway. Fortunately, they weren't in the mood to confront a superior armed and trained force. Some of the children even waved as they past. They weren't always ferals. They were once suburbanites just as he used to be. Fate had left them to scavenge the wastelands while he was a citizen of a civilized community, albeit a small one. The Rochelle Sovereignty wasn't anything the size of Lynchburg and certainly nothing like West Virginia, the energy and commercial capital of the Mid-Atlantic. But Rochelle was a slice of sanity where his children could grow up as civilized human beings and not be forced to scurry about, foraging for food like the people passing him by. A vehicle with a bumper sticker he passed along the way summed it all up perfectly. *Shit Happens.*

Life had been enormously good to Chris since the Shift, and he knew it. It wasn't just that he and his family endured the Great Suck, the first months of the Shift, where a majority of the US population had died en masse of violence, starvation, dehydration and the dreaded flu along with a host of opportunistic diseases. Chris had become a post-Shift success story in the land of post-apocalyptic opportunity. Between his commission as a captain in the Vicious Rabbits and his vehicle armoring business, he was comfortable.

"So, what in the hell am I doing here?" he asked himself. He just wanted to get home to Rochelle. He wanted to kiss Meredith and hold his three kids Aidan, Rhiannon and Baby Charles. But he knew the answer. Rochelle and its allies were surrounded. The Dominion of Lynchburg, led by the barking mad televangelist turned-dictator Regent Gordon Boche, threatened to wipe out the Rochelle Sovereignty and its allies in the Orange Pact. And to Rochelle's east and north was the vast untamed urban wilderness where bandits attacked relentlessly.

The First Bicycle Mounted Cavalry pushed onward another few miles, passing another traveling band of ferals. More people had survived the Shift and the flu than Chris had originally thought when he first returned to the Beltway. When he and his cavalry first treaded back into the Beltway a few years ago, he didn't see more than two or three people scurrying away from their presence. Like the civilized, the ferals were wary of outsiders not only out of concern of being attacked but because of the devastating flu that spread through the entire Mid-Atlantic region.

Today, with the flu having passed and with their numbers growing, the ferals seemed less skittish. They still eyed the bike-riding strangers warily, though. It was only natural. There were no laws, no social contract. One had to presume hostile intent of a stranger in order to survive. Years of living in a state of nature with roving bands of rapists, gangs and bandits re-instilled a survival instinct that lay dormant for thousands of years. Chris felt it every time he left the wire of civilization.

The Vicious Rabbit on point turned left, crossing the median of the highway. Chris raced up, knowing he was their ticket inside. As Chris crossed the highway, he instinctively looked both directions as if watching out for any oncoming cars.

The entrance to Occoquan Estates was marked by a marble slab out front which proclaimed it was a golfing community. Surrounded by gates, the entrance was manned by some rough looking trade, huddled inside one of those security checkpoint huts. Chris dismounted his bicycle. German Shepherds prowled behind the gates, the same breed that Rochelle used to help patrol its perimeter. One of the gruff guards came out of the hut, wearing a black, red, and yellow leather jacket with an eight ball on the back.

"Whatchu want, cracker?"

Chris raised his hand in a nonthreatening gesture of peace not unlike cowboys did with Native Americans in the old Westerns. "Afternoon. I'm Chris Jung, a friend of the Grand Sheriff."

The guard noticed the rusted orange armband on Chris and the others, which displayed the Rochelle Sovereignty's emblem. It was the sole uniform article of clothing they had to identify themselves.

"You one dem Nasty Rabbits?"

"Vicious Rabbits, sir, and yes. Hank is a friend of mine. Saved his ass once. Tell him Chris of the Vicious Rabbits is here."

The man's hard features softened a little, knowing that the Vicious Rabbits did business with the Occoquan Estates Tribe. The man scratched his beard ponderously.

"Ai'ight."

The man called out to one of the boys, presumably to summon the Grand Sheriff, when Chris heard the clopping sound of hooves. Three men on horses approached from the other side of the gates.

"Hey, civilization slicker!" called out the man in the lead. He dismounted and walked up towards Chris.

Even before he spoke, he knew the man was Hank Conrad, the Grand Sheriff of the Occoquan Estates Tribe. Having a horse out here was a dead ringer that he was an important man. Ferals weren't particularly good at maintaining livestock or beasts of burden. They required a lot of food and care. Only the grand Pooh-Bah would be able to wrestle the resources necessary to have a horse. And forget about vehicles. Even if they happened across a late model vehicle that could function in the EMP prone environment, fuel was too precious for ferals.

"Grand Sheriff," Chris said and shook the man's hand. Hank Conrad didn't look like the Grand Sheriff of anything. He would have been a mild-mannered nutritionist in the real world, but fate gave the shortish man with the strikingly well groomed flowing black mane a big promotion. Like most men out here, he wore a beard, but it was trimmed. He could pass as a citizen.

"So, what brings you out slumming with us?"

"You know, the usual. Cruising."

Chris didn't care to elaborate about his business. Besides, the Grand Sheriff knew what the First Bike Mounted Cavalry was doing here. Civilized folk didn't travel here unless they were coming to put a hurt on someone. Hank didn't mind that and Chris knew it. After all, it was his cavalry that saved him from an ambush a few years back. Chris was out on a scavenger hunt for his wife searching for some Swan secret squirrel thing that he didn't even know what he was retrieving when he happened upon the scene. Chris mistook Hank and his guards as citizens, stupidly strolling out in the wilderness, and lent a hand to take out the bandits who ambushed them. Saving Hank won the Vicious Rabbits a new ally in the wilderness. So, Hank didn't mind when the Vicious Rabbits went around cleaning house, for it only benefitted the Estates Tribe.

"So, I suppose you'd like to a place to stay for the evening."

"If you wouldn't mind."

"Not at all. Now, is this going to be me repaying the favor, or would you like to save that for another time?"

Chris exhaled wearily, letting out a giant plume of steam. He unbuckled the CamelBak Motherlode Pack from his MOLLE gear, and reached for a pack of Cream of the Crops underwear. Hank's eyes widened with excitement.

"This is small, so I believe it's the right size for you."

Chris knew Hank was petite, so before the gunny started handing out the acquired Cream of the Crops, Chris grabbed a couple of smalls for the likelihood that he was going to have to pay for entry into Occoquan Estates. He really didn't want to waste the favor Hank owed him to crash for one night on his proverbial couch. A six pack of pre-Shift underwear was too much even still, but what the hell? It was a spoil of the raid that bought more good favor with the Estates Tribe's boss man, and what with Christmas and all. A Vicious Rabbit handed Chris a satchel who in turn presented it to Hank. He opened it, took a generous whiff and grinned. Rochelle's number one cash crop, tobacco, was pure gold. It was worth its weight in pre-Shift underwear, especially out here. This brand wasn't Rochelle's finest grade of tobacco, but it didn't matter. Hank had just solidified his hegemony for another year with this catch. Had they had enough room, they would have also carried fuel for barter as townies like the Estates Tribe did have a few generators. But by the look on Hank's face, Chris knew he was satisfied.

"You and your men…and women," gesturing to Lieutenant Baraka, "shall be my personal guests." He turned to one of his guards. "Slate, see to it that the pool house is stocked for a party tonight! Tell the maids to get my guest house in order and to stoke the fires. We're having guests."

"Thank you, Grand Sheriff."

Hank fondled the package. "Thank you. Cream of the Crops were my favorite, especially the boxer briefs."

Indeed, Occoquan Estates had once been a posh golfing community as the landscape bore decaying evidence of the grounds. The once manicured fields had been converted to farming, a credit to the Grand Sheriff who had the wisdom of not relying purely on scavenging to eat. Though still feral, the Estates Tribe was the closest to civilized as Chris had come across, and what distinguished them was agriculture. It made a world of difference between living hand to mouth constantly fighting for diminishing cans of Chunky Soup, and living with a modicum of reassurance and hope for tomorrow.

They passed several upscale homes and McMansions on the way to the Estates community pool house. The homes were now falling apart. It was odd how this tribe made such strides in agriculture, yet completely neglected their living conditions. Chris also noted that newer homes tended to fall apart quicker than older homes he had come across. It probably had to do with cheap Chinese construction material used in the millennium.

Gunnery Sergeant Birmingham caught up with Chris. "Sir, we've got plenty of undies to reimburse you for the cost of lodging tonight."

Chris shook his head. "Don't sweat it, Gunny. I've taken my share of loot over the years and these kids need to build up their capital a lot more than I do. It's just the cost of doing business that's all." Besides, Chris still had a stash of no nonsense panties for Meredith. That was going to go over very well for Christmas. At least, he could scratch her off his list of gift buying. He just wished they happened upon a Frederick's of Hollywood as well. But that would be more for him than for her.

"Aye, well, I'll be buying first round." The gunny said. "It's safe, the booze, right? Won't be going blind or dying would we, Captain?"

Chris was amazed how much the Scottish/Australian legacy Marine loved to drink. Then again, he was Scottish/Australian and a Marine, so why should he be surprised? He never met an Aussie or a Scot that wasn't holding a drink. "No, you won't go blind, but it is about the worst tasting swill you'll ever guzzle down."

"Aye. I'm just looking forward to getting on the bus and getting my arse 'ome."

Chris saw the ragged looking women offering themselves out along the crumbling boulevard in the freezing cold. Some would have been very attractive if they had bathed and kept up with oral hygiene. But none were as beautiful as his wife Meredith. She was so beautiful in a natural, unassuming way as well as brilliant. Chris' longing to get home started to break through his concentration. He, too just wanted to get back on the bus and get back home.

"Word, Gunny. Word."

Chapter 2

Charlottesville, Virginia
Greater Monticello
December 2012

Fog kissed the tops of the snow-covered trees that hugged Highway 20. Rita Luevano loped as fast as she could while being mindful to plant her feet on the parts of the highway that weren't covered in ice. Strands of her thick black hair escaped from her ponytail and clung to her frozen cheeks. With the temperature falling rapidly, she regretted wearing a light Old Navy hoodie and Lycra running tights. As she ran, Rita could only hear the crunching of her feet upon the freshly fallen snow and the rhythmic pant of her breathing. She looked behind her to see Neko Lemay just a few yards back. Rita grinned inwardly. She had turned forty this past year, but despite having officially hit middle age, Rita was giving her twenty-four-year-old running companion and personal bodyguard a run for her money.

True, Neko was wearing heavy boots and lugging an HK MP5 sub machine gun along with a backup pistol and knife while Rita wore a well-worn pair of running shoes and carried nothing more than a compact Smith and Wesson revolver model 642 holstered in the small of her back, but Neko was in excellent condition. So, being able to even keep up with Neko was a good sign that she wasn't over the hill yet. That being said, it was particularly difficult running on the rapidly deteriorating highway, especially considering that having only one eye reduced her depth perception considerably.

"Come on, chica! You're letting an old woman show you up."

"Whatever, Rev. You try being five-three, lugging a sub machine gun and outrun an Amazon with something to prove."

Rita laughed despite being out of breath. "Always with the excuses, girlfriend. Come on. Let's see you outrun the one-eyed witch of UU."

The spritely redhead was half a foot shorter, but she didn't let that stop her from being one of Monticello's fiercest fighters and the commander of the Thomas Jefferson Martyrs Brigade, Greater Monticello's elite fighting force. Originally from Washington State, Neko was competing in the National Archery Finals in Charlottesville when the Shift hit. Fellow competitor and local resident Ezra Rothstein introduced the visiting archery troupe to Rita's congregation as they fled to Monticello.

The snow was beginning to pick up. They made their way onto the road that led to an unyielding climb up to the estate of Monticello itself, and jogged past the remains of the makeshift barrier hastily erected in the first months after the Shift to protect the fledging community from the hordes of refugees seeking food. A flood of memories rushed just underneath Rita's layer of conscious thought as they passed the defunct barrier.

Rita remembered how scared she was facing off against the Blue Ridge Militia. She hadn't been in so much as a fist fight since her early days of sobriety and that was way back in her early twenties. Who was she to lead these people against an armed militia? She was a Unitarian reverend after all; Unitarians weren't known for opening a can of Whupass. Well, at least back before the Shift, they weren't. The events since then sort of changed the lone surviving Unitarian Universalist Church—UU for short—in several ways.

The event that Rita credited for transforming Monticello, her church as a whole and herself was the seminal battle against the Blue Ridge Militia. When the Blue Ridge Militia attacked her people and broke through the gates of Monticello, it was Neko, Ezra and the archers, who jokingly referred to themselves as the Thomas Jefferson Martyrs Brigade, who stood against them. The archers proved crucial in the defense of Rita's ad hoc community comprised of over-educated (and utterly useless) suburbanites, college students, and migrant farmers. The archers were the only ones who knew how to shoot. They fought the wave of over-zealous militia back and vanquished them in what later became known as the Battle of Monticellan Independence. That battle united the people of Monticello and gave them a sense of identity. But it also came at a steep cost for Rita, for she lost her left eye and a few teeth in that engagement.

Rita and Neko waved to the people grooming their horses outside of Michie Tavern and the Grist Mill. Along the way, they passed a wagon carrying lumber down to the town. The final stretch up from the gates of Jefferson's property was at a steep grade. Rita had to watch her footing lest she slip on ice and twist her ankle. Neko was picking up speed and forced Rita to the envelope of endurance. They sprinted up the rest of the mountain, passing farmers tending to winter crops. Right after the Shift first struck, they had to rapidly convert to life sustaining crops over marigolds and rosemary, and they did so just in time for the first winter. These days the farm ran like clockwork.

As they reached the steps to the west garden, she and Neko broke from their sprint. Rita immediately crouched down and placed her hands on her knees. Panting, Neko gave Rita a thumbs-up, her bright red hair now matted on her face. "Good run, Rev."

"Thanks," she managed to say between gasping breaths.

People passed by, greeting them as they did. Some were laborers in the field, some were archers of the elite Thomas Jefferson Martyrs Brigade, and others were regular civilians of varying post-Shift professions. Monticello was no longer shelter to an entire community as it had been in the early days. Most of the population now lived in their own homes down the mountain and in the rapidly repopulating city of Charlottesville. Thomas Jefferson's estate was now the executive mansion and office for Greater Monticello's chief magistrate, that being Rita herself. Only she, Akil and some support staff slept in Monticello now, leaving it eerily quiet at night, but it was bustling with life during the day.

Neko pulled her hair back into a tight ponytail and took a scrunchy from her teeth to bundle it. "Reverend, may I ask you a question?"

Rita sighed. She knew that whenever Neko referred to her as "Reverend," she was addressing Rita as her reverent follower.

The Battle of Monticellan Independence had also transformed the Unitarian Universalist beliefs. Before the Shift, Rita was a world-weary secular humanist who was rapidly losing her faith in humanity, which was a real problem considering her profession. But after the Battle of Monticellan Independence when a Blue Ridge Militia member beat the crap out of her, giving her the massive head injury that took her eye, she had her first vision of Gaia, the living earth who appeared to Rita in various forms, but most often as her dearly departed grandmother. Had she not experienced it herself, she would have thought the injury had caused the visions. Maybe it had, but those visions helped Rita lead

Monticello through the desperate first years of the Shift. It certainly helped the recruiting effort that the Earth was the cause of the Shift. It's hard to argue against a belief that has roots in cold hard reality, even if the theory the geologists proposed about the Earth shifting the magnetic poles as the cause of the EMPs hadn't been proven conclusively just yet.

She knew there were a lot of old UUs rolling in their graves right now seeing how the church transformed into this Gaia worshipping, gun toting cult. But to be fair, they needed a mascot. Besides, Rita thought that the seven principles in UU segued into the whole "Earth Mother Goddess" thing nicely.

There were plenty of times when Rita doubted her own sanity. But then Gaia would smack her upside the head to remind her she didn't have time to contemplate her own mental state. Her job was to preserve and protect the human spirit through reason and openness against the seething tide of fear, ignorance and tribalistic savagery emerging in the post-Shift world. Rita had to be the most reluctant and skeptical prophet in history. Perhaps that's what made her so convincing.

But no matter how much she had come to accept her role as the prophet for Gaia, she never felt comfortable being treated with the kind of awe that the new converts to the transformed Unitarian Universalist Church displayed. At least Neko was one of the original converts and knew Rita to be excruciatingly human and flawed like anyone else. But even still, she had that tendency to fawn over the ethereal. Rita didn't know why. Gaia hadn't spoken to Rita in a vision in over a year.

"What's up?" she asked.

"How do you feel about a lot of these new arrivals?" Neko asked in a hushed voice. People were walking about nonchalantly, waving to each other as though they were living inside a Norman Rockwell painting.

Rita chuckled. "What do you mean? I like them just fine."

Neko rolled her eyes revealing that she wasn't too many years gone from a teenager who said things like, "what-ever."

"I'm serious, Reverend. I mean, people have been flooding into Monticello lately, a lot of them. We can't even keep track of the influx."

"I know, Neko. And isn't that just wonderful? Not seventy miles from here, Regent Gordon Boche and his Lambs of God have been running their own little Authoritarian theocracy."

"Little?" Neko retorted.

"Poor choice of words." Rita certainly wished the Lambs of God were small in number and not an overwhelming mass that out-numbered Monticello and the other members of the Orange Pact alliance.

"But my point is, as Gordon Boche goes around building his empire on the backs of others he deemed as 'unclean' and morally corrupt, people reject his false theology, and they choose to risk their lives to escape Lynchburg and join us."

"Exactly, Reverend. Hundreds, maybe thousands of people from the Dominion of Lynchburg, living among us."

"They're asylees, Neko. They risked their lives to come here to freedom."

Neko shrugged her shoulders. "Many perhaps, sure. Maybe even most. But certainly not all of them. There are a lot of these so called 'refugees' who are agents of the regent. You know that. Lucille's most recent report is undeniable proof."

Monticello's Sheriff, Lucille Schadenfreude was part the first waves of refugees from the Dominion of Lynchburg and one of the earliest and most enthusiastic converts to the Unitarian Church. As a former prosecutor, she was very effective in maintaining order with the rapidly rising population, but she was also more than a little paranoid.

"I don't deny that the regent has sent agents disguised as refugees to live among us. But so be it. I'm proud of what we've achieved here, Neko. Aren't you? Let them see how we live. We don't tell anyone who lives here how to think or what to believe. We teach the inherent dignity and respect of all individuals and live according to those core values of openness. We let people discover their own path. Maybe it will be us influencing the regent's so-called 'agents,' and not the other way around."

"Hmm," Neko responded skeptically. "You are too trusting, Reverend."

"No, Neko. I have seen the worst in humanity. I know what people are capable of. And that is why I must have hope and stick to my ideals."

"Truthfully, I don't know what that means."

Rita held Neko's hand. "I understand your confusion, Amiga. I often struggle myself."

Neko took a deep breath and let her words sink in. "It's not easy, you know, having hope. It requires trust in people. I trust in Gaia, I trust you. That's about it."

It was times like these that Neko dropped her façade and showed herself to be the beautiful and searching soul she was, not the deadly redheaded spitfire with an attitude who could kill with the flick of her fingers. Despite the age difference, Neko and Rita were as close as sisters.

Then as if the moment was too profound for both, Neko perked up. "In any case, Rev, you should get back inside and get ready. You have that dedication this afternoon. We can spar tomorrow."

Splendid, she thought morosely. Rita knew Neko loved her dearly, but that didn't mean that she treated her with kid gloves when it came to teaching her defensive tactics. For such a young woman, Neko was awfully intense and didn't allow Rita to let down her guard when they sparred, her one-eye handicap be damned. Between the Israeli martial arts being ubiquitously taught throughout the alliance, the archery and rifle drills, Rita was becoming modestly dangerous in her own right. Truthfully, she wished she knew what she knew now back when that militia man attacked her years ago. Instinctively, she touched the left side of her face where she lost an eye and some teeth.

An archer cadet walked a freshly groomed horse to Neko and she jumped on. After tucking her MP5 in the saddle and checking that her bow was fitted properly, Neko saluted and clopped down the mountain. Her red ponytail bobbed humorously in contrast to its lethal owner.

Rita shivered after the run as her body cooled off by the sweat that the Pre-Shift running gear didn't wick away. She was about to head back inside to wake up Akil when in the distance across the west garden, Rita saw a hooded figure dressed in black. Even through the snowfall she could tell by the stance that it was her hubby, Akil. Having lived with someone for so long gave her that ability to find him in a sea of people –if there were such a thing still. She walked across the garden, her feet crunching on the freshly fallen snow.

As Rita approached Akil, she could see the restoration taking place down below in Charlottesville. The re-emerging town centered on the University as it had sustained the least damage and housed Greater Monticello's offices.

Rita could sense that Akil was in deep thought. It was no wonder. He had just returned from Asheville, North Carolina yesterday. In his continuing quest to find his son Jamil, Akil set out to the distant city hoping against hope that he would find him with his ex-wife's parents who lived there. It was a long shot, and dangerous. But she wasn't a parent. She could only imagine how much Jamil's disappearance addled him. Akil was by no means the only one whose child disappeared in the chaos when the Shift hit. He was on his way from his home in Maryland to pick up Jamil from Ruth, his ex-wife who lived in Charlottesville, for the week when the first EMP hit.

After finding Ruth's place abandoned without a clue as to Jamil's whereabouts, Akil stayed in the burning city searching blindly for his son. Eventually, he stumbled upon Rita lying on the road, still infirmed with her injuries from the Blue Ridge Militia. It was a mystery how she slipped through Monticello's barrier undetected from the makeshift hospital at Michie Tavern and walked all the way down the mountain in her condition. Akil later told Rita that in her delirious state, she said that Jamil loved him, which would have been impossible. Uttering Jamil's name coincided with Rita's first and most profound vision of Gaia; she suspected Gaia slipped those words through her mouth to bring Akil into her world.

Akil was smoking a hand rolled cigarillo, the only kind of cigarette around.

"Hey."

Akil turned to give her a kiss but she playfully pushed him away. "Eww, you'll taste like an ashtray."

She stroked his head. His beard now had more gray in it, but he still was a handsome devil, a Don Cheadle with the voice of Morgan Freeman. Just looking at him, she felt weak all these years later.

"How was your run?'

"Not too bad. Although I think Neko forgets I'm not her age."

"No, you're a grown up," Akil said.

"When did you get up?"

Akil took another drag from the cigarette. "Just a few minutes ago. Sorry, I know there's a lot of work to get done."

"It's fine, mi Coriño" She said gently. "I know you were up all night."

"Yeah. Sorry if I woke you. It's just difficult unwinding after getting back."

"You don't need to apologize. I'm just glad you made it back in one piece." She shifted her weight. "We haven't discussed the details since you returned. Are you okay to talk?"

"Sure. There's not much to add. Jamil wasn't there. Asheville is as bad as most urban areas. There's nobody checking Lynchburg's six. They could take all of North Carolina if they wanted to."

"I'm sorry you didn't find him."

"You told me it was foolish to go."

"God, I can be so cold sometimes. Did I say that?"

"It doesn't matter. You were right."

"Yeah, but I wish I wasn't."

"I wish your patron Goddess would hook a brother up on my son's whereabouts. That's what I wish."

"Mi Coriño, she hasn't so much as coughed around me in almost a year. I think I bore her."

"Now that is insane. You? Boring? You're the sexiest gun-toting pirate Unitarian priestess I've ever seen, and I've seen some sexy eye patch priestesses in my time."

She smacked him on the shoulder and he feigned pain. "Come on, you lascivious strumpet."

"No," she cried out playfully. "We've got to get ready for the dedication."

He went to grab for her, and she used one of the moves Neko had ingrained in her, and tackled him into the snow with his arm pinned at his back and her knee hovering over his neck. If she were sparring, she would put her full weight on him.

"Hey, woman. I thought you said we had to get ready for the dedication. What's this—foreplay?"

She twisted his wrist ever so slightly and he laughed constricted by his chest on the ground and in pain.

"I told you that you taste like an ashtray. Now, I'm going to let you go, mi Coriño, and I don't want any tomfoolery. Agreed?"

"Agreed."

She let go and helped Akil up and dusted himself off. "Um, Rita."

"Yes."

"Remember how I agreed to no tomfoolery?"

"Yes, I remember."

"I lied."

Rita took off running. "Akil Roulston, you deceitful oaf! Don't you dare!" Rita couldn't stand being tickled.

Although the structure itself had remained as it had when she was the church's reverend, the building of the Unitarian Universalist Church of Charlottesville had undergone significant changes. Fire had swept through the early 19th century brick building. After being completely gutted, the volunteers renovated the church with utter disregard for the conservative, dignified American Colonial sensibilities. The red brick, which had been severely scorched, had been painted over in Technicolor. The assault of vibrating colors formed a mural of a cosmos filled with exploding stars, crescent moons, Indians shooting arrows on horseback, rams, eagles and squirrels coalescing around a gregarious, topless green woman sitting with huge milky breasts, sitting cross-legged, hugging her pregnant belly that was painted to resemble the earth.

Rita had thought of herself to be a liberal minded type. She was born and raised in San Antonio, so she was used to seeing loudly painted houses. But seriously? Taking something as historic as the Unitarian Church in Charlottesville, and recasting it as the bad trip part in the Beatles animated movie *Yellow Submarine* would definitely not have passed the city ordinances in the old days. Maybe the quarter German in her otherwise pure Mexican heritage had just about all the wackiness it could handle, and cried out for order.

Rita grinned widely, trying not to laugh as she exited her strange Beetle wagon and walked up the steps of the church with an exuberant crowd applauding her arrival. Most of those present today for the dedication of the restored church weren't even the original members. Some unfortunately had died as a result of the Battle of Monticellan Independence, the Obsidian War, and living without modern medicine. The original ranks of her church were dwarfed by the numbers of post-Shift converts. They were the most enthusiastic, especially the converts who escaped from Lynchburg and Roanoke. Rita tried to understand why that was so. Although a slim majority who fled Lynchburg remained Christian, the rest who escaped the regent's grasp embraced Gaia with such stunning devotion, it was almost as if Gaia herself had appeared to them and led them to safety. Many claimed she had in some form or another. Rita felt a mixture of bemusement and sympathy for them.

Despite the snow, people packed the street to the end of the block and covered the front lawn of the church. Among the people in the crowd was her husband, Neko, and Monticello's Sheriff Lucille Schadenfreude. Rita's deputy, Juan Ramirez, was absent, which was okay. He was a Christian, after all. Rita was here in her capacity as a Unitarian Reverend, not the executive of Greater Monticello. She knew such distinctions were blurred, but she at least tried to make them.

Rita slipped her hands inside the sleeves of her fur coat—it was PC to wear one so long as it was a Unitarian who bagged the poor animal—and gazed at the cheering crowd. The stole that denoted her as a minister draped down her front with flowing patterns that resembled the mural behind her. Across the street stood a statue of a nude female warrior with a compound bow, standing victoriously on top of a muscle car. It was beautiful, inspiring and preposterous all at once. Judging by the facial features and contours of the statue's figure, Rita surmised Neko had volunteered to be the model.

As the crowd settled down, Rita cleared her throat ready to project her voice to the person in the back. Monticello and its emerging settlement of Charlottesville had managed to generate electrical power using a variety of methods, but the power generated was not reliable nor of an impressive amount. As a result, electricity in Monticello was used sparingly. Rita would not bother wasting valuable energy for a microphone.

"It seems a lifetime ago now since I stood here," she said without preamble. The audience immediately fell silent. The light snowfall muffled out the sounds of construction a few blocks away.

"It was, in fact, another lifetime for all of us. Who I was, who we all were…we were settled in our lives, driving to work, to school, meandering through life unaware and utterly dependent upon the complex menagerie of gears that powered our civilization."

She smirked and kicked her foot into the powdery snow. "You know, before she visited me, I thought Gaia was just some scientific hypothesis that liberals co-opted to use for Earth Day events. I used her for my own ends, or at least I thought I did. Gaia was simply the focus for my next book, because professors need to keep publishing."

Some chuckled. "I know, right?"

As ridiculous as it sounded to the followers now, it was true. Rita recalled how before the Shift she felt like a fraud selling some jargon about the collective human spirit and social justice when she was just trying to put it into a book that would sell. There were times she was almost tempted to pick up the bottle and be done with it. Fortunately, living a couple of houses down from her sponsor Eric Starke kept her head together enough not to relapse. She was hanging on, but just barely.

"And then it all came crashing down when the first EMP struck. Terrified, we saw friends and loved ones dying. We thought it was the end for us all. And that is when she found us. So many died as a result, upstanding and malevolent alike. There was no justice in the Shift as we know all too well. We lost loved ones, and we mourn for them to this day."

"As I stand here today, I remember watching my church burn in the fires. So much death and destruction. I thought there could be no restoration. Gaia did not send the Shift to punish the wicked, nor to punish humanity. But we were thrown back to a state of nature. And out of that wilderness, Gaia spoke to me, and she found each of you."

"I had once thought I was using her to get on Oprah, but it was she who sought us out. She had done so, because we have to be the light against the darkness. The value of the inherent dignity of all humanity, the respect for balance and reason, these are the values that will guide humanity to survive these times and to evolve."

"The values we hold dear of respect, reason and spiritual exploration are in short supply today. Out there beyond the perimeter, people prey upon each other, people enslave and rally others to kill in the name of God."

"So, we must stand together. Whether we be Unitarian, Christian or anyone else who cherishes the values of mutual respect and reason, we must be a guiding light. It is why Gaia has led us here today. Your creativity and your toil resurrected something I never thought could be restored… this little church. And with this little church, let us serve as a beacon to humanity. For those still out there struggling, clawing onto life, we say there is something better to live for. Let this church serve to help bring everyone home."

The crowd applauded enthusiastically. Some started to chant, "Liberty, dignity, equality."

Rita walked down from the steps and into the crowd to press the flesh. If not by name, Rita was familiar with most of the faces in the crowd. Greater Monticello, though growing at an exponential rate, was still a small community compared to even a modest-sized city before the Shift. There were also several visiting devotees from others towns. Some even came from as far away as the Republic of West Virginia, though her mission was a small affair out there.

Hands reached out desperately wanting to touch her, and she moved slowly to shake as many hands as she could.

Neko and Akil stood beside her serving as a wedge to help Rita move through the crowd. Hands seemed to be sprouting out from nowhere. Rita stopped to thank everyone, kiss a baby, hand him back, move slowly and shake more hands. Neko was nudging her to step on it a little.

A scream rose above the cheering. There was a sudden commotion, but Rita couldn't identify where. In the next instant, Neko grabbed the reverend forcefully by the fur coat and pushed her forward.

"Gun!" someone cried out.

Rita tried to see what the commotion was about, but Neko used her smaller frame to protect the reverend and pushed her toward the carriage, the ridiculous one with the frame of a green VW Beetle that she reluctantly used for these religious occasions.

A shot rang out and a red mist sprayed onto Rita. The crowd screamed in horror and rage. Neko's screams for her to move were choked off with a shocked cry of pain. Rita nearly slipped on the snow, but Akil grabbed her left arm and kept her upright. In the chaos Rita saw behind her that a man was being attacked by a mob. She turned to Neko whose face was pale and splattered in blood as she struggled to push Rita to the carriage. Rita grabbed Neko.

"No! Go, damn it!" Neko barked.

Rita ignored her and wrapped her arm around Neko's waist. Akil was calling out for support as a team of archers in plain clothes tried to rush through the crowd to her aid. Rita turned to face the carriage only to see a short teenage boy wearing a black duster silently stepping towards her with a determined look. She immediately looked to his hands, which were wielding blades. It was as though he materialized out of nowhere and was invisible to all but her. The man stomped past the melee effortlessly, a cold look on his face. He bore on her and flicked the blades, preparing for a slashing motion with one arm and a parry with the other. Rita was transfixed on the blade arching in its trajectory towards her.

BACKGROUND MUSIC: "Gold Dust Woman" By Fleetwood Mac
Visit www.michaeljuge.com **on the *A Hard Rain* page to listen**

And then the motion of his arms slowed, impossibly so, and he froze in place. Everything stopped. The cacophony of screams and cries fell into silence. Time itself halted as the attacker's blades hovered over her. The world outside seemed like an indoor stage as she cried out belatedly, giving voice to her horror.

"Sorry to interrupt you, mi Querida."

Rita shot around and saw through the frozen crowd sitting at a table atop the steps of the church was a diminutive elderly woman, exquisitely dressed, resembling her maternal grandmother who died a few years ago.

Rita raised her hand over her brow. "Abuelita?"

It wasn't her grandmother—Rita knew as much. But since Gaia had taken the form of her grandmother, Rita chose to address her as such most of the time. It was just easier that way.

Gaia sipped from her teacup and placed it back on its saucer just as her grandmother did. Although her grandmother was of Mexican heritage, she was educated by Anglo nuns who instilled many of their traditions upon the students. The elderly woman wore white gloves and a fruit basket hat to accessorize her Sunday best, which was seasonably out of place with the snow. It was Gaia, so Rita imagined Mother Earth didn't get the chills.

"I see you're in the middle of something," she said understating the scene of violence before her.

Rita gingerly maneuvered around the attacker, Neko and Akil, careful not to displace them. She has had these visions before, so she was familiar with the sudden halt in the space/time continuum thing. Yet it had been a long time since her last vision, almost a year in fact. "Abuelita," she repeated as she approached. Out of the corner of her eye, she saw Neko covered in blood. She tried to push it aside. There would be time for that later. Rita slowly walked past the frozen crowd, crunching through the snow and ascended the steps.

"Please, take a seat," Gaia gestured to the empty chair across from her at the table.

Seeing Gaia, she felt a welter of emotions. She wanted to either hug the little woman or shake her. Why hadn't she shown herself to her in so long? And why at this very moment? Not knowing how to respond, Rita chose to take a seat. The elderly woman pulled a tissue from her sleeve and rubbed her horn rimmed glasses that were straight out of the 50s.

"It's been awhile," Rita said with practiced calmed, trying to portray herself as casual as the woman sitting next to her. It was difficult seeing the freeze frame bedlam a few feet away.

"Yes, mi Querida. I do apologize. I have been busy."

"I can imagine. It's good to see you, Abuelita." The elderly lady reached out her gloved hand and cupped it with Rita's."

"You are doing such fine work, my dear, and under such difficult circumstances." Gaia stood up from her seat and walked down the steps and along the church walls, studying the mural before her.

"Oh, my. Such imagination, such creativity you humans possess, filled with dreams, music, cheese filled foods. You are so tender, and…" She ran her fingers along the mural as she examined the artwork carefully. She turned to face the melee. "And so violent."

"It is a part of us," Rita conceded.

"As you are a part of me." Gaia strolled onto the street where bicycles and horses were hitched. An archer of the Martyrs Brigade dressed in the snow camouflage uniform was in mid stride with his AK-47 hefted in the air. Gaia knelt down next to him and caressed a patch of flowers near a bush that grew in spite of the icy conditions.

"Abuelita, what is it? What's wrong?"

Gaia facing away from her answered dully, "What makes you think anything is wrong?"

Rita moved passed the archer and knelt beside her. "Gaia, you haven't spoken to me in a long time. And then you show up in the middle of my assassination. And you're here but you're…I don't know, you're dawdling. Tell me, Abuelita. Tell me, why are you here?"

She then saw tears rolling down Gaia's cheeks. Gaia tried smiling though her dark brown eyes awash in tears. She took another tissue out of her sleeve and dabbed her eyes under her glasses.

"Sorry, mi Querida. I do get attached to things. Help me up, would you?"

Rita offered her hand and helped the elderly woman back up. Something was very wrong.

"Gaia?"

"Yes, dear, you are perceptive. There is something happening. I cannot say what, but I do know that all of us are in great danger."

Rita wanted to ask "What kind of danger," but Gaia already said she couldn't say. Also, she learned that Gaia tended to be cryptic. She didn't know if that was by choice, screwing with her head for the hell of it to make life more interesting, or if it had to do with the fact that being an entire planet hindered her ability to speak English and Spanish. In either case, she said nothing and let Gaia speak.

"Humanity has such potential, mi Querida. You look upon the stars and wonder who else is out there. None but you speak of such high ideals and yet are capable of such horrible crimes. You are my most confounding children. I had hoped that you would have the chance to grow, to evolve beyond what you are today. You don't know how satisfying it is to see a species evolve."

"But there's a problem…" Rita finished nervously.

Gaia nodded.

"What is it?"

Gaia stroked her hand, which made Rita all the more terrified. She had never seen Gaia upset before. Even during the height of the Obsidian War,

Gaia was as relaxed as a house cat lying on a summer deck. And while the Lambs of God rattled their sabers and amassed in numbers, Gaia seemed nonchalant, telling her to just add some Christian saints to the emerging Gaian religion. But now, Gaia looked deeply upset.

"Nothing in the universe is guaranteed, mi Querida. Our time, even mine is finite. Eventually one day, the sun will expand to swallow me. And I would hope that you will have evolved by then. But it seems you must grow faster than I thought. We are all mortal in the end."

"My God, Abuelita, will you please stop speaking in prose and answer me?" Rita had lost her cool, she admitted, but it sounded like Gaia was inferring that humanity as a whole was in peril.

"You must go to Jamil. Jamil might know."

Rita was already confused, but now Gaia was throwing Akil's son into this? Gaia continued. "With Laurel you will find Jamil."

It was times like these that Rita wanted to pick up the little old mushroom and throw her across the lawn to knock some sense into her. "Gaia, I'm trying to understand, but you're talking nonsense."

"I know this is frustrating. It is for me, too. I still have difficulty communicating with you. Your mind is so muddled."

"Yes, I get that a lot."

"What I know is with Laurel you will find Jamil, and Jamil will know what to do."

"Who's Laurel and where is she and Jamil?"

The next thing Rita knew she was standing in front of the attacker ready to slash her throat.

"I must leave you now," Gaia said.

"But I don't understand!" she cried out unable to move from her position.

"Mi Querida?"

"Yes," Rita responded anxiously.

"Duck."

The next thing she knew, Rita narrowly missed the assassin's blade.

Chapter 3

Montpelier Station, Virginia
Rochelle Sovereignty
December 2012

It was turning into a banner day for Meredith Jung. Her husband's crew, which was due back home yesterday, was laid over another evening out in the wilderness. Baby Charles kept her up half the night with colic. She was awaiting—more like dreading—Ezra's findings in Asheville and comparing it to what Ross discovered. Meredith didn't look forward to reading what Ezra brought back from Asheville or the report from Ross. She wouldn't understand what the reports said, anyway. She would have to have her people in Stokesville translate it for her, but again, she did not look forward to that. Actually, she hoped something more pressing would pull her away, and then she regretted making such a foolish wish, because something did pull her away, something horrible.

Meredith, the young director of the Swan, the intelligence agency that was comprised of and served the members of the Orange Pact, sat at a communications console and placed the telephone receiver up to her ear. Greater Monticello and Rochelle had laid down old-fashioned copper wire for telephonic communications, which was relatively reliable and provided clearer transmissions compared to radio communication. The communications office was clamoring with frantic activity, making it difficult for her to hear the receiver. Men and women were running into and out of the suite of the late 18th century mansion, which overlooked James Madison's estate, or would have if they ever opened the blinds, which she never allowed.

Back in the real world, Meredith had been perfectly content serving in DHS as a simple GS-12. She never had any desire to be a manager and hold a leadership position. She never dreamed that she would wind up as the founder and leader of an intelligence agency herself, and she never would try to compare herself to her former boss Michael Chertoff. But she took her cues from what she remembered of him as best as she could in creating the Swan.

As she waited on the line, reports officers handed her scribbled notes. She would have to put it all together within the next few minutes to brief the constable.

"Mrs. Jung? Are you still there?"

"Yes, Ezra," she answered expectantly. "I am. Sorry, it's difficult to hear. Was the chief magistrate harmed?"

"Quick answer, the chief magistrate is unharmed. Repeat, Rita's fine."

Meredith sighed with relief and gave herself a moment to catch her wits. "Thank God."

"What were the casualties?"

"We have two archers injured, but no bystander fatalities."

"Thank you, Ezra. Once your boss relieves you, I want you to come over."

"I'll get my night bag and I'll send you a status update in the next half hour."

After hanging up, Meredith took off her glasses and squeezed the center of her forehead just above the bridge of her nose trying to massage the massive headache away. Her Montpelier souvenir mug was filled with a viscous dark brew of chicory. It tasted dreadful, but it served to substitute coffee, which was now a precious commodity available only in pre-Shift vacuum packed bricks. Even with the vacuum seal, such gems were losing their freshness. Right now she either needed some coffee or to go into the complete opposite direction and partake in some cash crop cannabis.

She took a few moments to read the decoded cable traffic sent from Monticello, which gave more sensitive details about the would-be assassins. Meredith gathered her team and over the next few minutes, they hashed out what they knew, making sure they didn't miss anything. When she was satisfied that she had enough information, Meredith gathered the cables, which were nothing like the cables in the old days, but rather handwritten notes jotted from a telegraph, and headed to see the constable.

Meredith sat patiently near the center of the long conference table while Constable Jon Early and the others read the report. She brushed aside a few stray strands of her brunette hair that came out of her bun and readjusted the glasses sliding down her nose. Unlike the Swan's offices upstairs where the shutters were always closed, the expansive windows of James Madison's home let in copious sunlight. The majestic 18th century mansion had been gutted before the Shift, undergoing a massive restoration project. When the people of the neighboring town of Orange petitioned to become part of Rochelle less than a year after the conclusion of the Obsidian War, everything in Orange County to include President Madison's former estate of Montpelier had been annexed into the Rochelle Sovereignty.

The mansion was impressive even by the McMansion standards of the early millennium. It was an obvious choice for Rochelle to move its executive office there. The property of Montpelier, once a vast expanse of open fields used primarily for equestrian sports, had been converted to growing tobacco and the more ignoble cannabis plant, both of which were Rochelle's major cash crops. The mansion's location on top of a hill gave Montpelier a commanding view of the Blue Ridge Mountains.

Jon read through the report slowly while Vice Deputy Thuy Mai gave Meredith an encouraging smile. The Commandant, Dean Jacob, rapped his pencil on the table. Outside, snow was beginning to fall. Meredith thought about her husband out there in the Beltway region slogging it out in this weather. She had no idea how he was doing. It was late in the afternoon, the unseen sun cresting downward.

Sitting beside Jon was his wife Dr. Sharon Wessinger, Elizabeth Hughes' sister. Sharon's hair had more grey in it than Jon's—she was eight years his senior, but he was catching up fast. As he rubbed his chiseled jaw, Meredith noticed that Jon had neglected to shave again. He had been doing that a lot lately, not that Meredith had a problem with facial hair. Her husband had a chin beard with the hair braided into two prongs like some Viking warrior, which she found completely absurd. But Jon had always been clean shaven. It was the Marine in him. Even during the Obsidian War, Jon kept his clean cut look. Lately, though...

"Hmm." Jon's squinty eyes and high cheek bones, which in years past made him a dead ringer for a young Richard Gere, seemed a little less defined and striking than they used to be.

On the wall hung a painting of Constable Jon Early on top of his horse rearing on its hind legs as he brandished his great-great-grandfather's saber. Following him was a column of armed men and women on foot and on bicycles, bellowing out savagely. One of the citizen warriors hoisted the flag of Rochelle with the grey silhouette of a rabbit with preposterously long ears, whiskers and fangs over crossed battle axes, set against an orange field. It was an interpretation of the Rout at Exxon Heights, a pivotal battle that changed the course of the Obsidian War, a scene that Chris swore he witnessed firsthand and made sure was enshrined in a painting.

There were a couple of inaccuracies. For one thing, there was no Vicious Rabbits flag at that time. In fact, it was only at that precise moment in the epic battle that Jon first called them by the name Vicious Rabbits, which would later become official. The artist illustrated the smoldering carnage below of men burning alive by the balloon-thrown napalm, but it was spun with glory rather than raked with naked horror.

Comparing the man in the painting to the man reading the report before her, Meredith judged that they resembled each other in gross physical terms. But Jon reading the reports across the table from her seemed to be more of a shadow of the man in the painting that day years ago. The image portrayed Jon with a ruthless, fiery glare that bore through the fabric of the painting into the souls of the living who set eyes upon him. The Jon straining to read the fine print report next to her seemed anything but determined and alive.

Jon looked up from the report. "So, Rita is all right?"

"That's correct," Meredith answered. "She's at the hospital right now visiting with one of her bodyguards, Neko Lemay."

"Isn't she the commander of the Martyrs Brigade?"

"Yes, she was shot by one of the assassins. I do not know her condition. A bystander was hit by a fragment, but didn't sustain any serious injuries."

Meredith took a sip of chicory and continued. "There's a lot of confusion down there right now. Some witnesses claimed there were numerous attackers while others say they saw only one or two making for the chief magistrate. The sheriff's agents down there have rounded up a dozen potential suspects, all of them were armed. Of course, that by itself means nothing considering that pretty much everyone is packing these days. But, Constable, given the information I have, I can tell you it is the three individuals mentioned at the top of the report who are responsible."

"How is that?" Commandant Jacob asked. The tall African American had grown into his role as the military leader of the Vicious Rabbits, having served as Jon Early's executive officer in the US Marine Second Mar Div Fourth Battalion Eighth Regiment.

"Well, it was a Unitarian event and two of the boys weren't Unitarians," she said flatly. There was an uncomfortable stir around the conference room. Rochelle was roughly half Christian and half Unitarian. Jon was himself a devout Christian. Monticello on the other hand was predominantly Unitarian, though it had a growing Christian minority.

It wasn't as though there were ACLU lawyers waiting outside the gates to pounce on the constable of Rochelle or the mayor of Culpeper with a lawsuit if they put a nativity scene in front of their offices. But Jon was personal with his faith and also knew there were certain sensitivities with his community, namely a community divided between Christian and Unitarians who worked well together so long as they weren't reminded of their differences. With Monticello, not so much. Although their charter specifically forbade the promotion of a state religion and was very specific that religion would never play a role in deciding who was elected, in reality, Monticello was the home of the Unitarian people.

What's more, Rita Luevano had two primary roles. She was the chief magistrate, the secular leader of Greater Monticello, officially elected by the people when they realized they hadn't really officially elected her before then. Her other role was as Reverend Luevano, the prophet priestess of the transformed Unitarian Universalist Church, which was also known as the Gaia Piety Society. Meredith had never known Rita to be a demagogue or to have any delusions of being a theocratic autocrat. Meredith would never feel comfortable incorporating Monticello's intelligence officers into the Swan, otherwise. But at the same time, no one could say that Greater Monticello wasn't heavily influenced by their Unitarian heritage. Sensing the discomfort in the room, Meredith pressed on with an audience that was significantly more Christian than Unitarian.

"The Unitarians were dedicating the re-opening of the very church where Rita had preached before the Shift. This was a Unitarian function. I'm not saying that there wouldn't be any Christians there, but we also know that the regent has sent assets into the Orange Pact under the guise of refugees."

"Do we have any information from the suspects yet? Did they confess?" Deputy Constable Thuy Mai asked.

"Not yet. They're being held but haven't been questioned yet."

"What do we know about them?" Jon Early asked.

"All three were refugees from Lynchburg between the ages of sixteen and twenty-two. Their names are in the cable. Two arrived in Greater Monticello roughly two years ago, one four years ago. Two of them are soldiers in the Defense Forces."

"Shit," Dean muttered.

Thuy Mai added, "If they're operatives of the regent that means they've infiltrated Monticello and entrenched themselves."

"We don't know that they're Gordon's men," Jon cautioned.

"Not yet, sir, but when they do talk, I'd put my retirement that they were sent by the regent, and then we're screwed," Dean said fatalistically.

"Constable," Thuy leaned over to Jon Early, "I'd like to interview the suspects."

Jon raised his eyebrows. "I think Rita's people have experience with interrogations."

"Yes, sir, they do; however, to be blunt, I don't think the Monticellans are in the right frame of mind to interview them."

"Is that because their leader was targeted or because they're Unitarians?" Jon was not particularly fond of the Unitarian faith, neither its earlier secular humanist form nor in its Gaia Piety Society transformation. He shared many Christians' skepticism that Gaia worship was akin to paganism. That being said, Jon had worked very closely with Rita, and Meredith knew he considered her to be a good friend. He also valued the close working relationship between Rochelle and Greater Monticello.

Thuy shook his head. "Their being Unitarian doesn't figure into it. It's just that these kids don't have the experience in interviewing that I do."

"What, because you were once an agent in Diplomatic Security," Dean asked coarsely.

Thuy nodded. "That and my years on the force in San Francisco. I've interviewed more people than anyone in the Martyrs Brigade."

"Actually, Thuy, Monticello's sheriff will be interviewing them," Meredith answered. "Lucille Schadenfreude was the district attorney in Roanoke before the Shift and has done plenty of cross examination in her time. As the sheriff, she's done a remarkable job helping us in the Swan gathering intelligence, I might add."

"Still, I'd like to offer my assistance."

Jon ran a hand through his receding black hair. "I'll bring it up with the chief magistrate when she's available to talk."

"I'm just glad the plot didn't succeed." Dean's expression transformed into his trademark scowl. "If Christians were responsible for assassinating the mother of the Gaia Piety Society, well, that would be destabilizing for all of us, not just Greater Monticello."

"I'm afraid when this all gets out, it might have the same effect regardless," Meredith countered somberly.

"Wow, Meredith, are you always such an optimist?" Thuy chided. The Asian American with an absolutely perfect flat top that defied the collapse of western civilization had a way of staying chipper even during the worst of times. Meredith was glad that Chris had been in the same basic special agent class with Thuy and befriended him. Despite his incessant joking that sometimes grated on her, his cheery outlook and can-do spirit kept Rochelle above water during the brief months after Constable Charles Early died of the flu and before Colonel Jon Early's arrival.

Meredith smiled with as much sincerity as she could muster. "If I was an optimist, I wouldn't be working here, now would I?"

Everyone around the room chuckled before continuing. "Ezra Rothstein just got back into Monticello from North Carolina the night before last. Good timing, because he's the one who gathered the information we do have. I'm pretty sure he will have more useful intel to share when he is able to make it over."

"What was Ezra doing in North Carolina?" Dean asked.

Before Meredith could answer, there was a knock on the door and an elderly woman peeked in. "Sorry to bother you, Constable. Mrs. Jung, you told me to tell you. We just got word from Culpeper. The cavalry has safely returned."

Meredith sighed gratefully as though a weight had been lifted off of her. Her husband was safe and sound back in settled lands. She and Chris seemed to have lived several lifetimes together and yet she was still in love with that goofy neurotic man.

"Thank you, Mrs. Lanningham."

"Your husband sent a message. It reads," the elderly lady put on her glasses to read the note. "'What's happening, hot stuff? Be sure to get the sausages for the party. See you in an hour. Kaplah,' did I get that right? 'Kaplah?' What does that mean anyway?"

"It's an expression, Mrs. Lanningham, a Klingon one."

Meredith looked around and saw all of the men smiling with shit eating grins, and she felt mildly embarrassed having a slightly intimate message being delivered in the middle of an emergency meeting.

Jon slapped his hands together. "Look, unless there is anything else, I believe the meeting would just descend into wild speculation. Mrs. Jung, you have a reunion with your husband to get to. We can all meet up tomorrow when Ezra arrives. Let's say oh' eight hundred."

Addressing her specifically, Jon added, "Does that work for you?"

"Yes, Constable, thank you."

"Great. Unless there are any other disasters to discuss. No? Alibis, complaints? Okay, then I'll see you all tomorrow."

Everyone stood up and gathered their things while Meredith packed her valise. Mrs. Lanningham and another elderly gentleman cleared the table of any remaining classified cables. Meredith employed many of the surviving senior citizens, those who lived despite the death of pace makers and modern medicines, in the Swan's office. Though agents and operatives had to be young and fit, the elderly had served in more sedentary settings such as the Swan's operations center. Plus, they understood the old saying "Loose lips sink ships."

Thuy walked up to her and spoke with a hushed tone. "So, the party is still on then."

"Looks like it."

Thuy grinned. "The end of the world party. I love it."

Meredith thought it was funny too when Chris thought it up. He had remembered some talk about the Mayan calendar ending on the winter solstice 2012, which was a week away. She remembered Chris talking about seeing it on the History Channel or something and thought it would be a fun idea to celebrate the end of the world as an ironic gesture. The idea of an apocalyptic prophecy seemed a bit redundant, all things considered. That was Chris' point, to poke fun at a much-spoken about prophecy that, unless aliens were about to invade or something, was about to be debunked. The world had already gone pear shaped. It sounded like a great idea except that much of the actual nuts and bolts of the party planning, like arranging for an additional generator and food and drinks, were left to her. Some part of her didn't like tempting fate, though. That was why she didn't look forward to reading the reports Ezra was bringing back from North Carolina.

"Do we need to bring anything?"

Meredith grinned wryly. "To quote Chris, 'just bring your ass to kiss it goodbye.'"

Out front of the restored mansion waited her driver feeding the horses. Snow covered the landscape and was falling more heavily now. She bundled her designer overcoat, which was liberated on Chris' last deployment to the Beltway at a Neiman Marcos outlet store. The coat contrasted to the rugged hiking boots she wore. She was grateful for having a carriage and not having to ride a bike or go on horseback in this weather. The driver was a perk of the job, though her husband's business would have also paid for the driver's salary, paid in West Virginian Byrds, that is.

"Afternoon, Bob. Thanks for waiting in all of this," she said as snow caught on her eyelashes. "Let's pick up the kids and go to the staging area."

"You got it, Mrs. Jung."

Meredith's commute from work was rather short, just a few minutes ride north along a two lane highway. The carriage passed Funeral Mound, a mass grave where Rochelle had cremated its dead who fell to the flu that had claimed so many lives throughout the Mid-Atlantic in the autumn of 2007. In years since, people conjectured that the flu that wiped out whole towns came from Atlanta and was an experimental strain created by the government accidentally unleashed when the power first went out. Others said the strain that hit them was actually the New York strain, as it was slightly less virulent. The operating intel and forensics available lent credence to the theory that there were two separate strains of flu that infected the fleeing and desperate population along the east coast. Whether the two strains truly originated in Atlanta and New York City was anybody's guess. Nobody was going to traipse around either city to ascertain the truth.

Whether it was a government cooked strain or not, whether the strains originated from Atlanta or New York, the results were devastating, punctuating the term "The Great Suck" used in the Fredericksburg Union. As hooves clopped on the highway, Meredith stared out the window of the fiberglass carriage gazing at Funeral Mound recalling those first panicked months in Rochelle. She was pregnant with Aidan and had just cycled a hundred miles from DC with Chris. Charles Early, the town's constable and Jon's father, was a solid sort who seemed to instinctively know what to do to keep Rochelle safe from the enveloping chaos. When Charles learned of her profession, he put her to work making sense of people's accounts of what was happening in other towns and cities.

Charles was a gruff older man and a perfect Southern gentleman. When he succumbed to the flu, it was like losing a father. Dozens followed the constable, including the entire Early family save for Jon. The victims of the flu didn't even get their own service. In complete lockdown, the tiny hamlet carted their dead to the mound that had a dilapidated barn and set it on fire, cremating the flu victims' remains in a mass pyre.

Thuy Mai, Chris, Brandon and she became the only leadership left in a traumatized community. They didn't know how to organize the people like Charles did. They certainly didn't know how to defend themselves against the threats outside their gates. Before Jon Early arrived with the remnants of his Marine battalion, Rochelle was ripe for anyone to come in and take over.

Meredith recalled how frightened she was on the heels of Charles Early's death. With Rochelle in disarray, she pulled strings to install Thuy to take the constable's place; however, Thuy was in no condition to whip the town into shape. He was still in a wheelchair, having sustained a gunshot wound on the raid at Madison High. And as for her, Meredith was a week overdue.

Thinking back, Meredith smirked. She was trying to brief Thuy as the newly installed constable on what she and Charles had been working on before he died when suddenly her water broke. It was absurd. Here she was, detailing a plot she devised to overthrow the sheriff of Culpeper when nature stepped in to remind her that she had other business to attend to, like giving birth to Aidan.

And that was when she panicked. Meredith hadn't been able to prepare for Aidan, not with everything going on. She hadn't even taken a Lamaze class. How in the hell was she going to be a mother in this world? Fortunately, it all worked out, but Funeral Mound served as a daily reminder how desperate they had once been.

The carriage passed another set of fields as it approached the Jung's property. Off the highway down a snow-covered dirt road lay her home, a post-Shift construction that resembled a two-story farmhouse, something that she and Chris had often dreamt of one day owning while they were crammed in their tiny apartment in Falls Church. Chris had painted both the house and the barn next to it taxicab yellow.

Her kids Aidan and Rhiannon were playing out in the snow-covered fields, bundled in their winter coats, which made them look like blue and yellow ticks running around. The grazing sheep had the wisdom to run away from the kids whenever they ran toward them. From a distance, Meredith saw Aidan making snowballs and pitching them at the sheep. He was a five-year-old boy, after all. Rhiannon, who was three, followed her big brother's lead.

As the carriage pulled up to the driveway, a petite women past middle age carrying a bundled Baby Charles in the crook of her arms was admonishing Aidan.

"You stop harassing those sheep, you hear me, Aidan!"

"But they're those stupid Lambs of God, Mrs. Palfrey."

"No, they're not. They are your sheep, and you will treat the beasts with kindness."

Aidan fussed in the kid way, complaining, "Aw," elongating the word moving higher in pitch to punctuate his protest.

Mrs. Palfrey walked up to the carriage and carefully handed Baby Charles to her. Charles cooed when he saw his mother smiling at him.

"Thanks, Mrs. Palfrey. We're actually going to be picking up Chris now."

"Thank the heavens he made it back!" said the slight woman. Mrs. Palfrey had been a nanny before the Shift, which was evident with her expertise in corralling the kids to the carriage without having to scream and yell as Meredith often had to. Using her sweet voice Mrs. Palfrey broke the snowball fight up and Aidan and Rhiannon ran toward the carriage.

"Mommy!"

The events of the day, which weighed on her dissipated as her kids raced up to her. Aidan jumped into the carriage first with Rhiannon waddling behind. The two shoved their way inside the carriage and competed to be first to hug Mommy.

"Are we picking up Dad?" Aidan asked. Meredith nodded and the kids cheered loudly disturbing Baby Charles.

"I miss Daddy," Rhiannon said.

"I do, too," Meredith said as the carriage trundled back onto the highway.

"Why does Daddy leave so much?" the toddler who was the spitting image of herself when she was three asked.

Aidan jumped in to answer his little sister's question. "Dad is a warrior, Rhiannon. He has to kill bandits and ferals and Lambs of God to keep us safe."

Meredith opened her mouth about to correct him, because the way he described Chris, it sounded utterly preposterous. But she held her peace. As overly simple and glorified the child's explanation was, Aidan was essentially correct. That is what Chris did. And that was what he became, a warrior.

The once timid, sweaty, and quirky grad student who on their first date babbled so much out of sheer nervousness, was now a man who rode out into the wilderness to seek those who attacked their lands and he killed them. She knew he was still Chris. He had the same quirks, the same issues, even. But he was different now in ways that would have been impossible without the Shift. And so was she. Though her job description wasn't much different from before, the stakes were much higher and their fate rested on her. The assassination attempt, Ezra Rothstein's trip to North Carolina, all of these had consequences beyond the scale of anything she could have handled before the Shift.

Rhiannon started playing with Aidan's reddish locks. He pushed back. She screamed in protest and they were fighting again.

"Aidan, Rhiannon! Stop it!"

Whatever train of thought Meredith had just fell off the carriage as her role as mother took over and she wrestled the kids into place while holding a sleeping Baby Charles. Her valise, an old leathery case that was filled with documents that could shed light on the fate of humanity, lay next to the diaper bag. It was incredibly disorienting switching gears like this. But as frustrating as it was dealing with the battling siblings, Meredith was secretly grateful for the distraction that pulled her mind out from the dark recesses where matters of the Swan resided.

Chapter 4

en route to Rochelle, Virginia
December 2012

BACKGROUND MUSIC: "I Am…I Said" by Neil Diamond
Visit www.michaeljuge.com **on the *A Hard Rain* page to listen**

"I am…I said
To no one there
And no one heard at all
Not even the chair."

The armored school busses plodded along the slowly disintegrating roadway of Highway 29 as the Vicious Rabbits belted out Neil Diamond. The radio signal, emanating from a broadcast station in Culpeper, came in surprisingly strong today. The Shift had a way of scrambling the ionosphere, choking the airwaves with static, making radio communication touch and go. It didn't stop communities like Culpeper and Rochelle from transmitting. Within fifteen miles of a radio tower, the signal sounded like FM stations of yore. The mood on the bus was celebratory, not only because it was a sing along kind of song, but also because the clear signal indicated that the company was getting close to the wire, which meant that they would be inside the settled lands of Culpeper within minutes. Then they could take off their MOLLE gear and relax for the rest of the drive back home.

The forty-mile drive from Manassas to Culpeper took a few hours, about as long as the bike ride from their sleepover in Occoquan Estates to the staging area in Manassas where the busses waited for them.

The loosely welded armor slapped against the hull of the bus and rattled loudly whenever it hit a pot hole. It wasn't his best work, Chris thought with mild embarrassment. The armoring on this bus had been done before his shop learned how to armor vehicles properly. Each of the busses was painted with the flag of Rochelle, a grey silhouette of a rabbit's head complete with ears and deadly fangs over two crossed battle axes atop a burnt orange field. The busses groaned and coughed out noxious fumes as they chugged along. The engines would soon keel over and have to be replaced as a result of the caustic fuel they consumed and the thousands of pounds of armor they bore. They weren't a comfortable ride and they topped out at 30 miles per hour on level road. In fact, these things were worse than driving a Saturn, but at least they were operational.

"I am, I cried.
I am, said I.
And I am lost
and I can't even say why,"

The youthful Vicious Rabbits horsed around singing in the back of the bus while Chris sat up front rubbing his temples, trying to will away the shaky vision. The boisterous singing and the clattering metal coupled with the constant bouncing over mammoth sized potholes didn't help. Chris looked out one of the vision slits in the armor to see the occasional abandoned vehicle on the side of the road with the mountains looming in the distance cast lightly with snow.

His scars throbbed, his back ached. Plus, he was tired. Chris was in great condition, no doubt. He was in the best shape in his life, in fact. At the same time, he was turning 40 next month. He just wanted to get home to Meredith and his kids. To Chris' relief, the shaky vision began to ebb now as the bus approached a Culpeper watch tower. It was also nice to thaw out inside the confines of the bus. During the summer, these vehicles were tortuous hotboxes.

"What you got in the bag?" Chris was startled out of his reverie to see Lt. Kendra Baraka sitting next to him holding a bottle of whiskey. The attractive young African American woman suddenly seemed less intimidating than when she was suited up.

Chris picked up the gym bag resting on his lap. "This? Some presents for the kids."

Kendra sat down in the bench seat beside him and examined the contents. One item was a Princess dress complete with a wand and tiara. Then she pulled out what first looked like action figures. A closer inspection showed the figure to be a lunar astronaut holding the American flag. The spidery contraption turned out to be a lunar lander.

"Ah," she swooned sweetly. "They're adorable. You got them from the townies?"

Chris nodded.

"Which ones? The Estates or the townies hanging with the busses?"

"Occoquan Estates."

Some of the townies knew that the Orange Pact tended to stage at the same strip mall in Manassas. Whenever the busses arrived to release the cavalry to kick ass and take names, the townies would converge to trade. Chris never figured how the townies knew they were coming. It was a bit unnerving. Maybe they just lived nearby and could hear the busses groaning a mile away.

They were such a pathetic sight, the townies. Like any feral, they were unwashed. Chris could smell a human habitation from a block away, literally. Children around in the strip mall parking lot were filthy and bundled in ill-fitting clothes and they wore tattered shoes with tire treads used as soles. The adults had a traumatized look about them. The townies constantly looked over their shoulders as if someone was always lurking behind them. They lived purely off of scraps, constantly avoiding other people except maybe for the civilized who came to barter canned food in exchange for hard-to-come-by artifacts of the cities. Canning wasn't too difficult to do now with a rudimentary foundry. The most sought out items by the civilized, other than underwear and socks in original packaging of course, were vinyl LPs.

Chris caressed the lunar lander he was holding. "Aidan is all about space exploration."

"Really? That's odd. Most kids don't even know we ever went into space."

"You're right. Frankly, the first time I read him bedtime stories about pigs in space and what not, he didn't believe people ever flew airplanes, no less believe that we ever went into space. He thought it was just another tale we grownups made up like Sponge Bob, Star Wars and television. But I pulled out an encyclopedia and showed him pictures, you know, like that iconic photo of Neil Armstrong standing beside the American flag planted on the lunar surface. After that, Aidan was hooked. His entire room is plastered with posters of the moon landing and the planets. He has volumes of books on the subject, too."

Kendra nodded and lifted the whiskey bottle with the Hughes' logo. The label showing a drunken Native American chief slouched beneath the brand *Firewater* was offensive, but so overtly racist that it was meant to be taken ironically; therefore, it wasn't racist, which made sense in a post-modern sort of way. Chris realized that they truly were "post-modern" now.

"You care for a nip, Captain?"

Chris looked around. "You sure it's halal?" using an expression he got from the legacy Marines who served in Iraq.

Kendra pointed to the back of the bus. "It's fine Captain. We passed the first watchtower. We're safe."

Chris shrugged and pulled out his faded Starbucks titanium travel mug while she poured the bottle of clear liquid.

She raised her mug. "Welcome back to civilization."

The other passengers screeched,

"I am…I said
To no one there
And no one heard at all
Not even the chair,"

till their voices failed in the final high pitched notes.

"Shouldn't we be joining with the others?" he asked.

Kendra smirked. "I'm more of a Kanye West girl myself."

"Ah," Chris responded. They sat there silently as the chorus drunkenly butchered the song. Chris took another swig, the alcohol stinging his gums. The whiskey produced these days was much harsher, similar to Everclear in his opinion. But it warmed his gut and gave him a sense of wellbeing just the same.

"You ever think about the real world, Lieutenant?" he asked Kendra.

She stared back at him and scoffed. "Wow, already? Don't we usually wait until we're at least halfway through the bottle before getting into alcohol-fueled reminiscing?" Kendra's inflection revealed just a slight hint of an urban accent as a second generation Kenyan American from Brooklyn.

"Sometimes lately, I've had these dreams. And it's really unsettling because it's so disorienting."

"Dreams?"

"Yeah, dreams that I'm back in the real world."

"Well, a lot of you old timers dream in the old world, sir."

Chris let the slight go. "Those people we killed yesterday, if the Shift hadn't hit, they could have been decent people. They might have had jobs, had families, a mortgage to pay, a fantasy football club."

Kendra took a swig. "Well, Captain, the Shift did hit, and Gaia had her reasons for sending it."

Chris grunted, reminded of what a devout Unitarian Kendra was. Technically, it was still the Unitarian Universalist Church, but the cold secular humanism endemic in the old Unitarian creed resembled little of the transformed church led by the leader of Greater Monticello Rita Luevano. It wasn't as if there were any other surviving Unitarian congregations to contest this Gaia Piety Society. As it was now, it had a pant-load of momentum. Kendra was just one example of how widespread UU was in Rochelle. Nearly half of the population there belonged to the Unitarian Church. Kendra, like most of her fellow parishioners, was a zealous follower.

Oddly enough, a lot of the formerly fundamentalist Christian types, especially the ones who escaped from Lynchburg, completely turned away from Christianity to the Gaia Piety Society. Having a Masters in Anthropology, a minor in Psychology and having taken conversational French in high school, Chris figured he was an expert on the human mind and reasoned that those fundies who now embraced Gaia were completely flummoxed that the Shift, which was undoubtedly God's wrath, had left them behind. Seeing that they were shit out of luck with their Christian God, they decided to throw their fate in with Gaia. That was his read of the situation, in any case. With even the cold rationalist Unitarians finding religion, Chris felt like he was the only agnostic left in the world.

Chris continued. "Be that as it may, it doesn't take away the fact that those people we killed yesterday might have been people we would have worked with or even liked in another world. It's not like they had a choice."

"Everyone has a choice, Captain. You weren't there in the city when it was falling to shit." Kendra winced as she moved her injured arm about.

"When Miss Dawn was guiding us girls out of DC and we were stuck in Baltimore, I saw people choosing to feed on other people. The food hadn't even run out yet. But some people jumped on the chance to prey, literally prey, on their fellow human beings. And I also saw people giving their last scraps of food to hungry children. The wolves were no worse off than the Samaritans; they chose to victimize people. No, Captain, we always have a choice."

Chris considered what Kendra said. For such a young lady, she had wisdom beyond her twenty-two years. It wasn't just that she came of age during the collapse; that would have made her hard, but not wise. Chris suspected that Kendra would have been as perceptive as she was even if she had grown up in a normal world.

"So, what would you Gaians say of those people we liberated of their pulses?"

Kendra considered his question seriously and took another swig, passing the bottle to Chris. "We have a duty to pass the torch of humanism, a critical mind, science and the belief in the inherent dignity of all people whenever possible."

Then she frowned. "But 'there are times when reason falters under the cruel and wicked. And those who revel in chaos and wanton domination over others have forfeited their right to exist alongside us,'" she quoted something he heard commonly among UUs.

"Where reason ends, ass-kicking begins in other words," Chris observed. "I have to say, you aren't my dad's Unitarians."

Kendra shrugged. "Gaia has a way of inspiring even the most cynical."

Chris didn't know what to say to that. The two of them sat and nursed their rotgut whiskey watching the landscape transform from frozen scorched wasteland to tended fields that nourished winter crops. The young Vicious Rabbits belted Neil Diamond with jubilant disregard. Snowflakes danced in the sky as the bus groaned homeward.

The caravan of school busses passed the newest settlements in the Rochelle Sovereignty. His spirits were lifted now the nastiness of the operation washed away in Firewater and song. Chris wished he had designed the armor sheeting to have removable plates so that he could have a better view. One of the Vicious Rabbits announced that he saw Madison High, the staging area, the final stop where Meredith and the kids would be waiting for him. Chris rubbed his calloused, smudged fingers on the package of Cream of the Crops panties for Meredith expectantly.

Madison High had special significance for Chris beyond its use as the Vicious Rabbits armory and depot. It was where Chris first fought for his life. Back when Constable Charles Early learned about a gang who had taken over the school and held several refugees as slaves, the constable rounded up the fighting men to liberate the refugees, Chris included. He was just getting used to life without electricity, hacking out a living with his rudimentary blacksmithing skills. The hellacious panic that consumed him in the months leading up to the Shift had subsided, leaving Chris with a sense that he was sneaking under Panic's radar. Chris didn't want to go on the raid, but as the constable said, he needed every "swinging dick," and Rochelle was desperate enough that Chris Jung, the panic prone former intelligence analyst, was counted among them.

As the busses turned off the highway and into the parking lot of Madison High, Chris could hear friends and family singing the company's regimental song accompanied by the horn section of a marching band.

"I get knocked down
But I get up again
You're never gonna keep me down
I get knocked down
But I get up again
You're never gonna keep me down..."

When the bus came to a stop, the Vicious Rabbits all turned to Chris waiting for his order. Chris stood up, hefting the gear and helmet under his armor and walked up to the front of the bus.

"Alright, people, you did well out there. You all have leave for the next forty-eight hours. Dismissed."

The men and women cried out, "Ooh rah!" harking to their legacy Marine trainers. Chris never felt right trying to ape the Marines, because they were a class of their own. Chris had come to accept his role as a commander. It wasn't something he was exactly comfortable doing, leading men and women into dangerous seek-and-destroy missions, but he was good at it. Over the past five and a half years since the first EMP struck, Chris had gone from being a suburban head case with a cursory knowledge of weapons to becoming a battle-hardened warrior. That being said, he was reserved about using Marine jargon.

Followed by his company, Chris stepped outside into the blustery wind, echoing with cheers. Vicious Rabbits raced out from behind him running towards their wives, girlfriends, some boyfriends, husbands. Even through their winter coats, Chris could tell that most of the women were pregnant. And there were little ones running all around. People bred like, well, like rabbits since the Shift. Maybe that was a sign of hope along with a sign that they were fresh out of birth control pills. In this world, kids were a plus as opposed to his recollection in DC how people hauling children were seen as a burden.

Just behind a family waving Rochelle flags stood Meredith, elegant, alluring brown eyes, lovely, hot librarian Meredith, holding Baby Charles with Aidan and Rhiannon racing up to him. It was the loveliest sight in the world.

"Daddy! Daddy!"

Chris dropped his gear and his M4, and knelt down to take the kids in his arms. Aidan and Rhiannon nearly knocked him on his ass as Aidan always ran right into him without even slowing down. Chris hugged them as hard as he could without hurting them, smelling their honest sweat of children playing.

"I missed you, Daddy!"

"I missed you more, Daddy!" The kids battled each other for who missed dad the most.

"And I missed you most of all," Chris said cheerily.

After a couple of seconds, Chris put his helmet on Rhiannon, shouldered his rifle and lifted the two kids over to Meredith. Putting the kids down, he sauntered up to his wife.

"Hey, stranger," he said.

"Hey, yourself," she replied. He then grabbed the back of her neck and pulled Meredith forward giving her a deep kiss. Firewater was thick on his breath. Then he went to smell Baby Charles' head. Bob the driver took his rifle and backpack, loading it onto the carriage while Aidan and Rhiannon circled him and Meredith like puppies.

"You look beautiful," he said sincerely, because she really did, but she always dismissed it as she did now.

"Oh, that's the booze and a week in the bush talking."

Before he could protest, she gave him another kiss letting him know he was home where he truly belonged. After a couple of minutes, he and the family made their way over to another bus. Chris picked out *The Interceptor* from the line of other mountain bikes that were transported in a separate bus and walked it over to the carriage. *The Interceptor* had seen him through a lot over the years. It was worn and had been repaired numerous times, and it wasn't particularly attractive, but it was his lifeline out in the bush. He checked to be sure the spare tubes and duct tape were still where they were supposed to be. Tubes were like gold. You couldn't reproduce them, not yet anyway, and everybody needed them. That's why his tires had been retrofitted with car tire treads. And duct tape? That had saved his life more times than it did MacGyver. Once, a Vicious Rabbit's bike frame had bifurcated out in the bush of Tysons Corner. He didn't think it was possible, but the duct tape kept the frame together enough to get them back to the busses. He would have named one of his kids "Duct Tape" if Meredith would have allowed it. He hefted *The Interceptor* up to Bob who placed it on the back of the carriage.

He then helped Rhiannon into the carriage and turned to Meredith.

"Hey, did you get enough Petrol for the party?"

Meredith rolled her eyes, "Yes."

Sensing that she was annoyed, he asked, "What is it?"

"Well, you always come up with these crazy ideas but it's always left to me to actually work out the mechanics."

"That's not true!"

"Oh, really?"

Chris paused as Aidan kept bugging him to put him into the carriage. Then he relented. "Okay, yes, in this case. But c'mon. I was sent out last minute on this operation. What could I do? I was busy."

"Oh, and I'm not?"

Chris winced immediately realizing that he had just stepped in it. He knew that Meredith's responsibilities as the director of the Swan consumed her. He would never trade jobs. He quickly recovered. "No, of course not. It's just that…you know, um, I …never mind. I'm just happy to be back with you."

Meredith eased down and took his hand with her delicate long fingers. "Me, too, Hon."

Chris heard Bob prompting the family horse, "Giddy-up, Corolla."

The carriage left the high school and passed a sprouting of "X" shaped cabins, which were designed to maximize efficiency for less affluent arrivals. Each spoke of the "X" was for a family that consisted of a few rooms in a shotgun house design. The central hub was the common kitchen and living area and bathroom. After a few moments, he risked another question.

"Did you get the wine from Brandon? He still owes me for armoring his trucks, so the crates are supposed to be free."

She didn't answer and Chris suddenly feared he really screwed the pooch for dredging up the topic again. She turned to face him.

"Something happened in Monticello, dear."

Chapter 5

Charlottesville, Virginia
Greater Monticello
December 2012

Neko Lemay heard human voices whispering unintelligibly. She felt as though she was coming down from the worst trip since she went out to a cow pasture in high school and wound up with a nasty crop of mushrooms. Light pierced through her eyelids, so she didn't even try opening them. Over the last day, week or hours—she couldn't tell which—Neko had fallen in and out of consciousness. She was at the Our Lady of the Random Miracle, Greater Monticello's hospital. That much she knew. A nurse had tried to calm her down as he administered a needle into her. Before she slipped out of consciousness, her last thought was relief, seeing Rita standing over her safe and sound brushing her red locks back from her eyes.

Her shoulder wasn't in the searing pain it had been before her mind drifted off into a sinister version of *Toy Story* meshing with memories of *Grey's Anatomy*. As her mind emerged back into something she would call reality, she felt a dull aching throughout her body. The voices were becoming more distinct now.

"…was able…the arm…severe nerve damage…"

"But will she be able to use it again?" She recognized the concerned woman's voice. It was now coming to her. She had been shot defending the reverend. She saw fragments of herself spew out from her shoulder. The woman talking sounded like Rita and she was asking about her arm. Neko held her breath trying to hear the man's answer.

"Ma'am, I don't know if she will ever have use of her arm. If the wound doesn't get infected, we can save her."

"Jesus."

Neko froze at the words spoken, unable to buffer what she had just overheard.

The low male voice continued dispassionately giving an antiseptic report. "We won't know about the infection for another few days. Unfortunately, the antibiotics we produce aren't much against the super strains that emerged before the Shift. Even the antibiotics we had were beginning to waver in their effectiveness. I was able to get all the fragments out and it was a clean exit."

"Akil, how am I going to tell her?"

Neko must have given herself away because they abruptly stopped speaking to each other.

"She's awake," Akil whispered.

Neko strained to see in the light, her eyes refusing to focus. She felt hands clasping around her left hand before she saw that it was the reverend.

"Hi, Rev," her voice croaked weakly.

"Hey, girlfriend."

That was a bad sign. Whenever the reverend called her "girlfriend," something was amiss. But she already knew that.

"Um, everything's going to be fine." the reverend said as she brushed her hair with her long fingernails. Neko tried to act as if she hadn't heard the prognosis and sniffed a nod.

Out of the shadow another figure appeared. Despite the blurriness, she could see the tall dark stranger with the beard was striking. That was until she realized it was her friend, Ezra Rothstein, whom she always thought of as a little brother. It disturbed her that he looked so good. It must be the drugs.

"Hey, dork."

"Hey, psycho," he responded with his term of endearment for her. "I heard you saved the chief magistrate's life."

Neko nodded and touched his beard. Ezra chuckled. "Yeah, I got sick of trying to maintain a goatee out in the bush."

"You look hot," she whispered. *Oops.* She knew she was going to regret that later. When they first met right before the Shift, she and Ezra were competing in the National Finals that were taking place in Charlottesville. She had flown from Washington State to compete, but Charlottesville was Ezra's hometown. During the competition, he wouldn't shut up in his desperate play to impress her, but he was a boy still in high school while she was two years his senior sitting from the majestic height of nineteen.

It was a good thing Ezra was a local and had parents who were regulars at the Unitarian Church, for he guided her and the rest of the archers to Reverend Luevano, setting history on its course. Without Ezra, Monticello would not have the archers to defend her and Neko would have never found Gaia. Even if she had been home in Washington State when the Shift hit, she would have been just as lost as out in Virginia without finding Gaia. It was, in essence, why Gaia guided her to Monticello. Neko needed to be here so that she could help forge a new future for humanity, one where dignity, mutual respect and reason reigned. And she would kill anyone who tried to get in its way.

"You just try to get some rest," Ezra soothed.

As if his words were a spell, Neko slipped back into sleep.

Rita waited in the hall while Ezra was in the infirmary with Neko. Akil wrapped his arm around her waist tightly, in part she figured, because he narrowly lost his wife to an assassin's bullet, and second because she hadn't slept since Neko was rushed into the resurrected hospital yesterday afternoon and she was beginning to stumble.

The conversation with the surgeon was almost as upsetting as the event itself. Neko Lemay lived and breathed her archery. It was her use of the bow that helped saved Monticello in its most desperate hour and became a symbol of the upstart community. The surgeon had told her that the injuries Neko sustained tore through so much of the muscle and chipped at bone and ligaments that he couldn't see her ever having use of the arm again, much less wielding a bow. The surgeon probably hadn't seen many gunshot wounds before the Shift, but he had become savvy in those types of injuries since. He knew what he was talking about.

Rita squeezed Akil, smelling the residual smoke through the freshly painted walls of the hospital whose brick structure, like the church, had survived the fires. With fresh paint and gaudy naked electrical wire running along the ceilings, the hospital was pumped back to life. The doctors and nurses, the ones Greater Monticello was able to find and in some cases lure from other places like Lynchburg and even West Virginia, had to learn how to do their job with the limited resources of the Post-Shift world. As the surgeon pointed out, old antibiotics were scarce and most had lost their potency while bacteria had strengthened over the last several decades. Chemists made rudimentary penicillin, but they were no match for many varieties of bacteria propagating. Conditions once considered chronic were now death sentences. Congenital heart disease, type-one diabetes, those needing dialyses, all of them became conditions unsustainable in the new world. Their deaths hit Rita harder than any of those killed in battle. There was something callous about nature, the way so many good people died simply because they had some physical defect.

Nature could be cold blooded indeed, but you wouldn't ever know that if you heard the way Gaia explained it. She loves all of her creations and those that perish and the species that go extinct return to the soil; they return to her. As much as Rita understood that, she still found it unfair.

Why did she come to me? Who in the hell is Laurel? And what does Jamil have to do with...whatever she was warning me about? She was terrified about something.

Rita hadn't had time to process what she experienced yesterday. One of her dearest friends had been severely injured while saving her from an attack on her life. Added to that, after almost a year of silence, Gaia had chosen that very moment, the moment when the assassins went for her life, to make an appearance.

Plucking her out of time and space, the sudden shocking violence of the present froze in place reminding Rita of *The Matrix,* a movie which to her dismay was able to combine the solemn truths of Buddhism with action-packed gratuitous violence and S&M apparel. Rita tried to recall what Gaia said but to no avail. All she knew was that the fate of humanity hung in the balance and that "with Laurel and Jamil they would know what to do" or words to that effect. At least, that's what Rita gleaned from the vision.

Gaia was indeed terrified by something, yet she wouldn't explain exactly what it was. Maybe it had to do with not seeing her in a long time, but Rita couldn't tell if Gaia was having difficulty expressing herself in human language or if she honestly didn't know what was putting humanity in mortal jeopardy.

"She's asleep, ma'am."

Rita didn't even notice that Ezra had joined them outside in the hall. Like Akil, Ezra Rothstein had just returned from his travels to North Carolina, a mission at the request of the Swan. The young man who was once a lanky high school kid had grown up to become a handsome young man with straight jet black hair and a new beard that really looked good on him.

"She asked for you," Rita said.

"We've been through death and life together." After a moment's pause he added, "She will get through this. She's too damned obstinate to die."

Rita curled a slight smile, and felt her ill-fitting dentures slipping. She switched the subject.

"You came here to tell me something."

"Yes, Chief, Sheriff Schadenfreude has made a breakthrough in the interview of the three suspects."

"She has…so soon?"

"Yes, it seems they were quite willing to claim responsibility for the assassination attempt."

"Thuy will be disappointed. He wanted to come up for the interrogation."

Ezra titled his head. "That's odd. I was supposed to already be down there."

"Why?"

"Because, the director asked me to deliver some documents she had me fetch in North Carolina."

Rita didn't know how to respond, because there were a myriad of objections she had to that statement. First of all, Rita was given little notice about this mysterious and dangerous mission out into the recesses of North Carolina, a true no man's land. Secondly, Meredith Jung did not elaborate about why she needed Rita's people to go out on a most dangerous courier job. And now, the director was summoning her people to Rochelle for a briefing without advising Rita. Ezra's dual role as a captain in Greater Monticello's Thomas Jefferson Martyrs Brigade and as an officer within the multi-community intelligence agency the Swan typically did not conflict with each other; however, Rita found herself losing her good humor when it came to Meredith sending Rita's people out on missions.

"This is news to me, Ezra."

"I'm sorry, Chief, I thought they told you. There must have been a SNAFU in communications."

"I'm sure there was. So, you are to brief the director tomorrow."

"Uh huh. I was supposed to leave yesterday, but with the assassination attempt, I decided that I should stay until I could give her useful intelligence from the interrogations."

Rita suppressed her agitation. This is how things worked. Although the Swan was headed in Rochelle and run by a Vicious Rabbit, it was a multi-"governmental" agency comprised of the Orange Pact communities: the Rochelle Sovereignty, Culpeper, Greater Monticello and the Fredericksburg Union. In return for loaning her best and brightest to serve as officers in the Swan, Greater Monticello was not only privy to some of the best intelligence that it would not have gathered otherwise, it kept all of the allies safe.

Rita had to admit that Meredith knew her business. She was the architect behind an intelligence organization that would have rivaled the CIA, the FSB, MI-5 or the ISI. She had an intricate network of operatives, former DHS, FBI, CIA and other agency agents and analysts working for her, spread throughout the Mid-Atlantic region, possibly beyond. Few could ever spin the spider web Meredith had erected. It was probably the main reason the Orange Pact was still alive and kicking instead of having been run over by the Lambs of God years ago. Rita knew of many military buildups and coups that the Swan thwarted, averted or otherwise dismantled, saving them from the overwhelmingly larger force of the Dominion of Lynchburg. Given that, Rita knew she could not fault Meredith if she slipped on protocol every now and again. But still.

"Ezra, I'd like to see what it was she sent you out to get," gesturing to his backpack. Whatever it was, it was important enough that Ezra had possession of it at all times.

He looked conflicted, and she understood why. She figured that the director hadn't authorized him to share whatever it was he was sent to get with anybody but Meredith herself. But Rita was his sovereign. She didn't care to get into a pissing match with Meredith—that was for men to do—but she was not going to be ignored.

"Ezra."

"Um, yeah, sure, Chief." He took off the unremarkable Jansport backpack, opened it up and with some trepidation, handed her a stack of papers stuffed in a buff colored expandable wallet.

Rita skimmed through the tome of hand written notes. It was rare that anything was typed anymore with there being so few non-electric typewriters in existence by the time the Shift hit. She tried to make sense of it all, a series of mathematical equations. Surprisingly, she found she understood the equations and some unused corner of her mind started double checking the numbers written down. She experienced this weird knack for number crunching while trying to calculate the caloric intake of the community and the rate of the community's expansion. She had always been good at math, but these equations were complex, and yet she still understood. She chalked it up as another one of her quirks—that and her being the prophet of Gaia.

Her eye grew tired straining to see in the hallway with the dim electric light bulbs fluctuating from another power surge. Having one eye also forced the remaining one to work twice as hard, giving her headaches. Not to mention the fact that she hadn't slept since yesterday.

"Chief, I don't know what the hell this means. The folks I got it from were these people living a huddled existence at some observatory. They probably took over the place because it was stocked with food at one point and was secluded."

She turned to Akil who added, "I don't know, Sugar. I was doing my own thing inside the city of Asheville itself, what's left of it."

She handed the stack back to Ezra who looked relieved. "When you get to Rochelle, I want you to tell Mrs. Jung that I am going to ask her for a full and honest briefing of why you were sent out there, and what these documents mean."

"Yes, Chief."

"Now, you mentioned that the Sheriff had a breakthrough with the assassins. I would like to have a chat with them myself."

Chapter 6

Charlottesville, Virginia
Greater Monticello
December 2012

Rita, Akil and Ezra bundled on their coats and headed out of the resurrected early 20th century hospital to the turn-of-the-millennium parking garage where their horses waited for them. Her mount, a handsome quarter horse, neighed indignantly next to Akil's horse. Those two got along like the Turks and Greeks.

"It's okay, Prius," she soothed while brushing a dusting of snow from his mane.

Akil mounted his horse, a monster draught horse. Clicking his teeth he urged him down the ramp, "C'mon, Hummer."

As the three crossed the town, Rita took in the view. The old downtown area had been completely consumed in the fires. Most of the buildings had either toppled over themselves or had been demolished in resettling the land. Despite the snow, work teams were out in force erecting new homes along the pockets of town that had survived the fires. Prius clopped up and down the hilly roads, avoiding the ice patches.

Along the way, they passed an old pickup truck with the hood up. The driver was fanning the smoke from the engine, trying to see what he could do to resolve the mechanical malfunction. Truth was there was little he could do. The forty-year-old Chevy had been consuming grain alcohol and Hempanol substitutes for years now. The imprecise mixtures were far less efficient and far more corrosive than gasoline. There were mechanics working on building new diesel engines that would run on

Hempanol, but without an industrial base to machine new parts, there was no standardization for interchangeable parts.

Although most of the fraternity houses and bars had been wiped out, much of the main campus of UVA remained intact enough to be salvaged. Thomas Jefferson's pride and joy endured the inferno better than most of the more recent structures. Sheriff Lucille Schadenfreude had appropriated the Rotunda, the crown of the campus where the flag of Greater Monticello with the blue chalice and orange flame shaped like a bow on a green field waved. Built during Thomas Jefferson's waning years of life, the classical Greek columns seemed to hold the echoes of centuries. Rita felt it was rather presumptuous for the former district attorney to send her deputies to take the Rotunda when Monticello made its first furtive steps back into Charlottesville a few years ago. But as pushy as Lucille could be, she proved herself as one of the most capable lawmen or lawwomen she could ever hope for. After handing the reigns to a deputy, Rita and crew stepped into the warmth inside the Rotunda.

"Reverend!" Lucille Schadenfreude greeted Rita as she, Akil and Ezra entered an impressive office that was once used for ceremonies. Lucille gave a cursory kiss on the cheek, something that had become a common greeting in Monticello over the years, which Rita didn't mind. She found it more welcoming than the "man hug" style of their friends in Rochelle and Culpeper to the north. The Fredericksburg Union's greeting was rather cold, limited to a slight jerk of the head and a curt "sup."

Lucille Schadenfreude certainly didn't look like sheriffs in the real world. The brunette wore a stylish pair of glasses that Rita swore was just an affectation to contrast her no nonsense face to the more evocative attire she wore, ski tights and riding boots with a pistol strapped to her thigh. At the edge of civilization, who was going to call the fashion police, especially considering that she was the law in these here parts? Rita had to admit though, if anyone could get away with it, Lucille could. Every time she saw Lucille, she was struck by how familiar she looked. And then it hit her. The glasses, the hair, the smirk! She looked like that Saturday Night Live girl, the one who did the news. Rita forgot the comedian's name but she loved her.

"How's Miss Lemay?"

Rita sighed heavily. "It's too early to tell. The bullet didn't hit any vital organs. But infection is what we're concerned about now." Rita chose not to mention the prognosis about her arm. She felt it wasn't her place to announce something like that, especially since Neko herself didn't know it yet.

"Gaia watches over that girl, my Reverend. I know her healing spirit will wash over Neko. After all, she is the spear Gaia wields to protect us all, as she did for you yesterday."

"Let's hope so."

Lucille was as devout a convert to the Unitarian Church as Neko. But Rita was impressed by her off-the-cuff poetic response. She really did have a way with words. Then again, she was once an attorney, so why should she be surprised? Anyone who was the prosecutor for the City of Lynchburg had to have some eloquence in speaking about how a suspect drove a truck through the glass front of a stop-n-rob in a desperate attempt to snag an ATM machine.

"But as for the reason why you are here, did Ezra tell you?"

"He said that you got a confession out of the three suspects."

Lucille scoffed. "Well, not so much."

"I'm sorry?"

"Oh, they confessed to the attempted assassination, all right." She walked around an antique oak desk that might be as old as the Rotunda itself and grabbed a couple of manila folders. She leafed through the pages of notes.

"Terry Barrymore, age twenty-one, a cobbler. Born and raised in Lynchburg. Went to Mason High School. He arrived in Monticello back in June 2008. He was spotted by the archers patrolling the southern border near Scottsville. Terry admitted that he acted alone to assassinate you because 'God' told him to," she said mockingly.

"Douglas Winkelvoss, age twenty-two, a farrier. Also born and raised in Lynchburg. A Junior at Choate Academy in Connecticut, he was home for the summer when the Shift hit. He arrived in Monticello in August 2008 with a group from westbound on I-64. Two of his fellow travelers had their throats slit while in the old newcomer's compound. Nobody saw anything. Doug also confessed that he acted alone to," she adjusted her glasses to read his exactly words, "'to cap that one-eyed witch in the name of the Lord.'"

Rita couldn't help but grin. She had heard that pejorative before. Contrary to common wisdom, Rita actually liked it. "One-eyed witch of UU" evoked a frightful image that was greater and more intimidating than she was in real life.

"James Childers, age sixteen, currently actively serving in the Monticellan Defense Forces as compulsory for all boys and girls his age. He was a child when the Shift hit from Roanoke. His family died of the flu. He and his adoptive family arrived in January 2009. He also claimed sole responsibility for the attempted assassination."

"There's an obvious problem with their stories where each claimed to have acted alone," Ezra stated.

Rita rummaged through her memories. She was acquainted with Doug Winkelvoss and Terry Barrymore. Despite the fact that it was growing at an exponential rate, Greater Monticello wasn't a metropolis even by today's standards. A census taken earlier this year had put the community at about 20,000 souls. Today's population absolutely dwarfed the original community of a few hundred back in 2007, but it was just a modest-sized town at the end of the day. So, it would make sense that she would be familiar with two of the assassins.

"These were not new arrivals, Reverend. They have been here for years. Doug and Terry's parents attended the regent's church back when he was just a blow hard televangelist for Boche Ministries and Bible College filling the void left by Falwell's departure from the earth."

"How did you know about their parents?"

Lucille turned to Ezra and back at Rita. "The Swan. Terry is a member over at Pastor Dan's church; James goes to the Catholic Church. And Doug, well, Reverend…"

"Yes?"

"Doug Winkelvoss went to our church."

Of course. That's how she knew his name. Granted, the Unitarian Universalist Church's ranks had swelled into the thousands, comprising roughly ninety percent of Greater Monticello, and Rita had passed off her weekly duties as reverend to the younger upcoming ministers as she was tied down with her duties as chief magistrate. That being said, she still made a point to know everyone in her congregation.

Reading from the notes, Lucille added, "Doug Winkelvoss went to Pastor Dan since his arrival in 2008, and started attending UU a little over a year ago."

Lucille continued. "I can tell you Reverend, we didn't have any reason to suspect them before now or I wouldn't have allowed them near you."

"I'm just glad they didn't succeed," Akil said.

"Well, it's impossible to sift through potential threats, really," Ezra opined. "I mean, it's not like we photograph everyone who enters

Monticello, and besides, everyone is armed, so you can't just frisk everyone going to an event."

"Well, maybe when Rita is speaking we should."

"Well, I don't think the Chief is going to like that, right, Chief?"

Rita ignored the exchange.

"We're going to interview the friends, family and coworkers, Reverend," said Lucille.

Rita turned to Lucille. "I want to see Doug."

The holding cells and interview rooms were located nearby at the McCormick Road Residence Area, a set of dorms for freshmen. Along the way, they passed Clark Hall where several of her classes were located when she was a visiting professor there. Even though the building was for the environmental sciences, she found it worked out well with her religious studies classes. The dorms had been retrofitted with bars, making it obvious that it was a prison. Rita speculated that there were a number of Cavaliers who didn't find it a stretch.

There was no obvious electricity running through the building, as the halls were lit solely by kerosene lamps giving the converted dorm an appropriate spookiness that Lucille was going for. The halls didn't reek, there weren't sounds of whips lashing or muffled screams—Rita wouldn't have allowed any such inhumane treatment, having protested Gitmo and a variety of other facilities Amnesty International reviled—but the prison did have a dungeon sort of ambiance to it, something that she supposed was unavoidable.

A guard opened the door for Rita and inside the converted dorm room sat Douglas Winkelvoss, his right hand cuffed to a bare table. The lanky young man—most people were lanky these days—jolted seeing the would-be victim standing by the doorway.

"Leave us."

"We'll be just outside," Lucille said, wary of letting her in there alone.

"I'll be fine. Thank you."

Rita stepped over to Doug. She gently placed her hand over the side of his face, turned it to face her, inspecting for any signs of mistreatment. Outside of a few scrapes and bruises, undoubtedly from the angry mob of Gaians who pounced on him, he seemed okay. They even stitched a cut on his cheek just above his scraggly beard. His fingernails were intact, and there were no bruises where there shouldn't be. Other than the deer in the headlights look on his face, he didn't show any signs that he had been tortured. Nevertheless, Rita followed up.

"How are they treating you, Doug? Are you okay?"

The room was windowless, making it impossible to tell what time of day it was. The only light was a naked light bulb dangling from the ceiling, proving that electricity coursed through the building, after all. The unflattering light exaggerated Doug's haunted expression.

"They haven't let me sleep."

Rita chuckled wryly. "*Ese*, I haven't slept either, and it's all thanks to you and your friends."

"Friends? I don't know what you're talking about."

Rita knew that the Sheriff kept the suspects separate from each other and played up stories of one suspect ratting on the other even though that wasn't the case. Doug Winkelvoss wasn't an idiot as far as she could tell, but he was playing the part of one. Rita chose not to get into that argument with him and instead took a seat across from him.

"The Sheriff has enough evidence to hang you on the spot. You could request counsel, but your family would pay for the entire trial, and you will still wind up swinging at the end."

"Death doesn't scare me and neither do you," he spat out contemptuously.

"It doesn't matter, I suppose," speaking past his angry response. "But I would like to know why you did it."

The young man squirmed nervously. "I…I don't need to tell you anything."

"No, you don't. But I think you might like the opportunity to say what you always wanted to say to me before you meet your maker."

"Okay, *Reverend,*" he sneered, "I'll tell you why I did it. Because you are the queen of darkness, Satan's whore."

"Yes, yes, yes, I'm familiar with the litany of insults. But Doug, you went to my church for over a year. You listened to my sermons and the sermons of Reverend Loewy. Why after spending so much time with us are you still convinced of the regent's propaganda?"

Doug bristled. "The regent? You think the regent sent me? He had nothing to do with it."

"Right, and it was also just an enormous coincidence that three people plotted to assassinate me on the same day at the same time. You're going to have to do better than that."

"It absolutely amazes you that somebody else other than the regent might recognize your wickedness, doesn't it? You think you fooled the whole world, don't you? Well, you didn't fool me."

"I think the sermons and our actions alone should convince you we aren't Satan spawn."

"Ah, right. 'The inherent dignity of all people, the interdependent web of existence in which we are all a part.'"

"There are five more, you know. It's seven principles."

Doug snorted. "And they sound all pretty, don't they? Those 'principles' of yours are nothing but code for pantheism. Look how Satan takes the form of Gaia to turn you all from God."

Rita sat stone-faced as Doug went on in his diatribe.

"And you espouse the homosexual agenda that brainwashes children into thinking sodomy is an equally valid life. Why not bestiality or pedophilia?" Doug was on a role. "I submit to you, *Reverend*, I act in the name of the Lord and I will die as his martyr proud."

After he finished, Rita chose her words carefully, knowing there was no point in arguing with him. She had learned that debating someone who was convinced of something was futile.

"If you request counsel, tell me or the sheriff."

She stood up and heard the door unlocking to let her out.

"Man, that is one messed up *pendejo*," said Ezra breaking the silence with his butchered Spanish. In Monticello, the language took off. Every gringo in Greater Monticello understood Spanish, the language of agriculture and mechanics today.

"I swear, that boy is lucky he's in jail, or I'd break him off somethin'," Akil scowled.

"It's so sad." Rita had been silent on the long uncomfortable walk through campus back to the Rotunda.

"He's a tool who got his orders from the regent." Lucille seemed matter-of-fact as she said it.

"We don't know that, Lucille."

"In that we didn't get a confession from them admitting as such, no. But we all know the regent has operatives out here. The unchecked immigration from south of the border makes it all the more easy for his hounds to slip in and live with the normal."

Rita found it funny that Lucille referred to the unchecked immigration. After all, Lucille was once one of those immigrants herself. She was among the first to flee Lynchburg when it became apparent that the regent intended to establish a theocratic autocracy and those who didn't fit into his mold were considered unclean. After being cast out of Lynchburg to face the flu and the chaos, she made it to Monticello and jumped onto the Gaia Piety Society thing that UU was transformed into with unparalled zeal.

"It could have been the regent who sent them, but those boys could just as easily acted alone," Rita said. "Here's the rub. I don't know which one is worse."

Akil objected. "What do you mean, Sugar? I think the regent putting a hit on you is worse than some assholes acting alone."

"I don't," she countered. "We all know that the regent has a hard-on for me to bite the dust. But if there were kids, people who coordinated an attempt on their own, who lived with us and still feared us as Satanists, then who knows what's out there?"

"I will get to the bottom of this, Reverend," Lucille reassured. "If the regent is involved or not, I will find out. I will turn every cart over until I get to the truth."

"Thank you, Lucille, but remember we aren't at war with Christianity here. I know Father Duffy and Pastor Dan. We might not have voted the same way in the real world, but I know they are good people who are loyal to Monticello."

"Of course, Reverend. Nobody is suggesting otherwise."

Rita then turned to Ezra. "You can go and brief the director about what we've learned here, but, Ezra?"

"Yes, ma'am?"

"Tell Mrs. Jung, we need to have a talk about our MOU."

Ezra gave a confused look and she explained. " 'Memorandum of Understanding.'"

"Will do, Chief." And with that he ran off.

Charlene was nervous. She wasn't too good with strangers and she hated machines. Born after the Shift, the pure Arabian bristled as Ezra Rothstein helped guide his mare onto the cattle car.

"It's okay, girl. It's just a short ride."

She looked at him with eyes the size of walnuts. "What, you want me to ride with you?"

Ezra had been looking forward to catching some shut eye on the ride over to Orange. The Buckingham Branch Railroad Company operated a line that ran directly from Waynesboro through Charlottesville all the way to Orange to haul freight. It had lain idle during the first couple of years after the Shift, but the constant traffic between Charlottesville and Orange had created a demand to invest in resurrecting the rail line.

A rebuilt steam engine ran the line, the one type of engine that was absolutely one hundred percent reliable and unaffected by EMP surges. The only stitch was that coal was the preferred fuel, and that meant a reliance on West Virginia. But on the upside, people, beasts and freight moved effortlessly at a respectable forty miles per hour at its peak in the warm comfort of the passenger cars, which had electric light produced by the spinning coil from the wheels of the train.

Charlene snuffed and butted her head up against him affectionately. *Damn it.* Charlene always got what she wanted. Ezra took off his back pack, prepared to spend the next hour in the elements freezing his tail off, when one of the railroad employees came in.

"Sorry, son, but you can't stay in the cattle car. It's against regulations."

"Regulations?" *Is this guy serious? Since when were there regulations?* Still, though Ezra wasn't going to argue with the man even though it forced him to sit in comfort for the next hour.

"Sorry, girl," he said apologetically. "Regulations."

Inside the passenger car, Ezra took off his white poncho and overcoat and leaned his rifle muzzle up against the window. The car was an antique that had been given a second life. He heard the story of how they bought the car in Harrisonburg, took it apart to transport it, and reassembled it in Charlottesville. The train was packed with merchants, laborers and soldiers, some from the Monticellan Defense Forces, some Vicious Rabbit soldiers and a few fellow archers in the Martyrs Brigade. The patch on his sleeve that displayed a bow and Thomas Jefferson's silhouette identified him as an archer. His other job as an officer with the Swan had no such identifiers. The archer's patch worked wonders with the ladies.

*And speaking of...*there sitting across from him was an attractive coed with short bobbed blonde hair and blue eyes. He could swear she was the girl in the Noxzema commercial. Ezra sauntered over to her knowing he had some looks going for him. His jet black hair and high cheek bones under the beard were an edge. His patch was just a bonus.

"Hey," he said jerking his up slightly, playing it all casual. "There's some elderberry wine in the bar. Care to join me?"

She turned to face him and his eyes widened in surprise.

"Valerie?"

Valerie Blaine was one of the Swan's first operatives. Back during the Obsidian War, Valerie helped obtain vital intelligence to gain Culpeper's entry into the war. She used some of her feminine wiles on some poor schlubb in Orange. That was before the Swan existed formally. She had a brief flirtation with him and then disappeared off the face of the earth.

Valerie looked at him quizzically before registering recognition. "Ezra Rothstein? My, how you've grown. Love the beard," she said as he rubbed his chin with pride. *Man, I should have tried the beard years ago.* It was a pain to shave anyway with him being half Hungarian and all. He grew five o'clock shadow by lunchtime.

"Wow, what are you doing here?" he asked and then held up his hand. "Sorry, force of habit."

She giggled seductively looking every bit as alluring as when he first saw her years ago, if not more so. She offered him a seat and he sat just as the train lurched forward.

"Well, it has been a long time."

"So, you're heading my way?" she asked.

"Yeah," he said keeping aware of their surroundings. She knew exactly what he meant.

"So, how's life been treating you, Valerie?"

"Oh, it's been fair."

"And your husband?"

She made a face. "That was really subtle, Ezra. I'm not married."

Yes! He acted surprised. "Really? Oh, I thought, well, such a beautiful woman such as yourself."

"Oh, stop it, Ezra. Now, how about that drink?"

They both stood up and headed to the back, Ezra trying his absolute best not to screw the pooch and say something stupid, which was his way when around intimidatingly attractive women.

"Hey, you're going to be in town a few days," she asked as they crossed from one car into the frigid air and back into the warmth of the bar car.

"Yes I am."

"Cool. Well, after your briefing with…her, well, there's going to be this totally awesome party. You should come."

"I'd love to," he screeched out and then coughed. "I mean, I think I can make it. Who's throwing it?"

"The boss' husband, Chris."

"Yeah, I met him a few times. He owns the armoring shop."

"That and his other life as a captain in the Vicious Rabbits. He's throwing this end of the world party."

"A what?"

"An end of the world party. You know, the whole Mayan calendar is ending on the winter solstice this year and there was a lot of press about it before the Shift being the sign that the world was going to end."

Ezra laughed. "Man, people believed that?"

"Yeah, well, Chris, he's a weird guy. He thought it would be totally delish to throw a shindig, you know, to poke fun at it all. It'll be great. I heard the Fug Pugglies are going to play."

"Really?" He couldn't help but notice that she sounded a lot like a college sophomore now.

"That's unconfirmed, but I know Chris throws the best parties. So, you in?"

"Well, yeah, sure. Why not? I love end of the world parties."

As the train trundled slowly into the late winter afternoon, Ezra suddenly felt that if there really was a Gaia, she sent him on a long ride to North Carolina to fetch some banal documents just to put him on this train at this moment. Of course, being Jewish, he tended to distrust coincidences. But he was looking forward to the ride with Valerie.

Chapter 7

Rochelle, Virginia
Rochelle Sovereignty
December 21, 2012

Three years ago tonight Chris and Brandon came up with the idea for the Mayan End of the World Party. The devastation of the Great Suck that followed in the months after 7/11 and the Obsidian War was still on everyone's minds and was just beginning to soften in its raw intensity. He, Meredith, and kids were at a Solstice celebration being hosted by the local Unitarian reverend with Brandon, Anne and their boy when the thought occurred to Chris. He vaguely remembered seeing a series on the History Channel about doomsday prophecies. The prophecy getting the most attention on the show was related to the Mayan calendar, which ended on the winter solstice December 21, 2012. Its ending was supposed to herald the end of the world though there were several competing theories as to what exactly would cause the end. A sour memory flashed as he recalled lying on the futon listlessly watching the TV series late in the evenings during height of the panic-fueled, insomniac weary months before the Shift hit. Chris had decided at the Solstice party—he only went there for the free beer—that he was going to host the Mayan end of the world and make it a big celebration.

The yellow farmhouse Meredith and he had built a few years ago had a sizeable living and dining room, but it was rather cramped for tonight's festive gathering. Aidan and Rhiannon, dressed in their jammies ran with other children who were likewise dressed for bed. They wouldn't be going to sleep anytime soon though, not with this crowd. Chris and Meredith were trying to make sure there was enough food and wine to go around. Brandon had hobbled over with his one leg—the other one he had lost in an improvised explosive device hunting bandits—and started DJ'ing on the Stirling record player, and was drinking as much of the wine he lost to Chris in poker as possible while his boy carefully handed him priceless LPs to play.

The generator Chris slapped together helped to keep the lights going, but power was still spotty at times. The speakers took up a lot of energy. This was costing the Jung's quite a few Byrds, but what the hell? It was the end of the world, right?

BACKGROUND MUSIC: "Low Rider" by War
Visit www.michaeljuge.com **on the *A Hard Rain* page to listen**

"All…my…friends know the low rider….
The low…rid….er…is a little higher"

People boogied to War as though they never knew what had transpired over past five and a half years. The assault rifles stacked with the coats in one of the guest rooms stood as a reminder. But then again, nobody traveled without at least a sidearm on them. Even within the relative safety inside the settled lands, people still traveled with a weapon. There always was a scant chance that a small cadre of bandits had slipped through the wire and was looking for an easy meal.

A freezing waft announced the arrival of another guest. Chris walked over to see Kendra Baraka and a young man shaking off the cold.

"Hey, guys! Glad you made it!"

Taking off her white poncho, Kendra was dressed in a sleeveless glittery blouse, her arm still bandaged. The young man, one of the farmers, gawked foolishly like young men did when they found themselves on a date with a woman way out of their league.

"Thanks for the invite, Cap, I mean Chris."

Chris had asked Kendra and the gunnery sergeant to drop the ranks between the three of them when they were off duty, something that Jon had asked of him when he and Jon hung out just the two of them. Jon wasn't here, as far as he could tell, though with the crowd, maybe he was and he just didn't see him. Jon probably was stuck at the Christmas party at the Visitors' Center. That was the price of leadership.

"Here. Let me get your coats and rifles. There's beer outside on the deck and spiced wine in the kitchen. We're playing Twister and are gonna do some break dancing later."

"Great. C'mon Matt."

Right behind them came Valerie Blaine with a friend, someone he had seen here and there, but not a local. Even with the inclusion of the town of Orange, Rochelle was small in his pre-Shift view of world of demographics.

"Happy end of the world, Mr. Jung," the attractive young lady greeted. He wished she didn't call him "Mister" It made him feel old.

"This is my friend, Ezra Rothstein." "Ezra," he repeated. "We've worked together before." "I believe so, sir…about a year and a half ago."

"Right, the thing in Harrisonburg." Chris now recognized Ezra as one of Meredith's spooks. Chris had learned not to mention specifics in public gatherings. He liked the kid from what he remembered.

"Well come on in. Beer is chilling in the back outside."

"Is Meredith around?" Valerie asked.

"Yeah, she's around. Business?"

"Thankfully not."

"Ah, good then. In that case, she's with the ladies on the dance floor."

"Meredith? Dancing?" Valerie asked incredulously.

"Yes, Valerie, my wife did had a life before the Swan, you know. She can dance. Let me tell you. She loves to dance."

"Oh, of course. It's just that, well, she's usually so…so pensive."

"Yeah, well get a couple of beers into her and voila, she's a party girl, something I learned about her in grad school."

He understood their astonishment. The last couple of weeks or so, Meredith had been unusually "pensive." He figured the escalation of tensions with the Lambs of God had something to do with it. What did he know? She was the one who knew what was really going on. He just worked here. That was probably a blessing for him, he realized. But regardless, he started making her drinks as they prepared for the party. By nightfall she was as giggly as she was when they were grad students sitting next to each other at Cain and Abel's Bar during the Anthropology Department happy hour trying to not let the other cohorts know that they were dating and failing miserably.

"Val! Ezra!" Meredith called from the living room merrily.

Chris whisked them into the living room to join everyone including his wife dancing. Brandon was doing the robot, entertaining children and adults alike. Meredith winked at Chris, urging him to join her on the dance floor. Like Brandon, he would be doing the robot, too, because he really didn't know how to dance. At least Brandon had an excuse with having one leg and all. Some part of him was embarrassed to get on the dance floor. But Meredith looked delicious wearing that dress and heels. People rarely dressed up like the old days anymore.

The grandfather clock said it was getting late, but the party was still rolling, although the 80s slow dance song now playing helped to take things down a notch. With the sudden end to the microchip came the horrifying loss off all music that wasn't recorded on vinyl. The EMPs rendered CDs to drink coasters and wiped every MP3, WAV and every other digital file from existence. Even cassettes were erased of their magnetic recordings, not to mention the fact that all cassette players relied on the microchip. The only recordings still accessible were on vinyl. A strange byproduct of this reality was that pretty much all music available now was limited to a time when vinyl was still widely sold. That meant there were albums from the 60s, 70s and up to the mid 80s. Anything after that was really hard to come by. Outside of the retro fetish of a few select bands to record their music on an old school medium, most musicians stopped recording onto vinyl after the mid 80s. That meant that it was fossil rock all the time. It was either that or classic Country, which Chris found himself liking more and more.

Fortunately for Rochelle, Brandon's father James had been an avid collector of albums. His basement had been transformed into a music library long ago when Brandon was a kid. James had dreams of becoming a DJ in his retirement. Little did he know that he would be the sole source of broadcast music for an entire community. Most albums at the party were on loan from James.

The living room was now packed with people dancing, talking and drinking. Along the walls hung paintings and photos Chris and Meredith had gathered over the past couple of years. Brandon was shuffling his foot and peg leg with Anne, Gunnery Sergeant Birmingham in civilian garb was likewise dancing with his pregnant wife. It looked like that Ezra was doing well with Valerie.

As Chris headed toward the hallway, the shaky vision suddenly returned with stomach-turning intensity. The beer and wine with chili probably didn't help as a wave of anxiety emerged to fill his consciousness out from its hidden murky depths. Suddenly, it felt uncomfortably stuffy inside. Chris grabbed his overcoat and seeing his guitar standing by the doorway, he grabbed it and headed outside onto the porch.

He shut the door and found himself in sudden darkened silence. The moonlight reflected from the refrozen snow-covered fields. Plumes of steam floated from his nostrils as he exhaled deeply. Most found it too cold to be outside, but the chill was a welcome relief from the stuffiness inside. Chris sat down on a rocking chair and steadied himself, holding his temples with one hand. He breathed in slowly and deeply, letting the cold air dampen the nausea. After a couple of minutes, the nausea dissipated, though the shaky vision remained. Had he not known it was a migraine, he would have jumped to the conclusion that it was a tumor. Chris tended to jump to the worst-case scenario. It was his obsessive mind's way of trying to assert control over the uncontrollable. If he assumed the worst, then fate couldn't ding him for being naïve. That's what he read in the self-help books, anyway.

It didn't matter. Sometimes, the mind had a way of doing whatever the hell it wanted to. This migraine was its little way of telling him the demons were alive and well and were doing pushups in prison, biding their time to find a weak moment to make a break for it and pounce. In a world devoid of Phoketal and other antidepressants, people like Chris were left to find their own way of coping. No wonder why most choose Gaia or Jesus. *Christ, I'd give my left nut to believe in either of them. I don't care which one.* There were purveyors of the dwindling supply of pre-Shift meds; however, medications like Phoketal and Xanax were expensive, and there was a finite amount. Plus, there were several unscrupulous vendors out there who sold fakes. It just wasn't worth it. So many years on, Chris had learned to cope without it like temperamental pioneers in the days of yore had.

Sometimes the anxiety returned over a particular issue…like, say, being in the middle of a firefight; other times it returned for no particular reason at all and hit him out of nowhere. Five minutes ago, he was enjoying himself, dancing to Wang Chung, thinking about spending some quality time with his wife after the party, or perhaps sneak away with her quickly during the party, who was to judge them? And then the next moment *snap*! A pall cast over him and he became Morrissey whining over nothing.

Logically, he understood the underpinning fears and untethered anxieties were purely a function of his serotonin levels. Brain chemistry… the difference between a content, well-adjusted Vicious Rabbit, and a barking madman, flinging poo at the hated world he was involuntarily thrown into, was a matter of some miniscule neurons and chemicals working properly or not.

But logic only went so far to ease his troubled mind. On the bright side, this was nothing compared to the Panic of 2007. This didn't even rank in the top five episodes. It was just a generalized crappiness. Chris picked up the guitar and retuned the strings, which tightened in the cold. He started strumming with no song in mind. His playing had improved over the past few years. It was amazing what he was able to accomplish during his free time now that TV and the internet were no longer available to fill the vacuum. Aidan, Rhiannon and Baby Charles took up plenty of time, but even so he found the nights after the kids went off to bed strangely quiet.

During those quiet evenings when he wasn't being Captain Jung out in the bush, Chris got back into playing guitar. He wasn't Eddie Van Halen or anything, but he was competent. Chris even entertained composing his own songs. But he wasn't too astute with coming up with lyrics. Whenever he tried, he invariably used pre-Shift clichés. Chris figured hearing some middle-aged man bemoan the lost world wasn't something people wanted to listen to these days. If he had a Byrd for every bad poem called *A Lament to my iPod...*

Chris strummed, his fingers picking out a tune he wasn't consciously aware of until he recognized it. It was a song he hadn't heard in a long time, since shortly before the EMPs hit. Popular music had declined in credibility during the last decade so much so that perhaps the Shift was a way to spare humanity from Rock's long demise as bands became unrecognizable from each other and their songs immediately got picked up to be used in investment fund and car commercials. Playing was therapeutic, allowing Chris to vent while giving him something to concentrate on.

And then the song transformed into something else, something entirely new. It was strange how the chords just came together without even thinking about it as though he was someone else playing, because this song was something he had never heard before. And yet he somehow knew it. He could swear that whatever this tune was—he was convinced it was an original by now—it would be a great Rock ballad.

While his frozen fingers picked at the chords knowing them without knowing what it was, he saw a silhouetted horse-mounted figure approaching from the darkness. Chris adjusted his posture, placing his heel towards his right hand while he played. The .38 revolver tucked inside his boot had become a natural part of him.

When the figure appeared in the tiki torch firelight up the walkway, Chris recognized the man and relaxed.

"Evening, Jon. I was wondering when you'd get here."

Jon Early dismounted, latched his horse to the post, and carried over his saddlebag to the porch.

"Had to make an appearance at the other party first."

"Ah, how was it?"

Jon blew through his teeth. "Well, it would have been a helluva a lot more fun if you hadn't formed your own little soiree."

Chris just shrugged and continued to play until Jon took a seat in the rocking chair next to him.

"There's beer in the deck out back."

Jon lifted a bottle of Firewater. "I'm taken care of."

He took a swig, handed the bottle to Chris who then followed suit, which made his face contort. Firewater really was awful stuff, but it did the job most effectively if you're goal was to get shitfaced. Chris didn't care for getting intoxicated himself. He didn't like the feeling of not being in control.

But Jon Early drinking Firewater? Jon was a devout Christian, or he had been. When the two first met, he had never seen the man drink. But he had to admit, over the last few years, Jon seemed to get a little lax on his evangelical mores. As Jon reached into his satchel, Chris noticed how he stumbled slightly. He had definitely been helping the bottle attain liberation from its liquid. He wondered what the laws were about riding while intoxicated.

"Here, Buddy. Merry Christmas, or Merry Solstice or whatever it is you believe."

Chris was about to say that that the only thing he believed in was *Sto-vo-kor* when Jon handed him a bundle of cigars. Tobacco had been reintroduced the last couple of years after Rochelle was no longer living hand to mouth on subsistence farming. Jon would have been vehemently against the reintroduction of such a horribly addictive crop, which sapped the soil's nutrients more than any other crop; however, it had the benefit of being extraordinarily desired even years after those who survived quit smoking. There was a population out in West Virginia who wanted the feel of momentary bliss to inhale the robust smoke, hold it in their lungs and let it fill the void and just before they lost consciousness, exhale as the smoke dissipated into sinewy wisps. Along with tobacco, Rochelle also grew cannabis much to the constable's dismay. He tried to overrule the vote, but like tobacco, West Virginia was willing to pay top Byrd for some kine bud which Rochelle was only too happy to provide in exchange for ammunition, some remaining stockpiles of precious industrial chemicals and their superior form of petrol which ate the engines at a slower rate.

Chris took out a cigar from the box and with the Zippo in his pocket lit it. He inhaled the smoke and felt it saturate the bronchioli in his lungs. Finally, he let out a satisfying exhale. "Mmm. Thanks, Jon. I wish I wrapped your present."

Jon waved him off. "Come on. You can help me by polishing off this bottle." Jon took another swig and handed it back to Chris.

Chris sighed heavily before taking another swig. He really didn't want to get drunk, but it looked like he wasn't going to have a choice. He wiped his mouth brushing the two-pronged goatee before handing the bottle back and taking another puff.

"So, where's Sharon?"

"She'll be along," Jon said evenly.

The two sat in silence while a country song played inside. Chris hated silence. It wasn't just the tinnitus, it made him uncomfortable.

"Hey, man, you okay?"

Jon leered at him suspiciously with his squinty Richard Gere eyes as he took from the bottle. "Yeah, of course. Why?"

Chris shrugged. "I don't know. You're…well," Chris paused to choose his words carefully. "You're not the drinking type."

"I'm not, am I?"

"No. And your faith sorta prohibits it."

"So, you're gonna tell on me, Chris?"

"You know what I mean. I'm just concerned. That's all."

"Well, don't be. You're not my Pa, Chris."

That was a cutting statement for both of them. Charles Early, Jon's father, had led Rochelle during the first crucial months after the Shift. He had become a surrogate father and mentor to Chris, and when he died, Chris was there by his bedside holding Charles' hand. Jon had lost his entire family to the flu. Chris and Jon had come to become friends over the years and Jon confided that his dad and he had a falling out. There was no particular reason why, just two lions who were too similar to get along. Chris knew how much Jon regretted not being able to patch things up with his dad.

Jon sighed heavily as steam rose from his breath. "I'm sorry, that was uncalled for."

"Hey, it's cool."

"It's just that between the bellicose rhetoric by the religious factions pointing fingers at each other regarding the assassination attempt and the Lambs of God sniffing at our border..."

Jon stopped himself in midsentence, censoring himself from discussing business, a wise move as always from his constable. This was not the right venue to discuss such sensitive matters. It certainly was not the right time. Jon feigned a smile.

"Just a tough week, that's all."

Chris scoffed. "Just a tough past half decade; You know, billions dead, surrounded by savages and encroached by religious fanatics. It has a way of killing the mood."

"You want to get the fiddle out instead?"

Chris' eyes widened in surprise. "Why Jon, is that a classical reference I hear?" Chris didn't even know what the reference was exactly, except that it had to do with some insane emperor playing a fiddle while Rome burned.

"Contrary to what the liberal media fed you, most of us Devil Dogs can read. And some of us actually took an interest in history if you can believe it."

Chris snorted. "The media," he repeated the word, which sounded alien on his tongue. He probably hadn't uttered that word since...in a long time. That led Chris to another thought.

"Jon, you think they'll write about us?"

Jon took another swig and handed the bottle to Chris wiping his mouth with his sleeve. "Who?"

"Historians. In all the frenetic chaos these past years, I don't think there have been many people sitting and writing it down for posterity sake. I wonder if what we're doing now, what we've done up to now will be documented for future generations."

Jon nodded thoughtfully. "Hmm. That depends."

"Depends on what?"

"Well, you know the saying, 'history is written by the victors.' If we survive this, if by some chance, God delivers us from our enemies..." Jon's voice trailed to a whisper.

Although not part of the Swan, Chris had been privy to much of the intelligence as he was a forward reconnaissance officer in the Vicious

Rabbits Bike Mounted Cavalry. He had seen firsthand the rising tide of bandits, and their increasing brazen and sophisticated attacks. Then there were the Lambs of God. He knew less about them. Apparently it worried Jon as well as his wife. Suddenly, seeing what only could be described as fear on Jon's face frightened him. Jon wasn't scared of anything.

Puffs of steam danced between their faces as a kerosene lamp on the floor cast Jon's face in severe relief.

"Jon," Chris felt the chili and wine and Firewater in open revolt, "is there something I should know?"

Jon sniffed. "Shut up and drink your Firewater." He then patted Chris on the shoulder.

Chris put the cigar out to save for later. He didn't want to get addicted to tobacco again, but he had a sneaky feeling that it was inevitable. He picked the guitar back up and resumed playing the song he somehow mysteriously knew, but didn't know what song it was other than it was beautiful.

CHAPTER 8

Annapolis, Maryland
The Abercrombies
December 2012

Jean Paul Nguyen walked briskly, enduring the northerly wind speckled with ice crystals. For the first time in his life, he understood why the Navy issued pea coats as the one he wore kept his torso and arms comfortable despite the frigid wet wind outside. He just wished they came up with a hood and facemask to go with it. The nasty weather gave a plausible excuse for his hurried pace. The locals here seemed not to care for the Nor'easter any more than he, so there was nothing out of place with his clipped aggressive strides. He didn't want to appear to be scurrying off, which he and his ship most certainly were. The Abercrombie sentries would get suspicious if Jean Paul tiptoed his way around the docks. In his experience, if you acted agitated as you went about your business for the world to see, nobody questioned you. He hoped that rule of thumb held true with wackos like the Abercrombies here, because he was in essence making a getaway.

"Captain."

"Jesus!" Jean Paul jumped. He immediately crossed himself and muttered a corresponding prayer so as to not have taken the Lord's name in vain.

"Cody, dude, you scared the living shit out of me." He forced himself not to whisper, which was the natural response when one was trying to avoid drawing attention, but whispering caused the opposite, in fact.

"Sorry, Skipper, the girls always said I was a sneaky son of a bitch,"

Cody said with a sense of pride. "The XO says that we're ready to push off."

"And our stowaway?" Jean Paul asked trying to keep up with the unnecessarily tall passenger whom he had come to incorporate into his crew.

"Yeah, he's safely tucked in."

"Good. Let's get the hell out of here."

"Why all the rush, Captain? Aren't you enjoyin' the Abercrombies' hospitality?"

Jean Paul turned to face Cody just to be sure he was indeed being facetious, because his tone almost sounded sincere, and he didn't know Cody Robacheaux well enough to judge his character yet. Besides, he sported a handle bar mustache, which his people called a "porn star." And he tended to be wary of dudes with those. Likewise, he did not know the rest of Cody's companions Jean Paul and his ship was ferrying back home. It was a wonder Cody and his companions survived the journey that stranded them in Newfoundland where Jean Paul picked them up. Fortunately, Cody's smile suggested he had no love for the Abercrombies any more than he himself did.

"I just want to get out of here and back to somewhere sane. Home."

"I heard that."

Jean Paul winced. "Of course. Sorry, man." Jean Paul knew that however much he missed home, having been at sea for months now, Cody and his buddies had been away for years.

The *Jean Lafitte* undulated gently with the choppy waves slapping against Annapolis Harbor, her bow seeming to defy the rough currents beneath her steel hull. Seamen worked diligently out in the elements making final preparations, tightening seals, stowing the remaining equipment for departure, securing the ammo crates and most importantly hoisting the mast of the main sail. The massive golden emblem, which was likewise emblazoned on every crew member's coat and shirt, contrasted against the black fabric of the sail. The towering golden fleur de lis waved proudly with the wind, letting the world know who they were, and that, yes indeed, the Saints were coming.

Jean Paul stood to attention on the peer, saluting the symbol that united his people. Strands of his longish straight black hair escaped from his cap and matted his face. Other crewmen of the *Lafitte* stood to attention as well until Jean Paul lowered his salute to the fleur de lis and walked toward the plank.

"Man and I thought I was a Saints fan. Y'all really take it to a whole new level."

"A lot has changed since the EMPs, Cody," Jean Paul responded mirthlessly.

"Yeah, I noticed."

As Jean Paul stepped on board, one of the petty officers barked, "Captain on deck!" The seamen stopped to salute again and Jean Paul saluted back.

"Carry on."

Most of the seamen were either white or black much like in his hometown, Vietnamese being a distant third in the demographic. Back before the EMPs, these men wouldn't be seen working together so closely as they did now. They would have lived in different neighborhoods, gone to totally different schools, and wound up with completely different lives and with utterly divergent fortunes. But today they shared the same fate, the same heritage, and they all saluted one of the youngest captains, the son of a Vietnamese fisherman who once sailed across another dangerous ocean to escape the tyranny of the communists.

The Abercrombie sentries, walking along the peer and patrolling on motorboats, seemed not to take notice of the flurry of activity onboard the *Lafitte*, a good sign indeed. Once inside the dry and warm bridge, Jean Paul felt the burning of his cheeks and hands as blood began to flow again. The electric lights on the bridge were dim as to not blind them to the outside. His first officer saluted, which he could tell still seemed to impress Cody as Jean Paul was a kid compared to the older man before him, still twenty-five. Of course, Jean Paul being born to the sea moved quickly up the ranks of the Saints' navy.

"Where y'at, Commander?" Jean Paul asked, reverting back into his native accent.

"All accounted for, captain. We're ready at your order."

"The order is given."

With that the first officer blew a horn indicating to the seamen to cast off. As the *Jean Lafitte* reached open water, Jean Paul felt his spirits lifting. Annapolis was depressing. He had seen how most of the country had fallen apart, especially the Northeast. But as unsettling as it was to see how most of the population had died and the rest had turned into savages, it was far more upsetting to see a group of fanatics who enslaved savages and corrupted the word of the Lord to justify their ends. The Abercrombies weren't savages like the rest of the east coast; they were worse. They were slavers, though he had to hand it to them; they did wear their torn and faded clothes in a most stylish way.

Of course, the Abercrombies weren't too fond of the *Lafitte* and his crew either as the Saints didn't share their heretical vision of things. Jean Paul barely contained his contempt for them by being stridently Catholic in Corey Abercrombie—the boss man's face. The crew of the *Jean Lafitte* had been their guests, and the barrels of pure seventy octane gasoline bought them favor, but Jean Paul feared that they were about to wear out their welcome, especially when they would find their pet prisoner missing and who just happened to be safely onboard the *Lafitte*. Jean Paul just hoped to be far enough away by the time the Abercrombies found that out. As they sailed beyond the harbor and onto the open Chesapeake, Cody sighed with relief.

"You can breathe again, Mr. Robacheaux. We're on our way home… after we drop off our guest."

"Yeah, but what about that place? Is it gonna be like Annapolis, maybe worse?"

"I have no idea, but Mr. Spankmeister seems convinced it's civilized. And I heard the Abercrombies railing against them. And if the Abercrombies hate them, then they can't be all bad."

"You got a point there. The enemy of my enemy axiom worked for us well enough."

Jean Paul nodded and felt the weight of Cody's words. After a few quiet moments Jean Paul stroked his black locks. "Cody, may I ask you something?"

Gazing through the porthole out into the darkened molting seas, Cody answered without looking at him. "Sure."

"How was it over there? I mean, how did you all make it?"

"To Newfoundland?"

"No. How did you and your men survive Iraq?"

Cody scoffed. "What, you don't know?"

Jean Paul shrugged. "You could say we've been out of the loop on current events beyond our own neck of the woods the past few years. I heard rumors, but they're all jumbled and contradictory."

"Well, Hoss, we didn't all make it," he said, his tone turning sour. "In fact, there was a time it looked like the whole shit house was gonna go up on us." He paused as he recovered his balance. For a former Army Ranger, a land lover if there ever was one, Cody Robacheaux adapted to the sea better than most of the other passengers who like him were serving in the armed forces in Iraq when the EMPs hit. Some of the former Marines on board fared no better than the Army types they mocked. To Jean Paul who lived on the water, they were all land lovers.

"But thanks to the Sultan of Mosul…"

"You mean that General Petraeus guy," Jean Paul asked.

Cody nodded. "The one and the same. Thanks to a smart commander, the grace of God, and the Kurds' ingrained animosity towards the rest of the country, we did make it. It was getting out that was the trick. There was this matter of trekking through several layers of hell just to hit sea."

"So, the rest of the Middle East didn't fare any better."

Cody looked at him. "Captain, that place was falling to shit for decades before the EMPs." Cody pronounced the term for the phenomena the way most New Orleanians did, pronouncing it like "imps."

"Well, so was Nola."

"That's nothing alike. Anyway, yeah, the Middle East had pretty much turned into your garden variety cluster fuck like Europe and sadly, here as well. Most of us found life in Kurdistan to be pretty good, actually. Together with Sultan Petraeus and the locals, we carved a good life over there, especially compared to the hajjis dooking it out everywhere else around our AOR. We all integrated well with the natives, and a lot of us were given more respect there than we received back home. But enough of us wanted to go home. And when you want something bad enough, nothing will stop you, not even a minor inconvenience like a multi-faceted, multi-tiered sectarian war that makes other wars seem orderly in comparison."

"Captain," the first officer interrupted, "I brought Mr. Spankmeister as requested."

Jean Paul saw a scrawny character standing just behind his first officer. Helmut Spankmeister—he still didn't believe that was his real name—wasn't short. He stood about Jean Paul's own middling height, but he seemed smaller somehow. Jean Paul knew he wasn't a savage though. He was too articulate, too knowledgeable. Besides, if the Abercrombies kept him in a gilded cage, then he had to be worth something. But was it worth going on this diversion? It was another unknown and Jean Paul wanted to be back in NOLA as soon as possible. He was already going to spend the Lord's birthday out at sea. He didn't want to chance getting trapped in some savage backwater.

"Okay, Mr. Spankmeister, I've risked the life of my crew, the lives of these retired soldiers and my own in smuggling you out of the Abercrombies' hands. I want some answers before I agree to changing course." Both the proposed destination and his home were on the same heading up to a point. But as Father Boileau said about Origen of Alexandria, "why ruin good bluster with semantics?"

Helmut Spankmeister scratched his well-kept beard nervously. "Thank you, Captain Nguyen for saving me. If you would be so kind to drop me off..."

"Wait. Why should I divert my ship to go into another sink hole of humanity?" Jean Paul interrupted. Although Spankmeister was probably a few years older, he had gotten comfortable ordering men much older than himself around. It was necessary as captain. The way things worked in NOLA, a lot of the leadership on the seas fell to the younger generation, and it was upstart kids like himself who had random skills that wound up saving the city from the fate of the rest of the world.

"It's not a sink hole, captain. It's civilized land down there." Spankmeister's protest was cautious but sincere.

"Civilized? Out here? I find that hard to believe. Mr. Spankmeister, I haven't seen civilization since Newfoundland."

"Captain Nguyen, I need to go there. My people are depending on me getting there."

"And your people, they're not friends with the Abercrombies I gather."

"That's correct. And neither are the people in Fredericksburg. And they have a demand for your gasoline."

"Who doesn't? But do they have anything to offer in return?"
"I don't know. I've never met them."

"Wait. You never met these people and you want us to bring you to Fredericksburg?"

"Well, actually, I need to go to Monticello."

Exasperated, Jean Paul slapped his hand against his forehead. "Monticello? What is it?"

"It's the home of Thomas Jefferson, but that's not important. From what I gather, Fredericksburg is a close ally of Monticello. You drop me off in Fredericksburg and I assure you that you'll find yourself pleasantly surprised to find a new market for your gasoline. And they are civilized so they will be worth your while."

"How do you know any of this if you have never met them? Word of mouth from those Abercrombie jack wads?"

Helmut looked over Jean Paul's shoulder and walked past him.

"This is a radio, isn't it?" pointing to the cumbersome contraption, which took a significant portion of the bridge with all of its vacuum tubes and reinforced thick copper wires.

"That's right. We have radio technology back in Nola."

He turned to the communications officer. "May I?"

Jean Paul nodded and the petty officer moved. Helmut studied the contraption. "What's the range?"

The young man answered. "It depends. The ionosphere is still frazzled from the effects of the EMPs. We think it may be caused by the Earth preparing to shift its poles…"

"Yes, yes, yes, I know about the magnetic poles being the cause of the Shift," Helmut said impatiently and using an unfamiliar term that Jean Paul presumed meant the same thing as "the EMPs." In Jean Paul's experience, the theories about the cause of the phenomena and terms used to describe it varied depending on the region. The Cubans called it *los huevo fritos*, which if his Spanish was as good as he presumed meant "the frying egg," which totally made no sense at all. Oh well.

The petty officer continued. "We ran the antenna from the base all the way up the main mast. That gives us much better range than you would traditionally receive. On a good day, I'd say a seventy miles."

Jean Paul noticed that the lights didn't fluctuate meaning that there wasn't much disruption from the EMPs today and that the rotary spinning underwater that powered the electronics was running at full capacity.

"Let me see if I can find it." Helmut started turning the knobs gingerly. It was pure static out there, which was expected out where only savages and fanatics lived. He didn't expect to hear radio traffic again until he reached South Carolina when he entered Cuban territory. But then Jean Paul heard something out of the static. Helmut Spankmeister did too, and he stopped and turned back.

"Shh!" Jean Paul ordered.

Helmut moved the dial slightly and there it was; a high-pitched voice. It was hard to make out at first, but then Jean Paul recognized it as a song. The signal was faint and garbled in static, but it was clearly music—the Chipmunks, in fact, singing "Christmas Don't Be Late."

"You see? It's from Fredericksburg! It's the Fredericksburg Union! Do savages have radio?" Helmut asked rhetorically.

No, not these days they didn't. Having radio technology meant that you had to manufacture vacuum tubes and come up with a way to power it. The industrial base to produce anything sophisticated had been wiped out with the EMPs, but given an educated, disciplined populace with a division of labor and a sense of order, they could scrap up the materials necessary to build radios. And having enough spare resources to expend power to play music for entertainment purposes meant they had probably fared pretty well, meaning a civilized people. Whether they were in the market for gasoline or not, finding other civilized voices in the land once part of his country would be worth introducing himself.

Hearing radio communication again was a pleasant surprise for the crew of the *Lafitte*. The world really had been hit hard by the EMPs with few notable exceptions. The Northeast was especially unsightly. The men on the bridge cozied up to the radio and listened to the Chipmunks singing. This Fredericksburg place was a gamble, but then again, the church didn't consider gambling a mortal sin much to Jean Paul's relief. And besides, wasn't this his mission…to find new trading partners, "to seek out new life and new civilizations" as it were? Risk was part of being young.

"Well, Mr. Spankmeister, you're in luck. It just so happens I need to drop off a few veterans in Virginia anyway, and I guess Fredericksburg is as good a place as any."

"Helmsman, set a heading towards that signal. We're spending Christmas in Fredericksburg."

Chapter 9

Approaching Charlottesville, Virginia
Greater Monticello
January 1, 2013

Keep it together, Helmut. Hold on. Don't lose it here, not now. Helmut Spankmeister sat in the back of a late model Suburban beside Captain Nguyen and the lady who stood behind the mirrors in the debriefing room while her cronies grilled him for every piece of information they could squeeze out of him. Rochelle wasn't what he expected. Neither was the constable. Rochelle was a lot more rustic than he had imagined it would be, and the constable seemed much more human than he had built up in his mind's eye. He wondered what Rita in Monticello would be like. Frankly, he was amazed he made it this far. If he could keep his head together a little while longer, sell his story to her as he did to her Vicious Rabbits friends, he might get Rita to return with him and she can save the world.

"You okay, Mr. Spankmeister?" asked the puppet master lady sitting across from him. Her generous brown, almond shaped eyes looked at him with what he could swear was genuine sympathy.

"Just…you know, carsick." He shaded his eyes from the intense morning sun.

"The roads don't help matters much," added the regal looking constable with considerable charm. He could see why the whole community liked this man. He really did exude a kind of pheromone that made you want to follow him. It wasn't just that his father had been the previous constable—that's what he gleaned from the transmissions, anyway—Jon looked and acted like a leader, even if he was more down to earth than he had been built up to be.

"We'll be there in another fifteen minutes or so."

The caravan passed the charred ruins of the north end of Charlottesville trundling over the broken pavement at an impressive forty miles per hour, something Helmut hadn't experienced since before the Shift. Most of the vehicles travelling on the road were ugly tortoises covered in corrugated armoring that made them crawl. Not the constable's Suburban. Helmut figured that since the lands between Rochelle and Greater Monticello were settled and pacified, there was little need for such burdensome armor.

"It's impressive," he said. "What you all have done here."

"Thank you," Jon answered. "We worked hard to get here."

"I can see," added Captain Nguyen. "It's clear that your people are the guiding light of the Divine Logos."

Helmut found Jean Paul to be an interesting character. He was very philosophical for someone looking to sell oil. Of course, it was an unfair assessment to label everyone outside his compound as knuckle draggers, but it was true by-and-large. But Jean Paul seemed to defy his rough exterior and his Brooklyn accent, which he later learned was actually a New Orleans accent.

"The Divine Logos," Jon repeated. "Oh, the reverend's gonna love that one."

"It's a Catholic thing," Helmut added.

"Yes, Mr. Spankmeister. We have a lot of Catholics here."

"That's good to hear," Jean Paul said.

"I'm not one of them. And the reverend certainly isn't."

"That's okay. Nobody's perfect."

Helmut lost track of the rest of the banter between the captain and the constable. He rubbed his temples trying to massage away the nausea. His thoughts became more jumbled. He didn't know how long he could stay sharp. He lifted his head to find the woman staring out the window in deep meditation.

"You get carsick, too?"

She turned around. "Excuse me?"

"Are you carsick?"

She flashed a wan smile. "Yes, that's it." She turned back to stare out the window again and Helmut joined her seeing the new town emerging out of the ashes.

Rita Luevano had a feeling that this was going to be an interesting year. That wasn't necessarily good. One could say that 2007 was an interesting year, too. But if the latest profound if cryptic vision from Gaia followed by an assassination attempt last month was any indication, then the Chinese proverb "may you live in interesting times" would manifest. Something had brought the constable and Director Jung over on New Years' Day. She couldn't contemplate what fresh disaster was in store.

Rita and Akil were galloping back up to Monticello after visiting Neko at Our Lady of the Random Miracle. The doctor was encouraged by the fact that the wound had not gotten infected and believed that Neko might be released in the next week or two. But despite the good news, Neko was absolutely devastated. Rita told her about the prognosis of her arm and how she would never be able to draw a bow again. She would be lucky if she regained fifty percent of her strength and dexterity in her right arm where the bullet had torn up so much of her shoulder.

It was hard news to deliver to such a healthy, fit and spunky warrior such as Neko. Rita knew what it was to be mutilated in battle as she unconsciously felt the partials that replaced the missing teeth on her left side and touched the eye patch over her missing eye. She was once unscarred and now she woke up every morning with a reminder of the attack on her. She knew that the journey towards acceptance for Neko was going to be especially hard. As Rita and Akil pushed up the mountain to meet their guests, her thoughts went out to Neko.

Inside the dome room on Monticello's third floor sat Deputy Chief Magistrate Juan Ramirez, Sheriff Lucille Schadenfreude, the Rochelle contingent Jon Early, Thuy Mai, Meredith Jung and two guests she did not recognize. Despite the fact that one was white and the other was Asian descent, the two looked liked they could have been brothers as they both were roughly the same height, build and had straight black hair.

The late morning sun peered through the snow covered oculus skylight above them and through the circular windows from the quasi-octagonal walls, bathing the yellow room in light and revealing the classical yet innovative beauty Thomas Jefferson envisioned for his home. The room's majesty was highlighted by the Pottery Barn furniture, which replicated early 19th century classical architectural design modified for modern sensibilities better than any frontiersman could have hoped for.

"It's good to see you, Jon. It's been a long time. Happy New Year." Rita gave him a kiss on the cheek.

"Thanks, Rita. Merry belated Solstice," he returned with a slightly raspy voice indicating the beginnings of a cold.

She then made a face and hugged Meredith. As much as Meredith pushed the boundaries with her regarding using her people, it wasn't out of malice or inconsideration, but rather that the woman seemed to be so overwrought with responsibilities that little niceties slipped through the cracks. Rita could sympathize. Jon then handed her a present, a staff wrapped in precious aluminum foil.

"Oh, a stick. Thanks, Jon. Really, you shouldn't have."

"Open it, smart ass."

Rita smiled and opened the foil to see it was a bamboo stick, a fresh bamboo stick oozing something. She could smell that it was sweet. Putting her finger to it she tasted it.

"Sugar cane?" She asked completely befuddled.

Jon smiled.

"But how?" Rita knew that sugar cane couldn't grow up at these latitudes.

"Please allow me to introduce you to two guests staying with us. This is Mr. Helmut Spankmeister."

Rita fought back a grin at the preposterous name and extended her hand. The mousy man leered at her. He muttered something like, "Yeah, it's good to see you," but she couldn't tell for certain. He pulled his hand back and folded his arms and crouched back into his seat.

Jon ignored the social awkwardness and put his hand on the other guy's shoulder. "And this is where we got the sugarcane from. This is Jean Paul Nguyen, Captain of the ship *Jean Lafitte*, a vessel that sailed from New Orleans."

Rita's eye widened astonished.

They young man smiled warmly and shook her hand. "It's a pleasure, Chief Magistrate or is it Reverend? I hear both."

"Some people call me Reverend. Some people call me Chief Magistrate."

"Some people call her Maurice," Thuy Mai jumped in waiting for a laugh that never came.

"Well, Captain, you've certainly come a long way."

"Captain Nguyen led an exploration up the North Atlantic in search of viable markets interested in gasoline. His fleet made it to Newfoundland. On the way back, they picked up Mr. Spankmeister here in Annapolis."

Rita gave Jon a look and he nodded. "That's right, Rita, where the Abercrombies are said to be holding out."

Jon gestured. "Perhaps you should take a seat. This may take a while."

"We heard rumors about Newfoundland from the Cubans," said Jean Paul.

"The Cubans?" Akil asked.

"Yeah, they weathered the EMPs—the *Shift* as you call it—better than Americans did. They were living like it was 1959, so it didn't really affect them too much. It was a windfall for them in fact. But that's another long story. Anyway, New Orleans has a few oil rigs out in the Gulf operating again, those whose blow out preventers didn't activate when the first surges hit. Thanks to some old men who knew a thing or two, we were able to refine the oil without computer control, and we figured wherever there were civilized lands, there would be a need for gasoline. So, after learning about Newfoundland, we headed north carrying as much gas, rice and sugarcane we could fit in our hulls. There we found a number of veterans from Iraq who had made it halfway across the Atlantic when their own ship got caught in the currents, which tossed them all the way up to Canada. Lucky for them it was summer when they arrived."

He took a sip of chicory and continued. "The Newfies were happy to let us take them home. A number of the veterans lived in or had family in Virginia, Pennsylvania and Maryland, and we figured we could drop some of them off in Baltimore. They knew America was no longer what it was. They knew there weren't any cities anymore, I mean, except my town, of course. But they had family back in the States, so I guess I can understand."

"So, I'm off to Baltimore. It's sorta halfway between those states. I cut the other ships loose to head back for Nola and we sailed up the Chesapeake. And that's when we found the Abercrombies in Annapolis."

"At first we thought, 'awesome!' Another civilized town to cultivate a trading partnership with. We could use coal even with our supply of gasoline, and the North has a lot of urban mining potential, right? We need metal alloys. Their leader Corey Abercrombie seemed a gracious enough sort, but…"

Jean Paul shook his head ruefully. "Man, when we saw what the

Abercrombies were doing to the locals there, slavery, pleasure girls. It's not like that doesn't exist with barbarians, but these people did it in the name of God. Why is it when someone wants to justify something atrocious, they always go all Old Testament?"

"And then one evening, we found Helmut here hiding on our ship. I didn't know what his deal was, but I wouldn't send anyone back in the Abercrombies' tender care. He told us to bring him to you."

Rita craned her neck curiously. *How would he even know about us if he was up in Maryland? And why come to us?* Meredith seemed to catch her train of thought and spoke up.

"This is where things get interesting. Mr. Spankmeister was a captive of the Abercrombies, but he wasn't treated like the rest of the prisoners. That's because the Abercrombies wanted him for something important." Meredith urged Helmut Spankmeister to talk.

"I...I was, I worked for the Department of Energy," Spankmeister stammered. "It was an annex facility out by Fort Meade."

"That's in Maryland, yes," Juan asked. Rita vaguely heard of the place once or twice, but it was as foreign to her now as China.

"So, you were with the Department of Energy," Akil repeated skeptically.

Meredith adjusted her glasses. "That much I was able to confirm with some of my sources."

"Your sources knew him personally?" Rita asked.

"Not exactly. But some recognized the name."

"It is hard to forget," Akil added with some jest.

"I was out looking for food," Helmut interrupted. "I got too close to one of the Abercrombies' caches when they found me. They were going to kill me. I needed to stall them to keep me alive...so...I talked. I told them what I did."

Everyone leaned in across the conference table to listen.

"You see I used to keep track of the movement of all nuclear material throughout the country. Whenever the military was moving its missiles, X-ray machines were being transported, or whenever nuclear waste from a power plant was being hauled off to storage, my company was in charge of keeping track."

"Company? I thought you worked for the Department of Energy?" Lucille countered.

"I do, but I'm a contractor. I work...I worked for the Stubb Foundation, which contracted with the government."

"Christ, they even contracted nuclear security out," Lucille scoffed.

"Go on, Mr. Spankmeister," Rita encouraged.

"I was keeping track of a massive caravan hauling nuclear waste from a power plant in Pennsylvania when the Shift hit. It wasn't something I gave much thought about, you know, because I was just trying to stay alive. But when the Abercrombies picked me up, I was desperate to not be thrown into their chain gang or be summarily executed."

He gulped. "I heard about the Abercrombies, that they're a little possessed."

"You mean that they're eschatological madmen," Jean Paul added, which took Rita by surprise. Few used that terminology.

Lucille chuckled. "Yeah, they make the Lambs of God look reasonable and watered down in comparison from what we heard from Fredericksburg."

"I knew they wanted to have an edge, so I told them."

Rita held up her hand. "Told them what?"

Meredith sensing Helmut's reticence answered for him. "He told them what he used to do, and he told them about a caravan transporting nuclear waste that was presumably in Maryland when the Shift hit. He told them that he just so happened to have printed out the locations a couple of hours prior to the first EMP hitting. That means the information wasn't lost in the hard drives. He held it as a bargaining chip. He gave them the general vicinity of the caravan, but not the exact location. They want that nuclear material."

Everyone was stunned to silence as the gravity of the story hit them.

Lucille squinted. "Wait, I don't think they could build a nuclear weapon using nuclear waste, could they?"

"No, but they could develop dirty bombs," said Jon Early.

Lucille mouthed the words. "Oh, God, I think I remember now hearing something about them. Didn't some terrorist try to make those?"

"Yes. I think you might be referring to the case of Jose Padilla," added Meredith.

"A dirty bomb doesn't have any greater yield than the conventional explosives it uses; however, its shrapnel is deadly, dispersing highly radioactive material, irradiating acres of land, killing everyone slowly by radiation poisoning and making the land uninhabitable for generations. Take enough of those, use them in say, artillery shells, and you could completely destroy a small nation like ours or yours with just a few dozen such devices."

"Dios mio," Juan crossed himself.

Lucille then asked. "Well, if you have the goods on *all* nuclear material, why not use your knowledge to locate a missile silo and appropriate a nuke there? I'm sure the bombs within the missiles would still work even if the missiles don't."

Lucille's tone was openly hostile, which was understandable considering that Helmut just admitted through Meredith that he had given the Abercrombies the idea to create a dirty bomb. And the Abercrombies hated the Orange Pact. Normally, that wasn't a problem with DC serving as a virtually impenetrable buffer. But if they developed a dirty bomb…

"Yeah, but good luck in getting inside a silo," Akil answered. "Missile silos are buried deep beneath the earth and if the power fails, it automatically seals itself."

People around the table stared at him. "What? I did a stint with NORAD when I was in the Army."

Jon then added, "You would need more explosives to get inside than most of us possess."

A horrible thought crossed Rita's mind. What about the people inside the missile silos and nuclear submarines? What happened to them? She considered the tortuous death of being locked inside one of those silos or submarines when the Shift hit, unable to escape, to die suffocating beneath the ocean or deep underground. Rita shook off the thought and returned to the conversation.

"I can assume that you didn't really want to give them the locations at the end of the day, though, did you?"

"No, no, of course not! I learned about you all down here…um, through them, you see. They really have it in for you."

"Yeah, we get that vibe from them, too," Akil said.

"I don't know why. I was scared and I just told them. But as soon as I could, I started planning my escape. And that's when Captain Nguyen showed up."

"So, what we have is a bunch of fanatics running around Ft. Meade looking for Helmut's hideout that presumably has these printouts to show them where these radioactive Easter eggs may be hiding," said Rita summing up the story.

"Well, actually, it's not exactly Ft. Meade," Meredith corrected. "It's a town nearby Ft. Meade, some suburb called Laurel."

*Laurel…*The vision. Rita felt a sudden wave of vertigo hearing the word. She narrowly avoided knocking over a Monticello souvenir mug filled with hot chicory on the table.

"Sugar, you okay?"

Laurel. Rita's skin dimpled into goose bumps and her fingers went cold. She struggled to remember Gaia's words in the vision. "With Laurel you will find Jamil…Jamil would know what to do." *Do? Do what? Save humanity from destruction.* Rita implored Gaia to explain, but she would not say what it was that threatened humanity. "With Laurel you will find Jamil. Jamil would know what to do." The words made more sense now. All this time, Rita had assumed Laurel was a woman, not a place.

"You said Laurel?" she asked.

"Yes, it's a suburb next to Fort Meade." Thuy Mai added.

"The Department of Energy had an annex facility out there," Meredith said looking at Rita with concern. "That's where the printouts of the nuclear disposal sites are, where the Abercrombies were planning to head to until their little guide here left them. Now, the Abercrombies are supposedly looking blindly in the general vicinity."

"And we intend to get there before they find the maps," Jon Early said.

Gaia's words echoed repeatedly, beckoning out to her until she relented to Gaia. Rita knew now why this funny little man was brought here, and why Gaia sent him here. She needed to see this through. She needed to find this Jamil—it couldn't possibly be Akil's son. There are a lot of Jamils, right?—and make sure he does what he needs to do. She took a calming breath.

"I'm going," Rita said firmly.

Akil nearly fell out of his chair. "Baby, are you trippin'? Didn't you hear what he said? This isn't some stroll to Rochelle. This is out there in Maryland!"

Jon held up his hand. "Listen, Rita, I've got a team specifically trained for force recon out in the urban bush, the bike mounted cavalry; it's what they do. Now, if you want us to include a few archers along, I can talk to Dean and see what he can do. But Rita…"

Jon took a moment to choose his words carefully. She noticed how tired he looked, liked he had aged ten years since their last meeting a couple of months ago. Come to think of it, she remembered his appearance striking her last time, too. His hair was slightly tousled.

"You're the leader of your people. It wouldn't do to have their leader trouncing off into no man's land on a sui…" Jon looked over to Meredith who dropped her head slightly. "To go trouncing off on a very, very dangerous mission. You're too important to your people now."

"Yes, Sugar, please. To Jon you will listen if not me. You can't go out there. You're no spring chicken." Akil stopped himself realizing he had just committed a cardinal sin in marital conversations.

Rita raised an eyebrow to Akil for a long moment. She then took his hand and spoke softly to him. "*Mi Coriño,* she told me herself. She told me I had to go to Laurel."

Jon squinted. "Who told you?"

Lucille sat up excitedly. "She said 'Laurel?'"

Rita nodded. Jon then understood to whom Rita was referring.

"Look, Jon, I know you don't believe the visions I have."

"I believe that you honestly believe you have these visions."

"Fine, whatever. I understand your skepticism, but I need you to allow me to join your expedition."

Jon sighed before she pressed on. "I'm asking you as one leader to another. This is a class A request. I need you to do me a real solid here, and let me go."

Jon turned over to Ezra. " I know she's your boss. Your honest opinion. Can she hack it?"

Ezra scratched his beard nervously before nodding. "Yes, Constable, the Chief could outride most archers, and she could outshoot most of your legacy Marines."

Jon shot him a look. "Well, that's saying quite a lot, son. I sure hope you're right, because I don't want to lose the best ally I have."

Rita broke out in a smile. "Thank you, Jon."

"Don't thank me. I have a feeling your people are going to hate me for allowing you to go."

Chapter 10

The weather for Raleigh was expected to have a thirty percent chance of snow. Chris could care less; he was trying to find where this potential new employer was located. Chris scrolled down the screen till he found the company. The sun shown directly onto his computer screen making it difficult to read with his own reflection in the way. He noticed something odd about his reflection. It looked like he had a long chin beard. Then he noticed a figure walking up to him. From the reflection, it looked like a beautiful woman…with an eye patch of all things. He swiveled his chair around swiftly to see who it was. It wasn't a beautiful woman.

Shit. *It was the opposite of a beautiful woman, in fact. Chris quickly tried to exit out of the website, feeling rather conspicuous as he did. He knew his boss must have seen it.*

"Hey, boss."

"Chris. So, what are you looking at?"

"Nothing, really, just some company."

"Ah." The skinny redheaded man paused. "Does it have anything to do with work?"

"Umm." Chris was a terrible liar and he knew it. His nostrils always flared and his eyes shifted wildly. One benefit of having gotten to know himself over the past four decades was that at least he knew that about himself. He also knew that lying directly to the boss was a really bad idea, especially in the government.

"Umm, not really, Ed. I was just taking a break."

"Yeah, you seem to be taking a lot of 'breaks' lately when you are at your desk." He leered at him with yellow eyes.

Chris didn't know what to say.

"Yesterday, I went by your cubicle no less than four times, and you were never there."

"What?"

"You heard me."

"Ed, I was here all day yesterday. I don't know what you're talking about."

"Are you calling me a liar, Chris?" Ed moved closer to him, and he could feel his knees weakening a little. Ed Farcus was younger than he, but that didn't diminish his authoritarian attitude. In fact, it exacerbated it.

"I wasn't saying that..." Chris suddenly heard a voice that boomed from every corner of the office.

"Dad, Dad."

Rochelle, Virginia
Rochelle Sovereignty
January 2013

"Dad, Dad." Aidan whispered urgently, nudging his dad who was asleep.

"Come on, Dad. Time to wake up."

Somewhat disoriented from his dream, Chris muttered, "I'll get on it, boss."

"Dad," Aidan pushed again, more forcefully this time.

Chris awoke, seeing his strawberry blonde boy standing at his bedside intent on waking him up. Then he realized, today was the day he and his company were to depart to Maryland. Chris promised the night before to get up early and play with Aidan before he left.

"Okay, son. Just let me get some chicory."

Aidan's room was like any five-year-old boy's room, a complete disaster area. Tiny plastic dinosaurs, action figures, matchbox cars, LEGOs, and any other toy that didn't run on batteries swirled around the room in the most inconvenient places making navigating inside the room perilous business. Posters of the famous photograph of Neil Armstrong on the moon, the earthrise from lunar orbit, and other such pictures decorated the walls.

The radiator hissed, providing warmth in the pre-dawn morning. Chris hadn't used a radiator since his days in New York City when he and Meredith lived in an old brownstone. He never thought he would be installing such an archaic device in his own house. But such was the nature of things. This heater wasn't salvaged from the necropolis. This was manufactured in Rochelle, by the business he owned, Jung Armoring and Fabricators. While convalescing after the Obsidian War, Chris' duties as a blacksmith increased with the new demand to develop parts for home grown generators including wind turbines, retrofitting cow dung methane generators and rebuilding purely mechanical diesel engines that would work, at least better than their modern counterparts did, in the post-Shift environment.

Chris' old blacksmith instructor Frank Foreman who died in the autumn after the first anniversary of the Shift willed the blacksmith barn and all of its equipment to him, as Foreman had no living heirs, and Chris was the closest thing he had to a son, though the old man constantly berated him kind of like an abusive father would. Chris wasn't as skilled a blacksmith as compared to real craftsmen. He certainly wasn't much of an engineer or mechanic; he didn't even know how to change the oil in his car before July 11th. But there were men out there who did have such skills. He went ahead, took what resources he had to barter for more equipment—the Byrd hadn't become the standard monetary unit yet—scavenged out in Charlottesville, much to the dismay of the Monticellans, and set up a new shop. He hired mechanics and craftsmen who had skills but no resources, and since then he has become the post-Shift equivalent of Richard Branson, but without the neat accent and signature garish teeth.

Chris was tiring of his commission with the Vicious Rabbits. After recovering from his injuries sustained in the Obsidian War, he agreed to go back to duty fulltime, mostly because there simply weren't enough gunslingers in the Rochelle Sovereignty. The Obsidian War had thinned their ranks considerably. Chris wouldn't have felt right about weaseling out of the Vicious Rabbits Corps while he was able-bodied, minus a few toes and some scarring along his back, and experienced in war. They were vulnerable, small in number. Hell, even peg-legged Brandon with his seven fingers was still in the militia. So, Chris agreed to stay on. That being said, if he were Danny Glover, he would say that he was "getting too old for this shit." He had too much to live for now. He had a booming business. And most importantly, he had a wife and kids.

Chris wanted to stay home, to see Aidan, Rhiannon and Charles grow up, to watch them take over his business. Chris wanted to grow old and play with grandkids. And he was tired of leaving Meredith every month to go gallivanting into the wilderness while she was left holding the bag even though her responsibilities exceeded his. But the reality was that Rochelle was surrounded. This little sovereignty was in a precarious place in history and geographically. It was a tiny pocket of normalcy in a churning sea of chaos and depravity. His home needed people like him to stand on the wall, as it were. And that was why he was not going to retire today, why he was leaving his family, why he risked never seeing them again, because he had to do everything in his power to make sure his children would grow up safe and free.

Aidan played with the model Eagle One lunar lander Chris had picked up in Manassas and given to him via Santa. Chris watched his son act out the scene, which was told to him through books, speaking the parts of both ground control and the astronauts.

"Houston, the Eagle has landed. We're going to fit on our spacesuits and should be outside in five minutes."

Chris grinned at the innocent re-enactment according to a five-year-old. Sadly, Aidan and his generation would never become astronauts. Chris hadn't really thought about that up until now, but that was really depressing.

"Dad, are you okay?"

"Yeah, son. I'm fine." He realized that he had been overcome with emotion, and he quickly tried to recover.

Aidan put down the lunar lander and gave him a hug. "I'm going to miss you too, Daddy."

Chris embraced his son hard, because he didn't want him to see him completely fall to pieces.

The armored school busses choked to life in the parking lot of Madison High. If you ignored the arsenal being loaded into the back, the corrugated armor sheeting on the busses, and the assortment of armed folks coming to say goodbye, it could look like any school event. It was still freezing; however, most of the snow had sublimated, leaving brown earth in its place.

Chris, dressed in tactical gear, was helping one of his privates load the bicycles into the cargo truck. Chris hefted *The Interceptor*, outfitted with side bags, and which had been repaired repeatedly over the years—the only original parts remaining was the frame itself—and handed it to the private standing above him inside the bay of the cargo truck.

"Captain?"

"Yep?"

The sixteen-year-old Vicious Rabbit took his bike. "I've been meaning to ask you."

"Yeah, and what is that?" he said in his naturally friendly tone. Long ago, Chris quit trying to sound like a hard ass like Gunnery Sergeant Birmingham. That's what gunnery sergeants were for.

"Why did you name her *The Interceptor*?"

A wane smile crossed Chris' face as he realized the kid wouldn't have gotten the reference.

"Just old man humor," he said.

BACKGROUND MUSIC: "Cat's In The Cradle" by Harry Chapin
Visit www.michaeljuge.com **on the *A Hard Rain* page to listen**

The Vicious Rabbits began boarding the bus. Chris knew it was time. He always hated this moment, the threshold where his personal life clung onto to him as he walked off to his other life as Captain Jung, the bicycle-riding warrior of the urban necropolis. This happened on almost every mission, Meredith and the kids would see him off. Personally, he hated it. It tore at his heart and prolonged the pain of saying goodbye. He understood that Meredith did this more for the kids than anything else, but it was something he would rather not endure. If he had his way, he would have slipped out in the night. Then again…well, nothing could stop the heartache. He was a family man.

He held Rhiannon as she wrapped her arms around his neck tightly. Her honey brown hair wafted in his face as she sobbed. Aidan had gotten used to the frequent deployments by now, so the boy attempted to put on a brave face, which Chris admitted was more than he himself could muster at forty years old. Rhiannon, on the other hand, was three years old. She could sense her parents' distress, see the sobbing of other families around her, and she knew her dad was going away. And Chris' half-hearted assurances that he'll be back soon didn't satiate her.

"Don't go, Daddy."

Meredith held Charles who was asleep in her arms. Chris and Meredith had said their goodbyes the night before. Every deployment presented risks, but this one was like no deployment he had ever been on and both of them were well aware of that. Whereas he had previously been on jaunts to Northern Virginia to places he knew well, where he was even able to locate tribes of townies, this was a trek to uncharted territory; suburban Maryland. Chris couldn't say when he would return. If all went according to plan, if their eccentric tour guide Helmut Spankmeister was on the level and didn't fall off his bike and break a leg along the way, then perhaps they would be back in a couple of weeks. But Chris knew nothing ever went according to plan.

"Pick me up something pretty, okay?" Meredith said choking back her tears.

"Sure thing, hon. I hear there's a duty free at BWI."

Meredith tended to maintain an even strain even when he knew it tore her up every time he was deployed, but now he sensed she was openly distraught. He didn't know if it was just about him going out again or if it was something else. Even though he had been with her since the last millennium, she was still hard to read.

Chris pried Rhiannon off of his neck and handed her to their nanny Mrs. Palfrey. After giving Aidan one last hug, he placed his calloused hand on Meredith's cheek and gave her one last kiss. He was glad he used the homemade mouthwash this morning. He wished he had the use of deodorant, because he was already sweating beneath his tunic, armor and white poncho.

Others jumped into the school bus to join Lt. Baraka and a few of the archers from Monticello with Rita, who gave Chris a curt nod. Chris then waved goodbye, took his helmet off of Aidan's head and stepped onto the bus.

The driver had KVR playing on the radio while the busses idled. The song playing was a little too bittersweet for his taste, "Cat's in the cradle." As they started to drive off Aidan chased the caravan waving.

"Bye, Dad! I love you!"

The words rang out,

The cat's in the cradle, and the silver spoon,
Little boy blue and the man on the moon.
When you comin' home, dad? I don't know when,
But we'll get together then. You know we'll have a good time then.

The ride to Fredericksburg was uneventful. The stretch between Orange and the Fredericksburg Union wasn't completely pacified. Stray bands could be lying in wait anywhere on the stretch that the allies once used to degrade Obsidian Corp's reinforcements; however, the constant patrols made traveling between the two Orange Pact nations as relatively routine as a flight to Pittsburgh in the old days. Except in this case, there's a Kennedy on board, so anything could happen.

KVR faded out after Orange, the eastern edge of the Rochelle Sovereignty, but the bus driver found Fredericksburg's station, WTF. Jim Croce was crooning,

The caravan passed burnt out husks of vehicles as well as the occasional mass funeral mounds along the country highway. Chris tried to find a comfortable position to sit, but it was impossible wearing seventy pounds of equipment on a bench seat. He pressed his face against the vision slit to see an abandoned feed store next door to a Platinum Barrel and Petsmart looted years ago. This was his America.

"Hi, Captain."

Chris turned around to see Rita Luevano in the seat in front of him turning herself to face him. Eye patch or not, she was beautiful. Even when her dentures occasionally slipped out, which was understandable considering that there was no way to customize them for her, he couldn't help but appreciate her defiant good looks. Her husband Akil was across from them completely passed out, which amazed Chris considering how noisy the bus' engine was and the bumpy ride.

"Chief Magistrate," he said with unusual formality. They had been on a first name basis for years. Having realized a few years ago that their paths crossed back on September 11th cemented their friendship. But he was not pleased with her right now.

"I just wanted to say again, thanks a bunch for agreeing to this. I know that Dean Jacob wouldn't have approved my joining your company for this op if you had refused."

Chris was indeed reluctant to have Rita tag along. It was bad enough they were going to have to schlep Helmut Spankmeister, the crazy scientist, all the way through uncharted territory and past the Abercrombies. But Spankmeister was crucial to the mission. She, however, wasn't. Chris threw a fit when Dean told him that the Martyrs Brigade would be tagging along with the leader of Greater Monticello. He didn't mind the archers so much. He had worked extensively with them in the past. Though they were used to riding horses over cycling, the archers were able to keep up with the Vicious Rabbits Cavalry. The Thomas Jefferson Martyrs Brigade was the elite corps within the Monticellan Defense Forces, after all. And he was actually happy to be working with Akil again. The two of them met way back when the Shift hit and travelled from Manassas to Charlottesville together before he went on silent running to look for his son Jamil. He knew Akil's shit was squared away. But the leader of Greater Monticello?

"You passed my pre-quals, Chief Magistrate..."

Rita held up her hand. "Captain, on this mission you are the commanding officer. Chief Magistrate means nothing here. I follow your orders until a higher authority says otherwise."

Chris didn't know what she meant by that exactly. With some conciliation he added, "Look, I've worked with Ezra before. He's got a good head on his shoulders. So do the rest of your archers. At the end of the day I have little room to complain."

"Thank you."

"But what you haven't explained is why." Chris paused a moment, catching a glimpse as they passed another field that had reverted back to the wilderness.

"Why are you coming on this mission?"

"It's hard to explain."

"Well, it's a long ride. Tell me."

Rita got out of her seat and sat next to him. She spoke just audibly above the music and groaning engines. "I was given instructions to escort you to Laurel in order that you might do or find something that will save us...from I don't know what. But it's absolutely vital that I go."

Chris nodded matter-of-factly. "Instructions...by Gaia?"

Rita inclined her head as if to say, "Well, yeah."

"Rita, I don't know anything about any god, but I'm sure of this, maybe we can stop the Abercrombies from obtaining those nukes. But what about the Lambs of God? I don't know what can save us from them when they decide to come for us."

Chris broke off eye contact, feeling conspicuous having said it out loud.

"You've got to have faith, Chris."

Chris chuckled ruefully. "Faith, yeah right. I almost forgot 'the secret weapon,' faith."

"I'm serious. Do you think it was just coincidence that you, Jon and I were together on September 11th and then years later and hundreds of miles away after July 11th? Are you telling me it was just random happenstance?"

Chris blew through his teeth. Sometimes his agnostic resolve was shaken by such weird happenings as though there might really be something to what Rita was saying. But harsh reality would return him to the ground.

If there was any grand plan, what happened to all of the good decent people that died after July 11th? And faith that it would all work itself out, that there was some *deus ex machina* to deliver them from the Lambs of God? *Yeah, tell it to other communities who were swallowed up by the Lambs of God or by hordes of bandits.*

"I don't know, Rita. God never spoke to me."

Chris moved closer to her and whispered. "Has it ever occurred to you that this could be an elaborate trap? Maybe Mr. Spankmeister over there," Chris pointed to a scrawny man biting his fingernails sitting alone in the seat. "Maybe he got co-opted by the Abercrombies."

"I think your wife would have detected any deception."

"To be fair, my wife isn't a human lie detector. She has someone else for that job, and he could have been wrong. People who are committed, really committed, can come off calm when they lie."

"I know that, Chris. I had recent experience with such maniacally dedicated types," she countered bleakly.

"My point exactly. Maybe the Abercrombies wanted to lure us into a trap, capture a few grunts or maybe a mid level officer such as myself. They figured they could coerce us into providing them with some valuable intelligence. But look what they caught when they cast the net? The leader of Greater Monticello herself!"

"I hope you're wrong, Chris. And all I have is an assurance that I don't think she would lead me into a trap."

"Well, I hope she's right, for all of our sakes. I'm just trying to keep my people alive. God, the only reason I'm still doing this is to keep my family safe. I still wonder what in the hell I'm doing here."

Rita touched his hand in a friendly gesture. "You're a good man, Chris. I'm glad we have people like you on our side."

Rita sat back down in her seat and cleaned the stave of her bow. Chris thought about her compliment. He guessed he was still a good man, even after having killed so many people over the years. But what use was being a good man against the Lambs of God? Mathematics conspired against the Orange Pact. When you were outnumbered five to one, what good was being a good man? Chris pressed his face against the window slit again watching the train of corroded vehicles decomposing on the side of the highway.

CHAPTER 11

Fredericksburg, Virginia
Fredericksburg Union
January 2013

Chris had visited Fredericksburg on a number of occasions since the close of the Obsidian War. On the heels of the devastating defeat at the hands of Rochelle, Monticello and Culpeper at the end of the war, the remaining Obsidian Corp security specialists limped home to find they were no longer in charge. While they were off trying to amass more territory, the peasants in Fredericksburg, who had been treated rather poorly under Obsidian Corp., organized into a union led by Dave Richardson, a one-time student radical who later became a distributor for a pharmaceutical company. The Fredericksburg Union, led by Dave Richardson, joined the Orange Pact shortly thereafter. Chris had come over the past few years to aid the Fredericksburg Union in hunting down bandit groups who conducted hit and run attacks from their lairs in Woodbridge and Dale City.

Upon arriving into town, Dave Richardson greeted Chris, Rita and the bike mounted cavalry and led them through the old, once scenic, downtown. Fredericksburg was the absolute end of civilization or the absolute beginning, depending from where one was coming. Being on the eastern edge with the wilderness at their backs, the town's infrastructure took a backseat to maintaining some semblance of order, an extraordinarily thin mist of order at that. For instance, each home and business had to provide its own electricity. Even in the middle of town, it was dark at night unlike more settled towns like Orange or Culpeper. The port, where the large seafaring vessels were anchored on the Potomac River, was located fifteen miles east of town at Fairview Beach, while in Fredericksburg proper, a number of smaller fishing boats were anchored in the middle of town on the Rappahannock. Even in the dead of winter, Chris could smell the haul of dredged oysters and the catch of crabs co-mingling with horse dung and diesel.

Chris remembered going to visit the historic downtown in the real world. Back then, the streets were lined with antique and souvenir stores along with coffeehouses and bistros. Walking down the frozen cobblestone streets at night, they bore only a passing resemblance to the innocent storefronts they had once been. It had devolved since then, now pregnant with the trappings of a rowdy port city, underscored the seedy caricature of itself. The coffeehouse and gelato store where he once enjoyed an affogato had become a brothel, so too had the souvenir and antique store across the street. In fact, as Chris looked around, he realized he, his cavalry and the collection of sailors, fishermen and merchants were almost outnumbered by hookers walking out from the brothels to greet the men. Although it was below freezing, women, some tragically little older than girls, came outside to proposition his randy cavalry company.

Some of the prostitutes were dressed scantily, shivering in the cold, but some of the others were dressed rather prim for prostitutes. In fact, they seemed out of place in this world as several were dressed in business skirts and jackets complete with heels, briefcases and pantyhose, albeit torn and soiled. The brothels understood the post-Shift male psyche, the desire for more than just easy sex. A fair number of survivors had worked in the city and were accustomed to seeing beautiful women dressed in professional attire. Seeing women wearing clothing raided from Talbots brought them back to the world that once was even if momentarily.

"Howdy, big boy. Come on in. It's warm inside," a woman catcalled in his general direction.

Some of the young men in his cavalry stopped to make small talk with the girls. Men, they were hardly that. Most were no older than eighteen, and they were more animal than human in the presence of freezing women offering to give various parts of their anatomy a test ride. Their libido didn't allow them to appreciate the tragedy of fortune of the pathetic scene before them. Hell, despite his own moral compunctions, Chris noticed his other brain was waking up blithely unaware of how horrible it really was. *Men really are dogs.* It made him that much more fearful for his girl Rhiannon and the world she was going to grow up in.

He noticed how Kendra, Rita and the other archer, a young woman named Ilsa Jenkins, he believed, instinctively found each other and walked stiffly as though they were about to fend off a pack of wolves.

"I bet your lady won't do what I'll do, Colonel," a woman said to Chris directly.

"Ooh, you look like a strong one. You would do nicely," another girl said to one of his men.

"How much?" the eager young man asked without any tact.

Chris gave his gunnery sergeant a stern look.

"Roit! You boys just keep walking. I don't intend on you catching the clap on the way out!"

"Oh, you're no fun anymore!" a girl protested.

"Zhora is up on the next block," Dave Richardson advised.

"Who's Zhora?" Chris asked.

BACKGROUND MUSIC: "Brick House" by The Commodores
Visit www.michaeljuge.com **on the *A Hard Rain* page to listen**

Zhora was a place, not a person. The restaurant/bar and, of course brothel, that Dave Richardson brought his cavalry to had been a tavern before the Shift. Electricity wasn't completely reliable in Rochelle. Here it was downright sporadic. The generator outside coughed out smoke from a fuel that was little better than fermented potatoes. Fuel from West Virginia was hard to come by. Even still, neon lights lit the dank bar while, girls wearing lingerie and 2007's clubbing gear slowly swung around poles. At center stage a woman with a snake draped over her swayed seductively.

"She's a brick...house
She's Mighty mighty,
just lettin' it all hang out,"

The DJ played a severely scratched Commodores record while the lights lining under the bar fluctuated as the generator struggled to keep the place lit. Dave guided them through the crowded bar filled with a wide assortment of characters to another room he had reserved.

"She's a brick...house
That lady's stacked
And that's a fact
Ain't holding nothin' back,"

Dave called Chris over. “This way, Captain. Over here.”

As Chris walked over he saw a group of men all wearing black windbreakers with the golden fleur de lis. Meredith had briefed him about these men, the Saints, who would be ferrying his company over to Maryland. In the rush to prepare, Chris just sort of accepted Meredith’s report on an intellectual level. He didn’t have time to process it emotionally until this moment. The strange accents spoken around the table was the accent of his homeland, a distant land called New Orleans.

Dave walked over to a man several years younger with Asian features.

“Captain Chris Jung, I’d like to introduce you to the Captain of the *Jean Lafitte*, Jean Paul Nguyen of the New Orleans Saints. Captain Nguyen, this is Captain Chris Jung of the Vicious Rabbits.”

Jean Paul shook his hand. “Hey, Where y’at, Captain.”

Just listening to the men around the table, Chris could smell the mold from his hometown where the humidity was always ninety-five percent.

“Captain, you okay?”

Quickly, Chris recovered and shook the man’s hand. “Captain, Nguyen?”

“That’s me.”

“You all really are from New Orleans, aren’t you?”

The men laughed.

“Well, not all of us. I’m sort of delivering some veterans back home. Cody Robacheaux here is from Ville Platte.” A man with a preposterous mustache raised his mug. “But I guess that’s close enough, right?”

The young man cocked his head. “You from New Orleans, too?” pronouncing it “New Wallins.”

Chris nodded.

“Wow, small world. What part?”

“Lakeview area. You…New Orleans East, right?”

Jean Paul smiled, Chris guessed that it had to do with the fact that most Vietnamese Americans in New Orleans lived in New Orleans East.

“Well, glad to hear it. You got family over there?”

“I did,” he answered ponderously.

The young man smiled sympathetic to Chris’ sullen response. “I wouldn’t dismiss them. You’d be surprised. A lot of people made it who you think wouldn’t have.”

“Yeah?”

"We did a lot better than anyplace we've seen up here."

A waitress appeared and he ordered a couple of ales, and moved his seat closer to Jean Paul.

"Um, so, New Orleans made it?"

"Yeah, you right! I understand your skepticism, Captain. Everyone wrote off New Orleans long ago. But let me tell you, we had a lot going for us, and we owe it all to Katrina. Well, the blessing of our Lord and Hurricane Katrina."

Chris furrowed his brows. "I have to say that doesn't sound right."

Jean Paul chuckled. "Yeah, you'd think a place like Nola would be among the first to go to shit when the EMPs, I mean the *Shift* struck."

Chris pulled out a couple of cigarillos and offered it to Jean Paul who took it gratefully. Chris had noticed he started smoking more of these over the past few years. Jean Paul inhaled deeply and held it for several long seconds.

"Oh, yeah. I could see why there used to be so much whoopla about tobacco in the old days. There's gonna be great interchange of goods between your people and mine. This is what New Orleans really wants. Well, this and metals."

The young man looked like he was high, but it was just regular tobacco, not mixed with cannabis or anything. Abundant in Rochelle, tobacco was one of those crops that Chris considered a mixed blessing. It made money, but Chris could swear he was going to get addicted if he didn't watch it. Hurriedly he pressed on. "Jean Paul…Katrina. How did it save my city?"

"Yeah, I'm sorry. Where was I? Katrina, right. Look, you have to remember, by the time the Shift hit, New Orleans had just a fraction of the population it had before Hurricane Katrina. And many of the people were living life pretty hard. I mean, my parents were living without electricity still, and that was almost two years later! And their block was the only block for several miles that was inhabited. New Orleans East got it hard. They rallied with the other families on the block to keep the area secure, especially at night."

"This was before the Shift," Akil inquired.

Jean Paul nodded and inhaled his cigarillo. "I think that was part of the city's strength, you see. There were neighborhoods, blocks and streets that had already organized themselves. They were well armed, and they stored food just in case another hurricane hit. They weren't going to be caught off guard again. So, you see they lived in post-catastrophic mode before the Shift."

"Because catastrophe had already struck them," Rita concluded.

It made sense. Chris recalled how New Orleans had changed after Katrina. He was eking out an existence as an intelligence analyst in Northern Virginia when he saw on CNN his city get swallowed up by the surrounding waters. Shortly after the storm, he drove down to help his parents salvage what they could from their houses that were saturated in Katrina water and mold. He swore after ripping up the carpet that the smell would never leave his nostrils. The city itself became desperate and lawless even more than it was before the storm. Neighborhoods acted like autonomous sovereignties much like what existed today, where neighbors had to band together to keep watch for looters, especially at night.

As Chris thought about it, he realized that Katrina mobilized New Orleans into a state of emergency before the real emergency hit. It was the lone city in the US that had already practiced the end of times and test drove what to do when the shit hit the fan. So, as insane as it sounded, the fact that Katrina had wiped out its population and forced its citizens to endure hardship gave the city an edge.

"When the first EMP hit, the neighbors knew each other, knew how to work together and how to maintain their own security. And let's not forget the National Guard who were still out in force in the Quarters."

"The Quarters," Kendra asked.

"That's the French Quarter," Chris translated for her.

"Yeah, the National Guard's presence was a key component. The other was providence."

Jean Paul took a swig of ale before continuing.

"You see, there was a hell of a traffic jam that day on the river. There was a glut of cargo vessels coming up from the Caribbean and South America and even more cargo ships heading south down the Mississippi. The inbound ships carried things like coffee, bananas, what have you, but it was the outbound ships that saved us. Rice, wheat, potatoes, corn, the ships were loaded with the bounty from America's bread basket headed to feed the hungry planet. A lot of river pilots called in sick after they all participated in a raw oyster eating contest. Of course, anyone could tell you that it was stupid to eat oysters in a month not ending in an 'R' but their being sick saved the city. Without the river pilots to guide the cargo vessels, the ships were all stuck in New Orleans, and they just so happened to be caught in the city when the first EMP hit."

The significance of the story suddenly dawned on Chris and the other Virginians who now crowded around Jean Paul.

"Hundreds of tons of grain, rice and corn sitting in the cargo holds… enough to feed the majority of us, at least until we got our act together."

"That is an incredible story," Akil offered. "But there's something I don't get. I see that y'all had some fortune on your side, but even so, how could that city have organized itself until it got its act together?"

Jean Paul belted out in laughter. "Yeah, the city leadership wasn't too impressive. No, we didn't rely on elected officials."

"Then who?"

"We needed more than just someone who knew how to get things done and we needed a real leader, not a politician. We needed someone who could inspire, someone who could mobilize the people, someone who could break through the racial, class and political barriers."

Chris racked his mind trying to think of who could unite that city that he remembered as being fundamentally divided between black and white, and Vietnamese, rich, middle class and poor. Then he saw the fleur de lis on all of the men's coats. "The Saints?"

Jean Paul's grin confirmed his guess.

"Wow, you all really do love your football," Akil said amused.

"Say what you will, but the team's coach, and all the players for that matter, had come to the city and quickly made it their home, and the people responded. When things got desperate, it was that familiar sign that people looked to for guidance. Hell, they did get the team to the NFC championships for the first time in franchise history and only a year after Katrina."

His grin faded. "We didn't all survive mind you. There were opportunistic diseases that spread and then there was this flu…"

Everyone at the table sobered momentarily as they took stock of their own fortune for having survived the collapse. Every adult alive today lived with that shadow following them. Part of it was a survivor's guilt; part of it was recognition of their own mortality.

"We lost a lot that first year," he said staring into his mug, but then forced himself to smile once again. "But fortunately, we didn't receive outsiders coming into the city looking for help. New Orleans was the *last* place you'd go to find law and order."

Chris was awash in the young man's yat accent, which was the true New Orleans accent which most of Hollywood had seemed completely incapable of reproducing accurately. Directors and producers of movies like *The Big Easy* and *JFK* who hadn't spent more than one drunken weekend in New Orleans before filming insisted on making New Orleanians sound like either Foghorn Leghorn or have some dismal approximation of a Cajun accent. So, when tourists came to town, they were always surprised to find all these people from Brooklyn. New Orleans was the oddball of the South, not only because it surrendered to the north in 1862 without a fight, but also because of its subsequent history, which made it have more in common with New York in some ways than it did with other Southern cities like Atlanta.

The influx of German, Irish, Italian and Ashkenazi Jews came to the port of New Orleans at the end of the 19th Century just as they did New York and Boston, and hence developed an accent which most recognize as a "Brooklyn" accent. In New Orleans the same group of immigrants developed a similar "Brooklynese" accent but whose rough contours were sanded down by the smooth drawling of the South.

"Where y'at, dawling," was a common expression back home. The warm, inviting greeting hence became known as the "yat" accent. Chris' mom had it, so did his dad to a lesser extent. Had he grown up in one of the suburbs like Chalmette, he supposed that he would have spoken with an accent as well. As Jean Paul spoke, Chris felt as though he was coming back to a home he wrote off long ago.

"My God, an entire world out there and we don't know anything about it. Hell, we don't even know much about Maryland or the Abercrombies, unfortunately."

"Well, they're pieces of work," said the man sitting next to Jean Paul who sported a rude mustache. Cody, if his memory served correctly, was one of the Iraq War vets who survived the crossing over the Atlantic.

"Yeah, I'm glad we got our friend out safely," the captain added nodding to Helmut who was quietly sipping his beer in between burly Saints and Vicious Rabbits. "Isn't that right, Mr. Spankmeister?"

"Yeah, uh huh."

That was the first time Chris had heard Spankmeister speak.

Jean Paul turned his attention back to Chris and Rita. "Yeah, we didn't know what we were gonna find when we headed to Baltimore to drop off some of the vets we picked up in Newfoundland. But I didn't expect that I'd find people so hell bent on dying like those jackals. They seemed a bit odd when we pulled into port, but I soon learned they wanted chemical weapons, nukes, anything. They got a serious hate on for you guys."

"Yeah, we have that effect on a lot of people," Chris said dryly.

"Well, anyway we were looking for a way to just step out of the way quietly like you do when you've stepped into an Alanon meeting drunk, because your friends said it was some great secret bar, not that I know what's that's like, mind you. Just as we were preparing to set sail we caught our friend, Helmut here stowing away. And he told us about you guys."

Jean Paul leaned in really close to Chris, Akil and Rita. "He's a very strange character, isn't he?"

Chris politely acknowledged the undeniable truth. Jean Paul lifted his mug and turned his attention back to the nervous looking fellow ravenously eating a steak with not the least bit of attention being paid to the half-naked woman, pole dancing scant inches away from him.

"But who isn't a little post-traumatic these days? Isn't that right, Mr. Spankmeister?"

Chris has wondered about Mr. Spankmeister. There was no doubt he was eccentric, which these days was actually quite common. But he didn't act like a feral. He didn't talk much, and he ate meat like he would never eat again, but he didn't carry himself like he lived from hand to mouth. He was very hygienic and when he did speak, he was articulate.

"Aye, he doesn't seem like any of the wankers we've run into," Birmingham said with his mouth full of food while staring at another dancer who was upside down on the pole now.

"I don't envy what y'all about to get yourselves into," the young captain said grimly. "I'm just the delivery man here to drop y'all off. I hope you're right and he's for real 'cause, if it were a trap, well, you wouldn't want to be at the Abercrombies' mercy."

"I hope I'm right, too," Chris said in a macabre voice.

Chapter 12

Fredericksburg, Virginia
Fredericksburg Union
January 2013

All evening Rita tried to sleep but visions kept interrupting her. Being surrounded by pathetic souls in g-strings was disturbing. Rita knew that Dave Richardson didn't allow outright slavery, but these women, these girls were enslaved never-the-less. They found themselves selling their bodies either out of dire hunger, debt, or most likely from an addiction to alcohol.

The last one, Rita understood all too well. A little over nineteen years ago she herself had been teetering close to prostitution, sleeping with men who paid for her drinks. Of course, there was an array of drugs available back then, and she loved them all, but she always went back to the booze. Heroin and cocaine had virtually disappeared from the region after the Shift, but people's addiction remained. Even without a calamity, there were a percentage of people like herself who were just prone to addiction. After something as big as the Shift, nobody left alive came out unscathed.

Rita tried not to dwell on last night. Between the smell of alcohol and the pathetic looks on the faces of the girls shrouded by inebriation and aging Mascara, she was content to head back to their hotel with Akil straight afterwards. Akil was gentlemanly enough not to ogle. She appreciated how Chris, the young lieutenant and the gunnery sergeant were conscientious enough to forbid any of his Vicious Rabbits in engaging in any illicit exchanges beyond the occasional lap dance. Rita noticed how Chris declined Dave's generous offer of a young lady he placed on the Captain's lap. Visibly uncomfortable, Chris stood up and politely, even chivalrously, sent the girl on her way with a few Byrds in her string for nothing in return. The display of humility on the captain's face was reassuring. Some people maintained their manners even after civilization collapsed.

The twenty-five mile trek from Fredericksburg to the port at Dahlgren Naval Warfare Research Center took less than an hour thanks to a resurrected railway, one of Obsidian Corp's few beneficial byproducts. Cattle cars glided along the relatively smooth rails, tugged by an old eighteen-wheeler cab whose wheels had been converted to fit on the rails. It wasn't as reliable as the steam engine that ran from Charlottesville to Orange, nor were the cars as comfortable, but it was better than riding the distance on bicycle, something they were going to be doing a lot of soon enough. Rita had a feeling that this was going to be the last smooth ride she was going to experience for the foreseeable future, and that was if she made it out.

"Calm down, girl. Have a little faith."

"What was that, Sugar?" Akil inquired.

The husband and wife huddled together inside the cattle car more for mutual warmth than for affection as did several of the Vicious Rabbits and Saints. The olive drab wool blankets in the cars weren't particularly effective and the MOLLE gear and white ponchos they wore didn't insulate them any better. The Fredericksburg Union hadn't bothered to include a formal passenger car yet. Sailors heading to and returning from port suffered in the elements like the fish and spoils from the cities they hauled. The clouds were overcast again, meaning a potential for snow.

"Nothing, mi Coriño, just talking to myself."

"Ah, so it wasn't Gaia this time."

"No, no Gaia visions today." Something else was interrupting her sleep last night. It wasn't Gaia. This was different. She was dreaming in the past again, back when the world was sane, yet it wasn't exactly how she remembered it. Her sleep was also interrupted by Akil's constant blanket thievery. If she wasn't so taken by him, she would have slept in a separate bed.

Rita was beginning to have some real reservations about going along on the trip, which was a shame, because she called in a lot of favors to go.

If only Gaia was the type of being who understood that humans tended to lose their nerve and needed constant handholding and reassurance.

The port at the Dahlgren Naval Surface Warfare Center had been slapped together haphazardly in the few years since the Shift. Some ships docked at wooden piers that extended far from the beach while some of the ships with deeper keels were docked in the middle of the river tethered to a bridge that spanned the Potomac from Virginia to Maryland. That included the *Jean Lafitte*, which swayed gently midway between the two shores. Rita nearly lost her balance upon stepping onto the undulating *Lafitte* from the rope ladder connected to the low rise bridge. She had adjusted to life with one eye, but that was on land.

"Careful, there, ma'am." Jean Paul Nguyen extended his hand to steady her. "It's hella cold for a dip."

The Saints stepped onboard and seemed downright at home heaving from side to side, and excitedly chatted about the snow, a rarity down in New Orleans.

During the train ride from Fredericksburg, Rita noticed how Helmut Spankmeister kept staring at her. She was accustomed to catching men's eye, even since being reduced down to one eye herself and ill-fitting dentures. But Helmut didn't leer at her lasciviously so much. His stare was just odd. Rita smiled back at him to make sure he knew he was staring.

"Welcome to my house, Reverend, Captain." Jean Paul stood on the bow of his ship, arms folded and somehow seemed taller than he was on land. The *Lafitte* reminded her of a 19th century clipper ship although the hull was metallic and the decks were made of fiberglass. The .30 caliber machine guns and a World War II era cannon added to the anachronistic look.

"Thank you, Captain. You wouldn't happen to have any Pepto-Bismol would you?"

Jean Paul and the other Saints laughed heartily.

"Just stow your gear, sit back and enjoy the view. We got it from here." Chris walked up and put a hand on her shoulder. He looked as green as she felt, and they hadn't even undocked yet.

"I have a distinct feeling this is going to suck."

"True that, Captain."

The sailors of the *Lafitte* hoisted the black sail bearing the gigantic golden fleur de lis and within ten minutes, they were sailing towards the

Chesapeake. Jean Paul gave Rita, Chris and his lieutenant and gunnery sergeant a tour of the deceptively small ship. Below decks was a welcome change to warmth from the wet frigid conditions outside. There were a few electric lights dimly lit along the corridors. She assumed they had some kind of water-powered generator. But the big surprise was the existence of a diesel engine that ran a propeller.

"I'm sorry, but I don't understand," Lieutenant Baraka said, scratching her nearly shorn scalp. "You have an onboard diesel motor? So, why did you sail all this way to Virginia?"

The first officer answered. "We could only carry so much fuel with us, and we had no idea what we would find here. We had to assume all y'all were all a bunch of shit flingers. No offense, ma'am."

"Word, but now that you know we aren't and you have access to diesel, why are we *still* sailing instead of cruising up in style?"

"Why do you cycle your way through Maryland instead of 'cruising in style' with some motorbikes? Probably for the same reason that you don't want to announce your presence where people can hear you before they see you. It's the same with us."

"Ah, good point."

The cozy warmth Rita first felt now felt stuffy; the air was stale and choked with fumes. The deck kept swaying.

"You okay, Reverend?" Jean Paul asked.

That's when she lost her breakfast.

Fortunately, Rita wasn't the only land lover to hurl. Being a consummate gentleman, Chris felt the best way to save her honor was to join her in upchucking. So, too did many of the other Vicious Rabbits, many of whom never had seen such a large body of water before today. Akil held her hair as she fed the seas. Rita sucked in the icy air, which seemed to settle her stomach a little.

As evening approached, Rita and the other sorry passengers found their way to the galley and sat down with the other sailors who were tearing into their supper of cod. The lights flickered as they ran on the auxiliary water paddle generator that operated by the ship's movement through the water.

"Y'all care for music?" Jean Paul asked seeing a tepid affirmative response from his passengers. One of the sailors cranked a two-way radio that looked similar to the Stirling in that it was cumbersome and comprised of vacuum tubes.

"Fredericksburg's station should still be clear enough for a few more miles. Then it's all static the rest of the way."

Through mild static a tune Rita recognized came through. The music helped a little with her seasickness. Ezra Rothstein who had been almost invisible the whole journey sat next to her looking concerned.

"I'm sorry, guys. There's no quick cure for waves until you get your sea legs. But this helps ease the pain."

Jean Paul placed a bottle of rum on the table. Rita naturally declined and was grateful that the others did as well. She didn't need the smell of alcohol in her nostrils right now threatening to push her over the edge. She found herself surprised how much she desired to drink.

"We'll be in the Abercrombie's waters sometime this evening. God willing we'll slip past them."

Jean Paul unfurled a nautical map. Rita eased herself up as Chris and the lieutenant stood over the Saints captain's shoulder.

"From what we saw, the Abercrombies have fortified the naval academy and are really on their game. They own Annapolis all the way across the Bay Bridge onto the Eastern shore. That's why we're taking a roundabout right over here." Jean Paul placed his finger on the eastern shore of the Chesapeake just east of the Highway 50 Bay Bridge. "See right here? Prospect Bay. There's a clear path through Kent Narrows."

Rita strained in the dim light to see what he was talking about. There was a contiguous water way on the eastern shore with a bay that led to what had to be a canal, which led to the north end of the bridge and peninsula.

"It looks awfully narrow. You sure it's deep enough?" she asked.

"During our visit with the Abercrombies, I had a crew scout the area on one of our fast boats. The Abercrombies end their domain at the tail end of the Bay Bridge and don't patrol much onto the Eastern Shore. The narrows are deep and wide enough for the *Lafitte* to cross; however, the little causeway bridge is too low for our sails. We'll have to break the masts down."

"You can do that?" she asked in surprise.

"The *Lafitte* was designed to navigate through the unknown. That's why we don't depend on our diesel engine. And that's why we made our masts collapsible. We figured we might need to pass under some draw bridges that were locked in the down position."

"Aye, your designers weren't just pounding their puds were they, mate?" the gunnery sergeant said emphatically. Rita noticed he seemed fine at sea. Of course, he was a Marine.

"I'll take that as a compliment. I was the designer," Jean Paul replied. "Once we're back on the Chesapeake, we'll bear northwest towards Baltimore. We'll drop you right at the 695 underpass, which is practically curbside service. I just wish I had a GPS device to give me current weather conditions."

"Shit, I wish I had my iPod," Chris added.

Helmut Spankmeister who had been silent during the meal spoke up timidly. "I…I have an iPhone."

Everyone turned around to face Helmut and gave a collective "whoa." Rita noticed that he used the present tense, which confirmed her suspicion that Helmut had unresolved issues with reality. Yet she, like everyone else, couldn't help but be impressed. The iPhone had been introduced just a few weeks before the Shift hit, a lifetime ago.

"What was it like," Jean Paul asked enthusiastically.

"It's…it *was*…wondrous. It could do anything. GPS, iTunes, podcasts, compass, weather updates, email, internet access. It has these things… Apps! Apps for anything you want."

Despite his moving between the present and past tense, everyone in the galley sat in silent amazement. Hearing obsolete tech terms being uttered sounded out of place in the galley that could have been mistaken for a 19th century clipper ship save for the light bulbs and radio. The faux wood paneling almost passed for wooden planking, although a pin up of a soaped up girl straddling the hood of a Ferrari took away from the ambience.

Jean Paul returned to business. "Once we drop you off, you'll be on your own."

"We've been on our own plenty, Captain," Lieutenant Baraka added with a defensive edge. "I just don't like getting dumped that close to Baltimore."

The young lieutenant didn't have to explain why that was a problem, for everyone knew. Cities were the domain of ferals, those who refused to farm and instead fed off remains of the past and the unfortunate passing traveler. Cities hid feral bands better than the forests. Besides, there was little incentive for a feral to ditch the city for a forest anyway.

"We could drop y'all off further away, but you would be that much farther away from your destination."

"No, Captain. We have no idea what's out there. All things being equal, I want the shortest distance to Laurel at the furthest distance from the Abercrombies," said Chris rubbing his two-pronged goatee.

"We can handle ferals. I just wish the Abercrombies hadn't moved so far down the Chesapeake. We could have landed south of Annapolis, otherwise."

"At least they don't cover anything north of the town."

The nausea was threatening to return, either from the constant swaying or the discussion itself. Rita knew that Gaia wouldn't send her on this mission if it weren't necessary, but right now she felt more unprepared than she did since the opening days of the Shift.

"Cath, she stands with a well intentioned man
But she can't ...relax ...with his hand on the small of her back..."

Rita turned up the stereo playing Death Cab for Cutie as she cruised down the highway. She sang along as the car crested the hill and started its descent. There were few vehicles on the highway, so she decided to see what her new Audi A4 could do, and she hoped the cops weren't out this morning lying in wait. As the song reached the crescendo, it paused as her phone rang. She looked at the LCD screen and answered it.

"Morning, Jamil."

"Rita?"

"Yes, Jamil. Is there something the matter?"

"I had a bad dream. She came back."

Rita exhaled deeply holding back her frustration. She knew she had to be patient with Jamil. "It's okay, mi Coriño. It was just a dream."

"But it is not. She is real. I know it."

"Why do you say, she's real?"

"Because she knows things."

"Just calm down, Jamil. I'll be there in ten minutes. I'm just stopping to pick up a Methspresso." It was only at that moment that Rita realized how addictive Starbuck's newest and most controversially named coffee was.

"No, you cannot!"

"And why is that?"

"Because you have to wake up."

Rita nearly lost control of the car, but jerked the wheel just in time. "What? What are you talking about?"

"Wake up!"

The bark of men jolted Rita awake. She struggled to sit up but was caught in some sort of net. For a moment, she didn't know where she was, how she got here, and what was going on. Then she recalled that she was on the *Jean Lafitte*. The net was the hammock she slept in. Apparently, something not according to plan was happening.

A flashlight beamed in her face. "Chief!" It was Ezra. "Chief, we gotta motor. Get your gear, ma'am."

Rita struggled to her feet. The ship was rocking violently; it wasn't waves that were tossing the boat about.

"I trust everything is nice and fucked up?" she asked now on the floor prying on her boots. She was grateful that she followed the Vicious Rabbits' lead and kept her rifle and web gear ready to go and stowed on one of the hooks above her, because she couldn't see with her one bleary eye. Akil helped her with the backpack.

"Yeah, something like that. Though, I don't know much more other than we've been spotted."

"Okay, Ezra, get your gear, get above deck and find out where we are."

After suiting up, Rita placed her wind-up wristwatch in front of a light bulb. It was four thirty in the morning. It wouldn't be dawn for several hours still.

"Sugar!" Akil cried out.

"Yes?"

"I love you."

"And I love you."

Rita stepped up the ladder to the main deck where she saw all of the Vicious Rabbits suited up and ready. Just then, she heard a volley and felt the frigid spray of icy water.

Chris was speaking with Captain Nguyen and in the moonlight she could see him motion for her to come over.

"Well, the good news is that we're at the 695 overpass and made it ahead of schedule!" He didn't have to mention the bad news.

"I thought the Abercrombies didn't patrol this far north!" she yelled above the clattering of incoming and outgoing artillery. The onboard cannon rocked the boat as it fired.

"They must have spotted us back on the East Bay." Jean Paul turned to Chris. "Captain, it's your call."

"The rafts got motors, right?"

Captain Nguyen nodded.

"We're too close to turn back now. We'll take the rafts. Captain, you head back to Fredericksburg, and tell my people what happened. They're reimburse you for the rafts."

"I don't give a rat's ass about the rafts! We're sticking around to give you cover until you reach land!"

One of the .30 calibers opened up. Chris pulled out a letter from one of the pockets in his web gear and handed it to Captain Nguyen. "When you make it back to New Orleans, my family lived in Lakeview! Jung with a 'J'!"

Chris shook the captain's hand and grabbed his bike. "Rita, Akil! You ready?"

Both nodded. "Good, you're in my raft!"

Chapter 13

Chesapeake Bay, Maryland
Near Baltimore
January 2013

BACKGROUND MUSIC: "Gimme Shelter" by The Rolling Stones
Visit www.michaeljuge.com **on the *A Hard Rain* page to listen**

The inflatable rafts raced across the Chesapeake with the only the light of the moon to guide them. Chris was never particularly afraid of being on the sea, but he felt really vulnerable being weighed down by all of his gear. The life preserver was just a token gesture to give the illusion that you could survive if you fell off the boat. Another explosion landed nearby and capsized the raft next to him. Chris grimaced as some of his Vicious Rabbits plunged into the frigid waters of the Chesapeake.

"Oh, shit!" Kendra cried out involuntarily.

Chris couldn't see exactly where the firing was coming from. He just knew they had to cross the distance and reach the shore as fast as they could.

"I can see the boat launch, Captain!" Kendra called out. The original plan was for the *Lafitte* to coast up just a hundred meters from the boat launch at Fort Armistead Park, which lay about a quarter mile south of the 695 overpass, and disembark in an orderly manner with the shore only a few yards away. But when the Abercrombies spotted the *Lafitte* and started hammering them with 100 pounders, Chris had to grab his company and get them into the inflatable rafts while they were still in the middle of the Chesapeake. The engines screamed at full throttle sounding like a Cuisinart on crack. There was little point in worrying about making a ruckus now.

Another explosion sent another raft into the air and it, too, capsized. "Christ! That was the gunny's boat!"

Chris felt his testicles taking residence up in his stomach. Over the past few years, Chris had managed to become a competent leader of the First Bicycle Mounted Cavalry Company. He had come to accept the weight of leadership begrudgingly. But he always felt reassured knowing that Gunnery Sergeant Jay Birmingham had his back. The gunny acted as a safety net for the officer learning how to command. When the he was given a field commission of lieutenant to command the bike mounted cavalry during the Obsidian War, Chris had enough wisdom to defer to the gunny on almost everything including where to set up latrines until he felt confident enough to make decisions on his own. Chris still consulted with the gunny to get his take. Now with him gone, Chris felt as though he were in just a little bit more danger than he had been. Not that the mortars plunging into the water and machine gun strafing all around made him feel particularly safe.

"How far, Lieutenant," he asked as he revved the motor that started to sputter. He couldn't see between the heads in front of him and the water droplets crystallizing on his goggles.

"A few more seconds!"

Chris looked around and could see only two other rafts were still in the game. Chris swallowed the taste of bile realizing the rest of his company had been neutralized, an antiseptic term to mean that most of his company was either dead or dying. *Goddammit! What did I do?* Out in the distance motor boats, Abercrombie motor boats, raced towards them.

"Prepare for landing, Captain!"

Everyone on the boat prepared for a rough transition. Chris' bike was tucked beside him and he clung to it for dear life even though it wasn't secured to anything. There was a scratching sound on the bottom of the raft as it jetted over sunken boats near the launch. Chris gave one final twist with the throttle as the rotor blades made contact with something in the water and protested angrily and then ground to a halt.

They made it to land. Everyone on the raft immediately flopped out onto the field and grabbed their bikes.

"Form a perimeter," Chris barked. Lieutenant Baraka immediately pressed forward a few meters while Chris focused on the incoming crafts. Two of his cavalry's rafts were coming in fast, right on top of his raft being pursued by enemy boats. Chris took his M4, released the safety and took aim on the enemy crafts approaching closely behind. He didn't bother with automatic fire. In the predawn moonlit hours, he aimed for the boat's window reflecting moonlight back and shot. Rita knelt down beside him and with her M40 sniper rifle, cycled the bolt, took aim, and took out the driver in one shot within a second.

"You lay down cover for our friends," she called out.

Chris shrugged, mildly impressed seeing the reverend in action under fire. He heard stories how Rita was a prodigy behind the scope of a rifle, truly amazing considering that she was an anti-gun Unitarian minister who had spent most of time protesting war and animal cruelty. It seemed that irony could be…well, ironic. As she had the sharpshooting covered, he laid down strafing fire instead, hoping to get one of the engines that would result in some fantastic Hollywood explosion, but it never seemed to work out that way.

One of the rafts skidded onto land and people tumbled out.

"Over here!" he cried out.

"Roit! Get yer arses up and over!"

Chris spirits lifted hearing Gunnery Sergeant Birmingham's garbled Scottish/Australian bastardized version of English. He thought the gunny's raft had capsized. He was wrong. The tall buzzed-cut form grabbed his bike and raced up the mound to meet the others.

"'Ow are we doing, Captain?" he called out as he threw his bike over the last stretch of the uphill climb.

"Same as always!"

"That bad, aye? It's a dog's breakfast, wot?"

The decimated company, a few squads now, regrouped on the mound of the boat launch. It was a catastrophe, an utter rout of his people.

"Ezra! Ezra! God, where in the hell is he?" Rita called out blindly. "Wasn't he on our boat?"

Chris gave a helpless expression as he couldn't remember. The archer Ilsa hesitantly answered. "I…I didn't see him on the way over."

"Shit," she muttered.

"Ilsa, give me a status report! Bikes, supplies, ammo." Chris saw the *Lafitte* was still in position providing as much cover fire as they could. Their guns were now focused on the land, meaning there were enemies on the ground nearby. The horizon in the east was now a shade of dark blue with an orange trim telling that dawn was approaching. It would be foolish to ride off in complete darkness. The original plan was to push off on the I-695 after dawn had arrived, but they needed to get out of there now. His emotions desperately wanted to go back out into the water and to save as many of his company as possible. Those still alive in the water floating were certainly suffering from hypothermia. The shore was caked with ice. If he could just get to them beforehand…maybe he should abort the whole mission.

No, the damage is done. And if the Abercrombies get their hands on the nuclear material, all of this will have been in vain. Chris didn't know if it was the wrong decision. The best decision probably would have been to not disembark from the *Lafitte* in the first place, seeing as the ship had been spotted while the *Lafitte* was still a mile offshore. But that was hindsight.

"All but one have their packs on," Ilsa reported. "We have one carrier, missing one bike, no radio, but we've got Spankmeister!"

In the cluster flop, Chris had completely forgotten about Helmut, the man who would lead them to where the nuclear material was before the Abercrombies could find them. Without him, the mission would have certainly been a loss. He was glad the young archer had taken that into account when she was evaluating their status. Chris saw the lanky man, bundled in a thick white poncho huddled by his bike. Chris recognized him more for the fact that he had no pack. He didn't want the scientist lugging anything more than himself on the bike. He was no soldier and certainly he wasn't fit enough to keep up with his cavalry. He would have to remember to keep that in mind as they made a break for it. *Oh, and be sure you don't lose Spankmeister in the rear.*

"All right, everyone mount up and head to the road! Porkins, you're on point."

"Copy that, Captain," a husky Vicious Rabbit belted out.

Chris picked up his mountain bike, walked over to the huddled figure of Helmut Spankmeister and ran a cursory inspection of his bike for him. He then held out a hand to the scientist who looked ridiculous, wearing the Kevlar helmet the way news reporters wearing protective equipment as they reported via satellite linkups in war torn regions did.

"Come on, Mr. Spankmeister," he coaxed gently. "We can't stay here. We've got to go."

"I think I pissed on myself."

Chris chuckled until he saw the mortified look on Helmut's face in the dim predawn light. Then he explained. "Sorry, there's no shame in it. I did the same thing the first time I was in the shit. Hell, I think two drops came out just now."

He knelt down beside him. "You're doing fine, Mr. Spankmeister, but we need you to keep moving, okay? You can hack, right?"

Helmut nodded, stood up and mounted his bike. Chris had never been a hard ass. He tried once, and he wound up apologizing to a young Vicious Rabbit. He believed in positive reinforcement, especially with someone like Helmut Spankmeister who looked as frazzled as Chris felt just before the Shift. He realized his gentle style resembled his dad's.

He and Helmut cycled up to the rest of the team, no more than a dozen or so of them left, and onto the cracked pavement of the road that would lead up to the I-695. Chris' feet felt frozen having dunked them in the water. Unfortunately, his hiking boots weren't waterproof. Taking one last look at the Chesapeake, he saw the *Lafitte* starting to power southward with a continuous fart of diesel. His shaky vision was beginning to return along with it his tinnitus. *Of course it is,* he thought mordantly. *It wouldn't be fitting of me if I wasn't a wreck at this point.* He took a deep breath and felt the frozen air rush through the gaps where he lost a few teeth a few years back. The shaky vision wouldn't hinder him. It was just an annoyance, a stupid migraine, he reminded himself. He had much bigger problems on his plate.

Refrozen snow crusted the path along the C&O Canal trail making it too dangerous to cycle. Instead, Chris had taken up jogging during the winter months for lunch. As he made his way up from the K Street underpass, he heard Georgetown University's bell tolling. It was noon. "Oh, shit." Chris looked at his stop watch. He had been jogging over forty minutes. He lost track of time. "Damn it!"

Chris never thought in a million years that he would actually wind up missing his old boss Darryl. The pit bull-looking boss could be a pain sometimes. He was such a stickler. But at least he was dedicated and led by example. Plus, he rewarded good work. Chris had come to learn the hard way that his new boss was sort of an ass clown and made his old boss seem like a dream. Whereas Darryl had given him a wide berth and rated him on his accomplishments and work output, Ed Farcus was a clockwatching, micro-manager. Even worse, Ed made these claims that Chris was never at his cube when he knew he was. Chris didn't know what his problem was, but Ed seemed to have it in for him. Chris had to clock out whenever he exercised. It would be enough for most people to say, screw it, and not exercise.

But Chris didn't have much of a choice. He needed to get out of his cubicle and to get his blood flowing. Exercise gave his mind something else to think about. Furthermore, it pumped endorphins, which he needed. He had just gotten off of the meds recently, having gotten tired of not being able to lose weight. Exercise helped to regulate his mood a little. Now that he was off the meds and started jogging, the weight was coming off, but the anxiety was returning. He also noticed this strange shaky vision. Chris didn't know whether it was due to being off the meds, his new boss causing him grief, or a combination of the two. All he knew was that he was running late, literally, and Ed was going to ream him out for taking so much time to exercise when he should be at his cube working. That's what intelligence analysts do. They sit in a cube and work.

Chris raced across Key Bridge, which spanned over the partially frozen Potomac from Georgetown to Arlington, all the while trying not to slip on the refrozen snow on the ground. Cars whizzed past sending up fumes and flakes of grey ice in his face. Chris wheezed as he picked up his pace. It didn't matter. Ed was still going to be pissed…that was, if Ed chose to show up to work at all. That was the enraging thing. The scrawny redhead liked to tell people what to do, but was conveniently out on these late lunches himself. His vision bounced as his feet pounded the sidewalk. The high rise buildings across the river seemed impossibly far away. The iPod Genius app selected a song by The Rolling Stones.

"Okay, mate, what the bloody 'ell?" Gunnery Sergeant Birmingham cursed.

The ride from Fort Armistead Park had been a frantic dash from the pursuing Abercrombies, but at least it had been pretty clear going up till now. The I-695 Baltimore Beltway where they started had been desolate, which was a good thing considering that they were virtually blind before dawn. As they continued westward, they came across more dead traffic. Cars, SUVs, and 18-wheelers heading in both directions appeared sporadically at first but quickly congested both directions of the Beltway. There was hardly any effort, if any, to clear the vehicles off the highway, which suited the company just fine, so long as the breakdown lanes were clear. In Northern Virginia, whenever Chris' cavalry was forced to use a major highway, something he never felt comfortable with, they relied almost entirely on the breakdown lanes remaining clear as the highways themselves were completely congested. Usually they were. But standing before the dozen Vicious Rabbits and archers was a wall, literally, a wall of cars stacked three cars high that extended clear across from one end of the highway to the other. Unfortunately, they were situated where the 695 rose several feet above ground.

"What the frak?" Chris gasped.

"Christ, how could anyone stack cars without a forklift?" Lieutenant Baraka asked to no one in particular.

It was a good question. Chris had seen a good many ad hoc vehicular barricades over the past few years. Ferals marked and protected their territory with vehicle barricades all the time, but they usually were easy enough to weave around and they never looked like this. The wall in front of them was formidable, and Chris agreed no human hands could stack these cars like this. They had spotted a couple of ferals since setting off this morning. It wasn't surprising. This was the suburbs of Baltimore, the southern half of the city, which meant it also included bedroom communities from the northern edge of the Washington DC metro area. In fact, Chris remembered that there was no true line of demarcation between where the DC suburbs ended and where the Baltimore suburbs began, which kind of freaked him out even before the Shift. Originally from the South, Chris was used to there being at least fifty miles of sticks between one city and the next. But those buffers did not exist from DC northward, which made the Shift all the more deadly in the Northeast. Chris looked around from the vantage point of the crest of the overpass.

"We can push the top two down, sir," said Birmingham, indicating that he could topple the wall easily enough. They didn't look to be welded together.

Chris shook his head. "Nah, I don't want to piss off the locals. We can double back. I think there was an exit just a mile back."

"Aye, very good."

Huddled by the side of a car was Helmut. The skinny scientist had held his own on the ride. They didn't have to slow down for him, which was surprising.

"You okay, Mr. Spankmeister?"

"Uh huh."

"It's gonna be alright. We'll get to your hideout soon enough. I figure we're close to the 295. We'll get the map, suit up in the radiation suits." Chris stopped himself. "You do have radiation suits, right?" Helmut nodded.

"Good. We'll suit up, take the nukes out and the Abercrombies will be fresh out of ideas. And you'll be home."

"Good."

Chris wondered what kind of conditions allowed the rodent-like man to live. It amazed Chris how some of the unlikeliest people survived the Shift, himself included. Perhaps the man hid out in some warehouse, kept a garden and engaged in rat husbandry. Chris had seen all sorts of ways people came up with in order to survive.

Steam fogged in his goggles as he squatted in front of Helmut. He noticed how the man turned his attention to the reverend as she walked by. Chris thought to himself. *Well, he still is a man, after all.* Akil glared back and Helmut hurriedly turned away.

"Captain, we've got to get going." Ilsa's statement had the edge of urgency to it. She was looking through a pair of binoculars as she said it. Chris heard an explosion in the distance. Ilsa pointed back east.

"They're following pretty close. No more than four miles behind."

One of his people laid the tripwire shortly before coming across this barricade. It was possible that some animal or someone else other than the Abercrombies could have tripped it. He didn't want to take that chance.

"Alright, Gunny, let's see if we can crawl over this."

Over the years, the cavalry had perfected their operational best practices. That included modifying their CamelBak backpacks so that could attach their bikes onto their backs and climb. There weren't too many cliffs to worry about in the necropolis, but there were enough obstacles that warranted learning how to place a bike on one's back and humping it on foot. Horses could never hack it out here.

After delicately hoisting Helmut up and easing him down and getting a child carrier over, they continued onward toward the 295 with a little more urgency. It was almost above freezing, but the overcast sky hung a grey shroud over everything. The world was painted in shades of grey.

"Shit." Chris suddenly realized he left his helmet climbing over the barricade and forgot to retrieve it. There was no going back for it now. Chris wanted to get the hell off of the Beltway. If they were being pursued, then the Beltway was a sure way to find them. Once they got off into a neighborhood, they could always blend into the scenery. Although Maryland was completely unfamiliar to him, suburbs were suburbs, places to hide from pursuing marauders and religious fanatics. They pushed onward.

After another hour, Chris called for a break. Rita sidled up next to him while he put on a pair of dry socks.

"I'm sorry it all went to hell out there."

"Me too," he said lacing up his boots.

"It wasn't your fault. I would have made the same decision in your place."

Chris looked over to her and caught the empathetic look of a leader who knew what he was going through. "I sent a lot of good men and women to their deaths today." Chris' feet were still numb from the dip in the Chesapeake this morning even with the dry socks. The waters felt like knives. He figured no one would be able to survive in those waters for long. And he just left them. The shaky vision was getting a little worse again.

"Can I ask you something?"

"You may ask."

"You notice that Mr. Spankmeister has been staring at me?"

"Of course. He's a straight man with a pulse. It's only natural that he would fancy you."

"I don't think that's it. I know the difference between leering and gawking."

"Yeah, I did notice. Why?"

Rita sighed. "I don't know. It's creepy."

"You want me to kick his ass for you?"

She punched him in the arm. "I can handle myself, thank you."

"Helmut is no doubt *not* functioning on all four cylinders. I think he stares at a lot of things. I mean, you noticed how he spoke about the iPhone in the present tense."

"Yes," she whispered emphatically.

"Look, I know this is highly unusual circumstances, but my wife, she wouldn't be sending us, she certainly wouldn't be sending *me* out here if she wasn't convinced this guy was for real." That countered what he said before, but he needed to convince himself now.

Rita nodded. "And Gaia wouldn't have given me the message about Laurel if it wasn't vital to save all of us."

Chris hated it when Rita got all religious on him. She always seemed so reasonable and down to earth and then *snap*! She was Gaia's priestess again. Chris checked the tires of *The Interceptor* and mounted his bike.

"I think we'd better get going again."

As they continued, they passed a faded 7-Eleven billboard advertising the 100 oz. Ubergulper held by a bikini-clad woman who had often appeared in his dreams in the early days after the Shift. "You know you want it," the sign advertised with its double entendre.

Chris skillfully swerved around random junk lying on the road. *The Interceptor* had been beaten up and repaired more than all of the previous bikes he had in his life combined. But *The Interceptor* was tough. He had come to depend on it to always bring him home. With the M4 secured along the top tube of the frame, and with the array of packs containing repair kits, an air pump, duct tape and tubes, all of which were now exorbitantly expensive, and emergency rations, *The Interceptor* was his suburban assault vehicle, a Ferrari and Winnebago rolled into one.

Once they reached the exit for Highway 295, they stopped again to check for pursuit and to recharge with some hard tack and Power Bar mockups. He normally wouldn't be taking so many breaks, especially fearing that they were being pursued, but Helmut looked winded. Chris took out the AAA road atlas and laid it on top of the hood of a Subaru. While Lieutenant Baraka set up another trip wire and the archer Ilsa spied with the binoculars, he and the gunnery sergeant studied the map.

"Mr. Spankmeister, could you give us more precise directions?"

Helmut walked up and pointed to the street. "It's right here."

"It looks like an office park. You live in an office park?"

Helmut nodded. "It's where the printouts and radiation suits are."

"But this is where you live? How did you survive this whole time?"

Helmut hesitated. Chris was ready to press him when he heard gunfire in the distance.

"Trouble," Ilsa reported.

"So I hear." Chris and the cavalry grabbed their bikes and Chris stuffed the atlas under his poncho.

"I think someone else is shooting at them," Lieutenant Baraka said. "It sounds more like a firefight than them firing at us."

Just then there was an explosion nearby. "Doesn't mean they aren't completely occupied, though," she added.

The cavalry jumped on their bikes and started racing southward on Highway 295. Another series of explosions came nearer as they passed a Food Lion. Out of the corner of his eyes, Chris could see ferals fleeing from the parking lot. They didn't appear to be hostiles. At least, he hoped they weren't, though he feared they all just treaded onto their turf.

"LT, you set up the tripwire?"

"Affirm, Captain!"

Chris could faintly hear the rumbling of an engine. He prayed it wasn't the Abercrombies. Chris noticed that cars on the highway had been pushed off to the side of the road. There was an active tribe here. That was both good and bad. Another explosion went off several meters to his left. Could the Abercrombies be landing mortars? How would they know where to set up? It didn't make sense. As Chris tried figure it out all the while booking it down the highway, a vehicle pulled out in front of him. He was about to reach for his M4, but the driver wasn't interested in his people. It jumped the ditch and raced passed them. Chris had a moment to register that it was a purple El Camino with a .50 caliber, a Ma Deuce, secured in the truck bed, what the legacy Marines called a "technical." The purple El Camino technical tore down the highway coughing up black smoke with the gunner shooting the .50 caliber recklessly. He didn't get a good look, but he swore that the window painting on the back of the El Camino presented a busty Betty Boop wearing an American flag bikini straddling a motorcycle with the statement "Can't touch this" written in gothic letters over the overtly sexually charged kitsch artwork. The Anthropology grad student in him appreciated the odd beauty of the art in how it synthesized a witless form of patriotism and a defunct pop cultural theme with crass adolescent desires for sexual domination and a cool ride.

"Christ, I think we landed in the middle of a turf war!" Rita shouted.

Chris turned back to be sure Helmut was still with them and then turned his attention back on the road. Snow glazed the highway. Despite the frantic insanity of it all, Chris found himself whispering to a song by The Stones.

"War, children. It's just a shot away. It's just a shot away."

It was a weird selection, something he recalled from a dream, he believed, but it also seemed appropriate. There was another explosion, Chris swerved, narrowly missing a stranded car. His vision was getting really shaky and then he saw a deer standing in the middle of the road looking stunned by the team of humans on bikes rapidly approaching. Instinctively, Chris tried to veer, but his front wheel turned too far. His front tire slid on the ice, and he went flying. Chris tried to react, but it was too late. The next thing he saw was the pavement.

Chris sat languidly in his car behind a line of other cars at the stoplight listening to NPR discuss the disastrous day on the stock market. The Dow took another nosedive. Of course, it did. Did they think Mr. Optimism was going to make anything different? *After the inauguration, there was all of this talk of returning to fiscal responsibility.* Yeah right.

The economy had been so emaciated over the past several years, the country as a whole didn't even know what prosperity was any more. Well, at least I still have a job. *That consideration brought a bitter reminder of his day. Ed Farcus did, in fact, rip him a new one. He didn't even bother with shutting the door. Ed unleashed his bitchkrieg with the rest of the unit within earshot.*

"You think you're special, don't you Chris? While everyone else works, Chris just goes off and exercises."

"Ed, to be fair, the other people take off, too."

"I don't want to hear your excuses. You have an attitude problem. You have a problem with authority."

"Well factually…"

Suddenly, Chris' reliving of the day's events was interrupted by a loud voice.

"Out, mothafucka!"

He didn't even notice the man had opened the door. He didn't see the man's face. All he saw was the barrel of a pistol in his face. The man grabbed his collar.

"I'll blow you're fucking head off!"

"D...don't shoot. I'm getting…" Chris stumbled to unlock the seatbelt. He stared into the barrel expecting any moment there to be a blinding flash. The only thing of value in the car was his messenger bag. As the man pulled him out of the seat, Chris tried to grab it.

"Wait, my bag!"

"Fuck your bag, cocksucka!" Chris saw the man raise the pistol and heard the smack across the side of his head. Chris fell to the pavement and saw his car screeching off past the never-ending red light as he felt the impact of his head meeting the road.

Chapter 14

Montpelier Station, Virginia
Rochelle Sovereignty
January 2013

Meredith Jung sat at the conference table. Her face bore no expression, out of fear that if she did allow the slightest hint of emotion, she would lose her composure and bawl.

"It was a wonder that we survived at all. We certainly wouldn't have if it hadn't been for Captain Nguyen here." Ezra Rothstein sat at the other end of the long conference table along with Saints Captain Nguyen. Ezra's voice was raspy having been immersed in the frigid waters of the Chesapeake for several minutes. He, like the other survivors Jean Paul managed to pick up from the bay, had suffered from hypothermia.

Also present were Commandant Dean Jacob, Deputy Constable Thuy Mai, Constable Jon Early—sort of present, anyway—his wife Sharon and Monticello's contingent to include the Deputy Chief Magistrate Juan Ramirez and Sheriff Schadenfreude. The generators had been hit by a rare but particularly strong surge, overheating the coils, so the dining room, which became a conference room, was lit only by kerosene lamps and the waning daylight. The EMP surges were less frequent as far as they could tell—they could only detect the strongest surges that affected their bulky equipment—but they still occurred, ever reminding them how vulnerable they were to the forces of nature and that they could never truly trust even their own more primitive technology again. Trust in technology nearly led to humanity's demise once. Rochelle would never be so dependent on electricity.

Ezra continued with a gravelly voice. "My boat was closer to the shore when we capsized. I know a few of our boats made it to land safely."

"And we provided as much cover as we could while we scooped up your people" Jean Paul added.

"I'm almost certain your husband, Mr. Spankmeister and the reverend were among the people who made it ashore, Mrs. Jung," Ezra added reassuringly.

Meredith nodded furtively and attempted a smile. "Thank you, Ezra."

"We would have all been dead if it wasn't for Captain Nguyen here. He could have popped smoke and cleared on out. It would have been the smart thing to do."

Jean Paul held up a hand dismissively. "Listen, I've picked up sailors whose ship I had just sunk in battle. And I do that because I know it's a shitty way to die. So, of course I wasn't going to let your people bob up and down and wait for death."

"Well, regardless Captain, you have our warmest thanks," Jon said. The constable didn't speak much these days. Sitting there with his wife at his side, Meredith casually noticed his hand holding a coffee cup was shaking slightly. A beard had grown across his jaw, too, something she thought she would never see from Mr. Clean Marine himself.

"For what it's worth, New Orleans has a new friend in the Orange Pact," Juan added.

"I just wish we knew how many others made it," Jean Paul lamented.

After Captain Nguyen left, Meredith addressed Ezra. "I'm going need you to get in touch with your asset. He's sent signals our way but refused to talk to any of us."

"Something happened?"

Thuy leaned over the table. "Lynchburg is preparing to mobilize. Our sources in Roanoke confirm troop buildups."

"Also, we've seen a marked increase of ammunition sales to Lynchburg from West Virginia. They've been stockpiling for some time."

"Of course, so have we," Thuy added dryly. "We've run up our credit card with West Virginia this past year like there's no tomorrow as well."

"They've also stocked up on fuel," Jon Early added. "Anyone with any sense can see this is a prelude to invasion."

"Your asset may have some valuable insight to share on what Boche is planning," said Meredith, "though I think we already know what it is."

"I'll send out my signalers."

"In the meantime, we've got to mobilize ourselves. Juan, your people are in the direct line of fire. Whether they come up Highway 29 or I-81, you're the first of the Orange Pact communities they'll encounter."

Sheriff Schadenfreude scoffed. "We're also their top selling boogeyman. You'd think we had horns and hooves the way they've painted us Unitarians."

Meredith acknowledged that point though she didn't know why Lucille insisted on being here. Gordon Boche was a gifted speaker with a charisma that inspired the weary survivors of the Shift. She had read through transcripts of his speeches, and she had to admit that he had a way with words and with using the Shift to his advantage. The Unitarians were Satanists and the Vicious Rabbits were opportunistic drug dealers, the refuse that came from the dead cities. If you lived in the Dominion of Lynchburg, and your only source of information was filtered through the regent, and if you owed your survival to the regent's quick response during the collapse, it was no wonder why the regent had such a loyal following. And for anyone who thought to question the regent's great wisdom, there were the regent's Sheepdogs.

"Our operatives in Charleston aren't certain what the regent said to the West Virginian President, but we know they came up with some kind of arrangement that will appease the West Virginians. Otherwise, they would be upset by losing a customer such as ourselves."

Meredith was referring to the fact that the Orange Pact was West Virginia's most reliable customer for coal, fuel and rudimentary medications.

"It's almost as though the regent learned about the Chief's disappearance and decided to move now," Ezra added.

"I'm looking into that." Meredith didn't want to go into details.

"The regent has eyes everywhere. There are a lot of Christians inside the Orange Pact that are sympathetic to the regent," Sheriff Schadenfreude added matter-of-factly. "We need to keep that in mind."

Jon Early who had been aloof cleared his throat. "Listen, friend, I am a Christian. So is your Deputy Chief Magistrate Ramirez over there, and Dean. A lot of us are Christians, and we see the regent for what he truly is, a charlatan televangelist who knows nothing of Christ's love."

Lucille seemed to sparkle with her shrill yet somehow bubbly demeanor. "No offense, Constable, but you cannot deny the fact that the spies we have identified are Christian. I certainly don't mean to say all Christians are traitors. Most are good people. But the bad ones are out there, too. You see the difference between what I actually said and what you presumed I said."

Jon's blotchy face turned a shade of red as he quickly lost his composure, which was unlike him. He had always been professional. Sharon glanced briefly to Meredith who gestured to her.

"Come on, Honey," Sharon coaxed. "We should get you back home. You'll never recover if you keep getting out of bed like this."

Lucille, oblivious to the anguish she caused the constable said, "Sorry, I didn't know you were unwell."

"It's nothing I can't handle." Sharon squeezed his hand imploringly, and he relented after a few seconds and stood up. "Thuy, you'll apprise me of anything pertinent."

"Of course, Constable."

Sharon draped her arm around Jon's shoulder and the left the regal conference room to head back upstairs. Meredith saw the look of concern on Juan's face. She didn't want to open the topic about Jon's state with the Monticellans, not right now.

"Lucille, I agree with you that there are serious leaks within. I don't see it coming out of the Swan, but you don't need to have spies in the inner circle to gather what intel the Lambs of God have. The reverend's absence is well known, unfortunately."

"But how would they know about the disaster in Maryland?"

"We don't know that they do know." Ezra added.

"Well, it is awfully convenient that they're planning to invade right when we lost track of the reverend."

"I'll find out, Sheriff," Ezra reassured.

"In the meantime, we've got an army amassing on us." Dean Jacob's low voice resonated throughout the hall. "The Vicious Rabbits are offering whatever support you'll need at your southern and western borders. Mama Bell will mobilize her forces in Culpeper and the Fredericksburg Union President is scrapping up what he can."

"I hope it will be enough," Meredith said, losing her fortitude as the words left her mouth.

BACKGROUND MUSIC: "Wish You Were Here" by Pink Floyd
Visit www.michaeljuge.com **on the *A Hard Rain* page to listen**

Meredith held it in as long as she could. From the carriage ride home from work, to picking up Aidan and Rhiannon from school, Meredith forced herself to remain calm. While inside the kitchen of her farmhouse estate, Meredith helped Mrs. Palfrey with the cooking by cutting vegetables. As much of an introvert she was, she didn't want to be alone with her emotions. The kerosene lamps allowed for some light despite the power outage. Meredith volunteered to bathe the kids allowing Mrs. Palfrey to retire for the evening to her own house located in the back of the estate. Fortunately, the water heater wasn't dependent on electricity. Few things were.

Aidan played with his action figures attacking Rhiannon's princess collection. The kids squealed. Baby Charles was in good humor as well. Then it was time for bed. Usually Chris read to Aidan while she read to Rhiannon. Aidan wanted stories about dinosaurs or astronauts while Rhiannon wanted to read Thomas the Tank Engine. Both agreed to settle for a book about a dinosaur who rode through time on a train. Baby Charles fell asleep while she read to his elder siblings. Soon enough they, too, were fast asleep.

Still dressed in her work clothes, Meredith crept downstairs into the living room holding a kerosene lamp for light. She walked over to the raging fireplace for warmth and picked up a photograph of her and Chris taken back in grad school. It was one of the few precious photographs that made it out with them from the exodus from DC five and a half years ago. Chris always said he would come back for the rest of the photos when it warranted them making the journey that deep into the necropolis. It was one of the many things she had thought to take with them. While Chris was consumed with loading up on guns and ammo, she, six months pregnant at the time, considered other less drastic yet no less important necessities. She grabbed the Amish cookbook they bought on their first anniversary when they went to Schmicksburg, Pennsylvania. She also stuffed as much aspirin, Desitin, and Tylenol as she could haul.

She brushed off the light film of dust off the glass frame and gazed into the happy eyes of two young people freshly in love. Meredith remembered posing for that photograph. She had spent the summer in New York City doing an internship. She and Chris had only started dating and were ravenous in their passion, partly because of the distance apart. She looked at the clothes they were wearing. He wore a silk bowling shirt over a wife beater and she wore a black tube top with a red dragon. Meredith blushed seeing how ridiculous the two looked. *I cannot believe I ever wore that* she thought to herself mortified. But who cared? It was 1999. Moby was king, swing was in, the dot com bubble was never going to burst and they were young and hopeful. Anything was possible. She remembered how she looked forward to getting her Masters and hoped to get hired by anyone who had a decent health plan while Chris seemed to just find his way into his job with Diplomatic Security, applying online during one of the commercial breaks between episodes of *King of the Hill* and *The X-Files*.

From the slightly faded photograph, Meredith's deep brown eyes seemed to look right back at her and so did her husband, both who now struck her as woefully innocent. In that photograph, they had never known hunger, disease, or death. Chris was such a gentle soul who never raised his voice before. He hadn't known what it felt like to kill. And she was so skittish, afraid to confront people and to make decisions. That's why she liked being an analyst. She presented information to the decision makers without having to make one herself.

Unfortunately for her, for everyone in Rochelle, Constable Jon Early was an empty suit now, a figurehead who was too incapacitated to run the little country the Rochelle Sovereignty had become. The crucial decisions came down to Thuy, Dean and yes, to her, the very thing she hoped to avoid, being responsible for making decisions on things that extended way beyond the normal life decisions like when to buy a home. It was enough being the director of the Swan, but at least in the early days she had faith that Charles Early and later his son Jon would make the decisions based on her intelligence gathering and lead from there. Now, without Jon at the helm, it fell to the three of them and she feared that they just weren't up to it. Maybe nobody was, not against an army five times the size of the combined allied force. Meredith didn't know if it really was a prelude to an invasion—there wasn't an actual mobilization of Lambs of God yet, but she knew deep down what the signs were. And the signs were that their days were numbered.

In the firelight she caressed the photograph of the two of them. She could no longer avoid the truth. Her husband was gone, missing. Despite Ezra's reassurance that his boat had made it ashore, that did not ease her one bit. The Abercrombies were crawling all over the area hunting the Vicious Rabbits down. What were the chances that he was still alive? And if so, did the Abercrombies capture him? And what would they do to him if they caught him?

"Chris, where are you?"

And then in the silence, the truths she had hidden away from everyone began to surface. If the Lambs of God weren't enough, if having learned that her husband was lost out in hostile territory wasn't enough, there was more, something far more ominous that reared itself front and center, something potentially catastrophic just beyond the horizon.

She had placed the intelligence reports she received from Asheville, North Carolina and from Ross in the back recesses of her mind as best she could, just as she stuffed the documents themselves in the back corner of her office. But it was out there and remained what it was, something nobody could control or stop.

"Oh, God." She collapsed into the La-Z-boy, a torrent of grief rippling from her stomach as she began to bawl uncontrollably. She held it in as long as she could, but she could not contain it any longer. Her shoulders heaved as she let go of control.

Meredith woke up the next morning on the La-Z-Boy clutching the photograph and enshrouded in a quilt. The instant she awoke, the grim reality intruded on the moment where she had been blissfully unaware of time and history. Her eyes were sore from crying.

Baby Charles wailed from his room upstairs. *Get up, Meredith. Get up.* After several seconds she willed herself out of the La-Z-Boy to face the cold living room, which had plummeted several degrees during the evening once the fire burned out. Meredith draped the quilt over herself as Mrs. Palfrey had designed it to act like a comfy blanket with sleeves. Meredith had thought it a ridiculous, though thoughtful present. Later she had to admit it was rather comfortable to lounge around in during the winter. Mrs. Palfrey called her invention a "Snuggly."

After Mrs. Palfrey arrived from the guest house next door, Meredith dressed in her boots and overcoat, and walked over to the barn to grab the family horse.

"Giddy-up, Corolla, come on." She crossed the ice covered road slowly with an abundance of caution. Although Corolla felt confident on the icy surface, she never felt comfortable with riding a horse, even in ideal weather, but Bob, her driver, wasn't expected to arrive for another couple of hours. She rode slowly and cautiously and approached a lone cabin just a mile up the road and knocked on the door.

Thuy answered, also wearing a Snuggly. Rubbing his eyes, he asked with a hoarse voice. "Meredith?"

A male voice called from inside. "Who is it?"

Thuy called back, "My secret straight lover, Kyle. Go back to sleep." He gestured for her to come in.

Meredith wanted to cry again seeing the familiar face of Thuy, a friend from the old days, but her eyes ran out of tears. She walked inside the cabin to find chicory brewing in the kitchen.

"Sit down. I was just making some coffee." That's what they called chicory these days. Meredith sat at the kitchen table and gazed outside at the overcast morning through the frosted glass. Thuy poured two cups and sat down.

"Thanks," she said, noticing that Thuy still had the same flattop that he'd had years ago. She didn't know how he maintained such perfect geometrical proportions in this world, his exacting angular proportions defying a world losing its artificial angles.

After a momentary silence, Thuy spoke. "Meredith, I'm…look, Ezra said he saw Chris' boat make it on shore, and, well, you know what a lucky son of a bitch he is."

Meredith was never particularly tickled by Thuy's wit the way Chris was. She never understood it, really. It didn't even register with her now.

"Thuy, you and I've known each other a long time," she said stone faced.

"Yes we have. I remember when I was the constable and you went into labor telling me about the plans for a coup in Culpeper you hatched with Charles. God, those were the days."

"And here we are again." She heard Kyle snoring upstairs, and Thuy shrugged.

"What can I say? I didn't know he was a snorer until it was too late."

Meredith continued. "What do you think of Jon?"

Thuy rubbed his faced wearily. They hadn't really discussed it before, she realized. They just sort of intuitively stepped up to the plate to cover for the constable. But they never talked about the truth of their situation openly. "God, Meredith, it's really too early for this. I haven't even let the faux coffee kick in with its nonexistent caffeine yet."

"Come on, Thuy, we've skirted this issue long enough."

"You're right, you're right," he conceded. "I think you already know what I think. I think the constable is a great man who suffered enormously at the hands of the flu that killed off his entire family. I think the constable postponed any potential psychological fallout during that first year, long enough to see us through the worst of it. I think Jon was an incredible leader that managed to unite people from different walks of life and that his leadership saved our bacon."

She could tell Thuy was almost choked up as he paused. "And I think it all took its toll on him in the end. He's a wonderful man, but he's just a man just the same. We all have our breaking point."

"And you think he's reached his."

Thuy rolled his eyes. "He lost his entire family to the flu, Meredith. He served in Iraq and Afghanistan and came back only to find his entire family gone."

"He was at the Twin Towers, too. Let's not forget that." She saw the look of surprise on his face. "Chris didn't tell you? No, of course he didn't. Yeah, Jon was there. So was Rita. Chris told me about it a few years ago. I thought it was one of his over-imaginative memories, but Jon confirmed it."

Thuy shook his head incredulously. "I guess it's something special between them. In any case, Jon has served his country, he served his people with a dedication of his entire being."

"But he can no longer do it, can he?"

Thuy shook his head. "It just caught up with him."

"You, me, Dean, the three of us have been trying to gloss over it for a long time. We never dared discuss it to each other or even with ourselves. But the alcoholism has claimed him."

There, she said it. *Alcoholism.* It was a word they never spoke aloud. Jon Early was descending into an alcoholic abyss. The dossier on Rita Luevano revealed that she was a recovering alcoholic herself, nineteen years sober, she recalled. Meredith hoped to discreetly bring up the issue with her as they shared a similar plight; however, her absence made that a nonstarter now.

Thuy let the words sink in. "It crept up, didn't it? He showed up hung over a few times and we laughed it off, because it was so unlike him. But it became more frequent. And then I noticed his coffee cup, the way he always had it with him and how Sharon started joining him in the meetings."

"He's too proud to admit it to anybody, but he's falling apart." She took a sip of chicory. "Thuy, we need to have a discussion with Dean."

"You aren't suggesting we throw him out of office, are you, because..."

Meredith shook her head. "No, no, no. Of course not, Thuy. Jon is just as you say, a man who united our people. He's still that man. He's our constable whether he can sit in the stirrups or not. It's just that you, Dean and I are going to have to be honest with what we are, the true power behind the figurehead. We don't want it, we didn't ask to be it, but we are nevertheless. We are a triad."

"Great, just what my mom always wanted me to be."

"We're going to need to bring in Dean. Do you think he's open?"

"I think so. He's one of Jon's best friends, but that means he knows better than anyone."

"You know, Jon always confided in Chris. Chris never talked to me about it."

"None of us did."

"You're right, of course. It's just I always thought there were no secrets between us."

"Says the director of the Swan."

Somehow she felt…not better. Her husband was still missing, and Lynchburg was still amassing. But she felt less alone. She also felt a sense of clarity. She was the decider, or at least one third of a decider now. And now that there was no longer skirting the issue, she could move forward as the true power behind the throne, as it were, without feeling like she was wrong to do so. Maybe she would be wrong in her decisions, but she, Thuy and Dean were all they had.

"We're going to lose the way things look. Lynchburg will wipe us out in a stand up fight. I know nothing of military matters, but even I can see that."

Thuy nodded solemnly. "We were small potatoes even with the constable lucid and the reverend present. Now with the reverend gone, it will only be easier. Juan's a good man, but I don't think he can keep Monticello unified the way Rita did."

"I think you're right, especially with that firebrand sheriff of theirs seeing Christian conspiracies everywhere."

"I know! What is her damage?"

Meredith shrugged. "Lucille suffered at the hands of the Lambs of God." Mentally reviewing Lucille Schadenfreude's dossier, she recounted it as best as she could remember. "When the Lambs took over Lynchburg, they were seeking out enemies, nonbelievers, agitators. It was bad enough being a lawyer, but an uppity one who refused to submit was just asking for it. She barely made it to Monticello. I suppose Rita was her life raft. We've seen how the Gaia Piety Society has resonated with those with more metro sensibilities."

"Well, it's making keeping the peace difficult. Rita's gone, the glue that held Monticello together. We're fresh out of great leaders, at least ones so photogenic as the constable. Lynchburg has us right where they want us."

Meredith let out a macabre sigh. "There's more, Thuy. There's something I've been keeping from you, keeping from everyone. Once I tell you, I think you'll understand."

"Jesus, Meredith, what is it?"

She paused. After a moment, she stood up and put on her coat.

"Not here. Is there somewhere…your shed, perhaps?"

Thuy nodded as he grabbed his coat and put on a pair of boots. Meredith grabbed her valise and headed outside, desperate to finally divulge what she had been hiding for years. Thuy's cabin was isolated and the shed out in the back was practically part of the forest. Thuy unlocked the shed and led her inside. There was a lone window to let in the daylight. Meredith looked around, making sure the place didn't have any listening devices. It would be highly unlikely that the Lambs of God would bother placing a clunky bug in the deputy constable's storage shed. Even if they did, the technology available would make such devices easy to locate and it wouldn't be able to store its own power like bugs in the old days could. It was a prudent precaution to search, regardless. Meredith then considered holding off telling Thuy until they got to Montpelier Station.

"Meredith, we're alone. I think it's time you tell me what has you so petrified."

Meredith relented. She needed to tell him now. "A few years ago, before there was the Swan, someone, I refer to him as Ross, contacted me. Ross provided me with a lot of useful intelligence, but he also gave me something else." She pulled out a stack from her aged valise. "In this report…"

While Meredith spoke, she felt the horrendous gravity of it all finally coming to life, as though speaking aloud made it real. She didn't want it to be real, but it was what it was whether she gave voice to it or not.

Chapter 15

"Mr. Jung, Mr. Jung, can you hear me?"

Chris felt someone tapping his cheek. He could hear a voice calling his name, incorrectly pronouncing his last name with a "J" sound instead of a "Y" as it was intended in German.

"Mr. Jung, don't move. You're safe. We're taking you to Howard County General." Chris now heard the loud wail of…*a siren*?

Chris stirred and felt someone pressing down on his arms; his neck was likewise restrained. He was unable to move. He struggled to open his eyes and with a dizzying spin, he saw the face of a woman holding his arms down.

"It's gonna be alright, Mr. Jung. Just stay still. We'll be at the hospital in five minutes. Can you hear me, Mr. Jung?" she asked again.

Chris tried to nod, but couldn't. He struggled again, but the woman holding her down was strong. He managed to say, "It's Jung with a 'Y,'" before he fell unconscious again.

"Hon! Please wake up. Please."

Chris heard the sweet familiar voice of his love. "Meredith?" he whispered.

"Yes, Love! Oh, thank God!"

Chris blinked his eyes trying to adjust to the brilliant light. The last thing he remembered was cycling away from the mortars and the surrounding internecine battle as fast as he could. There was that El Camino technical that peeled away...the one with the busty Betty Boop in a bikini and the gothic writing. He remembered now. It said, "Can't touch this." He was pedaling over the icy road, he saw the deer, he tried to swerve and flipped through the air. That was out in Maryland, but now he heard his wife's voice speaking to him. She was in Virginia. Could he have somehow returned to Virginia, or was it…

"Am I…am I dead? Is this heaven?"

Straining from the bright light, he saw Meredith giggle through tears streaming down her face. "No, love. It's Maryland."

Chris lifted his head and placed a hand on his forehead which was bandaged. Someone helped him sit up. All he could do was focus on Meredith. She looked so beautiful, so perfect. Almost too perfect.

"You cut your hair," he said. She touched her bobbed hair that was perfectly shaped. It also had a reddish tint. His focus was beginning to come back; the world was no longer spinning. It hurt to look directly into the brightness. But as his eyes adjusted he could see he was inside a room, a clean sterile room with Meredith standing beside him. He heard voices, disembodied voices summoning people.

"What, where…" Chris tried to begin.

"Mr. Jung, how many fingers am I holding up?"

Chris saw a young man wearing scrubs holding two fingers in front of him. Chris answered him. "Two."

"Good. What's the date?"

"It's, uh, January…something, I forget, 2013; Thursday."

"That very good, Mr. Jung. And who's the President? Outgoing or incoming. Either one will do."

Chris squinted with confusion. "The President? Why are you asking history questions?" He scanned around the room and saw a monitor, a computer monitor making readings. He stared at the illuminated screen reporting his vitals. The screen looked so futuristic. Then it hit him. *It's a computer screen!* Sure enough it was a true-to-life computer monitor operating like in the old days. And he was inside a hospital room, at least as far as it looked, it was a hospital. The disembodied voices now made sense. It was an intercom. The lights in the room didn't flicker. It was a clean, steady light. Meredith was dressed in one of her business outfits the way she did back in the real world. Her hair, her face, they were done up.

Chris couldn't believe he was here. He was back in the past. Was this a dream? It felt too real to be a dream. He had a lot of dreams like this, but whenever he awoke, he always felt as though he should have known while he was dreaming that it was just a dream. Was this just another dream where he should know better? But this really didn't feel like a dream at all. It felt real. For instance, his head was really killing him and he felt sick. Maybe he stumbled onto a new wrinkle of dreaming, sort of like the times he dreamt of having insomnia.

"Mr. Jung, what do you last recall?"

Chris thought of the last moments during the furious battle between ferals and the Abercrombies. "I was cycling and I saw this deer. I swerved to get out of its way..."

"He often cycles during lunch," Meredith explained to the doctor. Chris was about to protest when the man in the scrubs spoke.

"Hmm, you don't remember getting carjacked?"

Chris shook his head, and immediately regretted making such violent movements with his head like that. If this were a dream, it was a particularly vivid dream. He waited to find an anachronism like his M4 by his bedside, a Vicious Rabbit or Lamb of God soldier on the TV, because dreams did weird crap like...

"My God, the TV's on!"

"Just try to relax, Mr. Jung. You sustained a concussion, so you'll have trouble with memory and things will seem a bit confusing for awhile, but it will pass."

Chris grabbed Meredith's hand, which had been caressing his forearm scratching it gently with her long red fingernails. "Hon, where am I?"

"You're at Howard County General Hospital. You were going over to that guy's house to pick up the guitar you found on Craigslist when you got carjacked."

"From what a witness said, the man who carjacked you struck you on the head with his pistol and you fell to the pavement, which explains why you have contusions on your forehead and your right temple." Chris turned to see a police officer speaking.

"I can get a statement later when you can remember better. And, Mr. Jung," the police officer said mispronouncing his name with a "J" sound, "next time, don't fight over a stupid messenger bag. Nothing in there is worth your life." The officer jerked his thumb over to the messenger bag under the TV. "Get well."

Chris felt sick. He thrashed out of bed in an effort to force himself awake. All that he managed to do though was get him nauseous. Meredith grabbed onto him and helped him back into bed. He realized he was wearing a pair of slacks and a shirt and tie.

"Oh shit, Hon, I don't...what the...what's going on," he implored desperately.

"Shh, Hon, you heard the doctor. You need to relax."

Chris rested his head. He couldn't get himself to wake up if this were a dream, which was something he was beginning to doubt. If it was not a dream he had no idea what this was. At least Meredith was with him, he consoled himself. He thought he would never see her again when he was dodging the mortars in Maryland or when he was being shot at in the middle of the Chesapeake. Whatever this was, he wouldn't mind staying so long as she was with him. Her hand felt warm, real. Then the wildest thought occurred to him. Maybe he had been transported to the past.

He knew himself to have an active imagination, and he really missed science fiction movies and TV shows. He read space operas in the first years after the Shift, as well as Kim Stanley Robinson and Doctor Who novels that he gathered in the ruins. No, he wasn't in the past, or at least, he wasn't going to allow himself to jump to that conclusion just yet. He was probably just dead or something and this was an unexpected afterlife. It's not heaven, but it's not bad. Maybe this is the agnostic's heaven. Zagat would rate it something like, "meh, I've seen worse afterlives."

Just to prove to himself that he was not in the past, he ventured a dangerous question. "The kids?"

"They're waiting to see their dad. Brandon and Anne are waiting with them."

Good. There, he wasn't in the past. Their eldest child Aidan wasn't born until three months after the Shift hit. He was born and raised in Rochelle proper, which they referred to the original hamlet itself to distinguish it from the nation state of the Rochelle Sovereignty to include all of Orange and Madison counties. So, too Rhiannon and Charles were born in Rochelle. They never breathed urban air. He thought of his children, his wonderful life back with Meredith and the kids.

"I missed you so much. I love you."

Meredith chuckled warmly. "Oh, Hon, it's been a hard day for you. I love you, too my sweet." She hugged him gently and he could smell the exotic scent of perfume on her. He peered down and saw she was wearing FMPs. He didn't know what this place was, but he smiled, nuzzling himself in her blouse.

Later that evening, Chris was discharged from the hospital. It was sort of like getting sprung from jail. A harried looking woman handed him a manila envelope, which contained his keys, wallet, a watch, ring and a very strange looking cell phone that didn't have a keypad. His last cell phone was a flip action variety. Then he reminded himself that he was in the agnostic afterlife, not the past. The hospital policy was that he leave in a wheelchair. He didn't mind. He was still dizzy. He didn't know if it was the concussion from the fall off the bike, the purported carjacking, or from the painkillers they gave him. He held his messenger bag in his lap and looked around.

"Missing something, sir?" asked the orderly.

"Yeah, my M4 and my sidearm. Where is it?"

The man laughed and wheeled him to the elevator. On the way down, Chris took deep breaths. He noticed something odd with his tongue. He had a full set of teeth. The four he lost to scraping with bandits and poor hygiene were securely attached in his mouth. He had no idea what was going on, but he knew he wasn't dreaming. He dozed off earlier and woke up. He never did that in a dream. The TV in the elevator, crazy as that sounded, was tuned to Fox News. His vision was a little on the blurry side, but he swore Tina Fey was speaking as a news contributor.

"What the hell?"

The orderly laughed again. "Yeah, she's a live one, huh?"

The elevator door opened and there waiting for him was Brandon and Anne. They looked great. Meredith was standing there holding Aidan and another boy's hand keeping them from running wild. Aidan looked funny wearing pre-Shift clothes, and his little friend looked just as excited to see him. Then both screamed, "Daddy!"

"Easy, now, easy," Meredith warned. "Daddy's still hurt, okay?"

Chris immediately quirked his face as she addressed *both* of the boys. Where was Rhiannon? Where was Baby Charles? The boys ran up despite Meredith's warning, but stopped short of tackling him.

"Daddy, I was so worried about you!"

"I was worrieder."

"No, you weren't, Yorick, I was."

"I was worrieder," the little boy protested.

"It's 'more worried,' you *baby*."

Chris was flummoxed, absolutely, stunned. He couldn't respond. There was his boy Aidan, but who in the hell was this kid beside him? The little boy looked eerily familiar, sort of like a brown-eyed version of Aidan when he was a toddler. He tried to recall what Aidan called him. *Yorick? Yorick?* He was about to ask, but then something he learned over the years kicked in, discretion. *Shut up, Chris, just shut up. Don't ask anything. Just go with it. We'll figure it all out later.*

"Hey…you." He opened his arms and embraced the two of them. He instinctively smelled their hair and was comforted by both of them. He still felt like he was missing something, not to mention the fact that he desperately wanted to ask Meredith where in the hell Rhiannon and Charles were. He had to find out what was going on, but he couldn't let on about his confusion. Why? Because, Meredith would think him crazy. Or if he were dead, he feared asking such direct questions would send him into another realm. He didn't realize that he was so superstitious. Then again, being an obsessive-compulsive, he learned that he had a lot of quirks without any logic attached to them, like always placing his untied boots facing west.

Hold on. What if the Abercrombies caught me, and they're pulling some Manchurian Candidate hypnosis on me to assassinate Jon or, God help me, my wife? That also could be what's going on. Dude, this is totally freaking me out! He was too dizzy from the hit on the head and to think this through logically. But alas, he knew from bitter experience. If the whole thing is confounding, just shut up and wait.

Meredith ran off to get the car when Brandon spoke. "Hey Chief, glad to see you're going to be okay." He and Anne hugged him gingerly. Chris noticed Brandon had all of his digits and didn't seem to walk with a limp, suggesting he had both legs. He also looked younger, more hip.

"Yeah."

"And you got your bag. Seriously, man, nothing in there is worth dying over."

"Lay off him, Brandon. It's just a good thing he's going to be all right," Anne said.

He noticed that Anne was pregnant, which he recalled she wasn't the last time he saw them, which was right before he left for the mission a week ago. They had one of their own kids back in Rochelle, but Avery wasn't here, wherever here was, supposedly a hospital in Columbia, Maryland, which was impossible.

Anne then turned to Chris. "Meredith called and we rushed over straight from work to watch the boys. I am so relieved!"

Chris nodded when he felt a buzz in his pocket. It buzzed again. It was his strange looking cell phone that was all LCD screen and sans keypad. The screen displayed "mom" and listed a phone number. A green "answer" option glowed at the bottom. Confused and without any other options, Chris touched the "answer" button and the phone came to life. A voice called out from the receiver, which didn't look like it was a receiver. "Chris?"

Cautiously placed the phone to his ear. "Hello?"

"Oh, my son, it's you! Thank heavens! I…Meredith called and told me you were injured and she…she had to rush to the hospital."

The voice broke down. He recognized this voice as he would his own. It was a voice he never thought he would ever hear again. Almost overwhelmed he asked, "Mom?"

Chapter 16

"Why do you insist on calling me at these hours?"

"I do not know. Because I get worried."

Rita was trying to catch up on her work. She was cozy, curled up with a laptop on the couch, reading an article on p-branes when the phone rang. She never got away from him.

"Worried? Worried about what?"

"The universe. What if it keeps expanding? What if there is not enough rest mass to stop the expansion and it just keeps spreading out until the force gravity becomes meaningless, the laws of physics break down and the whole entire universe dies a slow cold death where the stars die and nothing is left but the mist of what was once matter? Did you know that the rate of expansion is increasing?"

"You're kidding me, right? You called me at one in the morning because you're worried the universe keeps expanding?" Rita scratched her jaw and reigned in any angry comments. She knew she had to be patient with Jamil.

"But I knew you were awake."

"Really. How did you know that?"

"She told me you were still up."

"Who?"

"Gaia, silly."

Linthicum Heights, Maryland
January 2013

The row of mid-twentieth century aluminum siding and brick homes which lined the middle class neighborhood of Linthicum Heights looked ominously serene. The lawns had reverted to their natural state with the grass having grown several feet over the snow patches; there were signs of homes broken into as well. But the houses on residential street still stood, which surprised Rita. Looking at the map, they were close to BWI Airport. From her experience in Charlottesville and from eyewitness accounts elsewhere, she knew that most airports had been turned into infernos when the Shift hit. Planes on approach and taking off instantly lost all power, becoming falling bricks filled with jet fuel. Apparently, this neighborhood lucked out, not that it helped the former residents of this once quaint neighborhood.

In the fog of the melee, while mortars and machine gun fire rocked all around them, their mission commander Captain Chris Jung lost control of his bike. He flipped over and landed head first onto the asphalt. Unfortunately, Chris wasn't wearing his helmet. Lieutenant Baraka promptly took command. They hurriedly stowed his bike in a jumble of trash by the side of the road, dumped the gear from the Burley Bee child trailer, and stuffed the rather bulky frame of Chris into the carrier that was originally designed to carry only two small kids. Having been reinforced to carry crates of food, ammo and medicine, the Burley Bee trailer was more versatile than she figured. She had to admit, she laughed when she first saw the Vicious Rabbits with their bike-mounted cavalry and the child trailers during the Obsidian War. But after Neko, Juan and Ezra saw how the bicycle mounted cavalry put the child trailers into action and how effective the cavalry was in an urban environment, the Monticellans tried to replicate what the Vicious Rabbits had done with their own cavalry, though they still preferred horses over bikes.

While trying to flee the scene, mortar fire threw the cavalry into disarray while ferals scurried about, some peeling out in old vehicles, others on beat up bicycles, everyone else running in all directions. None of them paid any attention to the small party of strangers. Rita had assumed the mortars were coming from the Abercrombies and that the ferals were unfortunate souls caught up in the crossfire between two foreign powers.

Helmut Spankmeister did something unusual during the chaos. He took the lead, racing past Rita and signaling the cavalry to follow him. Kendra figured that this was closer to Spankmeister's turf, so they should go with his direction. It turned out to be a good plan. Nobody else knew what was around, but it looked like Helmut did. He led them away from the fighting and off Highway 295 to the little neighborhood they were now squatting. They were safe for the moment hunkering down inside one of the smaller Cape Cod houses.

Evening had arrived. Looking out from the kitchen, Rita saw a pack of dogs running by, followed by two human hunters. She quickly ducked to make sure they didn't catch site of her. She noticed how sudden movement made her feel nauseous, probably because she was dehydrated. Her vision was shaky like watching a film from the perspective of a running cameraman. She had been getting this a lot since leaving Virginia. She put her hand on the refrigerator as she stood back up. It hardly resembled a refrigerator now. When the power went out those years ago, the ice melted, the perishable goods rotted and nature came to claim the rectangular machine. The gases from the decomposed food burst the doors open, and became home to all sorts of insects. Fortunately, the rancid smell had dissipated in the freezing cold.

In the living room Kendra pulled the curtains before turning on a Coleman lantern. The living room of the stranger's home was unremarkable. Someone had broken into the home, probably years ago. But it looked like the kitchen was the only room that appeared to be scoured for goods. Lucky for them, there was some toilet paper left. That was a luxury item now. Their bikes were pulled inside and rested by the entertainment center while one of the Vicious Rabbits worked a Bunsen burner to warm up some ad hoc soup using the ice and bits of jerky and dried vegetables. The gunnery sergeant with that very peculiar accent sat on the couch with Helmut Spankmeister.

"So, mate, you're saying it wasn't the Abercrombies attacking us?"

Helmut was nibbling on hardtack and nodded. "I don't believe so."

"Aye, Gov," Rita had come to know the gunnery sergeant was referring to her. "You should take a seat and listen." He turned to the scrawny scientist. "Tell 'er what you've told me."

"Those people on the highway. They're the Targeteers."

"'Targeteers', like the store Target?" she asked. She remembered racing past a Target during the barrage.

Helmut smirked, which she had never seen before. "Yes, like the store. I think they were employed at the Target near here or something. That's what they told me, anyway. My peop…I sort of associate with them, a little. They're okay people, not cannibals."

"That's probably why they ignored us. They saw you and they know you, roit?

Helmut shrugged. "I guess that could be it. I didn't interact with them much except a little trading, but we…I, well, anyway, they're constantly battling against this other tribe, the Costcos."

Akil who sidled up next to her repeated, "The Costcos…Don't tell me. Let me guess."

"Yes," Helmut confirmed what she already surmised. "The Costcos and the Targeteers have been in a turf war for... since it all began, I guess."

Helmut took a moment to drink from his thermos before continuing. "The Costcos have all sorts of military hardware. That wall of cars, that's the border between the two groups, which they agreed to erect to keep the peace."

"You think we might have started a war between the Costcos and the Targeteers?" She couldn't believe she had just said that. Then again, she had come to say "Thomas Jefferson Martyrs Brigade" and "Vicious Rabbits" with a straight face. This world was anything but boring.

"Maybe. But they were always fighting each other."

"The good news is that it probably sets the Abercrombies back a li'le in their pursuit," the gunny added. Kendra Baraka walked in from the backdoor shaking off the cold as he continued. "But the LT was thinking that she and I go forward with our mission, and let you guide the professor here back to his 'ome."

"No, you can't!" Helmut protested with uncharacteristic passion. "I mean, you have to come to my place first…to pick up your radiation suits and the print outs. I don't recall the exact location where the material was. The nuclear material is actually closer to Columbia, anyway."

"Listen, mate, don't jerk me around. I've got a mission to complete, and as much as I don't fancy glowing green, we've li'le choice. Those bloody Abercrombies might be stalled, but if they get their 'ands on the nukes, my people are toast, roit!"

Rita held up a hand. "Wait. Let's just catch our breath and think a moment. Gunny, you said yourself that the factional fighting between the Targeteers and Costcos probably delayed the Abercrombies."

"And neither of the tribes like the Abercrombies," Helmut added.

"We want to approach this intelligently."

The gunny grunted. "It's all up to the LT, anyway. LT?"

Kendra Baraka took a seat on a coffee table next to Rita. Rita couldn't help but notice how beautiful the young lady was, which contrasted with her rugged BDUs. In that regard she was like Ilsa or Neko, but the similarities ended there. Whereas Neko was a spitfire, Rita had come to understand Kendra as more rational and wise beyond her years. The thought of Neko made her wince. She hoped she would come to terms with her injuries back home.

"The gunny and I believe that time is running out and that we should finish the job now with what explosives we have left. I say we send someone to retrieve the printouts..."

"We've got more explosives back at the office," Helmut jumped in before Kendra could finish. Rita didn't know what Helmut meant by "we," but it seemed to convince Kendra.

"Well, I certainly don't care to die of radiation poisoning if I can help it and if you have more explosives, then that works for me."

The gunny grunted an affirmation giving Rita some relief. She had hoped Gaia would return to her in another vision to comfort her, tell her they were on the right track. Instead, she had another one of those odd dreams during a cat nap. She dreamt of the past a lot. It was disorientating whenever she awoke. But the dreams of late were just plain odd. It wasn't a past that she remembered. And then she recalled some mention of Gaia.

Just as she tried to recall the last dream, Ilsa walked in from one of the bedrooms. Although disturbingly young—just over sixteen, the archer had surprised Rita how well she held her own on this journey. She should be in high school riddled with normal teenage angst over things like drugs, sex, SATs, finding true love, freeing herself from her parents' grip, fun stuff like that. Instead Ilsa was part of the Thomas Jefferson Martyrs Brigade, cracking skulls and kicking ass out in the wastelands. Yet she was still a teenager. She was painfully shy around the grownups and she blushed whenever she was around Ezra. *God, poor Ezra,* she thought morosely. His fast boat capsized. So many young souls would never live to become old.

"Captain Jung is stirring," Ilsa reported.

Rita, Akil, Lieutenant Baraka and Gunnery Sergeant Birmingham stood up and walked into the bedroom. The room apparently had been a boy's room. Toys were scattered all over the place. Rita nearly tripped trying to navigate over Legos and a robot in the dark room lit solely by a collection of candles. She figured it had been like this even before the Shift. Chris lay on a racecar bed, stripped down to his thermal underwear shirt and white and green mottled winter homespun BDUs. She thought he looked funny with his two-pronged chin beard. She remembered how she, Chris, and Jon Early had crossed paths years ago on September 11th. It was one of those insane coincidences, which Gaia reminded her that there were no coincidences. Chris was a brand new special agent, she was a divinity student at Columbia University and Jon was at a job interview when the planes struck the Twin Towers. She was on her way up the North Tower to meet her brother who worked at the Windows on the World restaurant and she got stuck in an elevator. When her elevator finally returned to lobby and the doors opened, she was greeted by a very handsome man she had mistaken for Richard Gere. She would later come to realize that it was Jon. He led her out the building. And when the North Tower collapsed, she was hauled off by a young man in a suit who carried her to a deli when the plume of smoke passed by them. She would later learn that that young man was none other than Chris Jung.

Both looked familiar to her, but she never would have connected the dots and figured that it was her experience on September 11th where she had met them. The mere idea was insane. Yet it was Chris who put it together and enlightened Jon who in turn told her about it. Knowing that both had been there with her, and had done what they could to help her on that day, she felt a special connection to them both. Examining Chris now, she felt particularly worried for him. He was moaning, struggling. Akil who had been trained as a medic during his days in the Army said Chris sustained a concussion.

"Stupid asshole," Chris grumbled.

Rita kneeled down by the racecar bed to be beside Chris. He had a bandage wrapped around his forehead.

"Chris," she whispered. "Chris."

"Micro-managing…ass clown."

Rita couldn't help but grin at Chris' cursing. Who was he talking about? "Chris, Chris, wake up."

"Don't shake him, Sugar," Akil cautioned.

"Chris Jung. Do you hear me?"

Chris nodded slowly. His eyes opened and he struggled to get up.

"No, no. Just lie down, Chris."

He rubbed his eyes and blinked again. "What…where am I?"

"We're in Linthicum, Maryland."

"What the hell am I doing in Maryland? Oh yeah, right. The guitar."

Rita leaned in close. "What guitar?" Chris looked at Rita and registered a look of shock on his face. He scrambled but Rita held him down.

Chris scanned his surroundings, his brows weaved pensively. Slowly, he asked. "Who…who are you?"

Not good. Rita knew concussions could do a number on people. Hopefully he was just a little confused, and would regain his bearings.

"Chris, it's Rita, Rita Luevano, you know, the reverend, chief magistrate, the one-eyed witch of UU?" Chris looked at her flummoxed. She took a candle and brought it up to her face. He stared at her as if he were looking at a complete stranger.

"Where in the hell am I?" he said this time more forcefully and he sat up. The sudden movement forced him to hold his head. "What's going on?"

"Just remain calm, Captain," the gunnery sergeant said. "You got yourself a nasty bonk on the 'ead, sir."

"Will someone turn on the lights, damn it! Who in the hell are you people? Where am I?"

"Oh, boy," Rita sighed. "Chris, just calm the hell down. Akil?"

Her husband shrugged helplessly. "I was told amnesia was just in the movies. But he might be temporarily confused."

"Confused? What's going on," Chris demanded.

"Relax, Chris. We're your friends. You were injured in the operation. You're in Maryland. You're bike flipped over while we were making a run for it."

Chris shook his head then winced painfully. "I…I don't remember cycling today. It's too cold, the roads are too icy."

"You can say that again, sir," Birmingham interjected.

"What's the last thing you remember?" Rita asked. She placed a candle between them.

"I was in…Maryland, that's right. I was on my way to Columbia, Maryland…to pick up the guitar."

"What guitar?"

"It was on Craigslist. Some guy was practically giving away a cherry Gibson."

Rita looked over to Gunnery Sergeant Birmingham who looked at Ilsa who looked at a Vicious Rabbit. He continued. "It was worth the drive to Maryland. I just got off the exit when this shithead carjacked me. He pistol whipped me and then…I don't know."

Rita feared that Chris indeed had amnesia and the last thing he remembered was a memory before the Shift, which would be really bad. Bracing herself, she asked. "Chris, what's the date?"

"It's January, I forget…the exact date, 2013. Thursday, right?"

Rita gave an inward sigh of relief. "That's correct."

"And who's your constable?"

Chris furrowed his eyebrows. "Shit if I know. I don't bother with local elections. And after the last presidential one, I don't think I'll ever vote again, period." The gunny and the other Vicious Rabbits in the room murmured amongst themselves.

"Okay, I've answered your questions," Chris pleaded. "Now, please someone tell me what in the hell is going on? Whose house is this? Who are you, and will someone please turn on the damned lights?"

"My God, he does have amnesia," Ilsa said.

"But he knows the date," Akil retorted.

"Screw you guys. I'm going home." Chris stood up, but his knees buckled and Rita caught him.

"Easy, easy," she coaxed.

"Fuck easy! I want to know what the hell is going on!" He searched his pockets. "My phone. Where's my phone? Which one of you assholes took my phone?"

Some part of her wanted to smack his memory back into place. Instead, Rita tried reason. "Chris, get a hold of yourself. There is no phone. You don't have a phone. You haven't had one since…"

"Oh my God!" Chris cried out. "What the hell happened to my teeth?"

"What do you mean, sir," Birmingham inquired.

Chris was sticking his tongue through the spaces where he had lost teeth over the past few years. "This," pointing to the gapes. "Did the carjacker do this?"

Rita lost her patience. She grabbed Chris firmly. "Chris, there was no carjacker. You have no phone. You haven't had a phone or a car for years, not since the Shift."

Chris froze, his mouth opened and shut again. "What Shift?"

"Oh shit," Birmingham muttered. He took the words right out of her mouth.

Chris hated Maryland. In Virginia, it wasn't normal for him to get carjacked and to wake up in some strange place with armed thugs surrounding him. His vision was blurry, still a little shaky, and the room was dark, but he could tell the guy at the foot of the bed with the God awful accent had an assault rifle in tow.

At first, he thought he was dreaming again. Over the years, he had a spate of these odd dreams. Chris examined the faces of the strangers in the darkened bedroom. They were people he didn't know, yet there was somehow familiar. This place…no, not the place…the circumstances were familiar in some fashion that was similar to the dreams he sometimes had. And then there was the face of the woman sitting beside him. He tried not to stare at the patch over her left eye or the scar on her face. She was definitely familiar.

Maybe he was dreaming. He tried to shake himself awake, but his head protested violently when he did that, so he decided against doing that again. If it was a dream then it felt awfully real. Then again, he supposed dreams usually felt real. Rarely, did he call bullshit on a dream. But this was something he could not wake up from. This was too vivid. He felt cold. He could see steam from his breath in the candlelight. It was too detailed to be a dream.

Chris was trying to make sense of what was going on. He went over the events in his head. He took his car to work today so that he could leave straight from there to pick up the Gibson guitar from that guy in Columbia, Maryland. His boss Ed Farcus was being his usual charming douche bag self, and he had a run in with him. After work, he set off to Columbia, got off the exit from the I-95. Then, while waiting in the traffic jam extending from the never-ending stop light to the exit, he got carjacked. Chris remembered reaching for his messenger bag, and he felt being hit on the head.

But the people around him, armed men and women, were trying to convince him that something else, something catastrophic happened. They called it…

"What's this Shift you're talking about?" Chris asked.

"The EMPs, Captain. Mother Earth Gaia, what 'ave you, sent up the EMPs that bloody wiped out all our gadgets."

Chris could barely understand the silhouetted figure, both because of what he was saying and how he spoke it in that accent of his. But he thought the armed figure said "EMP," and wiping out technology. He had read up on EMPs. Among other things, the candidates in the last election had competing defense policies, each citing the potential of Iran using a nuclear missile as an EMP weapon.

"EMPs? Like electromagnetic pulse, that kind of EMP?"

"Aye, Captain. Don't you remember when the EMPs first hit?"

Captain? Why is this dude calling me a captain? This was just getting more puzzling by the moment. He had to find out what was going on, and he had to figure it out one question at a time.

Aloud he asked, "Is that why the power's out?"

"Aye, sir."

"What time did this happen? How many days ago was it?" Chris was trying to fill in the gaps between the time he got carjacked and this EMP attack. How many days had passed? Why did these people pick him up? Why not an ambulance? Did the EMP attack happen to coincide while he was busy becoming another crime statistic? Was he certain he wasn't dead and in some kind of messy afterlife reserved for civil servants?

"Chris, the Shift…the EMPs…they started five and a half years ago," answered the woman with the eye patch.

"What…Five and a half…What are you talking…I don't…there wasn't an attack on the US in…what would that year be?" He struggled to do the math, but the woman answered for him.

"The Shift started in 2007. And it wasn't an attack. Chris, do you remember July 11, 2007?"

Suddenly, Chris felt his skin dimple into goose bumps and his stomach churn. He did remember that date. It was a seminal date for him. His mouth opened about to say something, but he thought again and said nothing. This was far too confounding to reveal anything else about himself to these people at this point.

Just play dumb as if the date means nothing to you, Chris. I have a feeling it means something else to them. "No, what happened on that day?"

Chapter 17

Charlottesville, Virginia
Greater Monticello
January 2013

Neko Lemay never had a problem with solitude. She had chosen to build her mountaintop cabin overlooking Monticello in order to have just that. Whereas most Monticellans chose to resettle in Charlottesville proper, Neko chose to be far enough away from the prattle of human voices. She had the whole mountain to herself. And back when she had full use of her body, there was no downside to it. Unfortunately, that was the past.

In the kitchen, Neko was trying to boil some water for tea, making an effort not to wince as she squatted to pitch more wood into the cast iron stove. Her red hair was in shambles, resembling the nest of a slovenly bird. She couldn't make a decent ponytail to save her life now. Strands of hair tickled her face and she burnt a few strands when she leaned over the stove. With her right arm securely fastened to her torso, it reduced her mobility as well as her dexterity. She tried to ignore it, to pretend that the loss of the use of her right arm didn't fundamentally change her life. The kitchen had windows, but the dark oak wood walls and the canopy of trees surrounding the cabin diffused the light coming in. She used a Zippo to light the kerosene lamp to search in the cabinet for a jar of strawberry preserves. The bread was already sliced, but when she found the jar, it occurred to her that jars required two hands to open.

Still in her pajamas, Neko sat on the floor, took off her socks, clamped the jar between the arches of her feet and attempted to open it with her good arm. It was difficult at first. The jar wanted to slide away from her grip, but with a little extra pressure, her feet kept the jar still and she was able to open the preserves.

She eased herself back up using the cabinet to support her, and got a butter knife. Steam started whistling from the kettle. She scooped up the strawberry preserves with the knife, but when she tried to spread it on the bread, the slice flew across the room and onto the floor.

"Shit."

The kettle's whistle grew louder. She searched the dark kitchen for the wayward slice of bread. The whistling beseeched even louder. She grabbed the handle forgetting that the kettle's handle was not insulated from the heat. The shock of pain made her jump, dropping the kettle on the floor, the boiling water gushing out on all directions.

"Goddammit! Shit! Shit, shit!"

Whatever patience Neko had was expended in one momentous explosion of rage, pent up for weeks, vomiting out alone in her cabin where no one else would hear her. Neko let out a howl of futile rage and angst, followed by tears and a string of inventive uses for the "f" word in a fugue of untethered anguish, making use of both English and Spanish. The kettle became the focus of her ire as she grabbed the handle—with a pot holder this time—marched through the living room, and threw the offending kettle into the snow as it sizzled. But that wasn't enough. Barefoot and in her pajamas, she stormed outside and grabbed an axe. Knowing that striking a steel kettle with the sharp end was a bad idea, she twisted the axe to show the butt end and proceeded to punish the kettle for its existence.

"Fuck…you…kettle!"

Neko managed to flatten the kettle with three blows. She felt light headed and collapsed onto the snow. Her shoulders heaved as she wailed, unhindered by societal constraints. Her hot tears froze on her face as she released a month's worth of pain.

BACKGROUND MUSIC: "Once I Was" by Tim Buckley
Visit www.michaeljuge.com **on the *A Hard Rain* page to listen**

It took her about an hour to clean herself up and change clothes. The hot bath went a long way to restore her sanity. Neko sat in the living room in the late afternoon staring at the fire draped in a strange quilt she bought in Rochelle, something called a "Snuggly." It was getting dark; she hadn't eaten since yesterday. The kettle affair this morning killed her appetite. Her wound bled, a result of her reckless acting out. She hoped she wouldn't have to return to the hospital.

Neko sat staring at the fire, feeling the pain which ran from her right breast through her shoulder down to her flaccid arm. There wasn't the availability of pain killers except cannabis resin. But the doctor forbade her from taking that so long as Neko insisted on going home and not allowing anyone to stay with her. That was fine with her. She didn't want the pain to go away. She was a cripple now. Her days as an archer were over. In one instant she had gone from the leader of the Thomas Jefferson Martyrs Brigade into a pathetic sobbing girl.

When Rita had broken the news to her, Neko already knew the prognosis. She would be lucky if she ever had use of the arm at all. She would never wield a bow again, and she could never ride—not the way the archers do, at any rate—again. Neko attempted to portray herself as being sanguine about the matter, at least in front of others, she did.

"It's okay, Reverend. I'm just glad the bastards didn't get to you."

Rita saw through the act. "Girlfriend, I don't know who you are trying to comfort, but please, don't try to spare me. I know what it's like."

Neko wanted to protest, she wanted to say that the reverend was being overly concerned. But then in the privacy of the hospital room, Rita took off her eye patch and then her partials, revealing the old injuries that had mutilated her. Neko had only seen Rita without her eye patch on a couple of occasions. And since she got the partials, she always had them attached. Seeing her stripped of the disguise, Rita looked different, her cheeks sallow, her scars more exaggerated. And when she spoke, the spaces where she lost her teeth affected her speech.

"I know what it is like to become damaged goods. You may not feel it yet. You may be trying convince yourself if not me. Whatever the case may be, I will be here when you are ready."

She kissed Neko on top of her head.

Staring into the fire, the memory of Rita's words haunted her. Rita wasn't here. She was lost. She, Akil and a few of her buddies from the Martyrs Brigade. They had presumably made it onshore on that ridiculous mission to that place in Maryland, but it was a disaster of a mission from what she had been told by her executive officer who was likewise her part-time boyfriend. He was being a pain in the ass trying to be all supportive, but he didn't know. Her best friend, her mentor, her spiritual guide was lost and she was tits on a bull now.

There was a knock on the door, which wasn't unexpected. The Martyrs Brigade sent an archer twice a day to provide supplies and check up on her. That was part of the deal in releasing her to her forest retreat.

"It's open!"

Neko saw the figure cut of a woman with riding boots, skintight ski pants under a leather duster. Instinctively, Neko straightened herself in her chair, wincing in pain as she did so.

"Sheriff."

"Oh, relax, sweetie," Lucille Schadenfreude said warmly.

"What are you doing here? I mean, what can I do for you?"

"I'm sorry to intrude, Neko. I just wanted to help out." Neko then realized that Lucille held a duffle bag full of supplies.

Neko hadn't spent too much time with Lucille just the two of them. She spent one-on-one time with very few people. Outside of Rita and the boy of the week fling, she rarely spent time with just one other person. Ezra was one other possible exception. Part of the reason for her aloofness had to do with her self-admitted socially stunted growth. Her abrasive question "What are you doing here" was just another example of her maladjusted childhood, living with her dad in the mountains of Washington State. She never knew how to socialize with her peers, so she shunned them.

That being said, she liked Lucille. She seemed to be a bird of a feather even if she was remarkably sociable and articulate to her own anti-social nature. Neko tried to make up for her abrupt greeting.

"It's no bother at all, ma'am. Please come on in. Take a seat."

"Thank you. Let me put these in the kitchen first." As she hefted the bag into the kitchen she added, "And then I'll check your bandage." Everyone had been trained in basic first aid and field dressing. Neko had already changed the bandage in an attempt to hide the agitated wound. That was delicate work doing it with one hand.

Lucille walked back into the living room and dug into the duffle bag. "I also brought these."

She pulled out a couple of things that looked like vises. "I knew that since you are by yourself and with your condition, simple tasks are really difficult. These should help. You see? You clamp this on the table and you can open jars using the pressure of the twisting motion."

"Thank you." Neko was sincerely touched. She wished it arrived this morning.

"Well, I know what an independent gal you are. You don't need a man to open jars for you."

"Thank you," she repeated again feeling her shyness creeping up.

"You mind?" Lucille asked indicating that she wanted to sit in the couch to her right.

"Please."

Lucille took off her duster and sat in the couch joining in a stare into the fireplace.

"I notice you don't have electricity."

"Huh? Oh, the lights. No, I don't."

"Good. I don't either, well, not at home I don't."

Neko cast a glance at her. "Really? But you're the sheriff."

"And you're the commander of the Martyrs Brigade."

Neko wanted to protest, because she wasn't anymore, or she wouldn't be for long. What good was a commander who couldn't lead her people into battle? But Lucille interrupted her train of thought.

"I never liked electric lights. I never understood why. I always thought myself strange for that. But I hated those stupid florescent lights."

Neko found herself nodding in agreement. "Me too. It's like it makes everything else seem darker somehow."

"Exactly. And when they started with the coal and wind generators and wired the new homes in the city…well, I just didn't want the return of false lights and fans to concoct weather as if I'm resisting nature. Sounds silly, doesn't it?"

"No, not at all," Neko responded with more enthusiasm than she could muster since the assassination attempt. "I know exactly what you mean."

"I had a feeling you would. The whole world had become so dependent on convenience, on comfort, on an unreliable technology. We were seduced by the lure of electric lights like bugs…just the way I was seduced by my own career, and how I was lulled into a state of submission by pharmaceutical drugs that they claimed would make my life better, would help me 'fit in,'" she sneered using air quotes.

"All of those wondrous things kept me from knowing myself. In the end, it abandoned us, because it was never truly legitimate, it was never sustainable. But despite all of that, despite how much we strayed, Gaia gave us a reprieve and had shown us a way to live pure, to live as full-fledged human beings, not consumers of a corporate machine, obeying their script."

Neko nodded more emphatically.

"And here we are, starting it all over again. Electric lights, cars belching fumes....Oh, listen to me. There I go again on my soap box as if I know everything."

"No, Sheriff, I totally agree with you."

Lucille smiled, her brown eyes glinting through the stylish glasses she wore. "You and I understand what the world is about, Neko. You and I...we were both lost before Gaia found us, just as the reverend was. And Reverend Luevano, when I met her...it was like..."

Lucille paused and Neko finished the rest of the sentence. "It was like coming home, and I never knew how much I longed for home until I got there."

"You took the words from my mouth," Lucille said softly.

The light was dying into sunset as the two of them shared a moment of silence save for the crackling of wood in the fireplace.

"She's alive, you know."

Neko turned away from the fire. "How can you be so certain? From what Ezra told me, he doesn't think her boat capsized, but that doesn't mean she's okay either. Things didn't go according to plan apparently."

"No, they didn't. But, sweetheart, Rita is alive. She didn't make it this far in life only to die. She's alive, I promise."

Lucille seemed completely convinced of what she was saying, which comforted Neko.

"But she's in trouble," her tone darkened. "All of us are."

"I've heard. Ezra told me about the Lambs of God mobilizing and the ammunition sales from West Virginia."

"Yes. All of that is true. The Lambs of God appear to be making preparations for a major campaign. But they're waiting for something."

"What?"

Lucille didn't answer. A spike of concern raced up Neko's spine. "Sheriff, what is it?"

After a tense pause, Lucille adjusted her glasses. "Neko, you and I have known each other a long time. Like you, I hadn't felt at home anywhere until Gaia guided me here. And when I arrived, I felt her strength, her grace. It was like being enveloped in happiness. I know this is the same for you as well. I love Monticello. I love Gaia. I love our dear mother with all of my being. She teaches us a responsible search for ourselves."

She took off her glasses revealing her inviting brown eyes. "What religion has ever done that without being hijacked by men who ensnare faith for their own ends? All around us, there are forces that seek to undermine us, Neko. The Lambs of God are just the most visible. But we've always been hounded by bigots and fascists, haven't we? Long before the Shift, long before Gaia acted in her own defense, we lived on borrowed tolerance in the very nation that we founded!"

Lucille stood up. "And now, when it is finally our time, our world to forge on the heels of the Shift, when we can finally, finally lead humanity to the path of reason and enlightenment, there the forces of the old order stand in our way. And they are not willing to go gently into that good night. And they are looking for any means to knock us off the face of the earth for good."

"The Lambs of God…" Neko started, but Lucille shook her head vigorously.

"The Lambs of God are a threat to be sure. But you can see them, you can identify them."

Lucille knelt down in front of her. "Neko, there are enemies who have conspired to bring us down from within. People you and I call 'friends.' The assassination attempt was just the most vulgar expression of a virus that courses throughout Monticello."

Neko shifted uncomfortably, her fingers were going numb again. "Sheriff, what are you saying?"

Lucille's voice softened almost to a whisper. "Sweetie, I didn't come here just to drop off the groceries. I've been conducting an investigation for some time. There are traitors that live among us. They say they're part of our community. They claim to be one of us. They hold offices and are privy to every aspect of our operations. How else do you explain how the Winkelvoss kid was able to get so close, or that the Abercrombies were able to find out exactly when that ship was coming?"

Neko felt cold as she absorbed Lucille's words. It all made sense. She didn't want to believe it, but Lucille was right.

"It's not just speculation or mere suspicion, my dear. My investigation has uncovered proof! There is a well orchestrated conspiracy operating in Monticello, in Rochelle and in Culpeper."

Neko felt the skin dimpling across her neck. "Is the Swan aware of the results of the investigation?"

Lucille scoffed. "The Swan? The Swan is part of it. They are polluted with traitors. Neko, it's just you and me. You know who I'm talking about."

Neko did know. She never voiced it out loud, though. "Christians."

"No need to be ashamed, Neko. You and I are two fortunate individuals who found Gaia. We fought and gave our blood defending our land.

You…" pointing to her lame arm. "You sacrificed yourself in protecting our reverend who has shown us the way."

"It was those people who did this to you. It is they who slip the regent our secrets, and it is they who threaten our existence. Now, it's not all Christians, mind you. Of course not. Most of them are good, loyal Monticellans, as loyal as you and me. You know that as well. That's why it's even more upsetting that these traitors hide among them. I need your help, Neko. That's why I came to you. I can trust you."

"Of course you can. But what can I do? I'm…" She felt an embarrassing amount of emotion welling up in her. "I'm no longer capable of defending Monticello. My days as a warrior are over. I mean, look at me!"

"I am looking at you, my dear. And I see a warrior. The fascist bastards may have struck a blow to your body, but I see your spirit is young and strong. Monticello needs you now more than ever. Not for your archery skills or your ability to fight in hand to hand combat or shoot on horseback. We already have our archers. No, we need your spirit and your voice, Neko."

Neko suddenly felt her self-conscious fear creeping to claim her. "But the reverend is our voice."

"I know. And she is gone right now. She needs your help. We need your help, your voice. I need you, Neko. I need you to be the force of nature that you know you are but have always denied yourself to be in order to expose these jackals."

Neko felt dizzy. In the span of the conversation, the sun had set and night had fallen. The fire was the only light now. Neko took a deep breath.

"You have proof?"

"Yes, I do. And the director of the Swan herself will confirm what I know. She's good people, but she's a little naïve. Don't worry. This is not a witch hunt, Neko. We're the witches, after all, aren't we?"

Lucille grinned and Neko let out an unexpected chuckle.

"Okay. What do we do?"

Chapter 18

Rochelle, Virginia
Rochelle Sovereignty
January 2013

BACKGROUND MUSIC: "Saturday Night Special" by Lynyrd Skynyrd
Visit www.michaeljuge.com **on the *A Hard Rain* page to listen**

"It's a Saturday night special
Got a barrel that's blue and cold
Ain't good for nothing
But put a man six feet in a hole"

Meredith hadn't expected anyone to be in the forge so late in the evening, yet as she walked into the barn, she saw Kyle Womack working on armoring a truck. Lynyrd Skynyrd was pumping out on the speakers Chris had bought a couple of years ago. They were the size of amps that belonged at stadium concerts. At least Rochelle's radio station KVR came in loud and clear inside Rochelle proper with very little static. Kyle was wearing a torn t-shirt and jeans and was soiled with grime. He looked very imposing, but the moment he spoke, his voice betrayed a slight effeminate inflection.

"Sorry, Mrs. Jung. I didn't hear you come in." He grinned sheepishly, having been caught using so much power to blast those huge speakers, with only himself listening. He walked over to the radio to turn it down.

"Don't worry about that, Kyle. I'm just here to pick something up. I'll be out in a second." He was a handsome young man if a bit rough looking, she considered. No wonder Thuy snatched him up.

Kyle went back to riveting plates onto a truck while Meredith took her gloves off and shuffled past a coal fire that kept the barn warm. Over past couple of years, Meredith had stepped inside Chris' business Jung Armoring and Fabricators only a handful of times. She hadn't much need to go there and her duties as the director of the Swan kept her from bothering Chris. This was Chris' creation, his brainchild. She never knew Chris to be an entrepreneur before the Shift. He was quite the opposite in fact, a civil servant. She had never known him to be a soldier either, though. He had never been anything approaching either of these things before the Shift.

She had to believe he was still alive. There was no evidence to the contrary, and some part of her told her that if he had died, she would know it. Going with intuition ran counter to everything she had grown up with, something she had a hard time trusting, but her intuition told her to have faith that he was still alive. With the fate of the world accented with a colossal question mark, what did she have to lose?

Hooks and light bulbs dangled from the barn's ceiling and one wall was covered with strange looking swords Chris had made. She believed he called them "Bat'leth." They were preposterous. In the back of the barn, behind Chris' desk, was a stack of papers and a toolbox. She gingerly removed the stack from behind the desk. On the floor was a safe. She didn't need to refer to any piece of paper as she committed a few select locations like these and their combinations to memory. She didn't know if she would ever need to open this safe and she prayed she wouldn't. She took a deep breath and turned the dial counterclockwise.

Inside was a folder stuffed with Byrds, a small satchel of gold pieces, and a pack of Cream of the Crops underwear still in its original packaging, something that traded better than tobacco. Underneath all of the booty lay a chrome snub nosed revolver. She took the handgun and felt its weight. It had been a dubious Valentine's Day present a few years ago, one she quickly stowed here, because she had no use for one and it was a danger to the kids.

She hurriedly placed the small fortune of money, gold and underwear back into the safe, and stuffed the handgun inside her valise, which could literally hold a small child. After shutting the safe, she returned the papers and toolbox to conceal the safe's existence once again. She left the barn without saying goodbye to Kyle, which she knew was rude, but she was just too flustered. Inside her valise, along with the revolver, were documents that held either meaningless data or her worst fears confirmed. And if that wasn't stressful enough, Rhiannon was sick.

When Meredith returned to the house, she walked upstairs and found Sharon tending to Rhiannon. Mrs. Palfrey was across the hall putting Baby Charles to sleep while Aidan was being entertained by Brandon and his boy Avery who was roughly Aidan's age.

"How are you doing, my sweet?" Meredith sat next to Rhiannon's right while Sharon fixed a vial of medicine.

"I'm sick."

"I know. Dr. Wessinger is going to give you some medicine and it will make you feel better."

"No," she cried.

Stroking her honey-colored locks Meredith said. "Stinkpot, you need to take the medicine. It will help you."

"It tastes bad," she complained. A three year old didn't need more reason than that to refuse.

"Rhiannon, take the medicine now," she commanded sternly. Rhiannon still refused, but Sharon eased the resistance by offering a lollypop, and Rhiannon relented.

Meredith kissed Rhiannon on head and followed Sharon downstairs.

"So," Meredith asked nervously.

"She has the mumps."

"The mumps?"

"Yes, I didn't know what it was at first, but the swollen salivary glands clued me in."

"Oh, my God," Meredith gasped.

Sharon quickly reassured her. "She's going to be fine. Mumps aren't serious, just a pain. It was a normal childhood disease a hundred years ago. Kids recovered without any long term effects…most of the time at least."

Meredith exhaled deeply. She took off her coat and sat down in the living room. She had been handed one devastating blow after another and she feared she was going to be hit again by Sharon delivering the news that her daughter was dying. But fortunately, that wasn't to be today.

Brandon's wife Anne sat down on the couch beside her and held her hand. "It's all right. She's going to be fine. Mumps are no worse than the chicken pox. Sharon gave her some Tylenol substitute." Meredith recognized the West Virginia brand. Another blessing the republic had were silos of chemicals that mixed to produce medicines. Maybe they couldn't make AIDS fighting drugs or relieve restless leg syndrome, but they could produce aspirin and acetaminophen, though they were exorbitantly expensive now that those chemicals were a finite resource until the day industrialization could fully get back on its feet. West Virginia was the only nation close to achieving that.

"Thank you, Anne. I was just so worried!" She tried to hold it in, but the emotions were too powerful, and Anne was a friend in addition to her colleague in the Swan. "My God, mumps? I'd never thought I would ever have to think about that."

"It's hard to accept, I know. Childhood diseases, diseases long thought dead, they've all made a resurgence since vaccinations all but disappeared."

Anne was right. Both of them were privy to information throughout the Mid-Atlantic. Meredith heard about feral children dying of things like measles and chickenpox. Malnourished as they were, feral children stood little chance. Other diseases had made resurgence as well, such as typhus and cholera. She feared that they would inevitably reach the settled lands - it was only a matter of time. And the worst part was, they no longer had the medications to fight it off. Vaccinations were a thing of the past. She had grown up in a generation that did not know death. All of her schoolmates survived childhood, untainted by disease save for mono and chickenpox and unscathed besides the typical emotional bruises.

Her children's generation was a different story. No matter how hygienic Rochelle was, come winter, diseases found their way into homes. Colds and flu, once a nuisance, now carried a potential for death. Aidan had schoolmates who had died, so too did Rhiannon. They were helpless before nature just as her great grandparents were. Meredith finally understood all of the old wives tales, the songs, and she now understood why people were so damned religious in the old days. They had no other recourse. Meredith found herself praying for her children's health every day.

Aidan had suffered from tonsillitis repeatedly. Before the Shift, Dr. Wessinger would have said, "bring him over to the office and we'll have them removed." Today, it was considered major surgery, and Sharon just did not want to risk such a procedure as it wasn't absolutely necessary. Rhiannon always got ear infections, poor girl. There was nothing to be done for her when they came save for home remedies, i.e. vodka. Now she was sick again.

Fortunately, this illness wasn't deadly. *This time,* she thought mordantly. How long would their luck hold out? Would all three children make it to adulthood? She knew the odds were better than fifty percent, but not comfortably so, and that was absolutely unacceptable. If one of her children died…if her husband died and then one of her children died…she didn't know how to finish that sentence.

"Sometimes," she paused to catch herself. "Sometimes, I feel like that somewhere out there it's normal, and we're just the unlucky ones still stuck out in the wilderness. I want to take Aidan, take Rhiannon and Charles, take them away from all of this, take them somewhere safe, where they can grow up with a *normal* childhood, and not have to worry that the next staph infection might require amputation! I would give anything I had to make sure they were safe. *Anything.*"

Anne wrapped her arm around her, providing Meredith with a shoulder to release her frustration. "I know. There isn't a sane mother alive who wouldn't."

Meredith waited for the kids to go to sleep. Meredith grabbed her valise, put on her over coat, and got on her horse.

"Come on, Corolla, giddy up."

She never mastered horse riding. That was partly her fault. She had a driver and it was so much more convenient to sit inside a carriage rather than fighting with a horse out in the elements. She struggled to get Corolla to obey her commands; the problem lay in the fact that she gave confusing commands, something that Chris often had accused her of doing with him.

At the gate near Highway 29, the old border of Rochelle proper before it annexed all of Madison and Orange counties, she found Thuy Mai standing next to an old Chevy Suburban and a garbage truck, both of which had been heavily armored. Nothing leaving the safe confines of the settled lands was unarmored. The few hotrod muscle cars they had were used for reconnaissance. Old Camaros and Trans Ams were faster than armored transport and fighting vehicles, being able to reach speeds up to fifty-five miles per hour with the substandard gasoline they consumed, but they were highly vulnerable to gunfire. A regular pistol round could tear through the metal, no less a rifle round.

"Evening. What's a nice young lady doing out on a cold night like this?" he said with resilient mirth.

"Looking for a big strong man," she said in a desperate attempt to lighten her mood.

"Funny. I was going to say the same thing." Thuy walked over to her and helped with the saddlebags towards the awaiting vehicles.

"Meredith, I can't tell you how bad an idea this is, you going out there. If Chris was here..." His voice trailed off.

If Chris were here, maybe he would talk me out of what I was planning, and maybe I would agree with him. But that was *if only.*

Thuy rephrased his statement. "Meredith if you hadn't heard from your latest intel briefs, Stokesville is in the middle of unsettled lands. Once we're passed Charlottesville, it's Thunderdome, honey, Thunder-dome. You have too many responsibilities here to be going out on this jaunt."

"You don't have to remind me. I have three children, one of them sick with the mumps. And they're going to wake up with their mom gone. They're already upset with their dad being gone. Aidan and Rhiannon keep asking when he'll be home. And I don't have the heart to tell them that I don't know if he'll ever return."

"So, why in God's name are you going? It's bad enough that Rita went on her vision quest to the suburbs. Shit, that's probably why the regent is gearing up for war. He knows Monticello is scrambling without their leader. We don't need to reproduce that here, Meredith."

"I have to go. I need to deconflict the information myself, hear it from the horse's mouth. You can understand that, can't you?"

Reluctantly, he nodded.

"The question is then with what you said about Rochelle needing its leaders in place, why are you going with me?"

"Are you kidding? Once Chris gets back and he finds out I just let you go on a mission like this, out to Nowheresville, and I didn't go with you... well, I know that will be the end of the little wrought iron decorations I get every Christmas."

Meredith rolled her eyes and snorted with bemusement. "I'm serious, Thuy. I appreciate you coming, but you haven't been the same since Madison High. I can see you're in pain whenever you force yourself to walk without a limp."

"You're very perceptive," he said with uncharacteristic seriousness. "I might not move as fast as I used to, that's why I have a few of our Vicious Rabbits coming along, but I also bring a lot of street experience. And to tell you the truth, I can't just sit around and wait to find out what the deal is until your return. I need to know *now* as bad as you."

Meredith grinned despite everything. She was indeed very grateful that he was going with her. She didn't know what she was going to find, or what to do if she heard the worst fears confirmed. She couldn't bear to think about it. But with an old friend by her side, they would learn of their collective fate together. Meredith gave Thuy a hug.

"Careful, people will talk."

"Oh, quiet, you."

Just as she opened the door to the Suburban, Thuy presented a pistol in the palm of his hand.

"Just in case."

She then pulled out the chrome revolver. "I'm covered."

"And I just thought you were happy to see me."

Thuy and Meredith then climbed into the 70s era Suburban relieved to get out of the cold. Along the way, they detoured off of Highway 29 and trundled past Stanardsville where she caught site of Flint's Exxon station, the site of the seminal battle known as the Rout at Exxon Heights. It became a part of Rochelle's illustrious mythology, propelled by her husband's colorful and grand retelling of the events. Back then at the climax of the Obsidian War, Jon Early was focused, driven, and sober. Thuy had warned against her leaving, citing that Greater Monticello had lost their leader. It hit her as they passed a plaque commemorating the battle that Rochelle had lost its leader some time ago.

The motorcade found its way onto I-64 and crossed past the western gates of Greater Monticello into no man's land and the Blue Ridge Mountains. The vehicles' engines groaned as they slowly wove up and down the mountainous interstate; their lights were dim to avoid announcing their presence to ferals. Bandits weren't too common between here and Staunton as the Vicious Rabbits and Monticellan Defense Force were religious with keeping their backyards clean, but this was the mountains. Staunton would be their first stop on the way to Stokesville. She briefly recalled going to Staunton with Chris once, sometime shortly before she got pregnant with Aidan.

Chapter 19

"Chris! RPG!"

The moonless night sky was bathed in light from flares slowly teetering to earth, their descent slowed down by parachutes. Through the trees, Chris saw an Obsidian Corp security specialist aiming a rocket-propelled grenade in his general direction. Chris raised the sights of his M4 and fired. The man was dead before he hit the ground, a headshot.

"Go, go, go!" he commanded as he slid down the muddy hill, half falling along the way, trying not to lose control of his approach or his bladder, incidentally. The thunderous tearing sound of the .30 caliber machinegun tore at men's will just as it did their bodies.

The flares' light died into the night as Chris and his platoon raced toward the barricade. He switched to full auto and fired behind a pine tree, which provided absolutely no protection from gunfire, but at least it gave some concealment. He turned to see the white eyes of Gunnery Sergeant Birmingham behind him, his face caked in mud.

"Push through!"

Chris nodded and cried out. "Push through!"

He charged the barricade avoiding rounds by mere luck, his legs pumping furiously to reach the other side. As he ran, he raised his rifle and heard a sound, a sound that wasn't right. It got louder, a pulsating wail that rang throughout the darkened forest. Mere meters from the berm, his brain registered what the alien pulsating wail was, some kind of alarm clock.

Falls Church, Virginia
January 2013

The wind rushed past, following the Metro train like a ghost, adding insult for anyone who was left on the platform at West Falls Church station. Chris didn't mind the cold. He had plenty of experience living with constant exposure to the elements and without the benefit of wearing a wool suit, a thick pea coat and fur lined leather gloves. They didn't wear well for riding or fighting.

Likewise, Chris didn't mind missing the train. In fact, he didn't *miss* the train at all, really. He let it pass him by, moving out of the way to allow other passengers to board instead. In fact, this was the fourth train that he chose not to board. The train status display overhead reported that another DC bound Orange Line train would arrive in four minutes, another two minutes behind that one, and a third one two minutes behind that. It was morning rush hour.

Rush hour...The term itself had become as alien to him as the scene around him. A sea of strangers stood, dressed in dry cleaned suits. Men were cleanly shaven, women had their hair done up. They were docile and acted as if nothing had ever happened. None of them were gangly, diseased, starving or dying. Below the station, sleek polished automobiles jockeyed for position along the ill-conceived Interstate 66; none of them were fitted with armor. A voice mumbled something unintelligible over the intercom while a woman standing next to him casually read a book on some "ereader" thing, completely unaware of how dangerous the world truly was.

Chris felt a sudden surge of nausea, due in part to his concussion, the rest due to his attempt to make sense of the world around him. The disorientation of it all threatened to swallow him whole. *Breathe, Chris, breathe.* Following his internal instructions, he drew in the frosty morning air.

Several days had passed since he awoke to find himself here in this place that just couldn't be. It wasn't the past. He knew that much. It was 2013, his time. But something happened, something that he couldn't comprehend, because in this place the Shift never happened. It sounded impossible, it sounded ridiculous, it sounded insane, but it was also the undeniable truth.

From the hospital, Meredith drove him and their *two* kids back to their apartment, the same dilapidated, cheap-ass, cramped little apartment he escaped from years ago. It was the same apartment where he, Meredith, Brandon, Anne and Thuy had last rested before setting off to leave the Beltway region and with it the world they had known for good. It was there where he endured the panic, the senseless and unyielding torment, the greatest betrayal of his mind that incessantly honed on the unbreakable thought about his tinnitus, his insomnia and his panic, which only reinforced the panic. It was where he lay, on the futon night after night, unable to sleep, watching TV hoping to be lulled into unconsciousness, yet as exhausted as he was, he was unable to rest. In truth, he wouldn't have minded if he never saw that cursed apartment again. When he left five and a half years ago, secretly, he was glad to leave, glad to see it all recede behind him like waking from a horrible nightmare and realizing it was only a bad dream.

While convalescing inside the dreaded memory of an apartment, Chris took the opportunity to acquaint himself with this "reality," for lack of better words. He made his way over to the iMac, which had been moved from the study to their bedroom since Yorick's arrival a few years ago—around the time his Rhiannon was born, interestingly. Gingerly, he pecked at the keyboard, amazed as the machine glowed to life, unmolested by any EMP. Chris' typing skills had fallen sharply over the past five and a half years. He typed with the dexterity of a lumbering oaf, eyeing every key suspiciously. While contending with headaches and slight dizziness, Chris searched through the collective mind of Google and the democratically congealed truth of Wikipedia in order to decipher what happened, where history changed course. Having seen *Back to the Future II* and having read Harry Turtledove enough times, he knew there was always a point of departure between one timeline and the tangent timeline, one particular event that altered everything else. If he could determine exactly when the timelines diverged, then he might discover what caused the divergence. Maybe he could find his way out of this place.

According to Wiki and BBC archived newsfeeds, everything up until July 11th seemed to coincide with his fading memory of historical events before the Shift. He was surprised by how much he had forgotten. It was as though the world before the Shift was distant a memory, much more than the span of half a decade. His life before the Shift had felt more and more like a dream, an increasingly bad dream, and then he awoke and with it the details of the world that receded into the ether.

That being said, Chris remembered the basics before the Shift. September 11th happened exactly as he remembered and Bush—the second one—was President at the time, not Al Gore, so that went according to the grand plan. The US went into Afghanistan and Iraq. Bush got re-elected, then there was Katrina, *American Idol* and inane reality TV shows saturating the airwaves, there was a brief war between Israel and Lebanon, *Friends* overstayed its welcome until it finally concluded. Everything added up to his recollection. There was nothing that strayed from his historical take up until the Shift.

At a loss, Chris typed "July 11, 2007" on Wikipedia and perused through events of the day. China banned diethylene glycol as an ingredient in toothpaste, 14 Filipino marines were killed by insurgents, in Britain four people who carried out the failed follow up suicide bombing in 2005 were jailed for life, CERN tested their particle accelerator, the Organization for the Prohibition of Chemical Weapons confirmed the destruction of the entire chemical weapons stockpiles in Albania, the Supreme Court in Libya upheld the death penalty for six Bulgarian and one Palestinian doctors accused of infecting children with HIV, Crown Prince Abdul-Aziz Al Saud announced increased production of oil from President Bush's Crawford ranch.

Except for the last bit about the Crown Prince's visit to the Crawford ranch, Chris couldn't confirm or deny any of these events having happened in his reality. It was a string of meaningless news snippets. But there was absolutely no news of a planet wide electromagnetic pulse wiping out all of the solid-state electronics, where everything with a microchip got fried. There was no mention about the industrialized world plunging into darkness. There were no reports of any EMPs at all, in fact.

July 11, 2007 was just another day at the office, another hot summer day where soldiers and insurgents from various nations fought and died in Godforsaken places, children starved, stocks rose, people went to work, children learned to ride bicycles, people died in car crashes, but the world turned just the same.

So what in the hell happened? As he waited for the next train, Chris was struck again by the thought that maybe he did die when he took the dive off *The Interceptor* and onto the pavement, and this was, well, it wasn't heaven. That was for damned sure. His idea of heaven did not involve living in an overcrowded, roach infested apartment with paper-thin walls where he could hear the upstairs neighbor's kids running back and forth, back and forth, back and forth, hear the downstairs neighbor's Latin pop as clear as if it were playing in his living room, and the next door neighbors arguing. But it was also too pedestrian to be hell. He knew what hell was, and as soul sucking as this place was, it wasn't hell. Maybe the Catholics were right and this was some form of purgatory, kind of like a shitty waiting room of an afterlife.

If this wasn't the afterlife, then maybe he was in a coma. "No, that's pretty thin," he muttered to himself. Nobody standing beside him on the Metro platform paid him any mind.

This place felt real enough, but it was some surreal, weird-assed, sideways world, the kind of wacky science fiction premise contrived from *Star Trek*, the one where the Federation and the Enterprise crew were the bad guys and Spock wore a goatee. Except here, instead of being thrust into a world where the Confederacy had prevailed or Kennedy—either one—survived the assassination attempts, Chris was thrust into a world where the Shift never happened. He and Meredith only had two children and Rhiannon was a slightly younger and was now a boy named Yorick.

He didn't want to tip his hand to anyone that he didn't belong here. The injury sustained in the carjacking was a plausible excuse to claim some form of amnesia, and he knew he was going to have to use it a lot, but he didn't want to exploit it more than necessary; otherwise, well, he just didn't want anyone to find out what his true situation was, which he himself didn't know.

In order to minimize the amnesia excuse, Chris spent the days at home going over the clues to his counterpart's life. The ID badge in his messenger bag told him that he still worked with the US Department of State, but he wasn't certain that he was still with Diplomatic Security, whether his office had moved to another building or not or if he worked in another agency. But then he picked up his professional journal. Thankfully, Chris had always been meticulous with his professional notes. There was some scribbling that he didn't understand, a new kind of meeting that he went to weekly, a database, he believed, but other than that it contained the same kind of notes he remembered writing back when he was here in 2007. He deduced from the notes that he was still an intelligence analyst and was still with Diplomatic Security's International Threat Assessment Division. He just hoped they hadn't moved the office.

BACKGROUND MUSIC: "Afraid of Everyone" by The National
Visit www.michaeljuge.com **on the *A Hard Rain* page to listen**

Chris left before sunrise, desperate to leave the confines of the apartment. But now standing on the platform after letting four trains pass, he found himself terrified to go any further.

The lights on the edge of the platform flashed announcing the arrival of the next train.

"Okay, let's do this."

The train screeched along the rails and came to a stop. When the doors opened, Chris stole enough courage to step into the train. For someone who was on the raid at Madison High, who had fought in the Obsidian War, who led forays into the wasteland countless times, who had faced his demons, the idea that stepping onto a train to head to work would paralyze him seemed absurd. Yet Chris knew his mental architecture was an intricate network of neuroses, memories and drives that wove a confounding tapestry.

After finding a comfortable place to stand, Chris pulled out his iPhone and thumbed through musicians on the touch screen. The device was pretty self-explanatory, but it was absolutely fascinating to scroll through whole albums with the touch of a finger. On the list, other Chris had compiled some classic rock, but he had his fill of fossil rock back in his world. One of the few things he missed from before the Shift was the contemporary indie bands whose music was all recorded onto CDs and MP3s. None of their music survived the Shift. Chris selected to play from the recently purchased list.

The train ran parallel to Interstate 66, racing past vehicles slowly creeping in both directions for the morning commute. He noticed how clean and new the cars looked. The only vehicles driving on the road in his world were built before the 80s. Newer vehicles, post millennium models like the ones on the road now, were rusting heaps back home. The train pitched slightly and headed deep underground, leaving the sun and the shiny automobiles behind as he and the rest of the passengers descended into darkness.

Rosslyn Station looked exactly the way he remembered it, the way it appeared to him in dreams. Indirect lighting from the floor cast shadows on the grey concrete arches that loomed over him as he stepped from the train into the station. The momentum of disembarking passengers pushed him from behind, as the boarding passengers squirmed into the cars and battled for seats. After the automated announcement chimed, the doors slid closed and the train screeched off. Chris suddenly felt particularly unsafe. Strangers were all around him in this underground tunnel, a place that carried with it horrible memories. Instinctively, Chris reached for a sidearm that did not exist, leaving him feeling naked, even though he logically knew that was irrational.

He walked along the cold tile floor, his steps echoing in the drab gray cathedral-like platform of Rosslyn Station. As he ascended the imposingly long escalator from darkness into daylight, he felt a freezing gust of wind blow battling with the temperate air below.

The last time Chris was here was a couple of days after the Shift first struck when he picked up *The Interceptor*—it was just his nameless Kona mountain bike back then—and was about to head back to Brandon's apartment when he conceived the plan that would save their lives. It was on these escalator steps alone in the eerie dead silence that he thought up the idea of fleeing DC to head to Brandon's parents' home in Rochelle. That plan wasn't conceived idly, but rather it was born out of his decision to *not* end his life right here, or at least to postpone his original plans for July 12th until he got Meredith to safety. The morning was turning up a lot of memories he had happily stashed away long ago.

Chris knew that he talked a lot of hooey in his life; he had a propensity for over- generalizations and gross exaggeration. But he knew down in his gut that the decision he made on the eve of the Shift to kill himself was not just talk; it wasn't just an empty threat. Chris knew he had every intention to "stumble" onto the tracks at the "wrong moment" when a train arrived at the platform. Chris had never been so intent on anything in his life. He *knew* he was going to do it. Nothing was going to stop him. But alas, something must have happened to stop him, because here he was, moping around all these years later. Lord knew what it was that stopped him in this reality.

Once above ground, Chris shuffled across the icy catwalk that overlooked Rosslyn and Georgetown University atop the hill just across the Potomac River. Arlington Police pulled over drivers for expired inspection tags, exacerbating the gridlock traffic in the morning commute. A siren blared, setting off a chorus of horns as drivers urged each other to move it. Men and women dressed in business attire and overcoats stood in line outside the Starbucks that he used to give a lot of business. A commercial jet airliner flew unsettlingly low over the Potomac as it approached Reagan National Airport a few miles away. Nobody else seemed perturbed by it. Civilization…the world of machines, of broadcast media, of daily international flights to London, it was here pulsating before him.

Chris became dizzy witnessing the impossible. He tucked his coat in closer and made his way over to the glittery façade of the skyscraper that housed Diplomatic Security headquarters.

"Hey, Chris!"

Chris turned around to see a young man with a blonde fro smiling and extending his hand. He was squat and looked kind of like a giant hobbit or a barely average height man, depending.

"Dude, that looks like it hurt," he said indicating to Chris' forehead.

Chris assumed that this young man was probably a coworker. He sure hoped he was. Without hesitating Chris answered. "Yeah, but not as bad as the side of my head," turning around to show where the doctors shaved part of his scalp and stitched up an inch long cut. Chris idly noticed how his counterpart had short hair as opposed to his shoulder-length mane and was clean shaven; this version of himself didn't have a two-pronged goatee like he wore. *The goatee again, just like evil Spock. Strange.*

"Ouch. Well, I'm glad to see you're well enough to make it back to work. It's been a madhouse without you, Chris, a madhouse!"

Chris smiled. "Well, I guess we should head on in then, shouldn't we?"

After a little trouble with building security for forgetting his PIN, he and the tall hobbit walked into the office. Chris followed him and mostly listened to names being thrown out, none of them he knew. It had been a long time.

"Farcus is going ballistic over last month's numbers."

"Hmm."

"I'd be careful around him right now. He's particularly premenstrual."

"I'll be sure to remember that."

Chris stopped in front of the cubicle where he worked five and a half years ago to find that he still did. A placard with his name on it was slapped up against the panel wall. *I wonder what that says about the other Chris.* The young man went inside the cubicle next to his. Chris discreetly saw the name posted in his neighbor's cubicle—Theodore Morley III. He sat down and stared at the computer screen with a floating login box. The same lock cabinet, the same six by eight foot space, the same cell of a world dead long ago had finally caught up with him.

In that moment, Chris felt the weight of those years catching up with him, feeling more a forty-year-old than he had running away from mortar shells and religious zealots. Here he had done none of those things, here that world had never been. All that happened in this reality happened inside this tiny cubicle. A terror suddenly welled up inside him. Were none of his memories real? Was this really where he spent the last several years? How could it be? His heart started to race. He was trapped. If this was another reality and not some delusion, he had no idea how to get back to where he belonged. The tinnitus cranked up again.

"Oh, shit. What in the hell am I going to do?" he whispered.

"Chris, what in the hell are you doing here?"

Chris knew that voice. It wasn't Ted—he presumed Theodore would go by Ted. It was a woman's voice, and he knew that voice almost as well as his own wife's. It was her all right.

"K…Kendra?"

CHAPTER 20

Linthicum Heights, Maryland
January 2013

Rita Luevano stood outside on the porch taking her turn at watch. Her feet were now officially colder than the concrete she stood on. The boots and socks she wore hadn't dried sufficiently since the landing at Fort Armistead Park several days ago. Next to her, a porch swing dangled precariously from a single chain. Squirrels, who made a nest in the collapsing overhang, scurried from her presence. She didn't mind taking her turn at watch. She needed to get out of the house. Tomorrow they would be making the push to Helmut's office for whatever good that would do. Rita knew they couldn't stay here, and Gunnery Sergeant Birmingham and Lieutenant Baraka were intent on completing the mission and denying the Abercrombies the chance of acquiring the nukes. Yet, something just didn't add up in her way of thinking.

"Abuelita," she called out into the cold night sky and paused before she chuckled mirthlessly. Gaia had chosen her for reasons she never quite understood. Gaia appeared to her in visions and guided her through the pivotal early years, and yet Rita felt reticent about calling to her for help just because she was scared and unsure how to proceed. As ridiculous it was, she didn't want to appear needy to the great Earth mother spirit; she wanted to maintain control over her own life and her destiny wherever she could. Rita was a reluctant prophet if there ever was one.

She had no idea why Gaia had sent her here; it didn't make sense. In fact, nothing made sense. She had just finished having another conversation with Chris who clearly was out of his gourd. Rita hoped that his apparent amnesia would subside and his memories would return after some rest. But it wasn't amnesia. It was something she couldn't explain.

And then there was that strange character Helmut Spankmeister. Something about him, his body language, his eyes...she couldn't articulate exactly what it was, but she was convinced he was holding something back, something monumentally important. Her spider senses were telling her that Helmut was lying. She couldn't explain why except that she started running numbers in her head; how many days he had been out in the wilderness, how many calories he needed to survive, how he was able to maintain his body weight. She couldn't begin to explain how she was able to do such complex mathematical equations—she figured it was a perk of being a prophet or something—but regardless, the numbers suggested that there was no way Helmut could have made it out here as long as he did by just foraging. He was skinny but not undernourished. She told Akil about her suspicions discreetly. He agreed, but had no better idea what it was Helmut was holding back.

"Am I disturbing you?"

Rita turned around to see Kendra standing before her wearing a man's overcoat, which she appropriated in the master bedroom. Rita hadn't realized how much time had passed. Lieutenant Baraka was her relief on the push schedule. Kendra continued. "You looked like you were in communion, Reverend."

Rita smirked. She would have surmised that Kendra was a convert even if she had just met her. Something about Unitarians, Rita figured. Perhaps Gaia gave her some sort of "Gaiadar" on top of her *Rain Man*-like mathematical abilities. Kendra's reverent demeanor towards her would also be a tip off not to mention the medallion around her neck. Rita indicated to it and Kendra understood allowing her to examine it.

"The Captain...Chris, he made it for me for the Solstice in the second year," she said meaning the winter of 2008. Rita noticed it was rather crude for Chris' work, a casting from a clumsily designed mold, but it was still clearly the emblem of the Unitarian chalice and flame.

As if reading her mind, Kendra added, "This was one of Chris' early works before his forge became a full scale factory. He made the casting for the new medallions going around now and tried to pawn one of his newer ones made of silver. But I didn't want it, and I refused to take it off." Kendra smiled mischievously. "It was the sweetest thing I ever got. No boyfriend was ever so sweet, and he's just my commanding officer."

"He's also your friend."

"Yes," Kendra answered. "His story, Reverend, it doesn't make sense."

"No, it doesn't."

Chris had spun a tale about a world that met July 12th with a mundane yawn as if it were any other day. In his version of reality, there was no Shift. And it wasn't just some vague meanderings about a world where the Shift hadn't happened. Chris was really specific, as specific as she would be if she were telling her life story these last five and a half years. Although slightly out of it from the concussion, Chris was lucid enough to give details about his supposed recollections. His telling of this fantasy world was so vivid; his personal life was fantastically dull. Nobody would make up such vapid and unworthy details. He talked about TV shows, viral videos on YouTube, getting "rick rolled?" and the latest video game where players ran around shooting Nazi zombie ninjas. He talked about some "social media revolution" that had spurred literal revolutions throughout the world. He seemed completely earnest as he spoke.

Rita almost believed that he came from that make believe world, but then he said some things that clued her in that his mind had crafted this fantasy world, things like that Obama guy becoming president and the Saints winning the Super Bowl. She had become familiar with the NFL teams as part of her study on human collective behavior and wound up falling for the loveable losers from New Orleans. She reasoned that Chris' meeting with Jean Paul Nguyen and his sailors, the Saints, from his hometown could have shaken him up a bit. It would then make sense that his mind constructed a fantasy around the Saints. Rita also remembered something about the young senator who was making Hillary Clinton nervous. Rita loved a good Cinderella story, but that was all it was, a fantasy. Everyone was taken aback by Chris and seemed equally confused, all except Helmut Spankmeister. Helmut just nodded expectantly. Helmut was the key to all of this, whatever this was. He was holding something back, something really important.

Inside the living room, a couple of candles glowed dimly. The small party pulled the mattresses from the other rooms and huddled together beside the entertainment center for combined warmth. A scattering of DVDs and CDs lay beside the TV while a couple of photographs of the previous occupants haunted the walls. Chris was sitting up now and was eating some hard tack and soup, which was a good sign. Next to him sat

Gunnery Sergeant Birmingham, Akil and Helmut Spankmeister who stood up as she approached and placed her assault rifle by the coffee table.

Wasting no time, she stomped over the mattresses up to Spankmeister who grinned at her in a way that hinted of a familiarity he hadn't earned. That seemed to annoy her more than anything else and reinforced her resolve that something was wrong.

"Helmut, what's going on here?"

"I…I don't understand."

With restrained calm, she continued with a counselor's tone, "Helmut, there aren't any loose nukes out on the road. Tell me, please, why have you brought us out this way?"

Helmut stammered. "Rita, I told you, the Abercrombies want to gather the nuclear waste to use in dirty bombs…"

There it was again, that casual way he addressed her, the casual way he looked at her. "Helmut, I'm asking you, please tell me the truth."

"But…I mean the Abercrombies…"

Gunnery Sergeant Birmingham moved with unexpected swiftness for someone with such a massive frame, grabbed the scrawny scientist by the fabric of his sweater and pinned him against the wall, nearly punching him through the cheap decaying sheetrock.

"You setting us up, buggar?"

Even in the darkness, Rita could see Helmut's face drain of blood. He gulped unable to make words, choked in fright as he was. Rita touched Birmingham's forearm, indicating to ease up on Helmut and put him down.

Practiced in the art of communication, she urged gently, "Helmut, now is the time for you to come clean with us, and tell us the truth."

"Rita…"

"You address 'er as Chief Magistrate, ma'am or Reverend, boyo!"

"Reverend," Helmut corrected himself, "I swear I'm not setting you up."

"But there is no loose nuclear material, is there," she coaxed.

Rita remembered Lucille Schadenfreude referring to this point of an interrogation as the "come-to-Jesus moment," the point in the conversation where the crook knew the gig was up and had an opportunity to save himself by confessing. Helmut stared at her imploring, almost as if begging her to stand between him and the gunny before he acquiesced. He shook his head, admitting that her intuition was correct.

"Why you, bloody…" Birmingham was moving in to swallow the little man whole but Rita's stepped forward to Helmut's defense. The gunny bellowed, "You sack of shit! You've got a roit lot of good people killed! And for what! Reverend, please allow me to extinguish the life out of this wanker!"

"It's not for nothing!" Helmut screamed out desperately. "I promise."

"Okay, everybody, let's calm down. Gunny, please give Mr. Spankmeister a little space."

The gunnery sergeant barked at one of the more meaty Vicious Rabbits. "Porkins, relieve the LT outside. She's gotta 'ear this." He moved a few feet back as Rita requested. A moment later, Lieutenant Baraka entered the living room, bringing in a snow-speckled gust with her.

Helmut slumped down on the mattress next to Chris, who was shooting glances at everyone in the room, trying to figure out what was going on. Helmut put his hands to his head. "I didn't intend for any one of you to get killed, but I needed to get you up here, Rita."

"Wait a minute, what's going on here," Kendra inquired.

"This buggar's been joshing us, LT. They aren't any nukes. He made the whole thing up!"

"What?" she gasped. "You led us to the Abercrombies?"

"No, ma'am," Helmut answered defiantly. "The Abercrombies are just as convinced about the loose nuclear material as you were. I made it up to give me time when they caught me."

Helmut wiped his nose with his sleeve before continuing. "I was outside the office when the Abercrombies picked me up. I couldn't tell them where I came from or what I was doing. They questioned me and I gave them a story to distract them. I used to be responsible for keeping track of nuclear waste disposal for the DOE."

Some people looked confused by the acronym. Helmut clarified. "The Department of Energy...well, actually I work with the Stubb Foundation, which contracted with DOE. So, I guess the loose nukes story just popped into my head."

"And then you told us the same story," Rita added. "Why?"

"Because, there's something I need you to see, Rita. I mean Reverend."

When he said "something I need you to see," he was referring to her specifically, not "you" in the plural as in the Monticellans and Vicious Rabbits. Slowly, Rita pointed to herself. "Something *I* need to see?"

Helmut nodded before she followed up. "What is so important that you need *me*?" Then another question popped into her head. "And if you're from some 'office' up here, how do you even know about me?"

Helmut stood up cautiously, eying the gunny warily for any sudden movements. "Let me ask you something. Have you been experiencing strange dreams or…I don't know, um, visions maybe?"

The gunny snorted. "You're talking to the One-eyed witch of UU, mate! That's like asking if a dog licks 'is balls every once in a once, no offense, Gov."

Rita completely ignored the colorful analogy, typical of the Aussie/Scot Vicious Rabbit, because what Helmut asked resonated with her.

"Yes, I have." The steam of her breath filled the candlelit room. "It's different from the visions I'm used to having." Rita would have laughed at that very comment before the Shift, as though there were pedantic supernatural phenomena like the spirit of the Earth speaking to her and then there were the weird ones. She continued. "It's not Gaia speaking; it's like déjà vu…but about things I don't remember."

"And it started happening here, right?" Helmut asked.

"Something like that, yes."

"Are you saying there's something…magical about Maryland?" Kendra asked.

Chris interjected. "Kendra, there is absolutely *nothing* magical about Maryland."

"No, not really," Helmut answered. He knelt down to Chris. "But Chris here, he's not out of his mind."

"Thanks, Dr. Strangelove, but as reassuring as your prognosis is, I'd like a second opinion," Chris said sardonically.

"You're saying that my déjà vu and Chris' memories are related?"

Helmut nodded. She could tell a burden was lifting from this man. He was telling the truth, even if it made no sense to her.

"Chris remembers things the way he does because in his reality, the Shift didn't happened."

"Excuse me," Kendra asked, raising her hand. "But I've seen a plethora of sad sacks out there who have been traumatized by the Shift. In their reality, they deny the Shift happened, too."

"That's not a reality, Lieutenant, that's a coping mechanism. I said Chris' *reality*. In Chris' reality, the Shift didn't happen."

"That's bullshit, mate. The Shift did 'appen; otherwise, we've just really overreacted over a power outage, wot?"

"Yes, the Shift did happen, of course," Helmut conceded before adding, "*And* it didn't."

The room fell silent, so quiet that Rita could hear a pack of dogs howling several blocks away.

"How?" she whispered.

"It is something easier explained if I show you."

"At your office," she finished for him.

"Wait a tic, Gov. You're buying this bullocks?"

"Gunny, are you saying you haven't experienced any of what Mr. Spankmeister has been talking about?"

Birmingham hesitated. "Well, I've not slept much lately. The mind's been known for jerking me around under duress."

"So, in other words you've been experiencing it, too," she concluded. "Helmut, you said you needed me to come. Why me?"

"Again, Reverend, it will all become clear at the office. I can't explain it here, but I can show you."

"Hold on now," Kendra said. "There are no nukes. It's a wild goose chase, right? So, why are we going to your office? I say we bug the hell out of here and limp our asses back home."

"LT, this is important," Rita answered. "I know you don't trust Mr. Spankmeister here, but I ask you to trust me. Do you trust me?"

Kendra nodded reluctantly.

"Good. I know we have lost a lot of friends on this mission. I do not intend for it to be in vain. Helmut has risked his life to get me over here. Whatever it is, I think it's something more than any of us can fathom right now, but our very future depends upon it."

"Well, the Captain's sort of out of it with all due respect," Kendra inclined to Chris. "So, Reverend, as they say, you're the decider."

"My office has more than enough food. And we might be able to help resupply you with ammo, too."

Rita knelt down. "Chris, how are you feeling?"

The burly Vicious Rabbit tugged on his two-pronged chin beard as if it was part of a costume. "Well, I feel a lot of anxiety, I admit, like I'm..."

"No, Chris, physically. How are you feeling *physically*? Do you think you're up to riding twenty miles or more?"

"Oh, right. Sorry. Yeah, I'm not really dizzy anymore. I mean, not more than normal." He gathered himself. "Yeah, I think I can ride."

"Good. Any objections, LT, Gunny?"

"I don't like it, Gov," Gunnery Sergeant Birmingham protested. "But we've run out of supplies 'ere and options. It's either go with the professor or throw our lot in with the Maryland ferals."

As the ad hoc meeting broke up, Helmut slunk away. She walked over to him and whispered. "Mr. Spankmeister, I don't know what's going on, but I know you're not lying to me. For whatever reason, you need me. So, I will indulge you on this for one day." She then pulled him closer and softly added.

"Maybe I trust too easily, but I assure you the gunny doesn't. If you're pulling something, I know he will make sure you don't die quickly. Comprende?"

Helmut gulped and managed to say, "Yes, Rit…Reverend."

BACKGROUND MUSIC: "The Lion's Roar" by First Aid Kit
Visit www.michaeljuge.com **on the *A Hard Rain* page to listen**

Chris hadn't remembered feeling this much anxiety since…well, it wasn't as bad as the Panic of '07, nothing had been that bad before or since, thankfully. That being said, "holy shit" were the only words to adequately articulate his situation since coming to a few days ago. Here he was, cycling with this smelly group of banditos or whatever, nursing his injury that made him more nauseous than he felt since he saw that monstrosity of a film *2012*. Getting hit on the head was disorienting enough. Waking up in some Cormac McCarthy inspired suburb was worse. When he first awoke, he was convinced that he had been kidnapped by some Liberty Party wackos, and they were going to have a little fun with a minor functionary of the evil federal government like himself. He started calculating the likelihood that the Department of State would pay for his release. But when he saw his colleague Kendra, he knew. These weren't some Liberty Party goons.

Whatever was going on, it was bizarre. Kendra and that reverend lady with the eye patch spun a wild tale, something that begged to be made into a TV series on AMC. Except—and Chris had a hard time explaining it—when Kendra and Rita told him about this *Shift* thing that supposedly happened five and a half years ago, it somehow struck him as true. Chris was familiar with this world. It reminded him of something, like an afterthought or a dream that dissolved when the conscious world wrested control. As fantastic as their tales were, he didn't believe they were making it up. July 11, 2007 was a seminal date for them. It was no yawner for him either, for that was the day Chris nearly ended it all. He hadn't told anyone, not Meredith, nobody.

It was that summer in 2007 when the tinnitus first appeared, and what would have been a slight annoyance to others sent him on the TSA Fast Pass to hell. The ringing in his ears sent his monkey mind reeling. He couldn't stop thinking about it. He obsessed over it. And then he couldn't sleep because of his obsessing, and then he panicked over not being able to sleep and not being to stop thinking about his tinnitus and insomnia and eventually he panicked over his panicking. There was no reprieve from himself, no escape from the senseless self-torment of a torturous mind bent on his demise. The self-loathing intensified daily as he repeatedly proved to himself how ineffectual, how impotent, how small he was before the demons.

His diseased little mind had it in for him. So, in one final act of defiance, he decided he was going to take command of how he was going to go out. He was going to end it on the tracks once and for all. He originally chose July 12th, but circumstances provided him an opportunity to push it up by one day. Chris remembered it all too well. He was intent, determined. He remembered stepping towards the edge of the platform in the crowded station, hoping no one would notice, making his peace, knowing the pain was about to end forever, and then…

"Captain."

Chris shook himself from the memories as he craned his neck to answer Rita who was the leader of the group it seemed. "Yes?"

"How are you doing?"

"Oh, I'm all right, except I'm not much with low riders." Ilsa Jenkins found Chris' Kona mountain bike just where she left it several days ago, but the back rim was bent. Fortunately, Helmut Spankmeister was friendly with the Targeteers and traded some canned food for a kid's bike wheel. Chris made the repairs and necessary modifications himself. Everyone was surprised he knew as much as he did, but he knew how to fix bikes. He had to back when he was a poor-ass college student and too destitute to buy replacement parts.

"You're doing fine, Chris. Just keep pedaling. We'll break once we're past Jessup. But you let me know if you're getting dizzy."

Chris nodded and returned his attention to the icy, broken road of Highway 295, weaving past a clutch of vehicles. Parts of Linthicum Heights and the highway leading out had been rendered to ashen ruins, and to his left he saw the cause—BWI airport.

This was really happening. With some self-satisfaction, he knew that he could accept this notion easier than most. After all, he had written a fair amount of *Doctor Who* fan fiction over the years. He watched the Discovery Channel regularly, so he could grok the concept of multiple realities. Of course, he hadn't heard of anyone accidentally slipping through the rabbit hole and winding up in an alternate universe as a result of a carjacking. But that's what you get for going to Maryland for a stupid guitar.

Chris tried not to think how much he missed Meredith and his two boys. Kendra had told him he had three kids in this reality. Three kids! How did they cope with *three*! At least Meredith and some version of the kids were alive and doing well. He just hoped that this Spankmeister guy could get him home to his reality, to his wife, his kids, his life. A tune he played in the car on the way to pick up the guitar before getting carjacked replayed in his head.

As he cycled along the eerily quiet road past another burnt out strip mall, his mind turned to his physical sensations. Besides the bitter cold, he felt the missing teeth along his left side, the almost constant burning sensation on his back, and the missing digits on his left foot. He didn't even know he was missing a few toes until he took off his boots to put on a less rancid pair of socks. Kendra explained how he came to be so busted up over the years. A war, several skirmishes with bandits, bad dental hygiene, crazy insane things he never imagined himself ever doing. Of course, he never imagined his friend Kendra as some warrior lieutenant in a group that worshipped Gaia—whoever that was—and ill-mannered rabbits either.

During the break, Chris took out a mirror and studied his face. It was him all right, but altered slightly by injuries he didn't remember receiving. He felt the bridge of his nose, which had been broken and was slightly incongruent, he was more wrinkled, and appeared to be older than 40. And what was the deal with the two-prong chin beard as if he were a Viking or something? But he also had to hand it to this version of himself; he was fit. He hadn't been this thin since the first time he got off of Phoketal when he was thirty-years-old and got into triathlon training. He had massive arms, and a flat stomach. Apparently the apocalypse looked good on him.

Chris tried his best to keep calm during the last few days, and he glommed onto Kendra. Although this Kendra was significantly better armed than his Kendra and sported a crew cut over intricate weaves, the two had essentially the same temperament, which comforted him. Before they left the house in Linthicum, she handed him an M4 and gave him basic instructions, all the while calling him "sir" and "Captain." He hadn't touched an assault rifle since basic training as a special agent over ten years ago, but it was easy enough to remember. He just hoped he wouldn't have to use it. From what he gathered, the group was from Rochelle—Brandon's hometown, and they called themselves "Vicious Rabbits." That explained the rusted orange armbands with the strange silhouette of a fanged-rabbit over battleaxes that everyone including himself wore, all except Rita, Akil and Ilsa. They travelled by ship to Maryland to stop a radical religious group from getting nuclear waste to use as weapons and had suffered massive losses in the process.

Throughout the ride, Chris leered at the rusting cars wishing to drive to wherever they were going. He had to remind himself that none of the cars on the road would start. He hadn't considered how completely dependent the world had become on computer circuitry. Power plants, water and sewerage pumps, cars, iPods, radios, all of it…to have all of them around the world suddenly fail must have been…well, bad enough to cause this. How did *he* survive in this world? How did he get Meredith out from a city that, without a doubt, must have become a scene of bedlam, and on July 11th? More sinister thoughts crept in. If the Shift happened when it did and it was so destabilizing to civilization and law and order as it was, he could have used the opportunity to take himself out for good. Why didn't he?

The mean looking bear with the oddest accent who Kendra and the others referred to as "Gunny" sat down next to Kendra and him while they were resting up. Although it was winter with flecks of snow falling, Gunny had a sunburn and was peeling around his nose. He pulled out an AAA road atlas.

"LT, Captain, we're about 'alfway to Spankmeister's lair, office, what 'ave you."

"We're making good timing," Kendra said optimistically. She looked at her watch, a Rolex from what he could tell. "I think we could make it before sundown."

"Aye. But lookee 'ere, LT. I don't much like the looks of things at this intersection. Could be a nasty pile up."

Gunny and Kendra discussed matters. Gunny threw out unfamiliar terms, both military jargon and phrases that seemed to have emerged since living together isolated out in the Shenandoah Valley. Things like "townies," "ferals," "Targeteers" were interspersed with "kill box," and "L shaped ambushes."

Kendra decided their course of action. "All right. When we approach the intersection, we'll divide up."

"Aye." Gunny slapped Chris' knee as his stood back up and walked over to the one eyed reverend lady named Rita.

"What was that all about?"

Kendra shrugged. "Just discussing how to approach Spankmeister's office, tactical approaches, that sort of thing."

"Oh." Chris waited a moment before continuing. "So, I'm the commander of this outfit?"

"That's affirm. You're the commanding officer of the Vicious Rabbits First Bike Mounted Cavalry Company, what's left of it, at least," she finished sullenly.

"Christ, I can't believe it."

"What?"

"That I could command anything, no less a," searching for the odd phrase, "bike-mounted cavalry."

"The Shift changed a lot of things, Captain, and Gaia touches people in ways that they do not expect."

"Ah, yes, Gaia," he answered patronizingly. From what he gathered, Rita was the leader of a new religion that was some strange offshoot of the Unitarian Church, something like a New Age cult on crack. *Great. That's just what I need to simplify my life, a bunch of militant Unitarians.* Kendra was obviously a dedicated follower. He noticed the chalice medallion around her neck. He decided it wasn't a good time to get into a theological discussion, but he was curious if his counterpart was a "Gaian," remained the agnostic he was, or perhaps he just went totally berserk and became a Scientologist, God help him.

"I hope you regain your memory soon, because you're a great commander although you can be a little temperamental sometimes, a real moody SOB."

Chris snickered. "Yeah, I can see that. But what about you?"

"What do you mean?"

"I mean, the Kendra I know. Aren't you curious how I know you in my world? Don't you want to know what the other you is like?"

Kendra abruptly stood up, and adjusted the straps to her MOLLE gear. "No, I am not."

Chris followed her back to the bikes. "Is it that because you don't believe me, that I'm making this up? Or do you think I went insane in the membrane?"

"I don't know what to believe right now. Maybe there is some way what you're saying is true, but I don't care to know even if it is."

"Why not? I sure as hell have been prodding you about the other me."

"It isn't important, Captain," she said emphasizing the formal title. "What became of me in a world that *didn't* happen is of no concern of mine. Gaia saw to it that I became who I am here. Anything else, any other permutation is wrong. And if what you say is true, then you don't belong here."

Chris was taken aback by her sudden abrasiveness. The way she described it, there could only be one reality, one truth, and everything else was a lie. If he didn't know better, he would have pegged her as a fundamentalist with sweeping statements like that. The statement "you don't belong here" rang in his head again.

"Yeah, I get that feeling."

CHAPTER 21

The wheels made contact with the ground about an hour after they were supposed to, which wasn't a surprise. Airline schedules were more like wishful thinking than reliable timetables. The indicator signal chimed and everyone immediately reached inside their pockets for their phones including Rita herself, who was sandwiched in the middle seat between two corpulent men. It always seemed as though she was assigned to a middle seat these days. If the folks over at MIT weren't so damned nervous and let her do her job instead of summoning her last minute every couple of weeks, she wouldn't have to endure the degrading conditions of modern air flight. The man to her left snored during the hour-long flight and the man to her right kept making eyes at her. It wouldn't be so annoying except that he had no sense of shame.

As the airplane taxied to the gate, one of the flight attendants announced. "Welcome to Baltimore Washington International Airport where the local time is four-thirty-seven. Use of cell phones and personal electronic devices is now permitted; however, please remain buckled in your seats until the captain has turned off the seat belts sign. We appreciate your flying with us on Conglomerate Airlines. We know you have a lot of choices with air carriers…"

"Yeah, right," the man to her right harrumphed. "Two major airlines left and each with different routes."

As annoying as the man was, she had to hand it to him. He was spot on. She powered on her phone, hoping beyond hope that she would be able to drive home and not to the office. No luck. An urgent text message from Helmut. She knew he was going to need her back at the office and sure enough…

"Come to the office ASAP. It is urgent."

"Shit," she cursed under her breath. She grabbed her purse, laptop and overcoat, from the overhead bin and waited while the passengers deplaned languidly down the aisle like sheep being corralled. She managed a quick voice text back to Helmut. "Okay, mi Coriño. I'll be there within an hour."

Laurel, Maryland
January 2013

Rita was getting concerned whether they were going to make it before dusk. They had set off early this morning; however, like everything in this world, it took twice as long as expected. They came across a feral band here and there, but fortunately they weren't hostile. Locals eyed them warily as they passed, brandishing their rifles defensively, but otherwise let them pass unmolested. She saw that many of the tribes, though not all, were distinguished along racial lines, a sad reminder of humanity's propensity to find differences among each other rather than similarities. Living among the allied communities of the Orange Pact where black, white, Hispanic and Asians lived together, racial identity dissolved. Even the Lambs of God fanatics were equal opportunists…so long as you were a devout Protestant variety of Christian. But here, where there was no civilization, the locals tended to fall back on their upbringing and their survival instincts they learned from the streets. Spiritual humanism was nowhere to be found here.

The sun was arcing over to towards the horizon when they finally turned off the highway onto a series of smaller streets that winded around with no apparent logic. Helmut started pedaling faster.

"Come on, guys. We're almost there!" beckoning excitedly like a kid coming home.

The gunny pursued him to ensure Helmut wasn't trying to break free while Rita tried to keep her tires from slipping on the ice patches. Helmut guided them past a Safeway and to the back entrance of an unremarkable office park with grass that sprouted over the snow-covered lawns. The triad of identical poo brown suburban office towers made a delta. At the foot of the lawn was a granite composite headstone identifying the decaying office park as "The Stubb Foundation" whose logo resembled a flower bud with a DNA strand inside it.

Helmut got off his bike and waved excitedly to the central building. The gunny immediately barked out, "Who are you waving too, boyo? You got snipers up there?"

Rita could see that Birmingham had stopped and held his rifle at the low ready, prepared to cap the scientist at a moment's notice.

Fortunately Helmut's response was open. "No, no snipers. Friends! Our friends. We're here. This is home. Come on!"

"This is home?" Akil asked incredulously.

Rita couldn't imagine there being any good reason why Helmut and his friends would choose to live inside a modern office building. Outside of the busted out windows, there probably was no ventilation, making summers quite unpleasant. Helmut walked through an opening with glass scattered into the inside of the lobby intermixed with a dusting of snow on the marble floor. Ilsa Jenkins pulled out a post-Shift flashlight, which she had to crank for power and scanned the lobby.

The security desk, the elevator banks and even the lounge chairs all had the Stubb Foundation logo, but there was no evidence of any habitation whatsoever. Rita could see the gunny's and the lieutenant's suspicion as they walked their bikes into the lobby. Helmut proceeded past a set of double doors and came to another door in the hallway labeled "Telephone Closet."

Helmut pulled out a key from his pocket and opened the door. For some reason the act of using a key to unlock a door inside this office building struck Rita as being out of place, like Helmut was coming home to his apartment after work.

There was a scuttling sound and the gunny quickly pivoted, zeroing his M4 on the source of the noise to see a family of cats scurrying away. He lowered the weapon and proceeded to follow Helmut who led them through the room, which was filled with wires randomly connected to inputs on an electrical board; they were telephone lines. At the far end of the room was a mainframe for the office's computer networks. Naturally, it was offline.

"You can stow your bikes here," Helmut said. "None of the locals bother with this place."

Chris shut the door behind them and everyone placed their bikes along the walls. Ilsa's bike, which carried the child trailer, barely fit, leaving them packed inside a darkened room filled with wires. Helmut walked over to the mainframe and unexpectedly, the massive dead computer, which towered over the scientist, swiveled out like it was on wheels connected to a hinge, which it was. Behind the mainframe was another door, but one designed with no knob whose seams could hardly be deciphered from the rest of the wall. Helmut pushed the door and walked through.

"I don't like this, Gov," the gunny cautioned and he moved right behind Helmut. The door was a hidden entrance to the top of a stairwell.

"Where do these stairs go?" Akil asked.

"They go down," Helmut answered nonchalantly.

Rita could see a faint light far below. It didn't look like firelight. They descended the stairs with as much caution as they could manage while Helmut raced down excitedly. They wound down several flights; however, there were no floors in between. Rita was getting dizzier and she couldn't tell if it was from spiraling down the way they were or if it was related to something Helmut hinted at being related to Chris' dementia.

Suddenly, Helmut came to a halt and cautioned, "This may feel a little weird."

As he continued down the stairwell, she saw Helmut and Gunnery Sergeant Birmingham shimmer slightly. "What the bloody…"

When she reached the landing where the gunny and Helmut had been a moment ago, she saw the walls around her shimmer briefly and felt this odd sensation sort of like static electricity. Her nausea, which she had stuffed away from her consciousness as best she could, evaporated with a suddenness that made her realize how dizzy she had been feeling these past several days.

Chris reacted as well. "Whoa, that's interesting."

Helmut looked back up at her with the dim light below and giggled. "See? I told you it would feel weird. Come on."

They continued down several more flights with no floors between them until they reached the bottom. The light that had guided them was an electric sign that cautioned to turn off all cell phones.

"You 'ave electricity down 'ere?" Birmingham asked.

"You could say that."

Helmut then pressed a button on a keypad next to the door, and a few seconds later, there was a click, indicating that the door was somehow unlocked. That confounded Rita. As the door opened, everyone covered their eyes from the blinding white light coming from the other side. When her eyes adjusted, she saw a group of people, frumpy, but otherwise clean looking people applauding. A comfortable looking woman raced up to Helmut and gave him a wet kiss on the lips and embraced him.

"Oh, honey, I'm so glad you're home!" The woman ran her fingers around Helmut's stringy black hair and kissed him passionately. But as she did so, she eyed Rita suspiciously.

The clean white light of the hallway stunned Rita. She suddenly realized it was warm inside. The people standing in front of her were dressed for room temperature and were conspicuously clean, now that she thought about it. They were somehow incongruent to the world outside. At first, she couldn't put her finger on what it was, and then she realized it was because they all looked like, well, nerds. Helmut and the woman finally broke off.

"Rita, these are my people. They're from various agencies, but we all work for the Stubb Foundation. People, these are some friends I made from Virginia. And this," he said as if presenting her formally, "this is Reverend Rita Luevano, the chief magistrate of Greater Monticello."

Everyone came up to Rita, completely ignoring the armed gunnery sergeant and moved to shake her hand. She was taken aback. She noticed that Helmut's girlfriend glowered at her. The woman strutted up to Rita. "So, this is the floozy?"

Rita had no idea what this woman's beef was with her, but it had been a long week and she had lost her "turn the other cheek and see the beauty in all people" attitude on the Chesapeake. Helmut moved in between them.

"Honey, please. The reverend is happily married. Nothing happened."

Rita guffawed. "Is that what you…oh, dear! Oh, I can assure you that your boyfriend remained quite chaste and untouched by *my* hands."

Akil backed her up. "Um, yeah, I can vouch for that, me being her husband and all."

The woman made a sound a skeptical cow. "Mmm."

"Andrea, please. We had a bit of a rough ride," Helmut said, and the woman Andrea reluctantly held out hand.

"Andrea Weber."

With a bit of caution, Rita took it. She noticed that the woman's hands were smooth. She even had on nail polish. What kind of queen lived without working with her hands? Rita suddenly realized how austere her own life had become and how her values would have been more in line with the Amish than her suburban congregants in the old days.

"Rita Luevano, a pleasure."

"And this here is Kim, and one of our engineers George," Helmut added, making the rounds. As he introduced the strangers, Rita gawked at the light of the hallway. Certainly, Greater Monticello had electricity at least half the time it did when the surges didn't bump the generators offline. So did Rochelle and the other allies, but the electricity pumping out in her corner of the world wasn't clean and steady. The methane and wind turbine generators were sporadic and wouldn't support florescent lights. They tried, but they lamps always flickered with the slightest disruption. But here, the florescent lights illuminated the hallway with reliable regularity. She noticed something else; it was a strange sound, hard to pick out from the voices, like regular background noise.

Rita stepped past the inhabitants walked furtively along the hallway to investigate the sound. Helmut caught up with her. "Ah, um, yeah…" he stalled. "Um, you're going to be a little surprised, Rita," he said emphasizing "little" with the space between his thumb and forefinger.

"Lead the way, Mr. Spankmeister."

He chuckled and bowed slightly. "Okay, right this way. Come on, guys. I guess you'll need to see this."

The humming sound intensified as they reached a set of double doors. Helmut opened the door for Rita and she stepped through.

It was impossible. It couldn't be, her mind protested angrily. But if she trusted her remaining eye, it had to be true. Computers monitors were alight, glowing with graphic images, charts, camera images, and resonance frequency charts. A mainframe riddled with blinking lights hummed contently in the background. Rita found herself needing to remind herself to breathe. She nearly dropped the AK-47 from the crook of her arm. A corpulent man sat at a desk at the far wall, typing on a keyboard. He froze, a Power Bar dropping from his hand when he saw the feral looking visitors. Rita didn't even acknowledge him. The brilliant white florescent lights of the immaculate room bore on her eye forcing her to cover it.

Behind her, Gunnery Sergeant Birmingham rubbed his eyes. "What the 'ell?" The other Virginians gasped out in utter exasperation and confusion, all except Chris.

Rita tried to speak, but found the words didn't come. She pointed to one of the flat screen monitors displaying, if memory served correctly, an *Excel* spreadsheet. "How?"

Helmut gently placed his hands on her shoulders and faced her. "Okay, I know this might come as a bit of a shock."

She walked over to one of the computers and touched the screen, studying how the pressure of her finger disrupted the cells displaying the image on the monitor.

"'oly shit, mate," Birmingham uttered. "It's real. They're…on."

For five and a half years, she lived in a world were a functioning computer was as anachronistic as a helicopter in a Spaghetti Western. *How could these machines be on?* The Virginians stood slack jawed with the exception of Chris who seemed unimpressed. He had been told about the Shift, but according to him, he was typing away on his desktop in his cubicle at work a week ago.

Chris snapped his fingers. "Oh, I get it. We're underground. That's why the computers weren't affected, right?" he asked Helmut.

Kendra shook her head. "I'm afraid not, Captain. The EMPs are being caused by Gaia. She is shifting the earth's poles, causing the EMP surges. No computer on this planet can escape her, no matter how far underground." Then she added. "Or at least, that's what I thought."

"You're right, Lieutenant," Helmut answered. "Every traditional computer that was plugged into a power source has been wrecked."

"But that doesn't seem to be the case here," Rita said gathering herself.

"There's more," Helmut said. "Rita. I need to introduce you to something. Come."

"Something?" she repeated.

One of the Stubb Foundation's people opened another set of double doors. On the other side was something that resembled the command center in the TV show *24*, a guilty pleasure that she had never admitted watching to anyone. How could she say "no" to Kiefer Sutherland? If the previous room was disorienting with its display of technology thought to be extinct, this auditorium was absolutely horrifying. The lights in the room were subdued; however, gigantic paper-thin screens covered the walls illuminating the room with moving images and creating a strobe effect. Some screens showed grainy green tinted night vision surveillance images patched through from vantage points located outside in the Stubb Foundation office park grounds. Some images were readouts, and some appeared to be recorded news feeds from CNN, Fox News and BBC America coming in with a lot of interference.

People were seated at stations attending to their desktops, some playing video games and others slept, while overhead, centrally situated, was a prominent screen, larger than all of the others. It showed an animated image of a boy's face with his eyes closed as though he were sleeping. He was blue, which reminded her of an Indian avatar. There were smaller screens around the main one showing the image of a green pregnant woman with the round belly painted to resemble earth, something hauntingly similar to the mural outside the resurrected church.

Helmut walked down a center aisle and addressed the central screen of the sleeping blue boy. "Jamil, I have returned and I have brought her to you."

Rita almost jumped back in fright as the sleeping boy's eyes opened. The image stirred, and appeared to be scrutinizing her intently. The boy's cartoon like features softened, and from the most impressive surround sound she had ever heard, the boy spoke.

"Rita! It is you! You are home!"

"Jamil?" she said stunned.

"Yes! I am your creation!" the boy exclaimed.

Akil staggered up to Rita as both stared into the face of the computer generated cherub blue boy's face. Jamil was the name of Akil's lost son. She grabbed Akil's arm as he approached the screen.

"S…son?"

"No, silly. Rita is my mother."

Rita collapsed in a chair dumbstruck.

Chris walked towards the screen and turned to Rita. "Yeah, I can see the resemblance."

Chapter 22

Stubb Foundation
Laurel, Maryland
January 2013

Rita Luevano wasn't the swooning type. She'd been through a lot in her forty-odd years of life. She nearly drank herself into oblivion as a teenaged Goth runaway, she'd had been in a lot of fights, she had fought in the Battle for Monticellan Independence; she had lost an eye and a few teeth to it, and she had witnessed the rise of the Gaia Piety Society. So, it was a little surprising when she nearly lost consciousness. She would have collapsed on the floor had her husband Akil not been there to ease her into one of the swivel chairs.

Akil knelt beside her as Rita shook herself out of the stagger of confusion. She placed her palms on her forehead as if trying to rub sense into the insanity.

"Okay, okay, just relax, Rita." Helmut who leaned over to her right seemed to have regained his faculties while she felt she had lost all of hers. "I know it's a lot to take in. Just breathe."

"Rita, are you feeling sick? Helmut, did you get my mother sick?" The computer generated face scowled at the people below.

"Just a minute, Jamil. She's a little disoriented. Please, just give her a little room and go back to sleep."

"Okay," the voice of a pre-pubescent boy sulked.

"Helmut?" she called.

"I, I know. From the beginning, right?"

Rita nodded not able to say anything more. Akil looked about as terrified as she felt. He pulled up a chair and sat next to the couple while the rest of the team sidled up to listen.

"It's real," said the gunnery sergeant as he pecked at the keys of a computer next to a Stubb Foundation woman who looked too frightened to protest.

"Please, Gunny, she's working," Helmut said. The gunnery sergeant must have been as shocked, because he obeyed the diminutive scientist.

"Okay, Rita, Akil, ladies, gents, Gunny, I know this is a lot to absorb here, so I'll try to tell you what I can. First, I would like to welcome you all to the Stubb Foundation. It's not often we receive guests."

"This is where you worked?"

"Well, actually, I didn't work in here. I was upstairs...you know, the abandoned floors above ground. I was part of the official operations of the Stubb Foundation, contracting with the US Department of Energy to keep track movement of all nuclear material, just like I said. But that is just the public face of the Stubb Foundation."

"What's going on here? How," trying to sort her myriad of questions out mentally, "How is this possible?"

"I understand your confusion. I'm trying to find a good place to start. Reverend, have you ever heard of molecular electronics?"

Rita's brows knitted. "Do you mean nanotechnology?"

"Well, close, kind of, but not exactly. What is your knowledge of computers?"

Rita rubbed her eye patch wearily. It was a funny question, like asking her about a subject she hadn't taken since high school.

"Not much except how to use them."

Helmut smirked as she continued. "I know that the micro circuits that formed the CPUs were made of silicon and that the Shift fried every one of them, or so I thought up until now."

"That's pretty good, Rita. Most people couldn't say that much. Essentially, you are correct. Silicon microchips act as microscopic switches, transistors, that make simple 'either, or' calculations, 'yes, no,' or more precisely 'one, or zero' calculations. Hence they are binary."

"Yes, I remember something about that."

"Yet, at the end of day, binary computers are limited. They always would be. Binary-based computers could never run the calculations needed at the speed required for the endeavors in the new millennium. As advanced or as fast as standard computers are, there is a fundamental debilitating limitation of binary calculations, making a series of ones and zeros. The more bits you have, the more transistors there are and at some point you run into the issue of how many calculations can be made per second, because of the universal speed limit."

"You're talking about the speed of light, aren't you?"

Helmut smiled. "That's exactly it. Electricity runs through a circuit at the speed of light. But the more transistors you have on a circuit, the longer it takes. So, as long as computers are dependent upon these switchboards, no matter how advanced they get, they will eventually run into the law of physics. We had to think of something completely different, a new way to make calculations beyond binary codes and transistors."

Helmut walked about as if teaching a class. "So, what if instead of the basic unit of information being either a one or a zero, what if it was a one, zero, or…a one *and* zero?"

"You're talking about quantum computing, aren't you?"

Everyone stared at her including Helmut. Akil leaned over rubbing his scruffy beard. "Sugar, you been holding back on me?"

Rita knew the substance of this conversation despite the fact that she had never been erudite in computers. She couldn't explain how. It was like remembering something that she didn't ever recall remembering before but somehow had been in the recesses of the mind all along.

"Yes, Rita. 'Superposition' is part of quantum computing, the ability to be a one, a zero or some combination of both at the same time. Instead of a bit, we call this calculation a 'qubit.'"

"Wait, mate? How can anything be one thing and another? That makes no bloody sense."

Rita sympathized with Gunnery Sergeant Birmingham's confusion. It conflicted with their experience. That was impossible in traditional physics.

"It's one of the confounding properties in quantum mechanics, Gunny. I still have a hell of a time wrapping my mind around it. Another property in quantum mechanics is *entanglement*, non-local connection. This means that two distinct objects separated by a distance can immediately affect one another, seeming to have defied the speed of light, because they are inextricably linked somehow in a way that cannot be rationally understood."

"In other words, two objects that seem to be two separate things are actually one, like being at two places at once."

"That's right. So, quantum computing would allow you to do calculations you weren't capable of doing before. Traditional micro circuits were limited by their very composition and would not be able to work well with qubit processing. Our research and development team realized the most effective medium to work with was not silicon based, but rather organic."

Rita turned her attention to the Stubb Foundation's logo on the coffee mug. The DNA strand wasn't simply a cute corporate logo. It symbolized what they did here. "Molecular electronics," the term Helmut threw out minutes ago suddenly made sense.

"DNA holds more information within its protein sequences than can be stored in 2007's greatest silicon-based supercomputers. You take DNA, re-sequence the proteins and you can store data and perform qubit calculations in a way no silicon-based circuit could. And when you're working with qubits, when you are conducting quantum calculations, you are not limited by the speed of light. Only organic computers whose hardware is DNA could maximize quantum computing because DNA is much more sophisticated than anything we could produce with silicon."

"Organic," Akil whispered. Then he snapped his fingers. "Organic computers. That's why they didn't blink out with the EMPs, right?"

Helmut smiled. "The EMP causes rapid fluctuations in the magnetic field producing currents that destroy the transistors in microchips. But Jamil here, an organic computer, it is not comprised of silicon circuits but rather an organic network. He…it is no more affected by EMPs than you or I are."

"I didn't know such things really existed," Chris observed.

"They weren't widely available, if that's what you mean. There are only a handful of organic computers in existence. They were developed by our R and D folks. A few competitors developed similar organics."

There was the word, "organic."

"Organic…" she repeated. "Helmut, are you computers alive?"

Helmut shrugged. "We think so. In the end we have to ask where life begins. Me, I'm a simple nuclear physicist. This isn't my bailiwick. I can't answer where that line is. That's for my colleague here to answer."

A slender woman with expressive blue eyes and an angular jaw line dressed in earth tone flowing fabric under her lab coat had joined the discussion while Rita had been engaged with Helmut.

"This is the Stubb Foundation's chief bio ethicist Dr. Ariadne Hunter. She knows more about this than I."

Bio ethicist. The career sounded about as useful as a poet or philosopher or a PR representative, thought Rita. The woman, roughly Rita's age, seemed eager to sit next to her and smiled.

"Why would you need to create an organism that could do quantum computing?" Chris asked. "It sounds like a rather pricey adventure even for a research and development company. I mean, what do you use Jamil for anyway?"

Helmut looked over to his girlfriend, Andrea, who was still staring laser beams at Rita. "Quantum computing had been developed to handle certain projects. Umm, one in particular…have you heard of the CERN Institute?"

"Yeah, the Large Hadron Collider in Switzerland, right? For making anti-matter to search for the Higgs Boson particle thing," Chris said casually.

Everyone in the room turned to gawk at Chris' unexpected expertise. He just shrugged. "I saw a thing on it last week on the Science Channel."

Right, she thought sardonically. According to Chris, he lived in trite fictional world of his where the Shift never happened. His nervous breakdown couldn't have happened at a worse time.

But then in a moment of clarity, it all clicked. Back in Linthicum Heights, Helmut had said that in Chris' reality, the Shift did not happen. Chris sure was convinced that it hadn't. And then they arrived in Laurel to find organic computers that operated in realm of the quantum mechanics where something could be one thing *and* another all at once, where one object could be at two distinct locations at once, where an event that happened in one reality didn't happen in another reality, and yet they both existed and were just as real.

Rita stood up out of the chair. "Helmut, you said that in Chris' reality that the Shift didn't happen. The quantum computing, qubits….Chris isn't delusional at all. Where he comes from the Shift *didn't* happen. He didn't construct that world of his. It's as real as our own, because just as on the quantum level something can have one distinct property and another simultaneously, so too an event, an event like the Shift. It happened *and* it didn't happen! Is that right?"

The room fell silent. Other than the hum computers, the Virginians sat dumbstruck buffering what Rita had just internalized. Helmut nodded, confirming that she was correct. She herself was trying to come to terms with what she had just said.

After a moment, Chris broke the silence. "Did you cause this?"

Helmut looked confused. "Cause what?"

"This!" He cried out, jabbing his finger to his head. "This, this…thing, this parallel universe, this whatever it is that put my head into this lovely fucking reality! Did you or that God damned HAL 9000 of yours over there…Do you send me here?"

Chris was seething, something Rita could sympathize with now realizing that the poor soul was torn from his world and into this, as he eloquently put it, "lovely fucking reality." She even began to feel guilty for having been short on sympathy when she thought he had just lost his mind. Where were *her* humanist sensibilities? But in her defense, who would have thought that Apple would have called their product an "iPad?" It really did sound like some sketch comedy spoof of Apple's foray into female hygiene products. Chris was on the verge of either breaking down, sudden violence or both.

"No, Chris, we didn't cause this," Helmut said. "Frankly, I can't explain how your consciousness got transported into your counterpart from this reality. You weren't anywhere near Jamil when the Shift hit, so I don't know how you arrived here."

"Whoa," Akil exclaimed. "Just rewind that last part, coz. What in the hell does proximity to Jamil have to do with the Shift?" He paused. "Did you cause the Shift?"

"No, hell no," Helmut protested. "For God's sake, you all know what caused the Shift, people! The earth shifting its magnetic poles!"

"Then why did you defend yourself by saying Chris was nowhere near Jamil when the Shift happened?"

"Look, *we* didn't cause the Shift, okay? Jamil is a marvel of human engineering, but it couldn't produce the energy that would prompt the earth to shift its poles. But…"

Helmut's eyes darted to Andrea and Ariadne. Rita could feel her gut tightening as Helmut whispered in Andrea's ear. She nodded and then addressed everyone.

"I was down here on July 11th," Andrea began. "The CERN Institute was going to run a test of the Large Hadron Collider. Jamil was responsible for receiving and processing the data on the test run."

"Here? I thought the CERN was in Switzerland?"

Andrea gave Rita a condescending smile. "Yes, well, if you recall we used to have instant global communications. Anyway, CERN was a European agency, but unbeknownst to them, the organic computer designed by their European company for the CERN was actually a subsidiary of the Stubb Foundation, and you see, well…"

"You were conducting espionage," Chris finished for her.

Andrea made a face. "The US was developing its own Large Hadron Collider before the CERN, and we know that the Europeans stole many of their designs from us, and then they managed to pull ahead of us. We were just keeping tabs on their work."

"I was observing the experiment through Jamil. The CERN started their tests. Jamil had a portal to view the experiment through its counterpart organic; it was as if we had a front row seat. The objective of the Large Hadron Collider was to create antiprotons. All the data coming in matched our projections. The collider was performing excellently. Protons colliding into protons creating antiprotons. It was magnificent. Then I noticed some static on the screen, and then…and then it all went to static. That was at 6:02 PM."

6:02 PM. That was the exact minute when the Shift hit. Ever since Jon Early arrived back in the autumn in the months after the Shift hit, Rita and everyone else in the Orange Pact for that matter, had accepted what Jon Early told them. Jon explained that the geologists in the Research Triangle believed that the earth had caused the Shift, that the Shift was a result of the earth preparing to shift its magnetic poles. Unitarians believed the earth spirit herself prompted it. Many Christians believed it was God. The rationalists believed it was just really bad timing for humanity. But regardless, everyone believed it was the earth, not man, that caused it.

"So, this Hadron Collider caused the Shift?" Rita asked.

Andrea sighed. "We think it may have helped facilitate it. Understand, as far as we know, the earth's magnetic field was showing signs that it was going to go through a reversal of its poles before the CERN started conducting its experiments. The collider couldn't cause a magnetic shift in the earth's poles with a stable field, but…well, Jamil started running the scenarios after it was all said and done, and well, the earth's magnetic field was fluctuating at just the right…I'm sorry, I mean, at just the *wrong* time, and at the wrong place. And you see, the power released when antimatter collides with matter is…well, it's complete destruction; there is a total annihilation of the matter. The energy released within a confined space is immense. Given the state of the earth's magnetic field and the resulting energy released resonating with the fluctuating field, we believe it resulted in what we are seeing here today."

Rita felt as though the world had collapsed into the confines of this room. She struggled to find the words. "They caused it?"

"It would have happened sooner or later," Helmut chimed in. "The experiment just sort of nudged the earth along by maybe, I don't know a hundred years or so. But geologically speaking, that's nothing."

"Nothing? A hundred years? Those hundred years could have been the difference between us having more of these organic Jamil computers and having an idea how to prevent a worldwide collapse and…" she stopped her growing tirade. "Wait…Jamil, how is Jamil related to Chris?"

"Jamil wasn't like what he seems now," Andrea said. "It was remarkably advanced, but when all was said and done, it was just a computer, that was until about eighteen months ago. When the *Shift*, as you call it, hit, the power fluctuated down here, but it didn't go out. While the rest of the world fell victim to the EMPs, this section below ground was unaffected. Even our cell phones still worked, though there was no coverage. Do you remember feeling a…static like sensation when you went down the steps?"

"Yes, and there was a shimmer, too."

"Is it some kind of force field or something," Chris asked.

"Not exactly, more like a bubble. Jamil was operating on the quantum level when the Shift hit. When the power went out, it should have gone out down here as well."

"Why so? I thought Jamil was unaffected by EMPs."

"Jamil still runs on electricity. Our generators upstairs are dead like everything else."

"So, what's powering all of this?"

"That's just it. The power is not from here. We cannot identify a power source here that is providing Jamil electricity and everything Jamil powers in this place. It just exists. The only explanation we had was that Jamil was tied to the Jamil in another reality somehow."

"The other Jamil?"

"Yes, Jamil…actually, we didn't call him Jamil yet, because he wasn't like…." Andrea stopped herself from getting into a tangent. "The point is we concluded that our organic was being powered in a reality where there was still electricity; in other words, where the Shift did not happen."

Everybody needed a moment to grasp what Andrea just said. It was times like these that Rita was glad they didn't carry their number two cash crop cannabis with them for recreational purposes, because it was right about now when her colleagues would be blazing up. And her sobriety was teetering dangerously.

"You're saying that Jamil is tied to another reality?"

"Yes. It shocked us when we left the operations center to find a world without power while we still had power. For the longest time, we didn't know why. But we started suspecting it had something to do with our organic's quantum processor. It was the only thing that explained Jamil's strange data that it spat out."

"I'm sorry, please, could you explain?"

"When the EMPs first hit, we got the other employees of the Foundation down here. Part of this underground facility is a biosphere."

"Wow, y'all sure do a lot here."

"We have a diverse portfolio. We hid down here while the world went to hell, and tried to make sense of what was happening. We had a linkup to one satellite in high earth orbit that didn't overload, and searched for anyone else who was still operational. We didn't even know why we still were online. But there was nobody else listening. The world just went quiet. We stayed down here for months, going up to scavenge for toilet paper and medicine only when necessary. But between the biosphere providing food and the underground providing protection from the flu and the gangs, well, we decided it was best to just keep our heads down."

Though it sounded cowardly, Rita understood. She and her folks did the same in Monticello, hiding from the hordes of starving and diseased refugees as well as the gangs that preyed upon them.

"Over time, we started having these dreams. At first I thought it was only natural, you know. You dream of home, right? I didn't mention it to anybody. We also noticed whenever we left the confines of the Foundation, the further away we travelled, it was like our minds would lose grip on reality. There, too, we just chalked it to the trauma of seeing the world as it had become. But it was more than that. It was as though our own reality started to slip away the further away we were from the confines of the bubble, and we couldn't explain that bubble either."

Suddenly, Helmut's earlier behavior made sense. In Virginia, Helmut was erratic, and appeared to be one of the souls who lost their minds to the devastation of the collapse, but as they reached Maryland, he seemed better and was completely lucid by the time they reached Laurel.

"And a couple of years ago, Jamil started showing images on the screens, images that didn't make sense. They came in with a lot of static, but we received messages and data feeds, and we even started receiving television signals showing the news feeds and TV shows."

"So there are others out there with the same technology reaching out to you, right?"

"No. These TV channels, streams of data and emails were local. But as you already know, that was impossible. Nobody, save for us down here, had anything like TV or internet once the Shift hit. We studied the data and the news feeds, and we concluded it could have only come from one place—another reality."

"So, you're saying that you were receiving alternate universe television?"

Andrea nodded. "I know it sounds incredible, but the video was real-time…in a sense. Between the dreams, the fact that down here everything was still working, powered by what we didn't know, we realized that Jamil was the key. Jamil was the portal to the world where the Shift didn't happen, but it was only about eighteen months ago that Jamil itself could explain everything."

Andrea turned to address Chris. "How you wound up getting juxtaposed as you did, I honestly do not know. I can say that some people are more sensitive to their other selves than others. We certainly have felt echoes of our other lives here at the Stubb Foundation. Sometimes it comes out in dreams, sometimes we remember things that didn't happen."

Andrea then turned her attention back to Rita. "It also explains why you have a remarkable grasp on topics that you have no knowledge of in this reality. Among other things, Jamil also told us about you."

Rita gave her a quizzical look. "I don't understand. What do I have to do with any of this?"

Helmut scratched his head. "Rita, in this world you are a reverend who led Monticello through the Shift. In the other reality, well, you gave up the Unitarian Church and the activism thing. You delved into Mathematics. You're a prodigy in fact!"

"What?" she said incredulously.

"It's true. Can you explain how else you were able to follow along so easily with this discussion?"

Rita couldn't. She didn't want to think of her life without Gaia, no less her life without her people. Why would she suddenly leave her community activism to go into something so diametrically opposite? Why?

Andrea picked up the conversation. "As I said earlier, a couple of years ago, we started receiving all of these signals. Shortly thereafter, Jamil changed. He became self-aware. And that's how we learned about everything including the fact that Jamil was the conduit to the other reality like we suspected all along. And we learned that it was *you* that made Jamil self aware."

"Me?"

"Yes," Helmut interjected. "You, other you, using your knowledge in mathematics were instrumental in Jamil becoming self-aware. Other you identified the mess of algorithms Jamil was processing, and other you sort of walked him through the jumble of confounding algorithms that threatened to shut him down. The confusing algorithms was self-awareness. And it was other you that guided Jamil to emerge from being a spiffy calculator to becoming something more. That is why Jamil refers to you as his 'mother' as it were."

"Okay," Rita said. This was a fire hose of information to grasp. But there was one question on her mind that she didn't lose during this *Alice in Wonderland* discussion.

"Why me? Supposedly, I helped an organic computer become self-aware…whatever. But why did you need to bring me here?"

"Because, Rita, I need you to help me save the world."

Rita nearly jumped out of her seat hearing the surround sound of the innocent voice of Jamil.

"There's a little more that Jamil told us about," Helmut added. "It's kind of horrible."

Chapter 23

Staunton, Virginia
January 2013

BACKGROUND MUSIC: "Baby Please Don't Go" by Van Morrison
Visit www.michaeljuge.com **on the *A Hard Rain* page to listen**

Meredith didn't expect such a lively crowd to still be loitering around when they arrived as it was well past 2 AM. But the Prancing Pony was packed. It had started life as a Chili's. Kitschy items such as a decorative stop light, street signs and a Marilyn Monroe print still decorated the family bar and grill and brothel, while a Van Morrison record played on the jukebox. Meredith was impressed. Anyone with a record collection was wealthy.

Thuy, Meredith and a small contingent of Vicious Rabbits stomped the snow off their boots and took off their overcoats as they entered tavern, dimly lit by oil lamps, and heated by the press of bodies inside. Four of the burly Vicious Rabbits, kids no older than eighteen, protectively surrounded her as she sauntered over to the bar. They made her feel extremely short but important all at once, as even the grisliest ex-biker saw her not-so-low-key protection detail and picked up his drink and moseyed off.

Laborers, coal and pot runners, hookers, arms dealers, pimps and desperados filled the joint. All in all, it wasn't much different from when it was a Chili's. The bartender, a woman who looked like she could double as a bouncer spat in a glass and polished it clean with a dirty rag.

"What can I get you, honey?" she said with a nasal voice, revealing she had few teeth left.

"I'm here to see the Ice Dragon."

The woman cackled. "Ha, no one sees the Ice Dragon."

Meredith leaned in closer. "You tell her that the Vulcan is here to see her."

The woman froze and lost her smugness. She stammered, "The Vulcan? You're the Vulcan?"

"That's right. I'm sure that the Ice Dragon would be most interested to know if you tried to keep me from delivering a very important message."

"That won't be a problem," the woman replied contritely. "Right this way, Miss Vulcan." She indicated to follow her through the swinging doors. The detail moved in front of Meredith to ensure there were no surprises as they walked into the kitchen. They passed the array of stainless steel tables and weaved around cooks, strippers and busboys till they reached a back office with two burly men waiting outside in the hall. With a look, the guards moved aside and the woman knocked.

"Yes," came an agitated voice from the other side of the door.

"Umm, ma'am, someone's here to see you…the Vulcan," she said nervously.

A second later the door opened. Meredith walked into the nondescript windowless office to see the Ice Dragon standing before her with her arms outstretched.

"Meredith!"

"Hi, Jen." The two friends gave each other a warm hug. Jenny Parker, AKA the Ice Dragon didn't give the appearance of being the local warlord kingpin or any kind of warlord for that matter. Most were tattooed, hairy ruffians, men who skirted on the frayed edges of civilization back in the real world, who didn't pay their taxes or recognize the social contract. But Jenny was a sweet looking blonde, about Meredith's age. Wearing a Lands End sweater, winter vest and white pants, Jenny looked like she should be hosting a book club rather than running the gun and Hemp trade for Rochelle through Staunton.

"My God, you look great! The apocalypse really suits you." she exclaimed with her tenor raspy voice.

"Oh, thanks!"

"How long has it been? Two years?"

"I think so," Meredith said plaintively. Meredith could feel her introvert nature clashing with her old college roommate's extrovert nature. When they met at American University, Jenny took it upon herself to take her roommate to all of the best functions and to expose her to DC's movers and shakers. But while Jenny went on to get her law degree and become a hired gun at one of DC's most prestigious K Street law firms, instilling fear in all who went up against her, Meredith chose the cerebral inward path of academia to obtain her Masters in Anthropology where she met Chris. Meredith often wondered why Jenny had taken a liking to her despite their obvious personality differences. Perhaps Meredith was her outlet to relax with someone not out to eat her lunch.

It was one of those small world moments standing before her old college roommate now, something that Meredith believed was beyond random coincidence that these two should both survive the Collapse and find each other.

She would never have been reunited with Jenny if it hadn't been for Ross. He was the one who gave Meredith the contact information to Sheldon Parker, Jenny's late husband, who was with the DIA. Sheldon didn't survive the flu; however, Jenny did, and she had taken the reigns for her husband.

Jenny was one of the many gifts provided by Ross. In fact, it was Ross who had given Meredith the contacts and the credentials to develop the Swan, which helped keep the Orange Pact one step ahead of their enemies. Before Ross, Meredith only had a handful of names, and it was anybody's guess if they were alive after the Great Suck. Ross was the intermediary for a growing regional network of spooks.

Meredith and Jenny caught up over the next few minutes while Thuy waited beside her patiently. She told about her husband's as well as the reverend's disappearance in Maryland, though Jenny had already received word through her own assets.

"I'm so sorry. I know this must be killing you not knowing where he is, but I know that Chris is a survivor. He will return to you."

Meredith forced herself from the direction her mind was veering. Jenny immediately sought to fill the void left in the last statement.

"But where are my manners? Thuy! It's good to see you again. Maude," she called to the bartender, "please get my friends something to eat and have the innkeeper set up decent quarters for them at the Stonewall Jackson and away from the ladies."

"I guess I wouldn't be good for your business," Thuy added.

Meredith waited until Jenny's employees left after handing them all mugs of hot cider. One of the guards closed the door leaving Meredith, Thuy and Jenny alone in a kerosene lit room without the benefit of a window, making her feel claustrophobic. Jenny's demeanor became solemn.

Without any further delay she pried, “Is it as bad as the communiqués say?”

“Things are not as I would hope,” Meredith said summoning her British ancestors’ remarkable talent for understatement. Meredith meditated on the warmth from the mug of hot cider on her frozen fingers. “The Lambs of God are coming.”

“When do you expect they will attack?”

“It looks like there are mobilizing,” Thuy answered and started counting off. “Forty-five regulars, plus another five thousand members of the Sheepdogs. Give the Sheepdogs the advantage of being on horseback, and I’d say we’re looking at a full on invasion in a few weeks.”

“Fifty thousand. My God. We can’t match that.”

“I’m afraid you’re correct. We’re looking at a five to one ratio even under the best circumstances,” said Thuy. “The commandant has run the numbers.”

“What does he say about our chances,” she asked hesitantly.

“A month, maybe two until they reach Rochelle. It wouldn’t be long after that to finish off Culpeper and Fredericksburg. Fredericksburg is not much of a fighting force. They’re definitely not organized.”

Jenny shook her head ruefully. “And West Virginia doesn’t seem to mind this at all. Everything I’m seeing indicates they made some arrangements with them.”

Meredith knew about the arrangements the regent proposed to the republic’s president, but as grave as the information was, it paled in comparison to the reason for her visit. Jenny, who had once known her well, could sense Meredith’s distraction.

“But this is not why you’re here, is it?”

Meredith shook her head. “We need to go to the observatory.”

“Oh.”

Meredith didn’t say anything else, and the absence of an explanation said more than anything.

“Maude will prepare some rooms for you and the boys over at the Stonewall Jackson in the center of town. It’s free of riffraff and comes with a free continental breakfast.”

“Jenny, we can’t expound on this, at least not yet.”

“It’s fine. I understand,” she said unconvincingly and then called out, “Maude!”

At least the stay over at the Stonewall Jackson was pleasant enough. Built in 1924, the upscale hotel was easily retrofitted to work with the original gas heaters and the solid brick structure had withstood the years of neglect remarkably well. Like the predominantly red brick town itself, it was old, functional and survived the Collapse better than the modern counterparts. The cheap motels where the Prancing Pony lay near I-64 and I-81 at the edge of town were falling apart. The Homestead Suites and Red Roof Inns weren't built to last more than a couple decades, and that was with the advantage of upkeep.

Thuy, Meredith and the small contingent of Vicious Rabbits drove off the next day continuing westward along winding two-lane highways, passing active and fallow farmland alike. They passed a ghost town along the way. Like many tiny bergs, this one fell because it was too small to protect itself during the Collapse. While large cities were certainly death traps, tiny hamlets were vulnerable as well. Rochelle was a notable exception to that rule. Midsized towns, depending on their industry, location and their luck were best suited to withstand the Great Suck, that is, if they weren't in the path of the flu. Meredith guessed that the former inhabitants of this place might have moved to Staunton, a town that was not officially aligned with either the Dominion of Lynchburg or the Orange Pact. It set its orientation towards West Virginia whose border was only a few miles from here.

The Suburban groaned as it slowed to a stop before a one lane bridge. To their left was a yellow house and an antique train caboose parked next to it at the base of a steep hill covered in trees. The road leading up the hill was blocked by a brown 1970's era Chevy Monte Carlo.

"This is it," Thuy said. They waited patiently for a few moments until she saw a few figures emerge out of the snow covered woods. One started the car and moved it to allow the Suburban to come up the hill.

The sight of the Monte Carlo prompted a memory of the one her parents had. Try as she might, Meredith couldn't help but reminisce about going to the grocery store every Friday with her mom in the boat-like vehicle, and how her dad managed to take down an evergreen from the woods and strap it to the car one Christmas with the roots splayed in front of them. The Monte Carlo stayed with the family long past its life expectancy. She drove it all the way from her home in Wisconsin to American University before it died the second semester of her freshmen year.

The sweet childhood memories stood utterly incongruent and in stark contrast to the grim reality of her world, especially considering what she was about discover. She never allowed herself to think about her parent's fate beyond forcing an optimistic outcome for them. Her brother operated a farm past the state line in Michigan's Upper Peninsula. He was a lifestyle entrepreneur who gave up the life of an investment banker to become an organic farmer whose livestock provided organic milk, eggs and cheese. Summers were pleasant in Wisconsin and her parents were in good health, she reasoned. Surely, they made it to their son's farm. If Meredith survived at six months pregnant in Washington, DC…if she survived, then certainly her parents in the upper Midwest where the temperatures rarely hit 90 degrees fared even better. That was the extent Meredith allowed for her imaginings.

Of course, assuming her parents and brother were in good health living the high life in the UP surrounded by stolid Swedish descendents and Canadians, she knew her parents would have assumed that she was dead. Considering her circumstances at the time, she wouldn't blame them. Funny, she hadn't seen it that way at the time. In fact, Meredith remembered feeling reluctant to leave the city, because she believed that by Monday morning the lights would be back on and her supervisor was going to have a few words for her taking leave without prior authorization. It seemed such a trite and ridiculous concern.

The Suburban plodded up the hill past the heavily fortified network of barbed wire where landmines and trip wire were planted. Beyond the clearing at the summit lay the cylindrical white building and conical dome of Stokesville Observatory and Museum next to a group of what looked like log cabin apartments. As far as observatories went, it was unremarkable. It boasted an antique telescope whose capabilities were limited to the technology of the early twentieth century. Largely a neglected artifact of the past and nestled out in the middle of nowhere, hardly anybody knew of Stokesville's existence, which served the Swan's purposes perfectly.

Outside the observatory stood an odd assortment of Vicious Rabbits dressed in white ponchos hefting various assault rifles and other people in civilian garb. Thuy and Meredith got out of the Suburban and stepped carefully as to not slip on the road which had melted and refrozen repeatedly since the snow began. They were met by one of the civilians, a man over 60.

"Mrs. Jung, Mr. Mai, what an unexpected pleasure."

"You may dispense with the pleasantries, Dr. Searles. I have the reports."

"Come on in. I have some chicory in the pot."

The inside of the observatory was little warmer than outside. Considering the fact that the roof opened every evening, the insulation was minimal. Troy Searles poured Meredith and the Vicious Rabbits escorts a cup of chicory while Thuy took the opportunity to study the observatory, which was once a museum. Unlike the burnt out observatory in Charlottesville, there was no modern equipment. The telescope was a vintage 14 inch Celestron Compustar. A series of old fashioned adding machines including slide rulers and several abacuses decorated the room.

"So this is where my tax dollars are going," Thuy said to no one in particular.

Stokesville Observatory was one of the black budget projects, not officially on Rochelle's books. As far as the Vicious Rabbit soldiers assigned here on temporary duty—TDY—assignments were concerned, Rochelle maintained a post here as a forward outpost for potential incursions by Lynchburg, West Virginia or other potential hostiles into the Shenandoah Valley. That was sensible enough. The hill on which Stokesville observatory stood provided a commanding view for several miles. In addition, the nearby neutral town of Staunton provided useful intelligence on trading activity of the other powers. There were other outposts south of Monticello, near Richmond, and north of Culpeper. According to the military, this was another such outpost. The observatory and the scientists within it were another gift from Ross.

Without words being exchanged, Meredith pulled the documents obtained from North Carolina out of her leather valise and handed them to Troy Searles whose bald scalp was beginning to show a few liver spots. He and a few of the other civilians started to put pencil to paper, making use of the slide rulers and the abacuses. One of the women unfurled a large blue print celestial map, clamping it to one of the worktables and jotting notes into a notebook.

As the team of civilians worked over the next couple of hours, Meredith was unable to stay seated. She stood up and joined Thuy who was studying an aged autographed photo of Leonard Nimoy with barely legible script requesting the observatory to "keep watching the skies."

"Your uncle?" Thuy asked.

Meredith nodded without hearing his question.

"You nervous?"

Meredith raised an eyebrow with her eyeglasses slipping to the edge of her nose and gave him a look as if to say, "Are you effing kidding me?"

He grinned sheepishly. "Right. Stupid question."

He put an arm around her and she rested her head on his shoulder, the two stood together for what seemed like hours.

Meredith broke the silence. "Chris always said he was grateful that you were gay. I never understood why until now." They stared at the photo of the TV and film star who would never be allowed to expand his considerable acting abilities beyond that of the bemused Vulcan.

Troy and his team used the abacuses and slide rulers, while a young Asian girl took notes. Meredith didn't have the faintest idea how they did what they did. She hardly believed that humans could do the work of computers, but here they were.

Troy's face was drained of blood when he broke away from his team and approached her and Thuy. On the other side of the room, one of the young women broke down. Meredith felt her gut tightening and she reached for Thuy's hand.

Troy squeezed the bridge of his nose with exhaustion. "The…uh," clearing his throat, "the calculations from the observatory in Asheville and from the latest report from Naval Support Facility Thurmont's observatory you provided to us both matches our own. It's going to hit, Mrs. Jung."

Meredith staggered back a couple of paces and nearly collapsed. She had hoped beyond hope the people in Asheville and Thurmont were wrong. After all, they made calculations with slide rulers and pencil to paper like the scientists here. It was entirely possible that they missed something. She was praying for human error. Still, she had to ask.

"Are you sure?"

"I'm afraid so. When you provided us the printouts a few years back from Thurmont, we were able to locate the derelict asteroid. If we didn't know to look for it, we might have never discovered it. We weren't able to give you an accurate prediction of its trajectory though, until it emerged from the far side of the sun. When it became observable again a couple of months ago, we started to run the calculations, just as our colleagues at the other two observatories did. The asteroid's trajectory had been shifted slightly, possibly from a close pass-by with another asteroid. Whatever it was that altered it, the other two teams' calculations were exactly what we came up with."

Meredith tried to find a hole in the prognosis. "No, there must be some mistake, something missed in the calculations. Is it possible your people were running your numbers based on their findings and you…"

Troy shook his head. "Our work was done completely independent from Asheville and Thurmont. We were running a comparison of their work to ours. And I expect we will be sending our work to them to verify once more the accuracy of all three of our separate calculations. Ideally, we would compare our findings with a multitude of observatories, but I guess we're lucky we were able to find even two other groups of astronomers and mathematicians. I grant, our team could be wrong, or their teams could be wrong. But all three of us? Even with human error, even if we were all wrong, we would at least have different calculations. We don't."

"So, what are we looking at?"

Troy rubbed his beard and took a seat. "The asteroid will impact on March 15th, probably in western Canada."

"Western Canada? We're hell and gone from Western Canada," Thuy said.

"The asteroid that killed off the dinosaurs was no bigger than the island of Manhattan," Troy countered. "The impact sent up enough debris into the atmosphere to block out the sun for several months, destroying much of the plant life."

"This asteroid," Troy took a moment before continuing. "This asteroid is eighty-five miles in diameter. It's composed of iron. It won't be the nuclear winter scenario of sixty-five million years ago. When it hits, the seas will boil, the atmosphere will sear."

"Our chances," she whispered weakly.

"There will be no place to hide. There will be," Troy stole a withering amount of composure. "We're talking about turning the entire surface of the earth into a molten state. There will be no survivors. No human being, no plant or animal will survive. Bacteria perhaps. I…I'm, oh, Christ…"

Troy collapsed into a chair and broke down. So, too did the other astronomers.

The afternoon passed into evening and the observatory, which had had never been warm enough, had descended to below freezing. Troy Searles and the other astronomers had retired back to their quarters, the makeshift log cabin apartments next door, leaving Meredith and Thuy alone just outside the observatory. The two sat warming their hands by a campfire. The soldiers who were oblivious to the content of the meeting patrolled the perimeter.

Meredith expected that hearing the confirmation of this news would send her over the edge, send her reeling into a fetal position, that she would vomit or faint. But she did none of these things. It was as if all emotion had been sucked out of her, perhaps an emergency response by her psyche. Maybe it was shock. Whatever the cause, she found herself to be remarkably calm.

"I hoped they would find a huge mistake in their calculations," she said sitting down next to him. "I hoped, dear, I prayed…"

The two sat silently a few moments listening to wolves howl beyond the confines of the observatory grounds.

"Do we tell the constable?"

Meredith pursed her lips. "I think he should know. As far as everyone else, I don't know. On the one hand, people should have the right to know their fate and make peace with their maker, and say goodbye to their loved ones." She felt a stab of pain knowing she wouldn't be able to be with her husband when the end came.

"True, but on the other hand, there's nothing that can be done. All it would do would send people into a panic."

"It's real, isn't it, Thuy? We can't see it yet but it's out there racing to us, sealing our fate, sealing the fate of all life."

"What's it called?"

"Sorry?"

"The asteroid. It's got to have a name, right. What's the name of the asteroid?"

"It was named after the amateur astronomer who discovered it in 2005. His name is…was Chester Rayne; It's called Rayne 2005."

Thuy sniffed. "The observatory Troy spoke about, the one at Naval Support Facility Thurmont. That sounds familiar."

"It should. It's the official designation for Camp David."

Thuy raised his eyebrows. "Camp David? Ross is connected to Camp David? I didn't even know they were alive."

"They are, barely." She gathered herself. "I have to get this back to Ross."

"I don't see why your Camp David contact is in such a hurry. They can't do anything about it, can they?"

There was an edge of hope in his voice. She couldn't blame him. Camp David was where the federal government evacuated in the days following the Shift. She, too, hoped that the federal government would come back and solve this pesky Shift thing. But alas, they were treading water. They certainly had no answer to the asteroid heading straight for them.

"Sorry, Thuy."

Meredith stared into the star filled night. She bet it was this dark out here even before the Shift, hence the reason for the location. She wondered if there would be anyone anywhere to observe the stars a couple of months from today. Somewhere in the night sky still too small for the naked eye to see, Rayne 2005 was coming for them all.

Chapter 24

Charlottesville, Virginia
Greater Monticello
January 2013

The ride up the mountain to Monticello was painful on a number of levels. Neko Lemay hadn't been on her horse Buffy since before the assassination attempt. She mounted her gingerly, careful as to not tear any of the stitches that replaced the other stitches she'd torn a week earlier. Buffy could sense Neko's weakened state and strode as steady as a beast could, yet each step reverberated right up her injured shoulder.

"Sweetheart, you sure you wouldn't rather take a carriage up," Lucille asked, seeing Neko wince in pain.

"No, Sheriff. What we're doing tonight is going to get real. And I'm not arriving like some pampered aristocrat."

"That's why no one else but you could do this."

Neko acknowledged the response and guided Buffy up the road passing the common funeral mound where members of the Blue Ridge Militia and the nascent defenders of Monticello were interred together. In some strange way, Neko had come to have a certain reverence for their first foes. Certainly, she had no love for their arrogance, their dismissive misogyny, their devotion to a dead patriarchal mythology contrived by 18th century slave owners. But as rotten as they were, Monticello wouldn't be the force they were without them. Neko had come to understand that the Blue Ridge Militia's attack on them tested their mettle and became essential in forging their identity as Monticellans. Monticello was borne out of violence, much like the pangs of being born, she supposed. The blood of their enemies mixed with their own, integrating and becoming an indelible part of Monticello's identity and for that, she placed her left hand, on her heart and lips, a sign of devotion and respect.

As she and Lucille Schadenfreude slowly trotted up the embankment where the wall once stood as a real barrier and not just a ceremonial entrance, she was reminded of that desperate struggle of survival. Back then she still thought of herself, at least residually, as a Poli Sci major, a student at Olympia, a New Pornographers fan. After that battle, she was a Monticellan and a daughter of Gaia. And one of the men who stood with her through it all was none other than Juan Ramirez.

Her lover Eric Starke, may Gaia guide him someplace peaceful, and Juan had together trained her in the basics of soldiering. Juan had taken his sordid experiences as a child soldier in the Salvadoran Army to benefit the community made up of upstanding suburbanites. He had fought by her side. The two shed blood together, and he risked his life to save hers. In sum, Juan Ramirez had been a rock for her.

That was what was going to make this all the more difficult. It's not as though Juan was some scheming traitor wringing his hands, and twisting a greasy mustache with a top hat. He was a friend, a good man, someone she had trusted. At the same time, she couldn't deny the evidence Lucille presented to her. But as shocking as it was, some small part of her understood his motivation. Had she family, if her father was still alive and he needed her help, she might have...*no*, she protested. Now was not the time for sympathy. It was that weakness that had allowed so many infiltrators into Greater Monticello in the first place. She would never betray Mother Earth, especially to that bug-eyed, imperialist crusader Gordon Boche.

She could not indulge personal sentiment over the greater good. The reverend was gone, who knew when she would return, if ever? Monticello was besieged with infiltrators as the Lambs of God were mobilizing for a full-on invasion. She needed to act to save Monticello now, and she would have to flush the remnants of her pity along with what was left of her innocence.

Juan Ramirez was sitting inside the study that the reverend had used as her office, scribbling notes under the light of a kerosene lamp. Electricity must have been on the fritz again. As they appeared at the door after being announced by the guards, Juan walked over and wore a friendly Cheshire cat smile.

"Neko! Lucille! Come in, come in!" he beckoned kindly. His English was more fluent than she remembered it being a few years ago, smoother. In typical Central American affection, he gave Neko a peck on the cheek, which made her feel awful, knowing that she was about to put him into the proverbial wood chipper.

"Let me take your coats." Juan gently helped Neko take off her winter pattern overcoat made specifically for the archers of the Thomas Jefferson Martyrs Brigade, showing extra care for her dead arm.

"Please sit down, my friends. I have some cider."

"Thank you, Mr. Ramirez," Lucille responded coolly.

Neko had been in Thomas Jefferson's study countless times over the years. Back in the early days, she slept here with dozens of other people, all of whom were crammed in the third President's crib like the refugees they were. Crates of ammunition, peanut butter, medical supplies were laid with little regard on the antique and historically relevant tables where Thomas Jefferson had once written some of his greatest treatises about freedom of religion and the evils of slavery, even if he was a slave owning hypocrite himself. The gravity clock in the antechamber built in the early 19th century kept time during the chaotic months where time would have disappeared otherwise. It began to toll on the hour.

Stirling radios whispered in the background. Most were two-way CB radios, but the largest wooden contraption near the window played Monticello's Classic Rock, "The only kind of rock in town, or the world for that matter," as the station loved to remind its listeners.

"I'm so glad to see you up and about, Neko. Blessed be," Juan said, making the sign of the cross.

"Umm, thank you."

"Why don't you two stay for dinner, yes? Mi esposa is helping the staff make sopa de pata. We have no plantains, of course, but it will keep you warm."

Lucille glanced over to Neko. With a cold authoritative voice Lucille said, "No, thank you. Mr. Ramirez, please take a seat and listen."

Juan stopped in midsentence, taken aback by Lucille's abrupt command and took a seat. "Okay, I'm listening."

Neko rubbed her injured shoulder. "Mr. Ramirez," she never used such formalities with him when it was such a small group, "Mr. Ramirez, I'm afraid I'm going to have to ask for your resignation."

Juan sat stone-faced at the table a few moments. When he spoke, his voice lost all of its warmth. “My English is pretty good, but every now and then I get confused. Did you just say you want me to quit as chief magistrate?”

Neko turned to Lucille who gave her a confident nudge. Neko felt sick knowing what she had to do, but she thought again of the evidence, which provided the anger necessary to do what she had to do. With conjured indignation she countered, “You’re the deputy chief magistrate temporarily acting as interim chief magistrate, and yes, that is exactly what I’m am telling you.”

Juan scoffed and stared at the medallion of the chalice and flame around her neck. “Ah, so, this is what it all comes down to, yes? Neko, chica, I always knew you were a little loco with the Gaia thing and everything, but I never figured you to become a bigot.”

“How dare you claim yourself to be a victim! After what you’ve done!”

“What are you talking about?”

“Don’t play innocent. I know what you’re doing to support your family in Lynchburg. I have the evidence right here, Juan!” Neko pulled a stack of letters from the utility pocket. She winced in pain slightly having moved a little forcefully.

Juan folded his arms. “Sending money to my family in Lynchburg is not a crime.”

“No, but embezzling public funds and sending the proceeds to them is,” Neko retorted. Juan tried to not react, but it was impossible not to see the color drain from his face.

“Neko, you don’t understand. They’re Catholic. They aren’t treated too good by those, those pendejos!”

“Not your nephews Jose and Angel. They’re converts, eager members of the Sheepdogs.”

“Neko, you don’t understand…It’s not as simple...”

“Bullshit, Juan! Your family has been living fat and happy thanks to our Byrds. If they wanted to leave, they could have left. They certainly could have bribed their way out. You’re not the only one here who has family over there. Lots of people have family they can’t help. But you certainly used your position like you’re above everyone else, like the rules don’t apply to you.”

Frankly, there weren’t any formal rules per se. Monticello evolved organically with a basic constitution and short on specifics, relying on common sense to lead the way; however, mobs tended to keep people in line. Juan opened his mouth to speak a couple of times, but no words came out. In the end, he covered his head with his massive calloused hands.

Lucille stood up and walked over to him, and gently patted him on the back, her glasses sparkling in the reflection of the kerosene light. "Here's what we're going to do. Tomorrow morning, you will announce that you are stepping down…for personal reasons, people can make whatever they want out of that. And you will throw your endorsement of Miss Lemay here to replace you as interim chief magistrate and will call for a vote the following week. We will be grateful for your service, and Monticello need never learn of your indiscretion."

"Are we in agreement?" Neko asked.

Juan hesitated a moment before relenting. Finally, he nodded.

"Good. You're not an evil man, Mr. Ramirez, just a little too human. I hold no grudge, and I hope we can maintain a cordial relationship." Lucille sweetly added, "And just to show how much I like you personally, I think your family can stay up here one more night.

The following afternoon, Neko rode back to Monticello. She still felt polluted with the unpleasantness from the night before. She knew she didn't have much of a choice in the matter. Juan was funneling Monticello money to his family for their personal gain. There was no excuse for it. Although none of the letters that were intercepted showed signs of espionage, she now began to question whether Juan wouldn't stoop to doing that as well. She had never known him to be a thief. He was never a scoundrel with the girls. He had always been a loyal husband, so the profile didn't fit. But if he was innocent, he would have put up more of a fight. Besides, two of his nephews were Sheepdogs. That was damning to be sure, because the Lambs of God didn't choose their Gestapo goons without a thorough vetting and indoctrination process. It was an ugly revelation about someone she had once looked up to, and that was more upsetting than anything.

Buffy descended the mountain where Neko lived and trotted up to Monticello. It was above freezing for a change, if barely, but her arm hurt just as bad, even a little worse. The weak, girlie girl part of her begged her to just drop the Zena Warrior Princess act and ride in a carriage, but the adult in her refused to submit to her wants. Injured or not, she was going to have to woman up and lead her people.

As she passed the funeral mound and embankment up to the gates, she was surprised to see the entire corps of the Monticello's Thomas Jefferson Martyrs Brigade lined up along the road, raising their bows in salute. Neko felt her face getting as red as her hair.

"Cheers to the interim chief magistrate!" the archer up front cried out.

A thunderous resonating chorus followed in a chant started by Ezra from something nobody knew the etymology to. "So say we all! So say we all!"

Slowly, she ascended up the hill to find Lucille standing beside her horse wearing the signature skin-tight riding pants and biker boots. One of the archers moved to help Neko off the horse with her injured arm. Neko wished she wasn't so prone to blushing, it made her…well, it made her blush even more.

Lucille gave her a hug and kiss on the cheek. "Welcome, Interim Chief Magistrate."

Neko rolled her eyes. "I thought there was going to be a vote next week."

"Oh there will be. It's just a formality, sweetie. Look at them all out there. It's all for you. They love you, Neko. They need you."

Neko hadn't heard it put that way before, but seeing the line of archers behind her, she knew they loved her, and she loved them. And with them, she felt that she could take on the Lambs of God and lay waste to the bastards who sought their destruction. A stray tear ran down her face, not realizing how touched she was by the moment.

"So say we all!" they cheered.

Lucille walked with her taking her left hand. "Come on, until the reverend finds her way home, you'll be keeping her seat warm. And we have a country to save. Let's get to work."

CHAPTER 25

Falls Church, Virginia
February 2013

BACKGROUND MUSIC: "It's Been Awhile" by Staind
Visit www.michaeljuge.com **on the *A Hard Rain* page to listen**

It wasn't so bad. There were things that Chris enjoyed about this reality. Coffee for starters. He had really missed coffee. Chicory just didn't compare to the true chemically-induced lift he got from his java. Food was another perk. After half a decade of frontier Americana cuisine, to taste a variety of spices again was a pleasure. Chris found himself frequenting Thai, Middle Eastern, Tex Mex, and Indian restaurants, not to mention almost daily visits to his all-time favorite Malaysia Kopitiam. It was also nice to catch up on TV. He got to see how *Lost* ended, though he admitted to feeling a little jipped at the end of it all. Soft toilet paper, Advil, Downy softness… And he was returned to his family, at least some version thereof, although Rhiannon was Yorick here—the two were extraordinarily similar in looks and temperament—but there was no Baby Charles.

But no matter how many niceties there were, this wasn't his life. This place wasn't supposed to be. It was wrong, and only he knew it. This was a world that had died or was supposed to have, in any case. Its presence struck him as a false reality, a Potemkin village that cast a veil of deceit over millions of people, people who were ghosts who did not know they were supposed to be dead.

Chris was the only one who knew the truth, and yet he couldn't tell a soul, not even his wife, a woman who he trusted with his life. There was no way to prove that he came from a different reality, and there was little point in trying. Knowing that made him all the more isolated. Chris was a veteran of wars that never were, a survivor of the apocalypse that never was. Those events that never happened were crucial in forming who he thought be became. Nobody here would identify, nobody here could.

Chris found himself waking painfully early each morning, sometimes waking in terror from nightmares that came from his world. He would dream of being on the inflatable speed boat with Lieutenant Baraka, while artillery and mortar shells exploded all around him in the dark, swelling sea. Machine gun fire, screams of men dying under his command, and in the next moment, he awoke in the silence with only the light of the clock on the cable box. Although it was 2013, to Chris, waking up every morning here in this apartment was returning to the past to 2007, to the time when the demons seized him and came frighteningly close to sending him over the abyss and onto the tracks in front of a speeding Metro train. He still did not know what it was that stopped him from going through with his plans for July 12th.

Chris avoided coming home from work as much as he avoided going into work. Panic imprinted itself on both places. He remembered the way these places smelled, the way they felt. The demons owned him and familiar places served only to remind of that every day.

Chris made excuses to Meredith to leave the apartment whenever he could. Yorick needed more pull-ups, they were out of ketchup and Aidan would not eat anything without ketchup. He would run to the store just to get out of the claustrophobic apartment into the brisk night air. He would drive in his rental car—his other one having been carjacked—and listen to the radio. He just wanted to get out for as long as he could, and he trudged back up the steps to the working-class apartment now worth way less than half of what it was when they bought it nearly a decade ago.

"Hon, tell me, what's going on?"

Chris was sitting out on the balcony bundled in his overcoat listening to some post-Grunge on his iPod when Meredith's voice broke through the ear buds.

"Sorry?"

"Hon, turn off the music and talk to me."

Chris knew Meredith was upset about something. She always said something like that or gave that look when he was being a lout, and he had a propensity for being a lout even when he wasn't inexplicably transported to an alternate universe. The kids were asleep finally. Chris hoped that this version of Aidan would be an early-to-bed sort. No luck. Fortunately, Yorick was like his Rhiannon counterpart and dropped off early. Meredith had on her coat and sat in the green Rubbermaid lawn chair next to him, clasping her delicate warm fingers around his frozen knuckles. Her almond shaped brown eyes met his.

"What's going on, hon?"

"Nothing," he said knowing that he was about as convincing as a feral posing as a civilization slicker.

"You've been distant ever since the carjacking. I can only imagine how traumatizing it must have been. It would be for anyone."

Chris didn't recall this carjacking incident, but apparently it coincided with his acrobatic mishap on *The Interceptor*. Regardless, the incident did provide him a modicum of cover, a plausible explanation as to why he didn't remember any of his passwords at work, or any of his projects for that matter. It also provided a plausible explanation as to his detached mood, although he had thought he played the part well enough. But Meredith was too insightful.

It would be easy to just say, "yeah, the carjacking really got to me." But as much as he knew he couldn't tell her the truth, he didn't want to outright lie to her either. He wound up saying nothing.

"Maybe you should consider going back on the meds, hon, under the circumstances. And you should make an appointment to see Doctor Randolph."

Chris didn't know how long the other Chris had been off his meds, but he found his decision to *voluntarily* abstain from meds to be insane. Sure, *he* had learned to live without them. But he had no choice. Phoketal wasn't something you could produce in the post-Shift world, and the peddlers of pre-Shift meds more often than not were swindling their customers with fakes. So, Chris learned to cope. But as he thought about it, he felt less of a need for them where he was from.

It wasn't that the demons didn't make an appearance every so often. But ever since he had that vision where he confronted Panic who took the form of his pre-Shift self, Panic had never since had the hold on him it once had. Sometimes, the tinnitus would ramp up and he would obsess over it. And then he would obsess over his obsessing, but then he stopped the cycle in its tracks. Instead of panicking over the obsessing, he just accepted that it was okay for him to obsess for awhile. And accepting his tendency to obsess took the wind out of its demonic power. Sure, obsessing sucked, sure, anxiety sucked, but it always passed, eventually.

As Chris thought about it more, he realized that over the last five and a half years, he had come to contain the demons. It wasn't that they didn't rattle his cage. Panic was always up for a game of "let's see how Chris likes this!" But the demons no longer owned him. What he never voiced aloud was how the Shift saved him from the demons. He owed his life quite literally to the Shift, because out of the horror of civilization's collapse something awoke inside him, a determination to last another day. It was in those desperate months, clawing to survive together with his wife, with his friends, with his people that became the Vicious Rabbits that forged the core of his refurbished soul.

It was that pure and tangible desperation for survival that saved Chris from the demons. Death surrounded him and threatened to swallow his people, his wife and son. Chris could see death all around, smell it, touch its presence. The demons had become physically manifest in the world and facing a physical actual threat was something he could handle. And every day he woke to defend his people, everyday he wrought life-saving tools in the blacksmith shop, it armed him, and imbued him with a sense of purpose and belonging; it aroused a tenacious spirit within him. So, when the demons inside his head returned, they seemed a bit weaker, less frightening.

Sitting on the balcony of this Godforsaken apartment now, the steady glow of street lights below and the strobe flashes from a TV in the neighboring apartment building seemed to negate all of that. In this world, none of it ever happened. In this world, Chris somehow muddled through.

But treading water as he did, this other Chris never faced his mortality and therefore he could not know how precious life was. And the sense of alienation. There was no community to whom he belonged. Rochelle existed in this reality, but it was not the home of the Vicious Rabbits. It was just another farming hamlet 30 miles north of Charlottesville. This reality was worse than death, it was a total negation of who he had become. He hadn't felt this lost since before the Shift.

Meredith squeezed his hands. "It's okay, love. I was terrified when I got the call that you had been attacked, but it's going to be okay."

Chris desperately wanted to scream out that it wasn't and that it had nothing to do with some stupid carjacking. It had everything to do with the foundation of who he was being ripped from him. Instead, he hugged her, feeling her warmth in the winter night and the two went back inside.

The car jostled, its wheels squealed on the rails as the Metro train ambled along its underground route on the Orange line. Arms and briefcases butted up against him as Chris stood flush with other passengers. He felt defenseless being trapped underground like this with all of these strangers without so much as a backup pistol for protection. He imagined ferals reaching for his messenger bag or a bandit slithering behind him ready to slit his throat. As he stepped off the train onto the platform at Rosslyn Station, his eyes darted around looking for signs of danger, his heart started racing. Arcade Fire playing "Modern Man" only seemed to reinforce his sense of being out of his element. There were too many people to identify a specific threat. They all were a potential threat for all he knew. Anyone of them could be a bandit or a Lamb of God.

"Stop it," he muttered to himself. He knew he was being ridiculous. He was safe; there were no Lambs of God, no bandits lying in wait, no biker gangs. Everyone here was cleanly shaven, well-dressed and well-fed. They were civilized, the world was civilized. As the song said, they were all "modern man." But walking among the mass of strangers, he felt utterly vulnerable out in the open like this unarmed. It was asking for it where he came from.

Sadly, nothing much had changed in other Chris' life over the past half decade in regards to his work. Well, that wasn't exactly true. He was now a GS-12 where he had been a GS-11 when the Shift hit. But aside from attaining the exulted level of a mid-level journeyman, nothing else had changed, not his work, not his responsibilities, not even his cubicle. After logging onto his desktop, Chris plugged in his iPhone to the speakers to listen to this new fangled Pandora "app." Windows had a snazzier look to it. The icons looked more futuristic to his eyes. Maybe it was simply that he hadn't seen a computer screen in so long that almost any graphic user interface would look futuristic to him.

As he went through his personal and government emails, an unsettling feeling washed over him. He was doing exactly what he did before the Shift, reverting to a kind of autopilot trained by countless hours of soul-sucking, ass-fattening, mouse-pushing drone work that drove him barking mad. The ringing in his ears started ramping up again. The years of close quarters combat fighting inside grocery stores and occasional run ins with Lambs of God-sponsored bandits with mortars didn't help his tinnitus. Then he reminded himself that this wasn't the body he fought those battles. Here, he had a full set of teeth, all ten toes, his nose hadn't become a crooked bulbous honker, there were no shrapnel scars along his back, and most refreshing he wasn't afflicted with the searing pain that often ran accompanied those injuries, though he was on the chunky side, just as he remembered himself to be before the Shift.

In fact, when he went to Wal-Mart the other day, he was struck by all the fat people in the store, himself included. It was almost like a caricature of Americans, but they were real. It wasn't so apparent inside the Beltway—too many type A personalities who wouldn't dare go over their optimum weight, no less be seen in a Wal-Mart. But normal people who lived out beyond the Beltway revealed the supposed "obesity epidemic" that plagued America before the Shift. Well, Chris knew of one easy solution to that one.

Chris turned up the volume on Pandora trying to drown out the ringing. Typing was a perishable skill as evidenced by Chris' fat fingering the keys like a Mongol trying to gingerly pet a kitten. Along with emails, Chris checked The Washington Post for news, though he really didn't know why he bothered. None of it mattered, really. This wasn't his world. He might as well get his history from reading Harry Turtledove. Besides, it was depressing. This world might not have had been hit by the Shift, but it wasn't much better off, just a lot more populated. The spiraling global economy was inflaming tensions around the world. There was an article that caught Chris' eye. It was about the presidential inauguration. Apparently, there were a mountain of controversies about the newly-elected president, but the one that stuck out was the minister who gave the benediction. It was none other than Gordon Boche himself.

Chris nearly choked on his coffee seeing the image of the pink-faced regent of the Lambs of God. No, here he wasn't the unquestioned leader of the Dominion of Lynchburg raising an army to topple the Orange Pact and set his home on fire. He was just a televangelist and president of Boche Ministries who barely escaped federal prosecution for firearms dealings. The bug-eyed son of a bitch looked just as smug and sanctimonious as the file photo Chris had seen of him when the regent made a speech to the neutral city of Staunton.

"Son of a bitch."

The phone rang and it took a second for him to remember to pick it up.

"H...hello?"

"Is that how you answer the phone?"

Chris didn't recognize the voice at first, but then it hit him that it was the other Chris' new supervisor, Ed Farcus. He didn't know what Ed meant by what he said.

"I'm sorry?"

"I said, is that how you answer the phone."

"Umm, yeah?" Chris answered casually.

"Wrong! You're supposed to say, 'State Department, this is Chris Jung. May I help you?' Got it?'"

"But you know who you're calling." Chris was confused and getting a little perturbed by the man's nonsensical argument.

"Are you trying to be funny?"

"I don't think so. I mean, I saw it was your extension calling." Though not technically true, it was factually accurate that Chris could see the extension number calling.

Ed was silent for a moment. "Come to my office."

Ed Farcus' office was the same as his former boss, Darryl. Darryl could be a real pain in the ass sometimes, and Chris never found a distinct neck between the massive bulldog head and shoulders of his, but at least Darryl was someone he respected. He was dedicated to the point of a workaholic, and he helped grow the unit's influence in the early days. And he did laugh at his jokes, so he was smart, too. This guy Ed?...well, Chris wasn't a psychological profiler, but he believed this Ed Farcus fellow had a real inferiority complex wrapped up with an unwarranted God complex, if that was possible, a real ass clown in laymen's terms. Though noticeably younger, he had a receding hairline with a shock of red hair to go with his yellow eyes. Various degrees and certificates comprised an "I love me" wall next to photos of Ed's exploits as a purported operator.

"Come in. Shut the door."

Chris sat down and stared as an airplane made its approach along the Potomac. He had to force himself to breathe regularly seeing the impossible sight.

"You got a problem with authority, don't you Chris?"

Chris didn't respond immediately. He studied the man's face, realizing he was dead serious.

"Um, no. No I don't have a problem with authority."

"Don't try to lie to me. You went to lunch with the Branch Chief without telling me first."

"Oh, sorry."

"Sorry," Ed repeated darkly. "That's what you have to say for yourself?"

Chris cackled "What?"

"This isn't funny."

Really? Because Chris had a hard time believing this guy wasn't just acting like an asshole. Now that he thought about it, if the other Chris was insolent, well, he could hardly blame him.

"Look Ed, um, I meant no disrespect. I just forgot." He had no idea why he needed to inform his boss that he was going to lunch with another boss first, but he was just playing along.

"Well, you're too old to be fucking up like this. I don't care what your excuse is. Now, get your shit together and don't do this again."

Chris walked out and shut the door. "God, what an ass hat."

"You said it." He turned to see Kendra sitting at the cube over. It was so disorienting to see her here and with long weaves instead of a crew cut.

"Kendra, you ever feel like everything is just wrong?"

"Of course. I'm a Redskins fan."

CHAPTER 26

Stubb Foundation
Laurel, Maryland
February 2013

Rita sat staring at the computer-generated projection of asteroid Rayne 2005, which will impact in a matter of weeks and destroy all life on the planet. Jamil, the organic computer, had delivered the devastating news to her in a voice that held both the innocence of a boy and the cold precision of an omniscient machine. She saw the calculations, and what's more, they made sense to her. Now, she knew how that was possible.

Apparently, some of the conspiracy theorists were right. There were things that the government hid from the people. It wasn't just this dazzling super computer that was immune to the effects of an EMP. More fundamental was the asteroid, the massive chunk of iron eighty-five miles across careening towards them. Jamil did qualify that back in 2007, Rayne 2005 was just another near earth object, a new discovery by this amateur astronomer, and there was still a lot of wiggle room in its potential trajectory at the time. It was just more data to a government too preoccupied with more concrete matters like the wars in Iraq and Afghanistan. Besides, what could the U.S. government do had it known? What could anybody do, even with the technology available before the Shift?

That was the question facing her now. Rita caressed the golden AA chip representing nineteen years of sobriety in her hand. The serenity prayer was about the most relevant prayer in her daily life. Every morning she asked her higher power, now in the form of Gaia, to grant her the serenity to accept the things she cannot change, the courage to change the things she can and the wisdom to know the difference. Now, more than ever, that prayer resonated with her.

Jamil had demanded the scientists over at the Stubb Foundation bring her of all people over to him because it said she would help save the world, though so far it was short on specifics. Why her? How was she going to save the world? She was good at math. So what? So were the Stubb Foundation scientists. And speaking of, how did they even know about her existence in Monticello? A lot of the questions remained that had not been addressed. More important matters came to the fore, matters like the end of the world, the real end this time, not the ambivalent scourge by the earth turning off the electricity like last time.

This was the end of all human history, the end of all life, the entire genetic heritage was going to be incinerated into the basic elements, everything that happened on the earth was to be erased in a global fire like none of it ever existed. The planet itself, the physical structure would survive, but everything that ever was special about it would be dead. If it had been a pandemic, genetically designed to kill all humans, Rita could live with that. At least the rest of the world, all of the plant and animal life would continue on. If it had been a nuclear holocaust even, she could make peace with that. Even then there would be survivors and a recovery.

As Jamil explained, the impact from this asteroid will completely sterilize the earth; the seas will boil, the air will burn, and the earth will become a molten rock. Rita now understood the content of Gaia's warning, and she now understood why she appeared unnerved. This wasn't just about one species. In essence, the very life of Gaia herself existed as the intertwined biosphere of all life. Once the biosphere gets extinguished, so too will Gaia.

Rita caressed the coin, and whispered. "Gaia, if you have something to share, now is the time to tell me."

Others sat throughout the command center, some gawking at the computers, others just sitting catatonic. The news was too much. Akil had disappeared. She knew hearing his missing son's name affected him more than anything else, perhaps even more than the news of earth's imminent end.

"I guess they were a few months off."

Rita turned to see Chris Jung taking a seat next to her. Physically, he was the same person that existed before the accident that apparently had transposed the conscience of Chris from this other reality of which Jamil spoke. But the way he carried himself now was just slightly off.

"I'm sorry. I must have been dozed off. Who was a few months off?"

"The Mayans. I guess they forgot to carry the one or something."

"You don't really believe in that, do you?"

"No, not really. I always thought it was bullshit myself. But now, I don't know what to believe. I mean, I was farting around in the world, happy, okay, well not happy, but close enough, and then this."

Chris paused to look away. "You know, I never really cared too much about anything. Shit, not even my own life. July 11th. It's crazy that this Shift thing happened on July 11th."

"How so?" Rita was suddenly distracted enough from the realization of earth's death sentence to see that Chris was struggling. "Chris, why was July 11th important to you if the Shift didn't happen?"

He shuddered. "Never mind, Rita. The point is that the only thing that ever really seemed to count for anything in my life was my wife and kids."

She smiled. "The other Chris is like that, too. Well, his family, and his troops and his home."

"Hmm. I hate my apartment."

"That's not what I'm talking about by home, Chris. I mean his people in Rochelle."

Chris waved off her objection. "The only thing that mattered was my family and now, everything will end, not just here, but in my world, too! As much as history altered between yours and my reality, the trajectory of planets and other shit in space are absolutely identical."

Rita nodded. It made sense to her. Even though events on earth to include human history were altered, to have the course of asteroids and planets altered, the historical divergence would have had to happen a lot earlier.

"And the worst part is that I won't be there with my family when it happens," Chris added. His voice softened. "I won't be there to comfort Aidan and Yorick, hold Meredith beside me."

Rita took his hand. "I'm sure the other you will."

"I wish I had your faith."

Rita held back the urge to laugh. The word "faith" was a relative term that rose and fell in value like a wild stock market of the old days.

"I've been hearing of this Gaia business from Kendra," he said. "She seems quite convinced by it, and from what I gather, you're Gaia's mouthpiece, right?"

Rita shrugged, not arguing the semantics of phrasing.

"I wish…I hope she is real. And I hope Skynet over there can find a way to save our asses."

"She is real," replied a female voice. Rita turned around to see one of the Stubb Foundation scientists, Ariadne Hunter, she recalled, the bioethicist or some other equally useless title.

The lady took a seat next to the two of them, her perky face seemed to cut through the gloom. "Gaia is real, and I know the reverend and Jamil will find the solution that will save the earth."

Rita snorted. "Thank you for your confidence, Dr. Hunter."

"Oh, please, Reverend. Call me Ariadne."

"Listen Ariadne, I don't have the faintest idea what I'm going to do."

"I understand that. But I also know Gaia will guide you and Jamil."

That stunned Rita. "How…how, do you even know about Gaia? How do you know so much about us?"

Ariadne smiled. "Wait? You don't know, do you?"

"Know what?"

"That we've been listening to you for years now, to you in Monticello, Rochelle, Culpeper, as well as Lynchburg," mentioning the last city with unveiled revulsion.

"How is that possible?" Rita was beginning to think that the Stubb Foundation had spies infiltrating the various communities and was about to raise hell when Ariadne clarified herself.

"We listen to your radio transmissions, ever since you started broadcasting."

"Hold on. Radio transmissions don't travel nearly as far as they used to. We lose reception of our stations before we're forty miles out and that's on a good clear day with little interference."

"I know, and if we had your limited equipment, we couldn't listen in. But Jamil uses the satellite in high earth orbit that wasn't destroyed by the EMPs."

"You still have contact with it?" Rita didn't even see Akil who joined the discussion. That was partly due to her having limited peripheral vision having lost an eye. He crouched beside her.

"Yes. It's a Chinese military satellite, but Jamil was able to convince it to play with us. The satellite can pick up the faintest, most jumbled transmissions and descramble and clean it up to stereo quality. I have to say, I particularly love KVR even if you all are stuck with Classic Rock."

Rita chuckled. She preferred Monticello's station WTJ, as it played a lot more Latino as well as Rock.

"Look." She slid over to one of the computer consoles and started working with the mouse. Rita realized the term "mouse" sounded funny to her now. "You mind some music? I'll turn to WTJ for you, Reverend."

Rita folded her arms slightly skeptical, but saw the actions on the flat screen where Ariadne intercepted a transmission and the computer started loading as if it were some online station. "There's about a second delay due to the cleanup, but…"

Ariadne clicked on the mouse, and Rita could hear a male voice singing and the strumming of an acoustic guitar. There was a slight amount of static, but it came in clearer than she heard most of the time inside Charlottesville itself. And sure enough, she recognized it was Bob Dylan singing.

BACKGROUND MUSIC: "A Hard Rain's A-Gonna Fall" by Bob Dylan
Visit www.michaeljuge.com **on the *A Hard Rain* page to listen**

"Oh where have you been my blue-eyed son? And where have you been my darling young one?"

Rita, Akil, Chris, and Ariadne were joined by the other Virginians. Gunnery Sergeant Birmingham, Lieutenant Baraka, and others hovered over the computer as if trying to listen the word of God Himself. She had heard this song thousands of times before. Being a Unitarian Minister and community organizer in the old days meant being an activist, and with that came a lot of 60s folk music. It hadn't been her thing growing up, but she had come to adopt it into her CD collection.

She whispered the lyrics along with Dylan, seeing that so too, were the others, even the gruff legacy Marine gunnery sergeant. Rita had spent her life clinging to booze, and then to the borrowed causes of others. When Gaia found her broken body and her broken spirit, she breathed into Rita something true, something that belonged to Rita alone, her soul. Now, listening to the words, she felt the weight of the world descending upon her. She was resurrected for a reason, after all. But it wasn't to simply guide Monticello through tough times as she once thought. The fate of the world rested on her, her and that computer "sleeping" over there. It wasn't arrogance to say this. She certainly didn't want this. She wasn't counseled on who should save the world. If she had her druthers she would have chosen someone like Jon Early…Jon Early of a few years ago.

But Gaia had chosen her. *How am I supposed to stop an asteroid!* She had no idea, but Gaia wasn't delusional. In her heart, Rita knew Gaia needed her now, as she once needed Gaia. She pushed away the images of the earth dying in fire. She would find out what she needed to do to save the earth. In Laurel, she and Jamil would save her.

Neko Lemay stood beside the podium while Lucille Schadenfreude spoke in front of a massive crowd outside Davenport Field. Like much of the UVA campus, the baseball field had been hit by the fires. Fortunately, being largely an empty field and benches, there wasn't much rebuilding to be done. It did make a good place to gather so long as the weather was cooperative, which it wasn't right now.

"And we will not back down from our responsibilities! The path Gaia has chosen for us is not easy, but she chose us because we are what is left that can stand up to the forces of darkness."

The crowd cheered in response to Lucille's fiery words. If it had been a couple of degrees colder, it would be snowing. Instead, a freezing rain doused the crowd. Neko herself was fine with the cold. She grew up in Washington State after all. She knew both about cold and rain. Her limp arm cradled in a sling ached with the moisture. While Lucille spoke, Neko tried to move her fingers, but to no effect. Were the nerves permanently severed?

"Old Gordo over there, thinks himself emperor of a Christian empire. And he wants to cleanse the land of unbelievers."

The audience booed. Lucille continued with her intractable chipper voice. "I guess he fashions himself after Caligula maybe."

The boos turned to laughter, most appreciating the reference to the insane emperor written in history books. The others played along pretending to get it. "But I have news for you, sunshine, we aren't the little pagan peasants you conquered. Read your history books, oh great Regent. Like the Visigoths before, we are your end!"

The audience roared in jubilation. Neko had to hand it to Lucille; she was a much better public speaker than she herself was. She hated this, though this was her first time speaking in public. Well, not exactly. Some years ago, before the Shift, during her senior year in high school she was chosen to present her team's product, a smoke alarm with a snooze button, before the rest of her peers in the Young Entrepreneurs class. She remembered stammering throughout, sprinkling her sentences with "uh," "like," and "but um" between every third word.

"We will stand together, and no amount of spies or goons can unravel the power of Gaia!"

Neko was about to pray for Gaia to send another surge, but realized that it was a selfish prayer. Instead, she thought of Rita, her mentor and friend who was out there missing. *Gaia, please guide her back safely. Please, I don't want to do this. You and I both need her now.*

"So without further delay, I give you the spunky spitfire who you elected to guide us to help those jihadi crusaders meet their maker. Interim Chief Magistrate Neko Lemay!"

The crowd cheered and Neko forced a plastic smile, waving with her good hand. Brushing aside a few strands of red hair that had matted to her face, she tried to will herself to look directly into the crowd the way Rita would. Her face pitched slightly downward, she tapped the microphone to produce a painful shriek. She cleared her throat. *Okay, don't say "um," "like," or "but um." Don't do it,* she warned herself.

"Um, yeah. Hello, I'm Neko Lemay." The audience cheered raucously more to show moral support for her right now than because they voted for her as interim chief magistrate.

She took a deep breath and spoke what she felt. "I miss, the chief magistrate. I miss her so much right now as do you all." The audience hushed.

"She brought us all together, kept us from killing each other back when we got on each other's nerves. Remember back in Monticello?"

People smiled, some laughed in communal remembrance of the insane first months when they were all crammed in the estate trying to eke out an existence while hiding from the throngs of refugees and gangs.

"She taught us about Gaia's guiding light, the earth spirit that unites us all. She gave us purpose."

Neko had to stop herself for a moment. With her voice strained, she continued. "I cannot replace her. I can only fill her post until she returns. But I tell you all this. I will not cower to the bastards out there who rape and pillage their way to power. I will not submit! My arm is now useless. An assassin's bullet made short work of it. But I do not grieve any longer, for it was a small price to save the reverend."

Neko unsheathed a dagger and hefted it skyward. "And with my good arm I hold this dagger and stand by you. And we will prevail! For Rita!"

The audience erupted, shouting "For Rita!" repeating the reverend name as the rain picked up. "For Rita!" was chanted for a good minute. Neko nodded, satisfied. Lucille placed a cloak over her and the two walked off the stage.

"You see, sweetie? I told you that you would do fine!"

Almost giddy, Neko agreed. The armed group guided them to an awaiting car. Through the rain and cheer, Neko could faintly hear the amplifiers now tuned to the radio station WTJ playing a song her dad used to play.

"Skyline Control, this is Echelon. Do you have our visual?"

"Copy that Echelon. We see your approach. You're clear to proceed… give the heads…Welcome back."

"Good copy, Skyline Control."

Meredith sat virtually catatonic with her face pressed on the rain speckled window slit of the armored Suburban not paying much attention to the Vicious Rabbit transmitting to Monticello's Western checkpoint on I-64. As the motorcade sped along at the thrilling speed of thirty-five miles per hour, the tires dispersing the water on the road created a constant whooshing sound.

A low layer of fog kissed the tops of mountains while Meredith caught sight of deer bounding off from the highway into the hills from the motorcade's approach. Snow, while still blanketing the landscape, battled to maintain its dominance with the freezing rain that ate away at it. A pair of feral dogs playfully wrestled along the side of the road. All of it would be gone in a matter of weeks. The snow, the mountains, the deer, all of it, washed away in a torrent of hellfire, sterilizing the earth, and erasing all evidence that it ever existed.

What were her personal problems to that? What was losing a war to the Lambs of God now? The world was going to end, for real this time. There were going to be no survivors. Her children would never grow up. They would never know what it was like to fall in love, to have one's heartbroken, to recover and fall in love again. It was wrong, so wrong.

Meredith had never believed in anything in particular, and she met the whole Gaia thing with as much skepticism as she did the whole Christian thing. She believed only what she could observe, but she also knew somewhere inside her, she was a spiritual being, they all were. If they all perished, maybe their souls would be remembered in some collective photo album. At least she hoped so.

The Vicious Rabbit in the front passenger seat of the Suburban placed the hand mic back in its cradle and turned to Thuy and Meredith.

"We'll be through the checkpoint in a couple of minutes, but we can stand down, now."

Thuy who sat next to her had been equally silent the whole trip. "Looks like we'll be home before dark. The kids will be happy to see you."

Meredith stared out the window. "I miss them," her voice cracked.

Thuy leaned over to the Vicious Rabbit in the front seat. "You think you can turn the knob over to WTJ? I'm kinda dying in the silence here."

"Sure thing." The Vicious Rabbit moved the dial on the Stirling and found the Monticello radio station playing a song she remembered Chris playing for her a few times back when they were dating.

"And it's a hard, it's a hard…"

Chris Jung waited in the customer service line holding a towel rack set and a thing that caught his eye, a Snuggie. Inoffensive music played on the loudspeakers while he tried to make sense of the inexplicable presence of so many shoppers on a school night. The Bed Bath & Beyond was stocked with items that hadn't sold over Christmas. Perhaps that had something to do with it. The checkout person scanned the items of the person ahead of him with rhythmic regularity, the scan's beep sounding like a heart monitor.

Chris surveyed the house wares store. It was well lit and warm inside and it boasted a nice selection of sheets he would love to get one day. There was a water fountain that worked, the place didn't reek of human filth, and none of the customers were shooting at him.

That's right, Chris. Nobody here is trying to kill you. Relax. And then he recalled the raid on the Bed Bath & Beyond nearly two months ago. He shook his head incredulously. This wasn't the same Bed Bath & Beyond where he and his First Bike Mounted Cavalry hunted down and killed the bandits who raided Culpeper and slaughtered a family and took cattle. That store was in Reston. But what did it matter? The layout was identical.

The same circular design was replicated in stores throughout the country, and made great hideouts for ferals…*there aren't any ferals, Chris.*

Waiting in line, he relived crossing into the threshold of the store, stumbling over a rack of useless digital clocks, hearing the din of machinegun fire reverberating indoors, tackling a bandit and slitting his throat. The checkout lady repeated her question.

"Sir, you have a Rewards card?"

"Pardon? Uh, no."

"Would you like to apply? You can save ten percent on your purchase today."

"Um, no thank you, ma'am."

Chris bundled his wool pea coat to protect him from the rain as he scurried over to the rental car. As he merged onto Leesburg Pike, he joined the evening rush hour traffic. The sheet of rain sparkled in the stream of headlights. He remembered that he used to play the radio in his old Corolla. While waiting at a red light, he pressed a knob on the radio, which came to life with a cacophonous rage, making him jump in his seat. He fiddled with the buttons scanning for stations while marveling at the digital display.

According to his memory, DC radio stations sucked. The radio waves were saturated with pre-approved playlists that consisted of maybe two hundred songs, most of them woefully lacking in any artistic integrity. Chris recalled how before the Shift, he had given up on the radio, appalled by the state of popular music. It was if a whole generation was being corralled into neatly segmented markets that could be sold goods and a self-image. The music reflected the soulless corporate generated sounds. Everything seemed that way around him now, fake, lacking any substance. It wasn't that way back home. Scanning through the channels, it was no different from 2007; it was worse, in fact. He was tempted to use his iPhone again, but he settled on a Classic Rock station playing some Zeppelin. What the hell, why not?

Chris plodded slowly along Leesburg Pike, past Tysons Corner Mall and over the 495 Beltway. The windshield wipers kept pace with the rainfall. Chris felt his heart racing again as he gripped the steering wheel. "Kashmir" faded out and was replaced by a song by Bob Dylan. He turned up the volume trying to drown out his anxiety and the world outside.

Thoughts about his irritating boss and spreadsheets colluded with memories of the Stand at Exxon Heights, the raid at Madison High, and blacksmithing at his forge. Memories of Charles Early, Jon Early combined with new faces here. Chris remembered struggling through the birth of Aidan, something much more traumatic to Chris than to his wife who was the one in labor.

Crammed in the little rental car, Chris struggled to maintain his sanity, to not let his thoughts of being trapped indefinitely overwhelm him. What was happening to his family in his world? Did the cavalry elude the Abercrombies? Did they take out the nuclear waste? Were the Lambs of God going to attack? How would the Orange Pact endure being outnumbered as they were? They were out there somewhere. His people were real, more real than this plastic construct of reality, and they needed him.

Chris knew his people's lives hung in the balance. Between the Abercrombies and the Lambs of God descending upon them, they needed every experienced fighter they could get. They were depending on him to take out the Abercrombies before they got their hands on the nuclear material, and here he was sitting in traffic being useless, stranded in a world for which he felt nothing. A world was on fire, and he was just a wonk sitting in traffic now. He desperately wanted to reach out to his Meredith to tell her he was alive and would find a way back. Every time he came home to his apartment, he had to hold himself back from telling this Meredith that. His Meredith needed to know he was alive.

Chris listened to Bob Dylan moaning away and recalled playing it for Meredith when they were dating, a time before it all fell to pieces. Somewhere back then, the man he thought he had become and the man who belonged here were the same person. He was trying to come to terms with that. He prayed that the other Chris would step up for him over in his world—presumably, the other Chris must have gone there, he reasoned—because he was certainly lost in a suburban malaise in this reality that shouldn't be.

Chris found himself whispering along with Bob Dylan, whispering the song he had once played for Meredith. And contrary to all logic, he whispered them to his Meredith, hoping beyond hope that she could somehow hear him and know he was alive. If there could be two separate realities, and if he could somehow slip through into the other, then who was anyone to say his voice couldn't reach past the layers of reality, past the quantum divide? Somewhere, Meredith, his Meredith, had to know he would get back to her some way. Stuck at another red light, he pressed his face against the cold window and sang hoping she would hear him.

The motorcade crossed the city wall of Charlottesville made of an intricate network of barbed wire and fences with tripwire, patrolled by heavily armed Monticellan soldiers on horseback ever watchful for bandits and infiltrators. Meredith didn't know if it was just her, but she could swear the border to Greater Monticello had been fortified even more since they passed through a couple of days ago for whatever good it would do.

Meredith pressed her head against the window and gazed out the vision slit into the rainy countryside. She found herself singing the Bob Dylan lyrics softly. Tears streamed down her face and she knew in a matter of weeks, everything that ever happened here would be erased. But then through the abyss something stirred in her, a glimmer of hope. Somehow, for some reason, she knew her husband was alive. Perhaps it was just that he played this song for her, but she could almost hear his voice singing. She had never been prone to believing in the supernatural, but she knew he was alive. It was ridiculous, really. The earth was going to die screaming, but if he came back, at least they would be together when it happened. Maybe that would be all that was left to hope for, but she held onto that feeling. Faintly hearing Chris' baritone voice through Bob Dylan's, Meredith sang back to him.

"It's a hard rain is a-gonna fall."